Irrefutable Evidence

C. N. Winters

Quest Books

Nederland, Texas

ISBN 1-930928-88-2

First Printing 2003

9 8 7 6 5 4 3 2 1

Cover design by LJ Maas

Published by:

Quest Books
PMB 238, 8691 9th Avenue
Port Arthur, Texas 77642-8025

Find us on the World Wide Web at
http://www.rapbooks.biz

Printed in the United States of America

Acknowledgments:

Thanks to Kate Orlando for always telling it like it is, and always being tactful in the process. Also, to Bridget Petrella for all her encouragement in all my endeavors and to a sea of online fans who've supported my writing over the years. And, last, but not least, thanks for my supportive husband and daughter who put up with the tempermental writer at times when I find it hard to put up with myself.

Dedication

This work is dedicated to my husband who never stops believing in my abilities and who gives me the focus to reach all our goals.

Chapter
1

September 16

"If I make it out of here alive, I am gonna *kill* Judith!" Sara mumbled to herself angrily as she drove along the ghetto streets of Detroit. The barred windows and graffiti-stained buildings were the only things diverting her eyes from the dirty street signs covered with residue from the area's industry. Nervously, she rounded a corner in her BMW.

"Damn it!" she whispered furiously. "Same party store...for the third time!" Her hands violently clutched the steering wheel, hoping the force of her fingers digging into the leather would somehow help her with navigational skills.

She had spent her life in the area and, with a little help from her assistant, had assumed she knew just where to go to look at a new property. With all the new subdivisions that had popped up recently, it was getting more and more difficult to say where anything was anymore; and she had definitely made a wrong turn somewhere along the way. She knew there was no chance that she would find a Cape Cod structure flanked by a luscious green front yard in this part of town.

She pulled to the curbside of the busy street to reread the directions, then shook her head in frustration. According to them, she'd made all the correct turns, but this definitely could not be the area for which she was searching. She realized ruefully that because of her unwarranted self-assurance, the trite expression "Never assume anything" was now appropriate.

Her attention, which was on the hand drawn map complete with directions, was abruptly refocused when a window cleaner approached her car and smeared a dingy rag across her windshield, leaving a dark smudge for her to view. Laying his palm flat, he mutely asked for compensation for his work.

His clothes were tattered and his face was dirty. She could tell by the thinness of his hands and wrists that it had been quite some time since he had eaten on a regular basis. Digging into her purse, she pulled out a five-dollar bill as she lowered the window.

"Here you go," she said as she handed him the money, her frustration beginning to melt as she met his needy blue eyes.

"Thank you very much, ma'am," he replied appreciatively.

"Make sure you eat."

"Yes, ma'am. Thank you again."

Sara's gaze followed him as he shambled off. Concerned that he might be on his way to purchase something other than the food he so obviously needed, a way to provide more immediate help occurred to her. She raised her window and shut off her car engine. "Wait a minute!" she called, exiting her vehicle with pocketbook in hand. She closed the car door and set the alarm. "Let's go over there," she said, pointing at a near-by diner.

The homeless man followed Sara obediently. He hadn't showered in quite some time and his odor was offensive. She managed not to cringe away as she held the door open for him to precede her inside. Every head in the diner turned to see the attractive, well-dressed blonde and the disheveled bum walking in together. Conscious of their stares, the vagabond tried to act dignified, brushing off his dirty, tattered coat and running even dirtier fingers through his greasy hair in an effort to enhance his appearance. Sara stood her ground, staring the patrons down until they returned to their meals and conversations.

"Come on," she said to the man. "Let's sit at the counter."

They each took a stool as a black, overweight man greeted them, taking in their appearance.

"What'cha need?" he asked as he cleaned the space in front of them with his washrag.

"What would you like to eat?" Sara asked. The man looked at the five dollars and then at the menu on the wall, calculating the costs.

"Don't worry about that," Sara said, grabbing the hand that held his money. "I'll pay for whatever you want."

The man seemed amazed as he looked at her hand on his. She'd actually touched him, when so many others simply passed him on the street, paying no attention, almost as if he was part of the scenery, some inanimate object and not a person.

"I'd like a cheeseburger and fries with a Coke," the man said politely.

"I'm buying, and you're only getting a cheeseburger? Wouldn't you rather have a steak?" Sara teased.

"Well, yeah, but—"

"But nothing. He'll have the T-bone with a baked potato...

What vegetables do you have today?"

"Green beans and carrots," the waiter said gruffly, a bit bewildered by the scene in front of him.

"How does that sound?" Sara asked her guest.

"Okay," the itinerant replied, his confusion mimicking the waiter's.

"Good. But there's one catch," she said with a smile toward the homeless man.

"What?" he asked, leaning away. He was nervous, almost fearful, the lines on his aging face growing deeper.

Sara sensed his apprehension. She knew he must be wondering what task he would have to perform in order to receive this meal. Maybe she needed a hit man to knock off a rich husband.

Sara smiled reassuringly. "No Coke. Something good, like milk or juice."

"Milk?" the man asked. He hadn't even considered that as an option.

"Milk it is," Sara replied. She was playing with him—teasing him, but he didn't mind. The bum simply grinned his approval and gave a slight nod.

"And you?" the waiter asked Sara.

"Do you have a restroom?"

"Yeah, straight back there," he pointed.

Sara turned to the homeless man. "What's your name?" she asked.

"Rick. Rick Edmonds."

"Okay, Rick. Go get washed up while they get your order, okay?"

Rick nodded silently and left for the restroom.

"Anything else?" the waiter asked in his urban accent.

"Yeah. I already had my milk today," she grinned. "I'd like a Coke for now, and some directions a little later."

"No problem. Lemme place this order and get the drinks," he said, walking to the cook's station before ringing up the bill.

Sara studied her surroundings and smiled at a table of people who kept looking over at her. She was definitely out of place. Her blue Anne Cline dress and Italian high heels were a statement of a level of wealth the other patrons didn't have and probably would never know. But she didn't feel nervous. In fact, she felt she was making everyone else nervous. Or perhaps it wasn't she who made them uncomfortable at all. Perhaps it was Rick—the man with nothing but the tattered clothes on his back. Perhaps seeing his state of homelessness made them question their own financial stability...or lack thereof. At any moment, perhaps one of them could become Rick—wearing dirty clothes, sleeping on doorsteps, and eating a decent meal only when a stranger fed them. Maybe he was the threat to their sense of security, not her, who was obviously well to do. She was what they dreamed of becoming; he was their worst nightmare. And perhaps their reality and destiny were closer to his than hers.

The waiter returned with the bill, which Sara paid with a fifty. He brought their drinks and placed her change on the counter top. Sara was sipping her pop when Rick returned.

"Feel a little better?" she asked him.

"Yes, thank you."

He took a big drink of his milk and a small white moustache formed on his upper lip. Sara chuckled softly as he wiped it away. Half the glass was empty, so Sara instructed the waiter to bring another one.

"I'm not sure what to say," Rick confessed. He looked at his replenished glass of milk as he spoke, shying away from Sara's engaging green eyes.

"Say whatever you want," she replied, placing her hand on his shoulder.

Rick delayed a moment, drinking some more milk. He could feel her touching him, but he didn't dare look.

"You've touched me twice," he said, still keeping his face averted.

"I have?" she said, self-consciously pulling her hand away.

"Yeah." It was spoken so quietly that Sara nearly missed his reply.

"I'm sorry if it bothers you. I'm a 'touchy' person I guess. I didn't mean to—"

"No!" Rick cut her off, meeting her eyes for a brief moment. "I'm not complaining. It's just...you see...the last time anyone touched me was over a year ago," he added, staring at his drink again.

"A year?" Amazement consumed Sara. She couldn't begin to imagine what it would feel like to go for without a year being touched by someone...anyone.

"Well, that's not entirely true. Last week some cops chased me from a storefront. And a month ago someone tried to get some money I had, which ended in a brawl, but...but I'm not sure that counts."

Sara's first reaction was to say, 'Are you kidding?' But she knew the man wasn't joking, and she held her tongue. She just looked into his blue eyes, pondering a response.

"Do you remember the last person who touched you?" she

asked gingerly, unsure of the reaction the question would bring.

"Yeah, a worker at the homeless shelter that used to be down here. I was really cold and she brought me an extra blanket she'd dug up. After she put it over me..." He paused. Sara watched intently as tears welled up in his eyes, waiting for him to continue, intrigued but saddened by his pain. "She stroked my hair... She thought I was asleep...but I wasn't. I still remember how she looked: long black hair, deep blue eyes, and gorgeous curves." A blush came to his face as he thought about the woman.

"She sounds like an angel."

"She was," Rick answered with conviction. "She was always nice, too. Always had a smile. But they closed the shelter. Lack of funding, I guess... I'm not sure what ever happened to her."

Silence filled the small seating area as Sara studied the man's face. At first glance he appeared much older, but he was actually rather young—perhaps early to mid thirties, her age. His face was now clean but just as shaggy, and she could see confusion in his eyes.

"Can I ask you something?" Rick asked, making eye contact again. She answered with a nod. "What do you want from me? You buy me steak. You clean me up. What can I possibly give you in return?" This time he held her gaze as he waited for an answer.

Sara was about to give him one when the food arrived. "Thank you," she told the waiter before turning to Rick, "Nothing, really."

"Nothing? There must be something you want. No one does something for nothing anymore."

"No, really. You just looked like you were hungry, and I thought you might..." Realizing that what she had been about to say would be an insinuation that Rick might have purchased something other than food, she amended, "I thought you might want to save that five dollars for another meal." When that answer didn't look like it was satisfying Rick, Sara continued. "See, I belong to a lot of organizations. I write checks to different causes all the time, but I never really see where my money goes. Today, I've spent a few bucks and you have a full belly. That's all. However, there is something I want." She shook her head as the apprehension flitted across Rick's face again. "I also need directions. I'm not where I'm supposed to be."

"I can believe that," Rick said with a smile. It was the first genuinely relaxed expression Sara had seen on his face. His teeth were maize in color but appeared to be strong, for the most part. Sara returned his smile with a brilliant white one of her own.

"What do you do?" he asked after a small silence.

"I'm in real estate. I was going to look at some property when I made a wrong turn somewhere," she said, rising from the table. "With any luck, that waiter down there can tell me how to get where I need to go. I'll be back."

Rick continued with his meal, watching Sara talk to the waiter. She leaned across the counter and he couldn't help but admire her body. Firm, full breasts, tight buttocks. *Looks as good going as she does coming,* he thought. Her golden locks weren't long. Stopping just past her earlobes, they were all even in length, except for some small bangs. It had been a long time since Rick had noticed a woman in a sexual way. Now that he was semi-clean and no longer hungry, he couldn't help noticing Sara. He watched as she scribbled some notes down on a piece of paper before coming back to him.

"Okay," she sighed as she finished her soda. "If my car isn't on blocks, yet, I'm in great shape."

Rick forced a smile.

Sara knew he was not anxious to see her leave, but she had to get going. Night would fall soon, and she had work left to do at the office. First on the list was to call her secretary/assistant Judith and read her the riot act for getting her lost.

As she was leaving, Sara paused. "Do me a favor?"

Rick nodded.

"Don't give up hope, Rick Edmonds. There are people who still care."

"I won't."

"Good," she said, putting her hand on his shoulder. A piece of her wanted to stay almost as much as he wanted her to. She wanted to make sure he was all right for the night, with a warm place to sleep. She wanted to see him clothed in garments other than the ratty old suit he wore; but she knew that she had to leave, and started out the door. Besides, she couldn't save the whole world. But perhaps she could brighten it for a few folks when the opportunity presented itself.

"Wait!" Rick said. Sara turned around and smiled. "You forgot your change. Plus, I don't even know your name." She could see the need in his face to connect some name with her deed, to have some person he could identify with as he remembered her generosity.

"Sara." She knew Rick wanted more. "Sara Langforth," she added, fulfilling his silent wish.

Rick looked at her, memorizing every detail: from the light shade of red in her blonde hair to the blueness of her high heels. He moved as if to return her change.

"You keep it," she said, "but on one condition."

"What's that?" he smiled. The nervousness he had experienced the first time Sara set restrictions on her gift had evaporated.

"You come back tomorrow and get breakfast. Some eggs, bacon and sausage—the works." Sara grinned at him one last time. "Promise?" she added, as Rick looked at her generosity in his hand.

"I promise." His grip tightened on the money as he spoke.

"I believe you," she said sincerely, reaching for the door.

"Sara Langforth," Rick smiled, making her stop, "you're my new angel."

Sara flashed a bashful smile. "Take care," she told him. Without another word she was out the door, walking swiftly back to her car.

A cool night breeze from the river had replaced the warm evening wind. The sun had almost made its descent across the horizon, shadowing the city against it. The sulfurous smell from a nearby factory assailed Sara's nostrils as she walked back toward her BMW. From a distance, the car appeared to still have all four of its wheels, and she sighed in relief. *At least something is going right.*

Walking quickly down the sidewalk, her attention was drawn by a commotion in an alley nearby. She could hear a struggle, and she slowed her steps. The last thing she needed was a broken arm from something flying around the corner into her path. She tiptoed to the building edging the darkness, and carefully peeked around to see what the noise was all about.

She saw four men: three surrounding another, who had his back to the alley wall. He resembled a caged animal, hoping to make an escape but finding every possible avenue of exit blocked, each attempt resulting in another punishing push against the wall. She could see the men were talking so she strained to hear the conversation, trying to block the visual images from her mind for the moment.

"Where is it, Jimmy?" the tallest man, and apparently the leader of the gang, kept asking.

Each time, the cornered man answered, "I don't have it," his voice quivering more with every denial.

Sara considered going back to the restaurant or making a break for her car, but any movement might alert them to her presence. She knew the people in the restaurant would probably be as sympathetic to this man named Jimmy as they were to Rick. And if Sara ran to her BMW, she might become the new target. So she decided to stay put, struggling to hear what the conflict was about, all the while planning her next move.

"It was a three hundred grand deal, Jimmy, and you're telling me you're empty," the ringleader insisted.

"I did the best I could," the man argued, showing more resistance than Sara had seen since the exchange began.

"Well, your best isn't good enough." With a raised arm, the thug hit the trapped man, and he fell hard to the ground. Judging by the way the victim fell so quickly, Sara could tell there must have been something in the attacker's hand when he'd struck. She watched Jimmy struggle to his knees in front of the menacing giant. "As a matter of fact," the thug added, "your best isn't worth shit! Anyone who 'misplaces' three hundred grand in dust isn't worth my time. And as far as I'm concerned, your time is up. You say you'll get the merchandise back, but the thing is, I don't believe you."

The shadows of the alley impaired Sara's view, but she could tell the attacker was pointing at the man; and she could hear Jimmy's tearful pleas.

"No. No, Carlos. I've been with ya for a lotta years... Don't end it like this. Please...no...Carlos! I'm telling ya the truth!"

The ringleader began to laugh, and helped the scared man to his feet. "You really thought I was gonna kill ya, didn't ya?" Carlos continued to chortle loudly, enjoying his own joke immensely.

A smile came to Jimmy's face and he, too, began to chuckle. "You really had me goin'," he said as he began to walk away.

Sara watched as Carlos turned around and watched Jimmy's departure, the grin disappeared from his face in an instant. The echo of two gunshots pierced Sara's ears, and she watched helplessly as the man's lifeless body fell to the street.

"Well, Jimmy," Carlos said, towering over the dead man, "you were right."

Shock. Denial. Disbelief. They all flooded through Sara at once as she watched the three men standing over the corpse they had created. Drawn by the sudden silence, Sara leaned further into the alley to get a better look at what they were doing. With herself more in view, suddenly their attention shifted away from the dead man and onto her. She could see the smoking gun, as well as the deep brown eyes of the murderer gazing at her.

Sara felt frozen. Her brain told her legs to run, but try as she might, they wouldn't move. Then the blaring of a car horn from the street behind her shattered her lethargy, and her feet took off.

She ran past the alley in an attempt to reach her car. Another shot rang out, this time aimed in her direction, but she kept moving. It had been years since she had run track in high school, but in her desperation, long-dormant speed and strength reappeared. She felt one of her shoes fly off, but kept up her pace, although her steps were now off-balance. She hit her car's remote, and the locks popped open. Shifting her momentum to a full stop, she crashed into the door, sending a shooting pain up her leg.

Sara flung the door open and hopped inside. Glancing in the rearview mirror as she started the car, she could see all three men in the alleyway moving toward her. They had all pulled their guns now. She threw the car into drive and sped out into traffic, narrowly missing a taxi.

"Put your weapons away," Carlos instructed. "I'll deal with the little blonde soon enough, and it won't be on an open street." He had to get out of the area quickly now, but he knew he had options, many options on how to proceed.

As the BMW raced away from them, he went out into the street, picking up the pump that had fallen during Sara's flight. The two other men, like trained junkyard dogs, followed instinctively behind him. He tossed the shoe in his hand once before slapping it with a thud against the broad chest of the companion to his right.

"Dead," he uttered, nodding back to the thug that now held the shoe. "I want Cinderella dead."

Sara's adrenaline levels surged, and she could feel her pulse pounding throughout her body. Next her nausea rose, and she felt herself starting to gag in response; but she wasn't about to pull over. She knew she had to keep it together. *Drive now, puke later,* she told herself.

She didn't know where she was going. She was just driving— driving as far and as fast as she could. Her thoughts were scattered. The image of Rick in the restaurant, the man, Jimmy, lying dead in the alley as the blood pooled from his body, the brown eyes of the murderer—all of these scenes flashed through her mind's eye. Clearest of all, however, were the brown eyes. She remembered them, as well as his other features—his tall stature, his fit physique, his tanned skin and large nose. This was not someone she would forget overnight...if ever.

Once her nerves and stomach began to settle down, she was able to focus on the buildings and street signs. That's when she saw it—a sign indicating the location of a nearby police station. Finding the station, she quickly parked the car and ran inside, shoeless, rushing past two uniformed officers, her breathing labored by the time she got to the front desk.

"Can I help you?" the officer asked.

"I just saw a murder I have to report," Sara answered raggedly as she tried to catch her breath.

Pointing at a small bench, he directed, "Settle down, Miss. Have a seat over there, and I'll get someone to help you right away."

Sara might have protested being told to sit down and collect herself, but his voice was comforting and concerned so she did as he instructed, trying to remind herself to breathe. She was doing well until the sound of someone shouting made her jump.

"No way!" the voice said.

Sara's eyes darted to two women as they walked through the double doors of the station house, arguing but laughing. They made their way to the front desk, debating something that obviously amused both of them.

"If that's what you think, Angie, you're crazier than I thought!"

"I'm crazy?" one of the women challenged. "I'm not the one who spent two hundred dollars on a psychic!" she added with a chuckle.

"For your information, I did not spend two hundred dollars on a psychic."

"Then how much did you spend?"

"A hundred and fifty."

"Oh, geez, what's the difference, Denise?"

A beat passed as they locked eyes. In synch, both women replied, "Fifty dollars!"

They both started to laugh. "Oh, partner o' mine," the other woman sighed. "You're getting too predictable, dear."

Sara watched their interaction with interest, sensing the easy comfort they shared. The taller of the two had long, dark brown hair that flowed just over her shoulders, and her laugh was intoxicating. Her deep blue eyes smiled when she grinned, and Sara wondered why someone so attractive would pay $150 for a psychic. It certainly couldn't be for advice on her love life. She was far too gorgeous to have to worry about being lonely.

The desk sergeant walked up to them and began to whisper. He pointed at Sara, and they looked over at her and nodded back at him. The sergeant resumed his place behind the counter as the two women walked over to her. Sara rose at their approach.

"Hello," the taller woman offered. "I'm Lieutenant Denise VanCook, and this is my partner, Sergeant Angela Michaels."

The lieutenant extended her hand, and Sara got the opportunity to assess her looks up close as they did the ritual, first meeting handshake. *Why can't the cops who stop me for speeding look this good?* Her appreciative once-over was interrupted by the sudden roiling of her stomach. *It has to happen now...right now...after all this... Just the thought of it...Oh, God, I'm gonna be sick. I know it.*

Denise looked down and noticed Sara's shoeless state. "That's a bold fashion statement." She smiled, hoping to ease the tension. "What's your name?"

"Sara Langforth," she said quickly. "Do you have a bathroom nearby? I don't feel real well."

"On the left, right through—" As Denise pointed, Sara darted away. "...those doors," Denise finished to no one. Denise pulled a quarter from her pocket and gave it a flip. She slapped it against the back of her hand and kept it hidden. "Heads or tails?" she asked Angie.

"Heads."

Denise lifted her palm and grinned. "Tails, you lose. I'll wait in the office for your return."

"Son of a bitch. I always get the sickly witnesses," Angie muttered as she headed to the ladies room. She walked with slumped shoulders but pulled together a professional demeanor as she knocked on the door. "Ms. Langforth? It's Sergeant Michaels. You okay in there?"

Sara's throat stung from the soda she'd regurgitated, and she let out a croak. "Yeah, just give me a minute."

"No rush," Angie called out as she took a seat on a wooden bench that sat against the wall. "You need anything?"

After the question was posed, Angie heard the toilet flush, as Sara emerged from the stall with an embarrassed grin, heading to the washbasin. She ran the water and cupped her hand to rinse out her mouth. Then she washed her hands and rinsed them, using the excess water to splash her face. "So, am I the biggest wimp you've ever met?"

"I spent months at the Academy," Angie began. "I was placed in all kinds of situational simulations. I was told what to expect, knowing that the unexpected could always happen. Then in my rookie year I answered a call to provide back-up at a suspected drug house. As I entered the premises, a bullet came within about three inches of my head. I managed to put someone in handcuffs a few moments later, but after that I went behind my squad car and threw up."

"Are you just saying that to make me feel better?"

"No, it really happened. I think it's both physiological and

psychological. Your adrenaline rush slows down, you start to realize what just happened, and well...nature takes its course." Angie
grinned. "It doesn't make anyone a wimp, it makes them human.
Of course, that was quite a few years ago, and both Denise and I
have been shot at since then," she chuckled. "Repetition builds
resistance, but it still gives us the willies."

With a small grin on her lips, Sara dried her hands and her
face. "I think I'm ready now."

"Okay, Ms. Langforth, come with me and you can tell us
what happened tonight." Sara nodded her agreement and was
escorted back through the waiting area, into the recesses of the
precinct, until they arrived at a small office partitioned from the
main room by wood and glass.

"Please, have a seat," Angie instructed, motioning to the
chairs. "Can you describe exactly what you saw? Take your time,
and remember as many details as you can."

As she sank into one of the two chairs in front of the desk,
Sara took a moment to soak up her surroundings. The lieutenant's
area was littered with manila folders and books. A bag of pretzels,
carefully rolled up, sat at the corner of the desk, along with a coffee mug. There were a few ring stains on the desk calendar that
covered much of the surface of her desk in the same area as the
cup. Sara would best describe it as an organized mess—she could
speak from experience.

"Well," she started, pulling her thoughts together, "I was on
my way to look at some property—I'm in real estate—and I got
lost on the Lower East Side, so I stopped at a diner to get some
directions. On the way back to my car, I heard some loud noises
coming from an alley...and that's where I saw it happen."

"Saw what?" Angie and Denise asked in unison.

"The murder, of course. The killer's name was Carlos; the
man he shot kept saying it. Anyway...as I was saying, I heard a
commotion, and when I looked into the alley, there were three
men holding this fourth guy they called Jimmy. They were beating
him up, and then they pretended to let him go; but when his back
was turned, this Carlos shot him...in the head, I think... I mean, I
know he shot him, I just don't know if it was the head. All I do
know is that Jimmy fell—quickly—and didn't move. And that's
when the other three noticed me."

"They saw you?" Angie questioned, exchanging glances with
Denise.

"Yes. At first I was in shock, and I think they were too. I
mean, I was shocked about the shooting, and they were shocked
about me seeing it. It looked to me like they had planned to kill

him, but they certainly hadn't planned on me being there." Sara rattled along in her explanation, her mind moving faster than her mouth; and she mentally kicked herself. She had to slow down and explain more thoroughly.

Denise and Angie guessed what Sara was thinking, and they both gave a reassuring nod to indicate they were following her account of the events to that point.

"Anyway, when they noticed me, I ran; and then I heard another shot, which I think was meant for me. I can't say for certain, because I started running and didn't look back until I got in my car. That's how I lost my shoe. It fell off as I was running, and I'd be damned if I was going to go back for it then." Sara felt a bit silly with the way the last sentence had come out, and she found herself grinning.

As Denise watched the woman, who looked half-embarrassed and half-scared, she had to grin as well. Even though this Sara Langforth had just experienced the most frightening moment someone could have—being a target—she still managed to keep her sense of humor.

"Okay, you've made a very good start. Now let's see if we can fill in some of the details. How long ago did this happen?" Denise asked. She pushed her chair back and started to type set-up data into her computer.

Sara looked at her watch. "Around seven, maybe seven-thirty. I didn't know where to go or what to do, so I drove around a while before I came here. After I calmed down, I found the precinct, and here I am."

"Do you remember what the gunman looked like?" Angie asked.

"I don't think I could forget if I tried," came the honest response.

Denise and Angie looked at each other and began to take down Sara's description of the shooter and the men who had been with him. The more Sara filled in the details, the more anxious Denise became. When the witness had finished, Denise turned to Angie and then her computer.

They all fell silent, and there was no sound in the room except for the rapid staccato of Denise's typing. After a few minutes, the printer produced a colorful printout containing the photos of six men, similar in appearance.

"No pressure here," Denise began gently, "but do any of these men look like the one you saw tonight?"

Sara studied the pictures. One immediately captured her attention, but she looked at them all carefully, one by one. Finally she looked up into Denise's eyes. "Yes, him." She pointed to the third man in the photo line-up. "But the man I saw looks about ten years older. His hair was beginning to gray—right here," Sara said, pointing to the hair at the temples.

Denise turned the printout back to herself and inspected the sheet. "Funny," Denise smiled. "This picture was taken eight years ago." She turned to her partner, Angie. "I want an APB put out on Carlos DeVittem. Armed and dangerous. And make sure you tell all the uniforms coming in and out. The shifts are changing, and I don't want to lose any time on this."

"No problem," Angie said as she quickly left the office.

"You're sure this is the man?" Denise asked Sara once they were alone.

"Pretty sure...I mean, the picture is old, but it's more than a striking resemblance," Sara said, scrutinizing it. She studied it again, then cocked her head.

"What is it? Do you remember something else?" Denise asked.

"This man doesn't have a tattoo," she said, pulling at the right neckline of her dress and pointing. "Right here. I couldn't see all of it because of his T-shirt, but it looked like one of those Celtic cross designs. Lots of bends, but sharp angles here and there."

"It's possible he's gotten it since his last arrest," Denise replied.

Sara nodded. "Perhaps."

"Well, we'll see if uniforms can round him up. Once he's in custody, we'll be in touch if we need you to make a positive identification. When we apprehend him, are you willing to testify to what you saw?"

Sara nodded and Denise began to take down Sara's information—phone numbers, addresses, and such. A few moments later, Angie came back in.

"Sergeant Wagner's taking care of the APB," she announced to the women in the small office.

"Good," Denise replied, getting her coat. "Can you start the report?"

"Yeah. Where are you going?" Angie asked.

"I'm going to escort Ms. Langforth home." Denise turned to Sara. "If that's all right with you."

"That would be fine," Sara calmly replied with a gentle smile.

"Good. On the way, I'll explain some things we might need you to do in the next few days, okay?"

"Sounds great," Sara replied.

They were leaving the office when Angie stopped them. "Are you coming back here?" she asked Denise.

"Yeah."

"Okay, if I finish before you get back, I'll wait for you. After all, you owe me dinner."

"Well, in that case, maybe I won't be back," Denise said, winking at Sara to get Angie's goat.

"You'd better be here," Angie ordered.

"Don't take that tone with me," Denise joked. "I'm your commanding officer."

"Ohh, don't even try to pull rank on me when it comes to food, Lieutenant," Angie countered.

Denise just chuckled as she made her way out the door with Sara. The cool air was a welcome relief after the warm station house. It was still a warm night, given the fact that fall was just around the corner.

Sara started for the visitor's spot where she had parked her car, but was stopped by Denise's gentle grip on her forearm. "I'll drive you to your place. If they got a look at your car, it's probably best if it stays here tonight. Call me tomorrow, and I'll bring you to pick it up."

Sara agreed, and they climbed into an unmarked police car. She gave her address and directions, and Denise pulled out into the light traffic. Sara's nerves had stopped jumping, and she covertly studied Denise as they drove down the streets.

"If the uniforms can bring DeVittem in tonight, perhaps you'll be able to identify him tomorrow. We'll put him in a line-up and ask you to pick him out. After that, I'll explain what we'll do next, okay?"

Sara simply nodded. She could tell Denise was a strong woman. Her voice and her body language conveyed confidence and reassurance. Sara felt rattled by the evening's events, but just being in this woman's presence put her more at ease. In addition to being beautiful, Denise also seemed experienced in her field. For the first time all night, Sara felt safe; and she allowed herself to lower her guard.

"Tell me something," Sara asked. "Does everyone get an escort home?"

"I wish I could say everyone who walks into my precinct gets this kind of service, but it isn't true. We can only do so much with the number of officers and the amount of time we have."

"Then why are you taking me home?" Sara responded with a smile.

"I was officially off-duty about an hour ago. Angie and I just got stuck filling out some back paperwork."

"My luck wasn't too bad tonight, then," Sara smiled. "I have an experienced cop taking me to my doorstep."

Sara couldn't disguise the joy in her voice. Denise, excellent detective that she was, picked up on it. She hadn't taken the time to notice as they spoke of the crime, but Sara was a strikingly elegant woman. Except for the fact that she was shoeless, her appearance was perfection. Nervously, Denise ran her fingers through her hair, trying to concentrate on her duties. She noticed women every day—at the supermarket, at the post office, at work or in a national magazine. A beautiful blonde could always turn her head, but this blonde would have to wait. Sara was her witness. Period. Letting her emotions interfere with her job duties could be deadly...for Sara and herself.

"You should know something," Denise said, attempting to defuse the charged atmosphere. Sara studied her intently as she spoke. "Any time someone witnesses a brutal crime, there's a chance they might become a target. I'm not trying to scare you, I just want you to be a little extra aware of people you encounter."

"Do you really think I could be a target for this man?" Sara asked in her clear, musical voice, a voice that Denise was enjoying more each minute.

"There's a possibility, yes. But that's why we're here. If you need us, or experience anything unusual, don't hesitate to call. My home number is on the back," Denise said, handing her a business card from her coat pocket.

"Thank you." Sara let her fingers linger a few moments on Denise's before pulling them away.

Sara's touch was soft, gentle. Her nails were well manicured, unlike Denise's short, brittle ones. Yet at the same time, their fingers were very similar, nearly identical in shape and size.

It had been a long time since Denise had felt another woman's hands on her. Of course she often touched her partner, Angie. Theirs was an intimate relationship, but their intimacy was emotional. The only physical intimacy they shared was like any other friendship—a light hug when things went wrong, a pat on the back when things went right, and a short caress on the shoulder to get the other's full attention.

Denise felt awkward. It wasn't often that a witness, female or male, had the style and grace to make her lose track of her thoughts. Sara, however, made her seriously unsteady. Denise, who had always considered herself to be bisexual, could feel the vibes this woman emitted, and it piqued her curiosity.

"Are you living with anyone, Ms. Langforth?"

Sara wasn't sure how to compute the question. "Why do you ask?" she queried.

"I was just wondering if someone else might be at risk."

"Oh," Sara answered, trying not to sound disappointed. "I live alone...now."

"Divorced?" Denise asked.

Sara didn't know exactly how to reply. Denise might not be so willing to help her if she knew she was a lesbian. But Sara had always said she would live her life on her terms and not deny who she was. Protection be damned, she knew she had to be as honest as possible.

"I lived with someone for five years. After many months of late hours at work, I came home early one evening. There was a blonde in our bed, and it wasn't me."

"I'm sorry," Denise said sympathetically.

"Thank you. But that was a while ago. I've gotten over it, but I still find my odd hours and late nights make it tough to find the right woman." *Okay. There. I said it.*

Woman? Did she say woman? Okay, Denise, play it casual. She's a witness. "I hardly work a nine to five, myself. I know how you feel," Denise answered.

Sara hesitated a moment. *She didn't reply or react negatively. Hmm, interesting.* Sara wasn't sure where to take the conversation at this point. *Turn it around on her,* she decided.

"So, I take it you haven't found Mr. Right?" Sara asked, as casually as possible.

"Or Mrs. Right," Denise said. "I like to keep my options open."

Sara chuckled. *So she did hear. And she's not offended. Great gosh o'mighty! And look at that grin on her face.* "So, what's it like to sit on the sexual fence?" Sara teased.

Denise took the jab in good spirits but replied, "I don't consider myself a fence sitter."

"Oh really?"

"Really."

"Well, let me ask you this. Would you consider spending your life with a woman?" Sara queried with a bit of disbelief regarding Denise's orientation.

"Is that an invitation?" Denise countered with a smile.

Nice way to send it back over the net. Sara smiled and a chuckle escaped. "No," Sara grinned. "Well, at least not yet."

Denise looked over and caught the playful, sexy smirk on Sara's face and had to chuckle with her. They came to a red light and Denise looked into Sara's jade eyes, trying to find a starting place for her explanation.

"It's difficult for both the hetero and the homo societies to believe that anyone can like both. And yes, at one point, I considered spending my life with a woman, but she didn't feel the same way."

"Too bad for her. She missed a wonderful opportunity, if you ask me."

"Well, it's not easy being a cop's wife," Denise explained. "I work late hours, too, but then there's the added worry that someone might shoot at me. I think it's hard to jump into a relationship and give it everything when you know you might be dead the next day."

"You make it sound much more grim than it needs to be," Sara answered.

"Well, you've never had to live it; and if you're lucky, you never will," the officer grinned.

The light turned green and Denise started smoothly with the traffic flow. Sara silently thought about her comments. Instead of debating that real love, no matter the situation, was worth any risk or sacrifice, she decided to drop the subject. Besides, the first topic had her intrigued, and she wanted to know more. After a brief silence, she cleared her throat and said, "So, tell me, how can you like both?"

At first Denise was lost by the abrupt subject change, but then she realized Sara was talking about her bisexuality.

"Do you like apples?" Denise asked, diverting her eyes from the road for an instant to look at the blonde.

Sara laughed. "What?"

Denise chuckled too but repeated the question, pressing for an answer. "Do you like apples, yes or no?" she specified.

Reluctantly Sara agreed to play along. "Yes, I like apples."

"What's your favorite—red or green?"

"I see where you're going with this, so let me save you the time. An apple is an apple no matter what color it is," Sara replied with a bored sigh.

"That's not true. Red apples are sweeter and green apples usually have a harder skin."

"Well, in that case, I like red apples," Sara laughed.

"I like both. Why should sexual preference be any different? And I've heard this from both sides. Hets think I'm a lesbian trying to act straight. Gays think I'm just afraid to come out of the closet. But both are wrong; they're trying to make my motivation more complex than it is. In truth, it's very simplistic: I fall in love with people, not genders. If I'm fortunate enough to find my soulmate, someone that I can connect with mind, body and spirit, I'm not gonna fret about the package."

Sara was intrigued. She sat up straighter and faced Denise by shifting her body sideways. "But doesn't being bi prevent you from finding a lifelong relationship?"

"No, why would it?" Denise replied.

"Well, let's take your apple scenario... Oh, take a right up here," Sara said, pointing. As Denise did as instructed, Sara continued. "Anyway, if you like both apples, red and green, wouldn't it get old after a while if you only had a red apple? I mean, wouldn't you like a green apple now and again?"

"For some folks, perhaps. But for me...not if I met the right apple."

"So for now, you're still searching the orchard?"

Denise had to laugh. "Yes, metaphorically, I'm still searching the orchard." Denise continued to chuckle. "Oh, God! How did we get on this subject?"

"You wanted to know about my love life." The comment was quick and direct. All indication of joking left Sara's face and was replaced with intent. Bisexual or not, this woman was someone Sara definitely needed to know more intimately. "This is my building," she said quietly, pointing out the window. "Mind if I call tomorrow to see how things are going with the investigation?"

Denise, putting the car in park, got sidetracked when she looked over at Sara, admiring her in the light of the streetlamp. She looked almost angelic, and Denise had to admit she was a tad smitten with the blonde.

Sara could almost read Denise's mind, and she had to chuckle at Denise's slip of reserve.

The soft laugh drew Denise out of her wandering thoughts, and her cheeks blushed red in response. "Oh, yes. Feel free," she said, nodding her head. "Tomorrow. I'll be there... Be careful, Ms. Langforth," Denise called out as her witness left the car.

"Sara," the blonde corrected. "Call me Sara. I'll speak to you soon." With that she winked and closed the car door behind her.

Denise watched Sara reach the doorway of her apartment complex and go inside. Denise realized, as she mulled over their conversation, her newfound curiosity would make for a long, sleepless night.

Chapter 2

September 17

The rush of morning filled the station house as Angie searched through the crowded precinct for her partner. Human chatter around the water cooler and clicking keyboards assaulted her ears as her eyes wandered around the busy room.

"Where's VanCook?" Angie asked one of her colleagues.

"Ain't seen her all morning."

Angie rolled her eyes and continued her search. An uncooperative perp fighting his way into the lock up cell almost knocked her over. Angie sidestepped the commotion as if nothing had happened, a testament to how long she had been on the force. She was on her way to the front door when the desk sergeant stopped her.

"Hey, Michaels!" he yelled, halting her movements. "Van-Cook called. She's at the 12th. They got your shooter, and they're bringing him back here."

"Great!" Angie said, walking back toward him. "Anything else?"

"Yeah." He handed her a folder. "Here. She needs you to call the witness. She's stopping by her house after she wraps up the details over at the 12th, and she needs the witness ready to go."

Angie took the folder with a small grin. "Okay. Thanks, Wagner. I'll be in the office until she gets in."

The desk sergeant nodded and took his seat back behind the reception desk.

Angie rushed back through the commotion that typified the office and dialed Sara's number. After the third ring, she got an answer.

"Hello?"

"Hello, this is Sergeant Michaels with the Detroit Police Department. Is this Sara Langforth?"

"Yes," Sara replied, trying to hide the sleepy tone in her voice but failing.

"Sorry to wake you, but I wanted to inform you that we have the suspect in custody, and we need you to come to the precinct to make a positive identification. Lieutenant VanCook is already on the way to your home. Do you think you can be ready when she arrives?"

Sara glanced down at her black satin nightshirt. She was about to answer when she heard a knock at her door. "No," Sara replied, rising from the bed. "I think she's already here. Can you hold on, Sergeant Michaels?"

"Certainly." Angie waited impatiently while there was a brief pause, and then she heard a door open and two feminine voices began talking.

"It's Lieutenant VanCook," Sara spoke into the receiver. "Would you like to talk to her while I get ready?"

"Please," Angie answered politely.

"Here you go." With that, Sara handed the cordless phone to Denise, who was mesmerized by the sight of Sara, half dressed. The nightshirt was short, exposing smooth thighs and curvy calves. She was shorter than Denise, but Sara's legs looked like they made up most of the blonde's height.

"It's Sergeant Michaels," Sara said as Denise took the phone. "I'm going to hop in the shower. Make yourself comfortable."

Without a word, Denise took the phone and watched Sara disappear deeper into the apartment. Denise studied the sway in Sara's hips and the way the shirt rose as she walked, exposing her cheeks slightly. Denise knew Sara was totally nude underneath, and the desire to follow her was compelling. Her thoughts, however, were interrupted by Angie's voice on the other end of the line.

"Denise? Are you there?"

"Hey!" Denise greeted. "What's up?"

"I was about to ask you the same question."

"Oh, right," Denise replied, being pulled from her distraction. Sara had left the room, but she still commanded a large part of Denise's attention.

"Are you okay?" Angie asked with concern, sensing something amiss with her partner.

Damn, that woman knows me too well. Instead of giving any details to account for her momentary lack of focus, Denise stuck to business. "I'm great, actually. Uniforms picked up DeVittem. They should be there any second. They found a weapon on him, but I think we're still waiting on the forensics report from the medical examiner to match the bullet with the one found in the vic."

"Well, I haven't heard from the M.E. yet. I've been looking for you."

"I'm sorry," Denise apologized. "I got an early start this morning. I told Wagner to tell you when you came in today, but he must have missed you."

"That's okay," Angie replied. "I'll call the examiner's office and see if they have anything for us. When do you think you'll be getting here?"

"As long as it takes Ms. Langforth to get ready. I'm hoping not long."

"Well, I'll get started on this end. I'll see ya soon. Bye, Den."

"Bye, Angie."

Denise grinned as she turned off the phone. She and Angie had been partnered ever since they were in uniform. In all their years together on the job, they had seen just about everything imaginable...and some things unimaginable. Through it all, they had guarded each other's backs. Denise felt lucky, even blessed, to have Angie at her side.

Hearing the shower running, Denise took a leisurely look at her surroundings as she waited for Sara. Pieces of ancient pottery sat on marble tables. White carpeting covered the floor. Black leather furniture gave sharp contrast to a room that was illuminated by standing halogen lights.

Across from the sofa stood a huge bookcase. A large assortment of books, ranging from Greek mythology to contemporary society, filled the shelves. Dickens, Poe, Shakespeare, Steinbeck, Rice, King—occupied the case alongside autobiographies, plays, and various non-fictions such as books on psychology.

Denise, with her keen observational skills, noticed that not only was Sara well-read, but all the books were hardcover—not a single paperback. She pulled down a book called *From Rape to Reverence*. The binding was bent, indicating that the book had been read—perhaps many times. She picked another and another and another. All the bindings were bent. Many people had large libraries that were mostly for show. This woman, however, seemed well versed on nearly every aspect of life and literature. Denise had to admit—this Sara Langforth was starting to have more appeal. *Beautiful* and *smart...killer combination.*

"*Death of a Salesman* is one of my favorites, too. Poor Willy Loman."

Denise turned around to see Sara smiling over her shoulder, cloaked in nothing but a wet towel. Denise hastily shoved the book back into its proper place. "I'm sorry," she replied, flustered at being caught prying. "I didn't mean to intrude."

"That's quite all right. Do you see anything you'd like to take home?" Sara asked. Her suggestive tone didn't go unnoticed by

Denise. She could feel the hair on the back of her neck rise to attention.

For just an instant, Denise forgot to breathe. With Sara dripping wet, and only inches between them, the officer felt her temperature rise and wondered if it showed on her face. She watched as Sara licked her lips, waiting for a response. To say one million erotic thoughts ran through Denise's mind in those two seconds would have been an understatement. Her libido, however, couldn't rule her actions or judgment. Yes, it had been quite some time since Denise had had anyone—man or woman—in her life. But Sara was important to her current case. She could not in any way be involved with the key witness who might testify against one of the biggest suspected drug dealers in the city.

"It's a hard decision," Denise replied, facing the bookcase again. *No kidding.* Sara stepped even closer, close enough that Denise could smell her recently shampooed hair. *Strawberries. My favorite.*

"May I make a suggestion?" Sara asked softly.

"Sure," Denise answered, trying her damnedest to keep her voice even but failing miserably.

Sara heard the effect she was having on the officer, and couldn't contain the satisfied smirk on her lips. It gave her a sense of power to hear Denise's voice falter, if only in the slightest. She reached past Denise, her breasts lightly pressing on the back of the lieutenant's arm. Without conscious thought, Denise found herself leaning back, straining to get closer to Sara's body under the guise of giving the blonde more room to search the bookcase.

With nimble fingers, Sara found the book she was searching for. Slowly she wrapped her fingers around the spine and pulled it from the shelf—gently handing it to Denise. "This is my absolute favorite," Sara commented. "I love ancient Greek literature."

Denise began to thumb through the pages, stopping at the table of contents.

"As you can see, nearly every great Greek story is in there, some written by Greeks and some by 'outsiders' who've written tales about ancient Greece," Sara explained, still looking over Denise's shoulder. "Everything from Oedipus to my personal favorite is inside."

Sara's index finger skimmed down the page stopping at a certain page number. Denise smiled when she looked over at the title— "The Isle of Lesbos."

Noticing the smile on Denise's face, Sara ventured, "I assume you've heard of this one."

"Yeah. It contains one of the first, if not the first, literary and historical reference to lesbianism."

"I'm impressed," Sara replied with both surprise and admiration.

"Please, don't be impressed. I had to take a course in lit at college; it just kinda stuck with me, I guess."

"Well, I'm still impressed. Not everyone knows that," Sara complimented, placing her hand on Denise's shoulder. *Oh yes, beautiful and smart. Nice shoulders, too. She's a keeper.*

Such a simple contact, and yet quicksilver shot through Denise's body. Suddenly the book felt like a ton of bricks in her shaking grasp. "Well, it's been a while since I read it. Maybe I will take this one," Denise replied. She waggled the book, trying to disguise her unsteadiness. *Pull it together. You're one of Detroit's finest; start acting like it.*

"Good." Sara gave Denise's shoulder a pat before moving away. "I'm going to finish getting ready. I'll be back shortly."

Denise gave a nod as she moved to watch Sara walk down the small hallway. As Sara neared her bedroom, she pulled the towel off, dragging it along the carpet. Her naked hips swayed back and forth. Enchanted by Sara's firm derriere, Denise remained mute. Realizing that her mouth was now hanging open, she quickly pursed her lips.

Sara was certain she had Denise's full attention. The officer's sigh she could hear from the living room was proof. *Now this should give her something to think about.* Before entering her room, she turned to face Denise. "I'll be out in a second," she called softly.

That's all she said. That's all she had to say. Denise viewed Sara's nude body for a total of five seconds, and she was utterly ensnared. The officer dug her nails into the book, willing herself to stay in the living room. Denise knew the beautiful blonde wanted her to follow. She also knew from the short glimpse of Sara's body that the woman was a natural blonde, and not modest in the least.

Denise began to pace. Her desire for Sara was blazing into an inferno. It felt unnatural. Intellect—that was what always attracted her to people, not so much their physical appearance. And she silently wondered why this beauty had her hormones on the verge of eruption.

You're being shallow, Denise told herself silently. *You don't know this woman. You've only spent an hour, hour and a half tops, with her. It's illogical to think of her as anything but a witness. Sure, she's gorgeous. Sure, she's obviously literate. Sure, she's a flirt, and you know how you love flirts; but...still...focus here.* Denise took a deep, calming breath, then recollected Sara's dripping body. *Oh, who am I kidding?* Denise finally conceded. *She's sexy beyond belief.*

Just as that thought came to the fore, Sara reemerged from the bedroom, fully clothed. "Are we ready?" she asked casually.

"Don't you want to dry your hair?" Denise asked, looking at the damp, combed strains. "It's kinda chilly out today," she added. Denise chastised herself silently. *What the hell am I now, her mother?*

"It's dry enough," Sara replied, intrigued by Denise's concern. "Besides, it's a low maintenance style."

"Okay then," Denise said, stepping outside as Sara locked the door. "Let's get moving."

The precinct seemed more crowded than usual as Denise led Sara toward the office where Angie waited. Angie rose from the desk when they entered the small glass enclosure.

"Good morning, Lieutenant, Ms. Langforth."

Given Angie's cheerful attitude, Denise surmised that things were proceeding rather nicely so far this morning. "You must have good news?" Denise asked, just to be sure.

"That depends," Angie smiled. "What kind of weapon did they find on Mr. DeVittem?"

"A .22. We've sent it to ballistics already."

Angie swung an evidence bag that held two empty bullet casings. Denise took the bag from Angie and held it up for closer examination. Slowly a smile that mirrored Angie's crept onto her face.

"Those were taken from the victim by the M.E.," Angie explained. "Seems the victim was shot in the cranium at close range."

"Yeah, a .22 is a preferred weapon—just as deadly, but not nearly as messy," Denise added.

Sara took a seat as Denise sat down. "I'm not sure I understand."

"The bullet is a small caliber," Angie explained.

"Size—length and width," Denise explained further, holding up her fingers to illustrate.

"Right," Angie continued. "Some bullets are bigger and do more damage; they are a better choice when shooting from longer distances. In this case, DeVittem had a very clear intent. He wanted to kill that man in the alley, but he didn't want to blow his brains out, so to speak. So, he used a smaller round..."

"Bullet," Denise clarified as she swung the bag.

"Yes," Angie directed towards her partner, a bit agitated. *Can I finish here, Den?* Denise took the hint and held her hands up in truce, conveying she'd keep her mouth shut.

"He used a smaller bullet." Angie paused and looked to her partner to see if Denise was going to interrupt her explanation again. When Denise remained silent, she continued speaking to Sara. "It did the job, and it didn't create much noise or mess, but he's got a major problem he didn't count on: he's got someone who saw him do it," Angie added, looking to Denise and then Sara.

Sara grinned for show, but inwardly she was just realizing the seriousness of her situation. The words of caution that Denise had spoken to her the night before suddenly struck home. This wasn't a random act of violence. DeVittem—apparently a very dangerous man who would stop at nothing—had a mission that she'd interfered with. And if he was vicious enough to lure that man into the alley to kill him, then chances were he would stop at nothing in order to ensure that she never made it to the witness stand.

Denise and Angie were engaged in conversation and hadn't noticed the slight uneasiness that settled over Sara.

"Were any more shell casings found?" Denise asked.

"Yes—one by the dumpster—similar to a dumpster where they found the body. Three total, just like our witness said," she smiled.

Denise put the evidence bags back on the desk and turned to Angie. "Where's DeVittem now?"

"Downstairs, in lock up."

"Okay," Denise said, rubbing her hands together, ready to get to work. "Have Wagner start the line-up. I'll take Ms. Langforth to the interrogation room."

"You got it!" Angie said, collecting some papers and making her way out. "I'll see you downstairs, Ms. Langforth," the partner added before leaving.

Sara gave a nervous grin and nodded. Soon Denise and Sara were alone in the small confines of the office. Sara's anxiety grew, and a deep sigh seeped from her mouth.

Denise noted the worry lines forming on Sara's face and the way the woman nervously played with her fingernails. "You'll do just fine," Denise encouraged optimistically.

Doubt still clouded Sara's dark jade eyes. "But what if I can't identify this man?" she asked. "Or what if I do, and he makes an attempt on my life?"

Denise could feel Sara's conflict: her passion in wanting to help catch the killer was warring with her concern for her safety. "The department will keep you safe, Ms. Langforth. And if you can't identify him, then you can't; it's as simple as that. But I have to say," Denise added more positively, "in the short time we've spent together, you strike me as a woman who pays great attention to detail. I think you'll do just fine."

"All night, I kept seeing the murderer's face and the way that innocent man died..." Sara looked out into the precinct's common area, away from Denise.

Although the death obviously disturbed Sara, Denise couldn't conjure up any sorrow over the loss of DeVittem's victim. "The man we found dead worked for Mr. DeVittem. Trust me when I say he was far from innocent," Denise explained.

"Perhaps. But he didn't deserve to die," Sara replied, meeting Denise's eyes in challenge.

Denise met her head on. "Ms. Langforth," she began formally, "it wouldn't surprise me if the 'victim' had killed another person exactly the same way he died. He was far from a model citizen."

"Don't you have any compassion?" Sara argued, her temper starting to get the better of her.

"Yes, I do," Denise said softly and sincerely, but not backing down one bit. "The teenage boy who overdosed on drugs the 'victim' helped push makes me very compassionate. But I see this as the murder of that boy's supplier, and that doesn't make my heart ache."

Denise's sarcastic intonation on the word "victim" troubled Sara. "How can you be so cold?" she asked in astonishment. "We're talking about another human being."

Denise didn't want to argue. But she couldn't summon up some fake grief to please Sara. "I believe in human rights," Denise began, "but I think you should act like a civilized human to be worthy of them. The dead man had a rap sheet as long as the Ambassador Bridge. He spent many years of his life victimizing others, when he wasn't in jail. Now that he's gone, that's one less person the courts have to spend time and money on."

Boy, did you ever misjudge her character. Sara sat slack jawed with amazement. "Do you really feel that way?" she asked in disbelief.

"One hundred and ten percent." The words were spoken succinctly. Both women found themselves facing off in silence.

Finally Sara shook her head. "Sounds like you've been a cop too long."

"Sounds like you've led a sheltered life."

Their eyes locked in silent battle once more until a knock at the door made Denise turn. It was Sergeant Wagner from the front desk.

Poking his head inside, he said, "We've got your line-up ready downstairs," and left just as quickly as he had come.

Denise and Sara just looked at one another for a few more moments, each wondering what the other was thinking. Denise pondered Sara's argument a few seconds longer before speaking. "Perhaps you're right," Denise started to concede. "Perhaps I do feel some remorse for the wasted life of the man that was gunned down. But believe me, if he wasn't dead, he would have gone on to victimize people far more innocent than himself."

Sara looked at Denise, her challenging attitude replaced by curiosity. "Do you honestly think he deserved to die?" Sara asked in a sober tone.

Denise paused, reflecting on many of the things she'd seen over the years. Perhaps in some way, however minute, she could see Sara's side.

"I don't think anyone deserves to die by another person's hand, but it happens."

Sara felt better, seeing that deep down Denise did have some compassion, no mater how little, for the man who had died. *So, the tough-as-nails cop does have a heart in there somewhere.* That thought made Sara grin, if only slightly.

Denise took it as an unspoken truce. "Let's get going," she said, interrupting the silence that was growing between them again. "You have a criminal to identify."

Sara rose, and Denise escorted her to the stairwell leading down to the dimly lit room where the line-up was to take place. Sara took a seat next to Angie, who was waiting for both of them. Denise grabbed the chair next to Sara, giving her hand a light pat for encouragement. Then Denise leaned over to Angie. "Send them in," she commanded.

The way Denise spoke was totally professional, almost regal, and Sara had to smile. She liked "take charge" women, and the police lieutenant certainly fit that description.

Angie spoke into a microphone, and six men lined up in front of a height board. Sara felt her pulse beating in her ears as she looked at each man facing her.

"Remember, Ms. Langforth, they can't see you, so relax and take your time," Angie instructed.

Sara looked at one man intently.

Denise watched as Sara's eyes moved up and down. "Which one are you looking at?" she asked.

"Number two," Sara answered.

"Number two," Angie said into the microphone, "please step forward."

He took two steps towards them, and Sara leaned forward in her chair to focus solely on him. After three seconds, she began to shake her head. "That's not him," she replied with certainty.

"Please step back, number two," Angie ordered. Then she leaned back behind Sara and mouthed something silently to Denise. Sara was so wrapped up in scrutinizing the men that she didn't notice the exchange between partners.

"I don't see him anywhere up there," Sara said despondently. "I was sure I could pick him out, but..." Her voice trailed off; she felt absolutely disgusted with her inability to identify the man who had managed to haunt his way into her dreams the night before.

Angie spoke into the microphone again. "Gentlemen, please exit to your left."

Denise and Angie remained quiet until a uniformed officer walked in. "Ma'am, we have another line-up after this one," he said, pointing toward the glass.

Denise turned to Sara. "Are you sure you didn't see him?"

"I'm sure," she answered.

"Okay." Denise turned back to the uniform behind her. "Officer Kline, send in the next line-up."

He did as he was instructed, and another six men filed into the viewing room. All of the men in the new line-up looked very similar to the one Sara had studied before, but the next-to-last man captured her attention immediately. He hadn't even reached his spot, before Sara was tugging on Angie's sleeve.

"He's the one," she told them. "Pick him." Sara was practically begging Angie to have him step closer.

Once they were all in place, Angie turned on the mic again. "Number five, please step forward."

Slowly, arrogantly, the man put one foot forward and then the other. Sara rose from the table and walked around to the front, an arm's length from the protective glass. She looked at his eyes—his brown eyes.

"That's him," Sara pointed. The certainty rang in her voice. "He's the one."

"Are you positive?" Denise challenged authoritatively. Often witnesses would buckle under at this point, the forceful nature of Denise's tone shaking their confidence. It was something that Denise insisted on doing, much to Angie's chagrin. She always wanted to make sure the witness was positive in his or her selection, while Angie was just grateful to get a perp identified. Between the two of them and their tactics, it always worked.

Sara studied the man for another three seconds. That's all the time she needed. "Without a doubt...that's the man from the alley."

Angie and Denise smiled at each other. The methods they used were at opposite ends of the behavioral spectrum—Angie coddling the witness, while Denise stayed hard as nails—but the end result was positive. Angie directed the line to exit, and once the stage was empty, the officer returned to the room.

"Office Kline," Denise began, "please escort Ms. Langforth back to my office, and return here when you're finished."

"Yes, ma'am." The officer nodded to Denise. "Right this way, Ms. Langforth," he added politely.

"We'll be with you shortly," Denise called over her shoulder as Sara was being led away.

Once Sara and the officer had departed, Angie turned to Denise. "Do you realize what we have here, Den?"

"Oh, I don't know," Denise drawled with a growing grin. "A drug dealer we haven't been able to convict on any drug charge, who's just been identified in a murder one case?"

"Exactly," Angie smiled. "Who'd have thought we'd nail a drug dealer on a murder charge."

"If it sends him to prison, I'm happy. After all, Ness got Capone on tax evasion. Why can't we get DeVittem off the streets with murder?"

"Now we can, and we will," Angie smiled.

"Don't start celebrating, yet," Denise warned, shifting in her seat. "This is far from over. And what was the deal with two line-ups? Did you arrange that?"

"Hell, no. That's what I was trying to tell you earlier. DeVittem wasn't in the first line-up, but I didn't want to blow it by saying otherwise in front of Ms. Langforth."

"Well, thank God you didn't. I'm sure DeVittem's attorney will be looking for *any* loophole he can find. This one has to be by the book and to the letter. This two line-up deal will either make us look extremely sloppy or extremely brilliant," Denise chuckled.

"We could be trend setters you know?" Angie teased. "A brand new way to hold a line-up... I've always loved serendipity," Angie laughed.

"That makes two of us."

Angie ran her fingers through her strawberry blonde hair as she smiled. "You realize if this works out, this is gonna look reeeeal good on our records."

"I realize that," Denise agreed, twirling the swivel chair to face Angie. "So, let's not fuck it up, shall we?"

"I'm with ya to the end, darlin'."

"Good. At least somebody is," Denise sighed.

Angie put her arm around Denise's shoulder in a show of support, and gave her a warm smile. "Some day your prince will come...or princess." The wicked grin on Angie's face forced Denise to smile herself.

"How about you?" Denise teased, wiggling her eyebrows. "You could be my princess."

Angie gave a hearty laugh, "Are you kidding! Me? Give up men? Besides, Denise, after working together all day, I can't see us together at night. We'd end up killing each other. Remember when I had my apartment fumigated and I had to live with you for three days?"

Denise remembered. The debate about how to properly squeeze a tube of toothpaste nearly ended in a fistfight after day two. She could chuckle about it...now.

"Nah, I love you but I could never live with you...and vice versa, I'm sure," Angie added for good measure.

Denise was going to reply, but the door opened and Officer Kline returned.

"You needed me, Lieutenant?" he asked.

"Yeah...what the hell is the story with two line-ups?" Denise asked.

"From what I understand, Sergeant Wagner sent the wrong line-up in. He had yours and Detective Brenner's. You got Brenner's line-up first. When he realized what had happened, he sent me to inform you of 'another' line-up."

Denise turned to Angie. "Wagner is a dead man," she whispered.

Angie simply smiled at her partner's antics. "Thanks for the info, Kline. We'll see ya," Angie said, cueing the officer to leave.

As the door closed again, Denise sat shaking her head in frustration. "Good help is soooo hard to find," she grinned.

"We could always take him to a ball game this spring and throw him off the top of Tiger Stadium."

"Commerica Park," Denise corrected. Tiger Stadium was now, like many icons in the city, nothing but a vacant space.

"It will always be Tiger Stadium to me," her partner and die-hard Tiger fan retorted.

Denise smiled. "Regardless, it would be too much work for Sanitation to clean him off the street."

"Okay. How about this?" Angie replied, anxiously squirming

in her seat. "We could strap him to the hood of our car and drive down the Lodge Freeway in rush hour traffic?"

"Nah... That's pretty scary, but not scary enough." Denise paused a few moments before brilliance struck. "I know! We'll force him to bungee jump off the Renaissance Center at gun point."

"Yeah, but who's gonna pull him back up? The guy weighs at least 300 pounds."

"Who said anything about pulling him back up?" Denise chuckled. "We'll head to Greektown for spinach pie and gyros instead."

They both began to laugh again as the door slowly opened. They turned to see Wagner standing sheepishly in the doorway.

"There he is!" Denise began playfully. "Just the man we're plotting against."

"I am so sorry, Lieutenant VanCook. I thought Brenner knew what he was talking about. I should have double checked before I sent anyone in."

"You're damn right you should have checked. You could have blown this whole investigation," Denise replied, her voice beginning to rise.

"I'll be more careful next time, I promise," Wagner said, starting to cower in the face of her temper.

"Don't promise, just improve. And I hope you do for your sake...aww, just...go! Get outta here before I get mad," Denise said with an angry wave of her hand.

Shoulders slumped, he left silently as Angie rose.

"Come on," she said, pitching a thumb toward the door. "Our witness is waiting."

Denise joined her and they walked to the door. "Wait," Denise said, stopping and grabbing Angie's sleeve. "Just for future reference, you're still a Tiger season ticket holder aren't you?"

"Yes, I am."

"Good. Because we never know when future Wagner trouble might arise and we'll be forced to go with plan number one."

Angie smiled and gave Denise a chuck on the arm as they started upstairs.

They entered Denise's office, where Sara was still waiting obediently for their return. Denise buried the growing smile that arose at the sight of Sara.

"We're back," Denise said unnecessarily, taking a seat behind her desk.

"I have some forms here that I need your John Hancock on," Angie said, showing Sara the paperwork and explaining each document as Sara went through, giving her consent.

When Sara had finished, Denise rose from her chair. "Your work is temporarily finished at this time, Ms. Langforth. We'll turn the evidence over to the district attorney's office, and we'll get hold of you as soon as we have more information and a court date," Denise explained.

"On behalf of Lieutenant VanCook and myself, I'd like to thank you for your cooperation," Angie said, shaking Sara's hand. "People usually don't want to get involved, so thank you for coming forward."

"Thank you," Sara replied, enunciating each word. "I'm happy to help."

"We know you must be busy, so we won't keep you any longer." As she led Sara to the door, Denise reached into her pocket and extracted one of her cards, which she handed over. "And remember, if you need anything, feel free to call us, okay? I've included my home number on the back again just in case you need to reach me after hours."

Sara paused a moment as if to memorize Denise's face before offering her hand. She wasn't sure when or where she'd see the officer next, so she wanted to take the mental picture with her. *She's certainly one to remember.*

Denise took Sara's hand lightly in her grasp, barely moving it up and down. *So warm and soft. No, not soft—delicate.* Sara favored Denise with a brief grin and sent a friendly nod to Angie before making her way from the office. Denise's eyes never left Sara until she was past the double doors.

Angie couldn't help but notice the non-verbal exchange that had passed between the two women. "You *like* her," Angie teased.

Denise was still distracted, but her attention turned quickly to Angie's proclamation. "She's a witness," Denise argued, making sure to avoid any eye contact with her partner, while at the same trying her damnedest not to look like she was avoiding her. As she took a seat behind her desk, she knew she was failing miserably.

"Sure she's a witness," Angie agreed, "and you *like* her."

"Look," Denise began as she searched through a folder, "my interest in this woman is strictly professional."

"If that's true, then why won't you look at me?" Angie challenged with a confident smirk.

Denise's head shot up and she glared at Angie, exaggerating the action. "There. Are you happy? I looked at you," Denise added, before stuffing her nose back in the folder.

Denise was certain that Angie was still wearing a smirk and it began to perturb her. But despite her annoyance, she wasn't about to look up to make sure.

Angie's mocking voice soon left her no choice. "'Remember, if you need anything, feel free to call me'," Angie exaggerated in a lovesick tone.

"I said us," Denise clarified. "Not, call *me*, call *us*."

"My home number's on the back." Angie then sat mute, her hands linked together over her heart while she batted her eyelashes.

"You're impossible," Denise said, throwing the folder down on her desk in exasperation.

"You're in love," Angie chuckled, not intimidated in the least.

"I am not in love."

"Okay, so it's not love," Angie relented. "Maybe it's just lust. But one thing's for sure..."

Denise waited for Angie to finish, but she was eventually forced to ask, "What's that?"

"You undeniably have the hots for that woman." Angie's grin widened and Denise sat back, giving up the battle. Angie collected her papers and placed them back into the folder before rising to leave. "Hey, Denise," Angie said, standing in the office doorway. A serious look returned to her face, and Denise could see she was being her "all business" self again. "Let's not fuck this one up, shall we?" Angie added.

Denise knew exactly what Angie was saying. It was the same thing she had been telling herself over and over since she had met Sara. Denise just smiled and nodded her agreement.

"Good." Angie grinned. "I'll be back in a few...lover girl."

Denise plucked a crumpled piece of paper from her desk and threw it at her partner. It missed when Angie ducked away, laughing. Denise smiled and settled back in her chair, thoughts of Sara returning to her mind while Angie's words echoed in her ears. *No, Angie—I promise, I won't fuck this one up.*

Chapter
3

It had been a long day. Following the early morning trip to the police station, Sara had unfinished business at the office that kept her there until well after nine. In truth, Sara didn't need to work, but she had become accustomed to it. And she enjoyed what she did.

The trust fund her parents had left her was more than adequate to keep her comfortably for the rest of her life. However, she found that real estate was a good way to keep her in spending cash. It also kept her connected to people in general. She couldn't live in an ivory tower as her mother had—appearing at different functions, being the country club matron her parents bred her to be. It had been a fine life for her mother, but it just wasn't for her. And Sara was happy with the choices she had made.

Curled up on the sofa as the kettle started to whistle, she went to the kitchen and made her cup of instant hot chocolate. She returned to the couch, mug in hand, and thumbed through her book, picking up where she'd left off—Huck and Jim just starting their journey on the mighty Mississippi.

It was typical for Sara to have at least three or more books she was reading at the same time. This week it was *Huck Finn*, *Little Women*, and *Taming of the Shrew*. Sara had never liked television, but her array of different reading materials seemed to mirror the inconstancy of a channel surfer—flipping to a different story or different characters, depending on her mood.

The apartment was silent except for the hum of her refrigerator and the tick of the wall clock. Once in a while she slurped on her drink, but even that wasn't noisy. She continued to read, getting deeply involved in the story as she always did, shutting out the world around her.

She was about to take another sip when she heard an unusual noise from the vicinity of the front door. It was the sound of metal against metal, much like a flat head bit drilling a screw. She rose and hurried over to the door, looking out the peephole. A man was standing out front, his arms and eyes cast downward. She stood on tiptoes, trying to get a look at what he was doing.

Realizing what it was, Sara dashed to the phone and quickly dialed.

"911. What's your emergency?"

"There's a man with a gun outside my door," Sara whispered, keeping her voice as soft as possible.

"Stay calm, ma'am. Is there someone in your home?"

"There will be if you don't send someone here now!" Sara kept her voice low, but her frustration level was growing.

"Stay calm, ma'am. We'll send someone out to help you."

Stay calm? You wouldn't stay fucking calm, lady, if somebody were outside your front door. Sara was on the verge of saying just that when she looked down and saw Denise's business card where she had set it next to the phone. *Fuck this.*

Without giving the operator notice, she hung up, fumbling with Denise's card for just a moment before she dialed with shaking fingers. The receiver held tightly in her grasp, Sara said a silent prayer as the phone began to ring. *Please be home, please be home, please be home.*

"Hello?"

"Thank God. Denise?"

"Yeah. Who's this?"

"Sara Langforth."

"Hi, Sara. What can—"

"Listen to me," Sara whispered quickly, cutting her off. "There's a man standing out in front of my door. He's got a gun with what looks like a silencer. I called 911, but I need your help."

"What?" Denise exclaimed. She felt the phone begin to shake in her grasp. *Jesus, keep her safe.* Sara began to repeat, but Denise cut her short. "Stop. I heard you. Is there any way out of your place?" Denise asked quickly.

"The front door," Sara replied sarcastically.

"Besides that," Denise pushed. She could feel her heart jump up into her throat. *If I could crawl through the phone line, I would.*

"The fire escape."

"By that alley before the driveway?" Denise asked.

"Yeah," Sara answered automatically. She then took a second to realize that—after being there for just a few minutes the other night and earlier that morning—Denise had managed to memorize the layout of her apartment building and the surrounding area.

Man, she's good. Let's hope she continues to be as good and gets her ass over here before it's too goddamn late.

"Okay, then," Denise replied before Sara could voice her astonishment. "Go out the window and head to the back of the building. I'm on my way."

"But I'm acrophobic!" Sara said. "I hate heights."

"He'll be in there before I can get there, Sara. Just don't look down. Concentrate on the steel beams around you, not the ground below. Okay?"

Sara sat silently with the phone pressed to her ear, staring at her living room window. The thought of going outside terrified her as much as the gunman that waited at her door.

"Sara?" Denise said urgently. "Sara!" she practically yelled to get the woman's attention.

"I'm okay. I'm goin'. Just get here."

Popping noises began to come from the front door, and almost made Sara drop the phone. At the other end of the line, Denise could hear them, and knew them for what they were.

"Oh, my God!" Sara whispered, her hand gripping the phone like a lifeline.

"Listen," Denise began, "he's coming in. Get out now! I'll be there in three minutes!"

Sara heard Denise slam the phone down. She quickly hung up, taking a deep breath. She ran to the bathroom and turned on the shower to give the illusion she was still in the house. Next she went to the living room window and fought with the locks. Once they were freed, Sara tugged on the sash and the window noisily shot up. Her shaking hands pushed against the glass to quiet the rattle.

Don't look down, Sara reminded herself. *Don't look down.* Slowly she put one foot out on the steel platform below her window.

Pop! Another shot connected with the door lock, followed by pounding against the door itself. Sara's body was half in and half out. She quickly ducked outside and closed the window behind her to buy herself more time. Once she was completely on the platform, she looked at the steel support bars wrapped around the fire escape like a protective cage. She didn't dare look at the sidewalk below.

With her heart pounding against her ribcage, she began her descent. The side railing looked secure and Sara walked slowly, pretending it was the stairway of her apartment as she made her way to the next lower platform. It wouldn't be long before the attacker realized she was not in the apartment, and she willed herself to speed up.

Once on the next level, she stopped and took in a deep breath, inhaling the cold autumn air. *One down*, she sighed to herself. *Two more to go.* She wasn't sure how much time had passed as she stood gathering her nerve to make the next leg of her trip. All she knew was she had a killer above her and a long, agonizing descent below her.

She felt her legs shake as she moved step by step to the next landing. Once there, she walked across to the next set of stairs. *This is getting easier. Of course you're not as high anymore, either, Sara*, she told herself. Finally, she was at the last landing.

She followed the railing, like on each of the previous platforms, until she came to the next set of stairs. She realized in an instant, she had a problem.

When she came to the end of the rail this time, there wasn't a stairway—just a huge ladder. She looked up and she saw a release latch. At that moment, Sara knew she didn't have a choice. She would have to look down. And she knew...she wasn't anywhere near the ground.

She closed her eyes and inhaled deeply again. When she opened her eyes and exhaled, she took hold of the ladder, releasing the latch quickly. With much commotion, the ladder clattered and clanged until it crashed to the concrete below, echoing through the alley. She knew by looking at the building across from her, she was still two stories up.

She began a deep breathing exercise she used whenever she got stressed at work. She had never thought that in a million years she would be using it to save her life. She was about to take her first step toward the ladder when she heard it—*Ping! Ting!* She looked up. The attacker was leaning out the window, and the sounds were two ricocheting bullets.

Suddenly she heard another noise. This one came from below. *Screeeeccchhh!* The sound of rubber against asphalt stung Sara's ears, and she looked down. She watched a car stop, swinging its backside so the grill faced her and the building. The passenger door flung open, then the driver side.

"Come on!" Denise yelled as she ran toward Sara.

She was far from safe, but the sight of Denise made Sara sigh with relief. The lieutenant moved like a cheetah, with quick, graceful strides. She was halfway to Sara when more shots rang out. The lieutenant leapt to the side, going into a roll and raising her hands. Two return shots rattled Sara's eardrums as Denise sprang to her feet, making her way over, revolver in hand.

"Let's go!" Denise coached as she stood underneath Sara.

Sara tried, but her feet just wouldn't budge. "I don't think I can," Sara wept, both in fear and frustration.

"Yes, you can! Just turn around and walk down."

Sara looked back up at the open window of her apartment. The assassin was gone...at least for the moment.

"Come on, Sara. You can do it," Denise said, trying to encourage her.

Sara looked down at Denise's smiling face. A man was trying to kill both of them, but Denise stood grinning at her, believing in her. With that, Sara began to make her shaky descent.

Denise stood looking up, watching every step Sara made. The attacker peered out of the window as Sara reached the halfway point. When Denise saw the man taking aim, she quickly drew a bead again. As she steadied her sights between Sara and the fire escape to get a clear shot, another set of shots rang out from above. Denise immediately returned fire, and the attacker ducked back inside.

Sara froze, gripping the ladder in fear, not sure who was shooting or if the intruder's next round might find its mark.

Denise knew they were running out of time and ammunition. "Jump!" she called up to Sara, who was stalled halfway down.

"What? Are you crazy?" Sara screamed.

"Jump and I'll catch you. I promise."

Sara looked down at Denise who holstered her gun and held her arms open. The sight gave her the confidence she needed. She sprang from the ladder, emitting a yelp of fear in the process. Her body plummeted toward the ground, and she prayed Denise would be strong enough to steady her. It felt like hours, but seconds later Sara's bare feet smacked the pavement and she felt Denise's arms go tight around her, holding her up. She was on the ground. Finally.

Not more than a second later, however, she felt her body slammed up against the bricks of the apartment complex. *Ow, geez. That's gonna leave a mark.* She watched Denise pull her gun from the shoulder holster and send two more shots back at the window.

"Let's go!" Denise ordered, nearly pulling Sara's arm from its socket.

They raced to the car and jumped inside, Denise slamming it into gear and careening down the alley toward the main street. Sara watched in awe as Denise opened the chamber with a flick of her wrist and took an assessing glance at her gun.

"Here," Denise said, setting the gun in her lap. "You'll have to help me reload," Denise instructed as they flew down the street. "Pull the bullets from my shoulder strap and hand them to me."

"I don't 'do' guns," Sara protested.

"You do tonight," Denise said in a tone that precluded debate.

Without further argument, Sara began to help reload the weapon. She could feel the softness of Denise's long black hair as she moved it out of the way to reach more ammunition. Pulling the bullets out one at a time, she could feel the officer's well-toned shoulders as she steadied the strap, as well as the shake of her own hands that held the bullets she had already extracted.

Denise could see Sara visibly quaking. "Are you okay?"

"I suppose so," she said softly, a pool of bullets in her hand. "Other than the fact that I feel like I'm gonna get sick again."

"You weren't hit, I mean," Denise clarified. "You weren't shot?"

"No."

Sara's answers were brief as she tried to catch her breath. Her adrenaline levels began to drop, and along with that came a series of involuntary shakes and spasms. The metal casings grew damp in her hand.

Denise held out her own hand, and one by one Sara started to give Denise the bullets so she could put them in the chamber. "Good," Denise said with a long sigh as she looked in her rear-view mirror. "I'm going to take you back to my place tonight. We'll make other arrangements tomorrow. I'll see what I can do."

Sara nodded her agreement and shifted to get more settled. That's when she first noticed Denise's left arm. "Oh, God, you're bleeding!" Sara exclaimed, peering over the armrest to get a better look.

Denise glanced down at the appendage in question. "So I am," she replied casually.

Sara did a double take at Denise's cavalier attitude. "We have to go to a hospital," Sara urged.

"No," Denise refused firmly. "I don't want to take the chance of letting you out of my sight. I'll be fine."

"But you've been shot, Denise. I think—"

"Sara," the officer stopped her. "Trust me. It's just a flesh wound. I know what being shot feels like. I'll be okay."

Sara didn't argue further. Denise was a trained police officer, and intelligent enough to care for herself if need be. She also wondered just when and under what circumstances Denise had previously taken a bullet, but she decided to save those questions for another time. The worried look, however, still showed on her face—her eyes were downcast and her lips drooped at the corners.

"Thank you for your concern," Denise said, noticing Sara's expression. "I do appreciate it, so I'm sorry if I got short with you. Aside from Angie, I'm not used to people worrying about me."

Sara suddenly felt a different uneasiness settle over her, something that took her thoughts away from the events that just occurred. She hadn't thought she was that easy to read. In fact, she knew she wasn't. But unlike anyone she had ever met, Denise had a way of pulling emotions out of her and bringing them to the surface. She could attribute it to Denise's observational skills as a detective, but for some reason it seemed to come from a deeper level, as if something touched her very soul. *But don't dwell on it now, Sara. Save it for later.* She cleared her throat and handed over the last bullet. "Here you go," the petite blonde offered quietly.

As she took the ammunition from Sara's hand, Denise felt a connection, too. *Look at her. She doesn't deserve this. Nobody does, but especially not someone this bright and giving. Admit it, Denise: this woman is becoming much more than just a witness.* Denise realized that she would have no hesitation in killing anyone that tried to harm this woman, and the longer she thought about it, the less her protective instincts seemed to have to do with the case.

They arrived at Denise's apartment, still a bit shaken but at least reloaded. The officer quickly escorted Sara into the complex and then the elevators. Denise got out first and checked the hallway of her apartment. Once she had ascertained that it was clear, she waved Sara out.

"When we go in," Denise whispered, "you stand by the entrance while I check things out."

Sara nodded mutely, following Denise's orders to the letter as they entered. The detective started by turning on the lights in the living room as Sara stood obediently by the locked front door. Sara watched as Denise checked the rest of the apartment. When she shouted an all clear, Sara finally released the breath she'd been holding.

"Make yourself comfortable," Denise yelled as she collected some medical supplies from the bathroom. "There's Coke and iced tea in the fridge if you're interested," she added.

"Got anything stronger?" Sara asked half-jokingly, while going into the refrigerator. "After tonight, I could use something a little stiffer than cola."

She noticed, aside from the drinks, a pint of Chinese take out, a head of lettuce, and one single egg were the sole occupants of the refrigerator.

"Sorry," Denise answered as she rounded the corner, supplies in hand. "The only alcohol I have is what's in this bottle," she said, shaking the disinfectant. "My dad used to drink, so I try not to." Denise didn't add more and Sara didn't press.

"Coke will do." She inspected a cupboard over the sink and found two glasses, pouring equal amounts into them from the can she took from the fridge. Sara took a seat at the small kitchen table, closer inspection revealing that it was simply a card table with a cloth thrown over it. With that discovery, she began to pay more careful attention to her surroundings.

She had never seen a "bachelor pad," but Denise's place seemed as if it would be a great example. Junk mail and unpaid bills cluttered the corner of the table. A sweat sock sticking out from beneath the sofa looked as if it had seen better days about two decades earlier. The TV was perhaps one of the first models that came out cable ready, since it actually had knobs instead of pushbuttons.

The refrigerator itself wasn't much better. It was almond in color, an appliance hue popular in the seventies. The wallpaper in the kitchen itself looked like a pattern one might find on an ugly polyester leisure suit. *Oh yes, this place is certainly refined. All that's missing is a picture of dogs playing poker.* Sara chuckled inwardly at Denise's surroundings. This was certainly a place where Denise simply crashed after long hours at the stationhouse. Nothing more than a warm roof over her head and a few cool drinks—the basics of survival.

Sara watched as Denise set the supplies down on the kitchen table. The officer then took the few steps over to the open area that served as the living room, and went to the phone by her end table, which was artfully constructed of milk crates. Avoiding her wound, Denise carefully removed her shoulder holster as she sat on the sofa. She dialed the phone and waited for a response.

"Hello," Denise said, as she untied her shoes. "What are you doing? ... Sorry for waking you. ... Well, I got a call from Sara Langforth. Seems DeVittem had someone pay her a visit ... She's at my kitchen table ... Okay, my 'excuse' for a kitchen table." Denise smiled and shook her head. *She never cuts me any slack.* Sara brought the drinks over, and Denise mouthed a thank you as Sara set her Coke on the coffee table before returning to the kitchen area to give her the modicum of privacy available in such a small area.

"Anyway, someone broke into her apartment. I'm sure the

uniforms I called are there now. ... Well, the short version is, she climbed down the fire escape and I picked her up in the alley. ... Yeah, there was a little gun fire. I got grazed, but I'm okay. ... She's good. A bit shaken, but okay. Can you call to see if the uniforms are there now? I'm going to the captain tomorrow to see about twenty-four hour protection, so can you get in early, around 7? ... She's going to stay here tonight. ... Okay, sounds good. ... I've got to get cleaned up, so I'll see you tomorrow, okay? ... You, too. ... Bye, Angie."

Sara felt a cold wave ripple over her as Denise recounted the evening's events to Angie. *It was a close call, too close. But she came and got me. She kept me safe.* Sara grinned in admiration at the thought, while trying to reassure herself and keep her attitude positive.

As Denise hung up, the perfect smile that Sara was coming to enjoy more and more appeared on Denise's face. *She's beautiful when she smiles.* Denise downed the Coke before closing her eyes and resting her head on the back of the couch. A deep sigh signaled a release of tension. Sara's eyes seized the chance to admire Denise's features—from the red highlights of her long dark hair to each digit on her feet.

Sara gave an appreciative grin, but soon her shoulders squared. *Now it's my turn to be helpful.* The blonde walked back into the living room area carrying the alcohol and bandages.

Denise could feel Sara's eyes on her, even though her own eyes were closed. She knew now the attraction she felt was anything but one sided. She figured she could be up front with Sara, tell her that as her protector the department wouldn't look kindly on any intimate relationship they might have. However, she didn't want to be presumptuous, either. If the situation ever presented itself, she would deal with it. But still, Denise couldn't help but remember how wonderful it felt to have a woman in her life. It had been a while since she'd had anyone in her life. But women...with the seductive way they brushed their hair behind their ears, or the way they would tease, licking their lips...she missed that. Those qualities that women possessed, and used, always made Denise's blood pump harder.

Watching Sara's body language was like looking at a fine work of art. Sara knew how to capture a woman's attention and hold it—hers to then shape and mold as she saw fit. To say Sara made Denise's blood pump harder was an understatement. Feeling the silence had gone on long enough, Denise sat up and opened her eyes, forcing Sara to abandon her covert admiration.

Denise stared into Sara's eyes, soaking up her delicate features—the small fluff of bangs across her forehead making her round face and high cheekbones more noticeable. The pale complexion was accented by her coral colored lips, further distancing Denise from her good sense. *She's a true angel...but why on earth did she come to me?*

"Take your shirt off."

The blonde's voice captured Denise. *Okay—tell her no. Tell her you can't. Tell her...*

When she didn't respond quickly enough to suit her would-be Samaritan, Denise watched mutely as Sara undid the buttons, one by one, hanging on her every movement. After Sara's task was completed, Denise pulled the fabric from her shoulders, and sat clad only in her bra and well-fitted denim jeans.

Sara grinned. She couldn't help it. Denise was by far the best looking woman she had seen in ages. With a slight shake of her head to regain her focus, Sara looked at the wound on Denise's arm. "Let's see what we've got."

It was only at that point that Denise realized that Sara was going to tend to her arm. *Thank God you didn't open your mouth, Denise, and look like a total idiot.*

She gently took Denise's strong arm in her petite hands, surprised by its feel. "You're very muscular," she complimented. "Nice definition, not too bulky."

Denise smiled. "Angie and I work out every Friday."

"How much can you press?" Sara asked conversationally.

"Around 230."

"Really? That's probably 100 more than you weigh."

Denise laughed. "Well, let's say I weigh more than I look like I do."

"Yeah, well, muscle does weigh more than fat, and you certainly have muscles."

Denise smiled as Sara grinned and began cleaning the blood from her arm. When Sara touched the wound, the smile disappeared from the officer's face.

Sara offered her apologies as Denise tensed. "I don't mean to hurt you. Just want to give you a hand."

"S'okay," Denise said, placing her hand over Sara's. "I know it's gotta be done. I just have to remember to get peroxide next time... Doesn't sting as much," she said, gritting her teeth. She released Sara's hand and let her continue. With the blood finally cleaned off, they could see that the wound wasn't deep; the bullet had just skimmed her. "If I'd jumped a second sooner, it looks like it would have missed me," Denise commented.

"Well, I'm sorry it happened at all. Maybe if I hadn't been

such a chicken, you'd be okay."

"Don't feel bad, Sara. I know how phobias can paralyze; you beat it tonight. Besides, a few years ago, I probably would have made it without injury. Must be slowing down."

The two exchanged a small grin. "You can't be that old," Sara told her.

"36."

"I'm 35, and I don't consider myself old."

"I don't think I'm old, either," Denise said with a sly grin. "Just not as quick as I used to be."

"I don't know about that. You were movin' pretty fast to rescue me." The reality of the night struck Sara again, and she gave herself a shake before rubbing her arms to warm herself.

Denise noticed, and she started to massage Sara's arms for her. "You're a tough woman, Sara. Don't ever doubt that. By this point, a weaker person might be a puddle, but you're still standing strong."

"I don't feel very strong."

"Regardless, I know you are. And I admire that, truly I do. And that's why I ran as fast as I did. You're one of the good ones, Sara. And with all the people I deal with day in and day out...let's just say that good people seem to be in short supply these days."

Sara looked into Denise's eyes. She saw the honesty so plainly written on Denise's face. It had been a long time since Sara had felt anyone cared that much about her. She could picture herself raising Denise's face with gentle fingertips and guiding those full lips to her own, feeling their warmth and responsiveness. But instead, she grabbed the bottle of rubbing alcohol and went back to her task.

"Thank you for saving my life, Lieutenant," Sara offered softly as she fixed the bandage. "I don't think I told you that before."

Denise lingered a moment, watching Sara's hand work on her arm with tender care. "My pleasure," Denise whispered, leaning down to Sara. Denise knew instantly the gesture might be considered inappropriate, but it felt so natural. Denise realized she liked the closeness between them.

For her part, Sara was not offended in the least. Hearing that softer side of Denise made her grin inwardly. *Bet the tough lieutenant can be a real teddy bear sometimes*, Sara thought as she finished bandaging Denise's arm.

As soon as the repair work was done, Denise quickly rose to her feet, going to the kitchen. "Would you like another drink?" she asked conversationally. The heated whisper from moments before seemed to vanish instantly.

Sara was momentarily confused. *What the hell just happened here? One second "my pleasure"; next, she's playing hostess.* Denise's warm nature just...disappeared in a matter of seconds. But the more Sara thought about it the more she realized, *She's retreating. But why? Am I getting closer, Lieutenant VanCook?*

"No," Sara said, pulling herself from her thoughts to respond to the question. "I'm still okay."

Denise returned with a glass of iced tea and took a seat on the sofa next to Sara. "Thank you for helping me," she said, motioning to her arm.

Helping Denise with her arm was far from an inconvenience when compared with the officer's contributions so far. "It was the least I could do."

An uncomfortable silence grew between them as Denise downed her second drink. Sara played with her fingernails, unsure of what else to say.

"Are you okay?" Denise's voice broke the quiet of the room. "I noticed you doing that in the stationhouse."

"Doing what?"

Denise imitated her. "Playing with your fingernails. You did it when you were nervous about the line-up, and you're doing it now. You sure you're okay?"

"Already picking up on my habits, huh, Denise?"

Denise smiled sheepishly. "Observation is what I do for a living." *Yeah, right. It's all about the job and not the gal.* "But really... *Are* you okay?"

"Honestly, I don't know. It's an odd feeling. I'm scared, but being here with you makes me feel safe. Logic tells me I should be cowering under a blanket someplace, but..."

"But what?"

Sara considered the question carefully, and then started to smile. "My friends always called me a duck."

The absurd statement made Denise chuckle. "What do you mean?"

"Well, my friends say things just roll right off of me—like water off a duck's back. My view is: if I'm conscious, breathing, and still have most of my mental capacity functioning, I'm doing all right. But I'll tell ya, Lieutenant, my level of tolerance is certainly being tested this week," she added with a light chuckle.

Denise grinned too. "Well, Donald," she teased.

"I like Daffy better," Sara piped in with a playful swat.

"Okay—Daffy then. I'm going to see about getting you 24-hour protection and having you relocated somewhere else in the city. At least for the time being," she added.

"I appreciate that. And thank you for caring enough to ask how I'm doing. For the record, I'm not the only good person still left in the world, Denise. I don't think just anyone would rush over to put themselves in harm's way like you did tonight."

"Like I said, you needed me and I'd made a promise."

"Then let me make a promise, too."

"What's that?"

"I'll do whatever it takes to get this scumbag off the streets. I'm serious...I know that I'm tired, I'm scared, but understand this...I'm not going to give up, because I know you won't. Agreed?"

Okay—beautiful and smart, I know. Now let's add resilient and determined to the list. That's it, Denise—keep the tally growing, why don't ya? Make it impossible to NOT fall for her.

"And how do you know that I won't give up?" Denise asked. "What makes you so sure that *I'll* stick it out?"

"For starters, look at this apartment. You're rarely here; and you don't strike me as the overly social type, which means you spend most of your time working. Police work is your life and right now—I'm your biggest case. So, I know...I've become your life at this point, and I know you'll protect me at any cost."

"Seems I'm not the only one with observational skills. I like that."

"You do, huh?"

Think fast, Denise. Give her a good reason why that's a good thing, besides the fact it's oh-so-appealing. "Yes...I mean...if anything else happens in the future, I think you'll be on guard and notice things around you. That might be a skill that very well saves your life. But once we get you to a safe haven, you should be fine, Sara."

Damn it. So much for being Ms Right. "So, do we have a deal, then?"

"Deal." Denise smiled before standing up. "Look, it's been a long night. Why don't we try to get some sleep so our heads will be clear for tomorrow, okay?"

"Okay." Sara rose and followed Denise, who waved her toward the back hallway.

"I want you to sleep with me." When Denise realized the statement could have a double meaning, she stopped and turned to face Sara. "I mean, in my bed. That way, I'll know you're safe."

Sara grinned. *What a lovely shade of red she turns. Maybe observational skills are a turn on after all.*

"I knew what you meant, Denise... Thank you. That will

make me feel much safer."

Denise let out the smallest of sighs, glad that Sara hadn't taken offense. She led her back to the bedroom and turned on the light. "This is it," Denise said, escorting her inside. "Not much, but it's home." She took off her jeans and threw on a clean white T-shirt.

She found an oxford in her closet and tossed it to Sara. As Denise turned down the sheets, she spoke to Sara over her shoulder. "If you'd like to change in the bathroom, it's right over...there."

Sara had quickly shed her clothing and was pulling the shirt over her head. Given their size difference, it made a nice nightshirt for Sara.

And Denise had to admit it looked damn good on her, too. "Or you could do it here," Denise chuckled.

Sara returned the light smile. "Where do you want me?" Sara asked, pointing to the bed.

Where do I want you? Just about anywhere would do. Lord, have mercy, Denise. Get your mind out of the gutter. Clearing her throat, Denise motioned Sara over to the other side of the bed so she could be next to the door. "I wanna stay on this side...just in case," she explained.

"No arguments here."

Sara began to climb under the covers, making herself comfortable. Denise turned off the light, and in a few moments their eyes adjusted to the darkness. Sara snuggled into the pillow that held a combination of Denise's perfume and her own scent. She inhaled deeply. *What a beautiful end to a lousy evening*, Sara surmised silently. The excitement of the night had tired her more than she'd realized, and soon she fell asleep. But not before curling up next to Denise, her arms wrapped around Denise's good arm.

Denise was drifting into a dream state when she felt the warm body curl up around her, clinging to her. Instead of being startled by the gesture, she simply enjoyed it. Sara fit her perfectly. Absolutely perfectly. With those tender thoughts, Denise drifted off to sleep.

Chapter
4

September 18

Denise's half-open, bloodshot eyes were the first things that Angie noticed when she walked in to the small office and closed the door tightly behind her. "Long night?" Angie asked with a grin.

"You have no idea how long," Denise said, sipping her coffee and trying to stay alert.

Angie studied the lieutenant's uncharacteristically dazed demeanor a while longer. "You look tired, Denise."

"I feel tired," Denise admitted as she rubbed her eyes. "I didn't get much sleep last night. I kept waiting for someone to break in."

"Was it a quiet night?"

"Yeah. No one followed us."

"Well, at least that's one bit of good news," Angie replied wryly.

The tone in Angie's voice set off a warning bell. "What's the bad news?" the lieutenant asked.

"Ballistics says the gun we found on DeVittem isn't the one that killed the victim."

Denise gave a dismal grin. "That would figure. The murder weapon is probably rusting at the bottom of the Detroit River. I guess our only evidence at this point is the testimony of our witness."

"It looks that way," Angie agreed. "And from last night's events, it seems that DeVittem is trying to clean up that little detail. Why don't you give me the long version of what happened?"

"Maybe later. I've got to go see the captain, and I didn't want to leave Sara until you got here." She nodded toward the blonde who was just outside the office getting some coffee.

"Sara, eh?" Angie teased. "What happened to calling her

'Ms. Langforth'?"

"Let's just say we got a little closer last night," Denise said softly.

"Oh no!" Angie exclaimed, bolting from her chair and starting to pace. "Please don't tell me you slept with her!"

"Did I say that?" Denise countered. She didn't offer more, but when Angie said nothing, she added, "No, I did not."

"Then what do you mean—you got closer?" Angie prodded, a hint of anger in her voice.

"We just got closer, that's all," Denise repeated. She could see the disbelief on Angie's face. "Honestly," Denise continued, "I didn't sleep with her... Well, we slept in the same bed, but you know what I mean." Angie remained stone-faced—doing that disapproving motherly stare that Denise despised. "Look," Denise said defensively, "I understand how important this case is, and I'm not going to screw it up."

"I'm not worried about you screwing the case, Denise; I'm worried about you screwing the witness."

Denise felt like she'd had the wind knocked out of her. "That's a cheap shot!"

"Is it?"

"Yes, it is," Denise retorted. "You don't have to worry."

"Well, I do worry," Angie replied, her pique fading. "And not just about this case. If you're going to be between this woman and the people trying to kill her, I want to know you're thinking with your head and not your—"

Angie stopped in mid-sentence as Sara opened the door. By the look on Denise's face, Sara knew the women were in a heated debate, but she wasn't sure how to make a graceful exit. Asking seemed the best course of action. "I'm sorry. Should I come back later?"

Denise's eyes flickered from staring at Angie to focus on Sara. "No," Denise answered.

"Actually, Ms. Langforth," Angie began, her back turned to Sara and her eyes still fixed on Denise, "I'd appreciate a few more moments alone with Lieutenant VanCook."

"No problem," Sara answered, assessing the staring match between lieutenant and sergeant. "I'll be outside."

Angie heard Sara close the door behind her, and only then did she speak. "I love you, Denise," she began sincerely. "I've spent the last fourteen years of my life with you, and I'd like to spend at least fourteen more. But understand me when I say this woman could be real trouble."

"She's harmless."

Angie ran her fingers through her hair in frustration. "I agree, *she is*. But the people who are after her are not. We've got to use our heads here, or we'll end up losing them. I don't know about you, but I know I'm too damn young to die."

Denise understood everything Angie was saying. Getting emotionally involved could cloud one's judgment. If a situation arose where a quick decision had to be made, having your heart interfering with your head could be deadly...for everyone involved.

"Believe me, I understand. That's why nothing happened."

Angie could tell Denise was being honest, but she was also aware that Denise was attracted to Sara. Given the right circumstances, that attraction could very well flare up at the worst possible time. "And that's why nothing is going to happen, right?" Angie prodded.

Denise shrugged. "Right."

The office went silent again as Angie and Denise locked eyes. "I know you can't control who you're attracted to," Angie said sympathetically. "All I'm asking is that you wait...wait until it's over and DeVittem is behind bars for good. Okay?"

"Okay." Denise grinned. "And for what it's worth, I love you, too. I'm not gonna endanger anyone here—especially not you."

"Okay." Angie nodded, feeling satisfied. "Now that the mushy stuff is out of the way," she grinned, "what's on the agenda for today."

"When is DeVittem's preliminary hearing set for?" Denise asked.

"September 25—one week. He already entered a plea of not guilty at the arraignment, but thanks to his prior record he's being held without bond," Angie provided.

"Not soon enough," Denise said, shaking her head, "Go to the D.A. and see if that young attorney that has the hots for you can move things up a bit."

"Why me?"

"Because he likes you."

"But I don't like him," Angie moaned.

"Please," Denise sighed. "Just put on a smile and ask real nicely. Desperate times call for desperate measures."

Angie chuckled. "Okay," she agreed reluctantly. "But you gotta buy me dinner again this week. Deal?"

"Breakfast," Denise countered.

"Lunch?" Angie offered.

Denise chewed on the inside of her cheek as she considered it. Angie was a shrewd bargainer. "Okay, deal," she agreed, breaking into a smile.

They sealed the pact with a spit handshake, and Angie collected some papers from the desk as she asked, "What about Sara?"

"Take her with you while I speak to Captain Genar. I want to see about getting 24-hour protection for Sara. I'll meet you back here. Let's say...around noon?"

Angie nodded and made her way to the door. "Good Luck with Genar. You know what a pain in the ass he can be."

"Thanks for reminding me," Denise commented sarcastically.

Angie grinned. "No problem. Well, I'm outta here." She opened the door, but didn't quite make her exit.

"Hey!" Denise called, causing her to stop. When Angie turned to face her partner, Denise walked over and slowly undid the top two buttons of Angie's shirt.

"What are you doing? Trying to make Sara jealous?"

"Giving the young D.A. more incentive." Denise smiled. "Now you can go." Her hands squeezed Angie's upper arms in a supportive gesture, as if she were commending her valor.

Angie shook her head. "I don't believe this," she chuckled.

"Men are very visual. He'll love it."

"I feel like I'm prostituting myself," Angie said as she walked toward Sara.

"Must make me your pimp, then, huh?" Denise chuckled. Angie simply waved her away and Denise retreated back to her office. She watched as Angie and Sara engaged in a short conversation before going out the door.

Denise went to her desk and assembled some of the paperwork she had filled out earlier in the morning. She knew it would be an uphill battle at Captain Genar's office, so she took a deep breath and prepared for war. Placing the requisitions neatly in a folder, she made her way upstairs.

She knocked on his office door, then waited a few seconds before stepping inside. The captain was concluding a phone conversation and after he hung up, he turned to face her.

"Lieutenant VanCook," he began, "what brings you here this morning?"

"The witness in the DeVittem case, sir," Denise answered, getting straight to the point.

"What's wrong? She decide to back out?"

"No. Although I could certainly understand if she wanted to," Denise said, trying to pique his curiosity.

"Why?"

"She needs 24-hour protection," Denise said firmly.

Genar laughed in the annoying way that always got under Denise's skin. "Doesn't everyone?"

"I'm serious."

"So am I," he said sternly, as the smile faded from his face. Genar was a large man, muscular and well built given his age. His crew cut and sharp jaw gave him a menacing demeanor. Many detectives had quailed before his dark, steely gaze. Many detectives, but not a certain lieutenant. Many was the time Genar would have written up VanCook for her insubordination if she wasn't so damned good at what she did.

"Last night an attempt was made on her life," Denise explained. "She called me and then managed to escape out of her window, where I picked her up. Uniforms arrived at the scene, but they found nothing in her apartment except the running shower she had used as a diversion."

Genar tugged on his tie in discomfort. "I wish I could help, but we just can't afford to take the uniforms off the streets to give her that kind of protection."

"We can't afford not to. If she testifies, she could put away a very dangerous criminal for a lot of years. But if his men have their way, she'll never set foot in a courtroom."

"I'm sorry, but there's not a whole lot that can be done. There are many witnesses to many crimes and I'd love to protect them all twenty-four hours a day, but that's not realistic. We just don't have the resources," Genar insisted.

"That's true. But this is not your average criminal, and this is not your average witness. She is extremely important to this case. We have her sworn statement, but that's not enough. If she dies, the judge will never allow her testimony in court. How many times have we seen the defense argue that they can't cross-examine a dead person? They would throw the statement right out, and DeVittem would walk."

"You have the weapon, right?"

"Actually, no. We learned this morning that it's not a match. And even if we did find it, that's not enough to stand on its own, either. Please, protect this witness."

Captain Genar sat and studied Denise's face. She was determined, stubborn, and he knew she wasn't going to go away.

"You want 24-hour protection, huh?" he asked, rubbing his hand across his cheeks, trying to decide.

"Yes, sir."

"Okay, you can have it," he agreed, throwing his hands in the air in surrender.

Denise rose from the chair. "Thank you, sir," she replied,

heading towards the door.

"Not so fast, VanCook. I'm not finished," he said, stopping her in her tracks. She turned slowly to face him. "If you want 24-hour protection for this witness, you're the one who's gonna provide it," he announced.

"What?"

"You heard right. If it's that important, you're going to have to provide it."

"But what about my other cases?" *How can he do this?*

"Well, according to you, this is more important than any of them."

Angie was right—he's the biggest pain in the ass this side of Chicago, Denise thought silently. "Yes, sir. But what do I do about the others?" she repeated.

"Give one case to each of your detectives."

"Fine," Denise agreed, growing frustrated. "But how do I stay awake 24 hours a day. Angie is going to Aspen next week."

"I hope your partner is willing to reschedule her vacation time. Otherwise, you'll be drinking enough coffee to get Brazil out of debt. After all, you'll have a lot of protecting to do."

Denise felt her cheeks growing hot. Genar always had a special way of enraging her. And, yes, was quite aware that he could get to her. She knew he delighted in it.

"But who's going to run the squad room? Angie is next in command," Denise replied, making one last attempt at reason.

"You'll find someone." Genar grinned pompously. Denise stared him down, but he continued to grin. "Be careful what you wish for, Lieutenant," he added in his usual arrogant style.

There was so much Denise wanted to say. She wanted to tell him off once and for all. If she did, she knew her fellow officers would regard her as a hero or, more accurately, a martyr; as she also knew she would be severely reprimanded, perhaps even suspended, if she spoke up. Aware that both Angie and Sara needed her, she could not allow herself that luxury. She held her tongue. Instead, she calmly replied, "Yes, sir. Thank you, sir."

"Good," he said triumphantly. "Now you're dismissed."

Denise left his office and returned downstairs to hers. *How on God's earth am I going to explain this to Angie?* she thought as she walked through the stationhouse.

Denise was just finishing organizing her caseload to reassign to the squad's other detectives when Angie and Sara walked in.

"The preliminary hearing for DeVittem is set for Friday,"

Angie said victoriously.

"Did you have any problems?"

"You mean aside from him trying to grab my butt?" Angie asked.

"I meant with Sara," Denise said nodding towards the woman in question.

"Oh, no problems. No attackers... And Sara was very well behaved, too. I only had to threaten her twice with, 'I'll turn this car around right now and go home'."

Sara giggled and Denise shook her head. "You'll have to get used to her warped sense of humor," Denise told Sara.

"But she isn't joking," Sara said with a straight face. "I have to admit I kept playing with the window and then the rearview mirror."

"Yeah, but aside from that she was really good," Angie said, patting Sara on the head like a young child.

"Beautiful," Denise said ruefully. "Now I have two of you to contend with."

Sara and Angie smiled at each other as Denise rubbed her temples.

"Anyway, how'd it go with the captain?" Angie asked.

"Well..." Denise said, looking over at Sara. "Why don't you get some coffee while I talk privately with Sergeant Michaels. Top secret police info and things like that," Denise teased. "I'm sure you understand."

"Totally," Sara said, heading for the door. "Just don't forget to come get me when you're done," she teased as she left.

Once the door was closed, Angie turned to Denise. "He denied the request for protection, didn't he?" Angie whispered.

Denise considered before answering. *Where to begin? Just stick to the facts.* "Actually, he approved it," Denise said cheerfully.

"Really? That's wonderful!" Angie said. "Now tell me the down side," she added, knowing there was more to it than Denise was saying.

Denise shook her head and smiled. "I can't hide anything from you, you know that?"

"Of course I know. I'm a detective; that's my job," Angie grinned. "Now, tell me what's up."

"Well," Denise said stalling, "Genar approved the protection, however we have to be the ones to provide it."

"But we can't," Angie argued. "I've got my Aspen trip coming up."

"I know," Denise muttered helplessly.

Angie studied Denise, noting the look in her eyes; and when she didn't add more, the light dawned. "Ohhhh nooo," Angie whined. "I've got reservations already. Damn it!"

"I know, and I'm sorry. He won't give me anyone else."

"But what about our case load?"

Denise held the stack up in the air. "I've got to disperse these to the other teams today."

Angie sighed and plunked down in the chair across from Denise. "So I'm losing my vacation *and* my other cases?" she asked despondently.

Acknowledging Angie's objections, Denise dropped the files back on the desk. "Look, you don't have to cancel your vacation if you don't want to. I can handle it the week that you're gone," Denise offered.

"Thank you," Angie replied. "But I wouldn't be able to have a good time knowing you're back here alone with target number one."

"I'm really sorry," Denise said with heartfelt sincerity.

Angie took a few moments and considered the whole situation. "It's not your fault, it's Genar. The man is an incredible jackass."

"I wish there was something I could do," Denise said, heavy-hearted. "If it's any consolation, I'll take the night shift. I know you're a day person, and they probably won't make a move on Sara during the day. Really, I wish I could help."

"There's nothing you can do except go home and go to bed," Angie said with disappointment. "I'll take Sara home to get her things, and I'll give you a call at your place to tell you where to meet us."

"Okay," Denise agreed quietly, not wanting to linger on the negative aspects. "I'll finish up here and take off. How does 7 to 7 sound?"

"Fine. I'll call at 6 tonight to wake you up."

Denise circled around the desk to where Angie was standing. "I know how much you were looking forward to this trip. I'll see if I can get you a few extra days on the department when this is over," Denise offered.

Angie was touched that Denise cared that much about her. "It's not your fault," she replied, flashing a genuine smile. "Besides, Mt. Trashmore will be open in a few months. This case is far more important than any vacation, so just go and get some sleep."

"Somehow a garbage dump converted into a ski resort seems like a poor substitute for Colorado," Denise said sympathetically.

"Very true. But, like I said, it's okay."

Denise gave Angie a gentle hug.

"I'll let Sara know what's up on the way back to her place," Angie said, going out into the bullpen.

Denise nodded and watched as Angie collected Sara and the two of them left. Grabbing her coat and the files from her desk, the lieutenant joined the other detectives. "Everybody listen up," she shouted. "Everyone has an extra case this week. When I call your names, come and pick up your folder."

Everyone moaned and groaned their displeasure.

"I'm not any more pleased than you are, folks," Denise said before calling out the first team. Finishing the reassignments, she called out, "Detective Brenner," and walked over to him. He looked up from his desk. "Sergeant Michaels and I will be protecting the DeVittem witness, so for the next few weeks, you're in charge. I'll call you tomorrow with the number where you can reach Sergeant Michaels or myself if you have any questions. Okay?"

"Aye, aye, Lieutenant," he said with a smile.

"Good man. Please don't let the place go to hell while I'm gone, okay?" Denise grinned as she took in her grimy surroundings. "Not that I'd really be able to tell if it did."

"Don't worry. It's safe in my hands," Brenner stated.

"It had better be. I'll catch ya later."

Denise walked out and informed Sergeant Wagner of the change in command, as well. After the short conversation, she headed out to her car. *It's going to be a long afternoon,* Denise thought. *And an even longer night.*

Chapter
5

September 23

Earlier that week, when Angie had offered to guard Sara at her place, Sara had voiced her preference to put them up at a hotel. Angie didn't argue. She and Denise had deduced that DeVittem had contracts out on Sara all over the city; so every low-life looking to make a few grand would be searching for her. Registering under an alias at a neutral location would make it more difficult for any bounty hunters to determine where the witness was staying.

Tucked away in the suite with Tiffany vases and fine rugs from the Orient, Sara felt safe. It was her own personal ivory tower, similar to the one her mother had had, the one in which she was raised. It had two spacious rooms with everything one needed for comfort—living quarters, a full kitchen with dishwasher, and a bedroom that put the boudoirs in the Ford mansion to shame.

Hell, Denise had mused the first time she saw it, *it's bigger than my damn apartment.* But for the moment, she and Sara sat at the large kitchenette table playing cards.

"Draw four."

"Son of a bitch!"

Sara couldn't help but laugh.

Denise was having a tough time. *Mental note: Never play Uno with Sara again...ever,* she thought silently as she picked up four cards from the stack—all yellow.

"I think I'll callllllll...blue!" Sara said next.

Denise rolled her eyes. "You would have to call blue."

Sara laughed heartily and laid down a blue 10. Denise laid down a yellow 10 and turned the pile back to yellow. Unfortunately for the officer, Sara wasn't going to let that happen. She held a yellow card that would bring her closer to victory. "Draw two," Sara told her. With a grumble, Denise took two cards as Sara got to take another turn. She laid down another "draw two" card, this time changing it back to blue again.

"You're heartless."

"Am not. Just competitive."

"Competitive? Oh no. It is not enough for you to just beat me, you've decided to mutilate me."

"Not so. You're just a lousy Uno player," the blonde countered, laying down another card. "Uno!" she added.

Denise looked at all the cards in her hands. This was not good. "This is going to be another naked defeat, isn't it?"

"Well, I'm not sure about the naked part—you could probably cover most of your body with all those cards in your hands," she chuckled.

"Smart ass," Denise muttered under her breath with a smile. She laid down a red 10 and waited for Sara's play. The blonde just smirked at her in response, but didn't make a move. "Oh come on," Denise grumped. "Pick a card or kill me here."

Quietly, and being exaggeratedly careful, she placed a Red 5 down on the deck.

Denise just shook her head and laid her cards flat on the table for Sara to count.

"Five cards alone with 10 points. Geez, Denise, I think you're getting worse at this game instead of better."

"Oh, please, feel free to not only win, but rub it in a little. Don't forget to gloat while you're at it."

"Oh, don't worry, I won't forget."

Denise sighed. "Son of a bitch."

"That's been your favorite phrase all night... While mine, on the other hand, has been *uno*."

As Sara wrote down the total, Denise rounded up the cards. "I'm dealing this time. You're marking the cards or stacking the deck. You've gotta be," she grinned.

As Sara finished the total, she turned to Denise. "Wanna know the total for this—"

"No," Denise answered, cutting her short. "Cut the deck."

Sara just smiled and did as she was asked, then slid the cards back to Denise.

"So, tell me..." Sara began.

"What? How I acquired my fine mastery of this card game?" Denise asked.

"No," Sara answered. "Tell me what you do when you're not arresting criminals."

Denise considered the question. "Trying to prevent having criminals to arrest." Sara looked confused, so Denise explained. "Every Fall, I help organize Fall Festival events. They give the kids in the inner city stuff to do at the area activity plazas. It's a self-preservation thing. If they're busy, they aren't breaking the law."

"I don't believe that's the only reason you do it. I think you care."

"Yeah, you're right," Denise conceded as she dealt out a new hand. "Some of those kids have got it tough—parents are either not around or in jail—but I think if they realize someone does care about them, then maybe their lives aren't going to be about gangs or drugs or all the other evils out there. Maybe having a cop smile and call them by name might have a positive effect. Guess I'm idealistic sometimes."

"Idealistic is good." Sara nodded her approval as she organized her cards. "I admire that. You're trying to make a difference with them."

"Well, what about you, Ms. Langforth? What do you do in the 'off-season'?"

"I'm not the humanitarian you are. I don't devote my time, but I have donated money to the festival. They repaved the basketball court over by Woodward thanks to my donation. Jesus, the way that came out sounded pretty damn pompous, didn't it?" Sara laughed. "Seriously, though, if I see a cause that's good, then I'll give to it."

"Doesn't sound pompous to me. They really need the money, and it's good to know that folks like you care enough to take the time to look into their organization. Told you, you're one of the good ones." At that moment Sara put down a "draw four" card. "Okay, I spoke too soon."

Sara laughed and laid down a green 8. "Do you do anything else? Sporting events, music, stuff like that?"

"Nope. Angie's a Tigers fan, and sometimes she drags me to the games; but only when they play the Yankees, because I'm a Yanks fan."

"The two of you at the ballpark must be a sight to see, I'm sure."

"We have our moments." Denise smiled. "So, what about you? What do you enjoy? I don't think TV is one of your choices, because I didn't see one at your apartment."

Sara put her cards face down on the table, which made Denise look up. "That's amazing, but I must confess—I feel like there's no sense of mystery here between us."

"Sorry, I just noticed there was no TV in the living room is all."

"Well, I do *own* a TV—it's in my bedroom. I like to curl up and watch old movies."

"Popcorn kernels in the bed?"

"You know it." She smiled, picking up her cards to continue the game.

"So, what's your favorite classic movie, besides *Gone with the Wind*? All women seem to like *Gone with the Wind* for some reason."

"I don't."

"Really?"

"It's okay, but about two hours too long, if you ask me." Sara chuckled. "But it's okay nonetheless. My favorite would be *Casablanca*, I think."

Denise smiled. *One of my favorites, too.* "It keeps you guessing. You keep wondering what's going to happen."

"Do you know why it keeps you guessing?"

"Good acting?"

"Well, I'll admit I like Bogart, but in truth, the reason is that when they were filming it, they were guessing too. No one knew how it would end. They didn't have an ending for it until they were deep into production."

"Really? I didn't know that. It won best picture, didn't it?" Sara nodded. "1942."

Denise gave a chuckle and shook her head. "Now *that's* amazing."

"What is?" Sara asked.

"That you would know that. You're like a sponge."

"Gee, you're a sweet talker," the blonde chuckled.

"It's a compliment," Denise insisted. "Everything you see or hear seems to stay with you. You soak up everything around you. Believe me, it wasn't meant as a negative of any kind."

"Yes, well, I'm a walking index of useless knowledge." Sara grinned at the officer and laid down a "draw two" card. "Uno!" she called again.

"But it's not useless—don't you see? You can find common ground with just about anyone because of it. I'm surprised you're not in politics. I take that back. You're too honest to be in politics."

Sara chuckled and laid down her last card.

"Son of a bitch," Denise said, quickly tossing her cards onto the pile before Sara could count them.

"Hey, you cheated! I didn't get a chance to count them," Sara complained.

"Trust me," Denise laughed. "You won—hands down. Don't make it any more painful on me. Give me 100 and have mercy, would ya?"

Sara happily agreed to that, rounded up the deck, and shuffled. "So tell me, Lieutenant VanCook, how does a female climb so high in the department?"

"I never go home. Like you said at my place, I spend most of my time at the precinct."

"Think that would ever change?"

"I don't foresee anything being more important than my job, but who's to say. Maybe I'll meet that perfect person who makes me want to rush home at night. So far, I haven't been that fortunate." Denise looked at her cards and laid down a green 8, starting a new game. "What about you? You work irregular hours, don't you?"

"Yeah, I do. I get calls at all times of the day and night. But I don't mind too much. I enjoy what I do."

"What do you enjoy most?"

"Umm, helping people. Granted, I don't offer the kind of protection that you do." Sara grinned. "But they say that next to the death of a loved one, buying a house can be the most stressful. I like to think I'm successful because people relax with me. I'm easygoing, and I take things in stride."

Denise smiled. "I'd have to agree, at least when you're not being a card shark."

"Speaking of which—*uno.*"

Denise let out a deep sigh.

"Go on," Sara prodded. "Say it! It's not the same unless you say it."

"Son of a bitch," Denise muttered. The bubbly tone of Sara's laughter made the officer smile. "You're really enjoying this, aren't you?"

"Yeah, I am," Sara said, not shying away in the least. "We should play this again tomorrow."

"I think not. I'd like to keep what little pride I have left."

A knock at the door made Denise look at her watch. 6:45 a.m. "Thank God! Angie's come to save me from getting butchered yet again," Denise teased as she tossed the cards on the table. She went over and looked out the peephole in the door before opening it. As expected, it was Angie.

"Glad you're here," Denise remarked. "You just saved me from a horrible beating."

"Too late," Sara interjected.

"Ha. Ha," Denise replied as she relocked the door. "You might have won tonight, Ms. Langforth, but I'm bringing over Monopoly tomorrow, and I'll be sure to smother you."

Angie looked at Denise with a wry grin. "Playing Monopoly

against a real estate agent. Are you sure you want to make that large a boast, Den?"

"She can't lose any worse than she did tonight," Sara teased.

"After I have Park Place and Boardwalk, you'll be singing a different tune," Denise countered.

"Why go for the big bucks?" Angie piped in. "Get the less expensive properties and build your hotels there. Then you can keep hitting her up for cash as she moves around the entire rest of the board."

"Shhh," Sara said, putting her finger to her lips. "Don't tell her that."

"That's not a bad idea. Thanks, partner."

"Yeah, thanks, partner," Sara said ironically.

"Well, I gotta look out for her," Angie answered, inclining her head towards Denise.

"So you're the brains in this duo, huh?" Sara joked.

"Hey! Do you two mind talking about me behind my back after my back has left?" Sara and Angie just chuckled. Denise smiled as she put on her jacket. "I'd better leave now with the tattered remnants of my ego." Denise looked out the peephole and unlocked the door.

"Denise," Sara called. "You know I'm just joking, right?"

So she cares about my opinion—interesting. "Yes, I know, Sara. And as for you, Angie, watch her closely. I think she marks the cards." She winked at Sara. "See ya tomorrow."

They both gave a wave, and Angie locked the door after Denise was gone. She turned around to see Sara cleaning up from the card game. "You and Denise seem to have hit it off pretty well," Angie remarked casually.

"Yeah." Sara nodded. "I enjoy her company quite a bit."

"Forgive me if this seems out of line but..."

"But what?" Sara stopped straightening up the table as Angie paused a moment longer, deciding on the best place to start.

"Let me preface this by saying that I think you're a very dependable person, Sara. We've had witnesses that turned tail and ran after being subjected to even less than you've had to go through. So, I respect that a great deal. I know you're trying to do the right thing."

"But?"

"But," Angie smiled to soften what she was about to say, "you are our witness, and our relationship has to be professional. Friendly is good, but anything more and..."

"I'm not involved with Denise, if that's what you're implying."

"No, I don't think you are, yet. But I see the way you look at her, the way you smile, the way you light up when she comes into a room. Your admiration is more than friendly... I'm just saying that I'm concerned here—for you and for Denise. If an attorney for the defendant thought there was anything unethical going on, they could put both of you through hell on the witness stand. Denise has worked damned hard to keep a clean record all these years, and it wouldn't look good for her if she was suspected of being intimately involved with a witness."

"She's not involved with your witness, Sergeant Michaels." The retort came off much more curtly than Sara had intended. She had thought that addressing Angie formally would be best, but as a result it just sounded sarcastic. "Look," Sara added, trying to salvage the conversation. "I'm not going to lie. I'm very attracted to Denise; I admit it. And given the chance, I would jump at the opportunity to have more than a friendship with her. I don't think life has to revolve around the 'rules'—especially when the rule makes little or no sense. I'll help you and I'll help Denise, but I'm not going to give you false assurances that nothing will happen. I don't know what lies ahead. Just know that whatever might happen, I will always keep Denise's best interests at heart."

Angie sighed. "I don't want to argue, Sara."

"Then don't. Just let it go."

Angie gave a reluctant nod, and Sara went back to clearing the table. When she'd finished, she put the stack of cards neatly on the end of the counter.

"You might want to know something else," Angie said softly. "Something between the two of us."

"What's that?"

"Denise has been real unlucky with love."

"Who hasn't?" Sara snorted.

"Seriously, she had a very bad thing happen."

"Such as?"

"She's had her share of lovers over the years, but there was one guy in particular, Joseph."

"What happened?" Sara asked, taking a step closer.

Angie paused a moment, questioning her decision to share the information. *Maybe you should have kept your mouth shut. Well, it's too damn late now.*

"What about him?" Sara prodded.

"Some punk that Denise had arrested early in our career made parole. He stalked Denise, found out about Joseph, and instead of taking his revenge on Denise, went after her lover."

Sara was too wrapped up in the story to utter a sound.

"He got beaten within an inch of his life, and needless to say, it pulled them apart. She's been love shy since, so please don't be sitting around and waiting for Denise to get close."

Sara just gave a nod. She couldn't even begin to fathom how that would feel: to have someone you loved hurt because of something you'd done in your past. *It must have made her feel pretty damn helpless,* Sara concluded.

"She never got over it?"

"Not quite," Angie answered. "She coped with it, but I think her way of doing that was to put up a wall around her heart. I think Denise has built a lot of walls. I know her better than anyone, but even I don't know everything. I just don't want you thinking you're going to fall for each other and find happily ever after. If you do, you're sadly mistaken, Sara."

Sara gave a sarcastic grin. "So you think that telling me this is going to deter me?"

"No, I think that telling you this will prepare you. Because if something does happen..." She sighed and shrugged. "I just thought you had a right to know, in case it all blows up."

Sara considered Angie's words. She didn't honestly know what to make of the sergeant. At times she seemed like an ally, but at other times—such as now—she seemed adversarial. Although the information wasn't promising, she was grateful for getting it.

"Thank you for the insight," Sara began. "And like I said, I'll do my best to keep things on a friendly basis. Now, if you don't mind, I think I'll be taking a nap. I've been up for a while this morning."

"I can imagine," Angie grinned. Sara just nodded and began to make her way to the bedroom. "Hey, Sara? I don't want any hard feeling, okay?"

"No hard feeling, Angie. We'll just agree to disagree." Without adding more, Sara simply walked into the bedroom and closed the door behind her.

Oh boy, Angie thought as she let out a sigh and sat down on the sofa with the remote. *You've got a spitfire on your hands this time, Denise.*

September 27

The week went by without incident. Angie was relaxing in one half of the suite reading a magazine when she heard the 6:45 p.m. knock. Denise always came 15 minutes early and Angie fully expected to see her partner standing in front of the door when she peered out to verify who was out front.

"How's it been?" Denise asked as she entered.

"Quiet," Angie responded. "Sara's taking a nap...again." Angie looked at Denise with suspicious eyes.

"What?" Denise asked defensively.

"The woman sleeps all day and she's up all night, isn't she?"

"I don't know what you're talking about?" Denise protested with a sly grin.

"Yeah, you do," Angie smiled back, putting on her coat. "I'm gonna get going. Call if you need anything."

"I will." Denise preceded Angie to the door and checked the hallway before opening it. "Take care."

"You, too," Angie said as she left.

Denise closed and locked the door. Hearing Sara stirring in the sitting room of the suite, she crossed to the communicating doorway. "Good morning," Denise teased, with a pointed look at her watch.

"Good afternoon," Sara admitted with a smile. "How has your work day been?"

"Let's see: I went home this morning, grabbed a bite to eat, went to bed, then came back here," Denise detailed.

"Do you hate the night shift?"

"Actually, when I was a rookie that was my first duty assignment. It wasn't that bad, I'm just out of practice."

"Not me," Sara replied. "I'm a very nocturnal creature. I love the night."

"Oh really," Denise said sarcastically. "All the hours you've stayed up talking to me—it was hard to tell." She gave Sara a coy grin. "As a matter of fact, Angie thinks I've been keeping you up all these nights."

"No offense to your partner in the slightest, but you're much more...stimulating to talk to."

"Stimulating, huh?"

Sara nodded and her grin widened. "Much more."

The feeling was mutual. Denise had slowly begun to realize that although her life had meaning, it had been a long time since she'd really had much fun in it. She enjoyed Sara's company, too. The way she tilted her head slightly when she smiled, the way she emphasized her words by using her hands, and the way she admired Denise silently in every conversation were mannerisms that were adding up to a grand attraction. Sara's laugh when something amused her, the way she could carry on a conversation about practically anything...

Long after Angie began her shift each day, Sara was still on

Denise's mind. The image of that short blonde hair bouncing as Sara walked through the suite haunted Denise every afternoon as she tried to sleep. Denise would close her eyes and see Sara's charming grin and shapely hips; she had never felt so captivated by anyone. Only one ritual would lull Denise to sleep, and it wasn't a cup of warm milk.

Denise hummed a moment, breaking the silence. "Have you had dinner yet?" she asked.

"I was thinking," Sara began slowly, testing the waters, "maybe we could go out for dinner."

"You suggested that two days ago, and you know what my answer is," Denise answered, obviously frustrated with the request.

"Please. It's been a week and nobody has tried anything. Besides, there are some very important papers that my secretary Judith has set out for me at the office."

"What?" Denise asked. "I'm not sure I heard that right. You want to go to dinner *and* stop by your office? The answer's no."

"Why not? I'm not asking for the world." *I'm not a child either,* Mom.

"You know why, Sara. There are people out there who want to kill you!"

"But I already spoke to Judith. Everything is all ready to go; I just have to pick it up. Then afterward, we could stop at the fast food joint."

"You called Judith?" Denise exclaimed in disbelief. "I told you not to have contact with anyone in the city. No! We are definitely staying here," Denise added firmly.

"Come on, one manila folder and one greasy cheeseburger. That's all I ask."

"That's too much, Sara," Denise stated seriously.

"Fine!" Sara said, glancing around the floor to locate her shoes. "I'll go without you!" she shouted as she picked them up.

"No you won't!" Denise retorted, grabbing the footwear from Sara's hands.

"You can't stop me!" Sara challenged, snatching the shoes back.

"The hell I can't!" Denise answered, reclaiming the shoes.

Sara growled, storming off into the bedroom, making sure to slam the door behind her. She began to pace. *Who the fuck does she think she is? Jesus, some fresh air would be nice! I'd die for a little human contact tonight besides the police department! Why is that so goddamn hard to understand?*

Denise threw the shoes on the sofa and ran her fingers

through her hair in frustration. *Good God, why doesn't she see that I'd let her go if it wasn't so dangerous for her? Why does she have to be so damn stubborn about it? I'm trying to be her protector not her jailer, but...Jesus Christ.* Denise slammed down onto the sofa, rubbing her eyes to release the tension that was building behind them.

After a few moments, Sara emerged from the bedroom. Denise didn't look at her at first. She was still too angry.

"I'm sorry," Sara offered. "I know you're just doing your job."

Denise looked up and realized how childish the argument had become. "Apology accepted," Denise began. "I'm sorry, too. I wish I could do as you ask."

"That's okay," Sara said softly. "I don't hold it against you; but please don't be too upset when I tell you that I'm leaving anyway."

The door was unlocked and opened before Denise had the chance to look down at Sara's feet. The broker had on another pair of shoes.

"Wait!" Denise yelled as Sara bolted outside. The officer shot to her feet and darted out behind her. She was just in time to see Sara squeezing between the closing elevator doors in the middle of the small hallway. By the time Denise reached them, the car had begun its descent. The detective frantically stabbed at the button, trying to reopen the doors, but it was too late. Denise slammed her fist on the door then spun to her left, where she knew she would find the stairwell.

Taking to the stairs, Denise moved as fast as she could, taking them two at a time to try and catch up to Sara before she got out of the hotel. When she was a few steps from the bottom landing, she lurched over the railing, judging the distance. Sara would be reaching the exit at any second, so she made a quick decision. She jumped.

Denise landed hard, sending a sharp pain shooting up her leg. The drop had been further than she gauged, and gravity worked against her. As quickly as she could, Denise hobbled to the door that led to the lobby. Pushing it open, Denise hopped wildly towards the elevator around the corner. She heard the signal bell indicate its arrival, but she waited. The last thing she wanted to do was play elevator tag. Once Sara had cleared the doors, she wouldn't have the chance to send the elevator back up and lose Denise all over again.

As Sara casually walked by, a satisfied smirk on her face, Denise grabbed her by her tan dress jacket and forcefully swung the young blonde around to face her. "Don't ever do this again," Denise panted firmly.

Sara's happy go lucky expression turned to one of shock. *How in the hell did she catch me?* Evaluating the look on Denise's face, Sara knew she meant business. Denise had the strength and the smarts to outwit her. Sara didn't dare speak, she simply nodded her capitulation. *Okay, Denise, you can let go now. I get the point.*

Denise felt Sara tense. She saw the genuine fear in her eyes and regretted having been the cause of it. *She's certainly an all-or-nothing woman. But still, that doesn't make it right and she should know better.* As much as Sara's actions had enraged Denise, she also had to admire them on some level. Realizing that Sara was stubborn and persistent, and that her mind was set on going out, she knew that things would proceed more smoothly if she compromised. Denise released her hold and carefully smoothed out Sara's jacket. "Let's go get your papers and your cheeseburger," she suggested, still trying to regain her breath.

Taken by surprise by the sudden change of heart, Sara only nodded. As they walked to the parking garage, she noticed Denise's limp. "Are you okay?"

"Oh, yeah," Denise replied ironically. "I just jumped about ten feet trying to catch you. I'm okay; just don't ask my leg how it's doing."

Sincerity filled Sara's voice. "I'm sorry. I didn't mean for you to get hurt."

"Just get in the car, Ms. Langforth."

Sara did as Denise ordered, hearing the officer's distress in the use of her last name. Sara knew it wouldn't be like their usual time together—stolen glances and innuendoes. *Romance certainly isn't in the air tonight.*

Denise drove in silence. It was only when they came to a strip of fast food restaurants that she spoke, ordering sternly, "Pick something."

"That looks okay," Sara said softly, pointing to the left.

Denise pulled into the drive-thru and stopped. She turned to Sara and asked coldly, "What do you want?" Her hostility spilled into the words.

Sara felt very guilty. "I'm sorry," she tried again.

"What do you want?" Denise repeated, ignoring the apology.

Sara paused, unsure if she should press the point or back off for the moment. "Cheeseburger with everything, small fries, and a cola," she replied.

Denise placed the order, pulled up, and paid. She handed the food to Sara, then pulled back out into traffic. "What's the address of your office?"

"It's not too far from here. Take a right at the second light," Sara instructed.

They continued in silence, except when Sara directed Denise where to turn. Her office was only fifteen minutes away, but it seemed like an eternity in the quietness of the car. It had never been this uncomfortable between them, and Sara hated it. *Jesus, Denise, say something—anything. Okay, fine, act like a brat, see if I care. I said I was sorry, for crying out loud, isn't that enough?*

When they arrived at the office, night had already fallen. Denise studied the surroundings as Sara unlocked the door. The office had two large bay windows in addition to the glass door. The street looked vacant, which was a good sign. There were a few cars parked along it, but nothing near the office. Except for the usual passing car, the street was quiet. Once inside, Sara broke the silence, distracting Denise from her observations. "Are you going to talk to me at all tonight?"

"I haven't decided yet," Denise grumbled.

"I wish you would stop being immature," Sara countered, placing her hands on her hips in defiance.

"Immature?" Denise said, raising her voice and approaching Sara. "I'm immature?"

"Yes. You're being immature by not speaking to me," Sara argued, not intimidated in the least by Denise towering over her.

"Look here, lady! I'm not the one who took off like a spoiled child who didn't get her way. And if you do it again, I'll kill you myself." Denise's breath was growing quick and ragged, her anger getting the better of her.

Sara could see the fury in Denise's eyes, but it didn't stop her from continuing. "I told you I was sorry."

"That's not good enough."

"Well, what would you like, Denise? Should I sign it in blood for you?"

"Promise you won't do it again, and perhaps I'll consider your apology!"

Sara couldn't bring herself to make Denise that promise and released a frustrated sigh. "It's got nothing to do with you. I feel like a goddamn prisoner locked up in that hotel room," Sara shouted.

"You think I like it any more than you do?" Denise asked, raising her voice again.

"At least you get to leave. I'm stuck there 24 hours a day. Hell, DeVittem probably has more freedom than I do, and he's a fucking murderer!"

Suddenly Denise could understand Sara's point. She was just as much a prisoner of the police department as the man she was to testify against. And Denise knew that for the time being there wasn't anything she could do to change it. *You're going stir crazy, aren't you, sweetheart? Not that I can blame you... Did I just think "sweetheart"? Did I say that out loud?* Denise watched Sara to see if it might have slipped out, but when Sara offered no reaction, she was certain it hadn't. *Cut her some slack, Denise. Go on—call a truce.*

The pain in Denise's leg began to wane, as did her temper; and Sara noticed the change. The tension lines in Denise's face began to smooth and the scowl was starting to disappear. Sara took Denise's lead.

"Look," Sara offered, "I really am sorry about your leg. The last thing I wanted was to hurt you. And I promise from now on to try my best to do what you say. I feel like..."

"You've got cabin fever?"

Thanks for understanding. "Yes, that's exactly what it feels like."

Denise nodded. "Apology accepted...as long as you accept mine."

The comment caught Sara off guard, and she quirked her head in curiosity. *What did she say? She's sorry?*

"I should have realized you were feeling penned up, and I'm sorry I didn't just agree to bring you here in the first place," Denise continued.

The tension that had marred the evening began to dissipate, and Sara found herself grinning again. "How's the leg?"

Denise smiled and rubbed it. "Looks like this old war-horse will be okay."

Sara was relieved to see the expression on Denise's face. She walked to her desk and picked up a folder that was sitting squarely in the center. Thumbing through it quickly, she glanced at the contents to make sure everything was in order.

"Okay," Sara said, waving the folder. "I'm all set. Let's get home."

As they turned to leave, Denise suddenly stopped. Her face turned ghostly white in an instant.

"What?" Sara asked.

"Oh no," Denise whispered.

Sara followed Denise's gaze to outside of the windows before she felt Denise twirl her behind the desk. Sara crashed against a steel file cabinet as she heard the sound of shattering glass. Denise pushed the desk over, giving them cover from something outside. Denise's strength surprised Sara. It usually took two girls in the office to move the big oak desk even an inch, yet Denise had flung it over as if it were made of paper maché.

"Keep your head down," Denise ordered as she peered over the top. She saw the broken glass, but the man in the trench coat with the sawed off shotgun who had been standing there moments before had disappeared. He was gone...or at least out of sight.

Sara watched the officer as Denise scanned the area. "Where is he?" Sara whispered.

"I don't see him," Denise admitted in frustration.

"Maybe he gave up," Sara suggested. She knew it was improbable, but she liked the reassuring feeling it gave her to say it.

"Maybe," Denise said, as she began to rise. "Maybe not. You stay down."

Denise slowly crept forward. She could hear the wind whistling through the fractured door. Broken glass crunched beneath her feet as she made her way through the office. Suddenly, from the corner of her eye she spotted a gun barrel outside. She leapt fast. More glass exploded, cascading to the floor. Without hesitation, she returned fire toward the corner of the building where she had seen the muzzle flash.

When things got tough for Denise and Angie, they always joked with each other. They figured if they were going to die, it might as well be with a smile on their faces. Sometimes their humor was the only thing that kept them sane in a dangerous situation. "In case you hadn't noticed," Denise said with a nervous giggle, "he didn't give up."

"So I hear."

It was an old habit, and Denise was glad that Sara was willing to play along and give her the calm she needed.

Denise rose again and waited for the assassin's next move. The attack had blown out the far right window. It was perfect. It gave Denise the option of inching along with her back against the wall to a point where she could look out without using the doorway. Now she could see perfectly if he was on her left, and if he was to the right she had the wall as cover. Slowly, she slunk along the office wall to the edge of the shattered glass.

She looked out the left window. He wasn't there, so there was only one other place he could be—standing next to her on the right, perhaps only inches away. She couldn't fire blindly around the corner. Protecting Sara was her first priority, but in case the attacker decided to back off, she didn't want to accidentally injure an innocent bystander who might be on the other side. So she waited. And she listened.

Her right hand gripped her .38 so hard that her knuckles began to turn white. She rested quietly against the wall for a few moments and then slid into a crouched position. She was wondering how much longer he was willing to wait before he came back for another try, when she heard some glass crackle outside under the shifting of weight. *Paydirt,* she thought.

Crouching, Denise swung herself around the corner just as he was making his move. Two shots rang out. Expecting her to be at her full height, the attacker never got a chance to fire. His body tumbled forward like a fallen tree, and Denise scrambled to get out of the way as he went face first into the broken glass. After the sounds died down, Sara peeked her head up above the desk.

"Is it okay?" Sara asked, seeing the man lying outside.

Denise was checking the man for signs of life and found none. The words she had spoken to Sara earlier that week haunted her. *No one deserves to die by another person's hand, but it happens.* Denise jumped a little when she felt Sara's hand on her shoulder.

"Are you okay?" Sara asked, seeing the emotion on Denise's face.

"Son of a bitch wouldn't give up." She was angry with the dead man for his disregard for his own life. She was angry with herself for being the one who'd had to take it. But more than all that, she ached because of what she had done. Her sense of duty and her sense of morality conflicted.

Sara could see Denise's pain. "It's not your fault," Sara said, trying to reassure her. "You did what you had to do."

Denise would have started to sob if her reflexive police training hadn't taken over. "Get back behind the desk," Denise ordered, pushing her back to the hiding place. "He might not be alone."

Without haste, Denise dialed 911 and gave the operator the rundown on what had happened, knowing that the emergency worker would notify the police in the proper precinct. Hanging up, she immediately dialed again—this time to Angie.

"It's Denise... All hell broke loose tonight," she said into the receiver.

Sara listened as Denise talked to Angie. She noted how Denise kept observing her surroundings even as she spoke of the incident that had occurred. Sara couldn't help feeling guilty for all the trouble that she had caused by insisting on this one little trip to the office. Her heart ached for Denise. She could see how shaken the officer felt—but even within that distress, there was a great deal of confidence and courage.

Denise hung up the phone. "Angie's on her way," she said, looking down at Sara. That's when Denise saw the tears. "It's okay," Denise said kneeling next to her on the floor, reassuring her. "You're all right."

"I don't care about me," Sara sobbed. "Look at what I put you through, all because I had to have my way."

Denise gathered Sara in her arms and held her close. "It's okay," Denise comforted. "You were right, Sara. You shouldn't live like a caged animal. You should have the right to come and go as you please. That's why you're leaving the city...tonight. That way, if you want to go out, you can."

Sara looked up into Denise's sympathetic eyes. "I'm not leaving without you. I trust you, Denise. Besides...we made a promise, remember?"

"I remember; we'll leave together."

"Really? What about Angie?"

"She'll stay and run the precinct. Besides, I feel much better with her in charge of the squad than Detective Brenner. Don't get me wrong. I like Brenner, but he's a bit of a himbo, if you know what I mean."

"No, actually I don't," Sara said, looking for an explanation.

"Male equivalent of bimbo—a superficial airhead, but he's a nice guy. In fact, we went through the Academy together."

"Ah, I see."

That's when Sara noticed that Denise hadn't let go of her. *Not that I'm going to complain*, Sara thought, as her hold on the officer unconsciously tightened.

Denise felt Sara's grip get stronger. Sara's head was level with Denise's chest, and Sara rested her head there and let out a long sigh. Automatically, over and over again, Denise stroked Sara's hair, letting her fingers travel though the even strands. Denise realized that the gesture had little to do with calming a witness. She was loving every moment of it: feeling the soft body clinging tightly to hers—depending on her, needing her. Being needed was something Denise had missed for quite a long time, and she was in no hurry to have the feeling end.

The combined scent of Denise's perfume and perspiration quickened Sara's pulse even more than the events that had just transpired. She rose to her knees and tilted her head up toward Denise so they could be face to face. Sara studied Denise's expression. She knew they were both thinking the same thing.

Sara took Denise's face in her palms and pulled her closer. The officer's skin was soft to the touch, and the contact made the hairs on Sara's neck stand on end. Sara gave a soft grin and took one last look in Denise's eyes before closing her own. "Kiss me," she whispered.

Denise felt helpless to resist. She wanted this. She needed this. And against her better judgment, she began to make her descent to Sara's waiting lips. That was, until she heard the car out front. Instead of the lip lock she was hoping for, Sara felt herself being pulled down protectively behind the desk as Denise peered over its top.

"The back-up's here," Denise said, as she got up and headed outside to greet them.

"Great," Sara mumbled to no one but herself. *Well, this proves the theory,* Sara thought. *There's never a cop around when you need one, yet they always manage to show up at the most inopportune moments.*

Sara watched as Denise spoke to the uniformed officers outside. She knew the lieutenant would be busy for a while, so she walked back to a large Monet poster on the wall, took it down, and opened the door hidden behind it, which fronted a safe. After three turns of the lock cylinder, the safe door was open. Sara pulled out a black satchel, then returned everything so nothing looked disturbed. She walked quickly to the front of the office where the destruction had occurred.

Angie arrived, and Sara watched as she held Denise tight. As Sara looked on, she couldn't help thinking there was more to their relationship—much more—than just a compassionate partnership. Sara suddenly felt threatened as she watched the two embracing. Immediately she chastised herself—she and Denise didn't have a relationship of any degree. Angie had said it herself: Sara was a witness; Denise was her protector. End of story. *But you want more and you know it.*

When trying to look at their relationship as a professional one didn't work, Sara tried to tell herself it wasn't wise to get too emotionally involved with Denise. She swore to herself that she would only be with a woman who loved women. She knew a select few of her friends would ridicule her for getting so worked up over a "part time dyke," someone who couldn't make up her mind about what she wanted. But it seemed as if Denise had made up her mind: she loved women and she loved men. Even if Sara couldn't understand the latter, she certainly understood her attraction to women. She knew Denise's attraction to the fairer sex wasn't just an experimental urge. It was a bona fide sentiment of the heart. Sara had met many game players in her time, and Denise wasn't one of them. She realized Denise's sexuality was her reality; and maybe, like the world, nothing is ever in black or white, just different shades of gray. Sara couldn't deny her attraction for Denise, and if given the chance to love her...

"How ya doin'?" Angie asked, her voice interrupting Sara's thoughts.

"All right, I suppose," Sara replied.

"So, when are you leaving?" Angie asked, turning back to Denise.

"Tonight, if possible. I'm going to take Sara back to the hotel and gather up her things. Then I'm going to go home and do some packing."

"Where are you going?" Angie whispered, not wanting to be overheard.

"I'll call when I get there," Denise replied.

Angie nodded in understanding. "Why don't you get outta here," she offered. "I'll take care of it from here."

"Are you sure? You're probably tired by now."

"Yeah, it's all right. You told me the story. Besides, it's best if you leave now before the press shows up. We don't need Sara's face plastered all over the city."

"Good point," Denise agreed.

"Just call me on the private office line tomorrow and let me know where you are, okay?" Angie said, planning their line of communication.

Denise nodded in agreement.

"Good luck," Angie added supportively.

"Yeah, you too." Denise smiled. "You're gonna need it when you go to Captain Genar with this story."

"No kidding. I'm always saving your ass with the boys upstairs," Angie joked. A moment passed and the smiles left their faces. Angie looked into Denise's eyes with deep sincerity. "Take care," she added softly.

Denise nodded. "You, too."

Angie pulled Denise into another tight hug. The possibility of never seeing Denise again swept through her, but her logical side took over. Denise was intelligent and quick. If anyone could face DeVittem's thugs and live to tell about it, it would be Denise. "Go on, get outta here," Angie said, shooing them away with her hands. She watched as Denise and Sara got into the car and drove off down the street past the arriving news crews. *Time to play ringmaster to the media circus,* Angie thought with a growing grin.

Denise's eyes were never still the entire trip back to Sara's hotel. She scanned constantly for a potential threat, not letting her guard down for a minute. Sara found herself looking around, too, watching for anything unusual.

Back at the hotel, Denise quickly escorted Sara inside. Her head, in a perpetual state of rotation, was making sure they weren't being followed. She scanned the area quickly but thoroughly. The bellhop, the man in the hotel bar, the clerk behind the counter—all of them fell under Denise's scrutiny as they made their way to the elevators. Once inside, Denise flashed her badge and prevented an older couple from occupying the car with them. She was taking no chances.

"Once we get upstairs, start packing your bags," Denise ordered as they stood in the ascending elevator car.

Sara nodded quietly. "Do you have any suggestions about where we could go?"

"Maybe north to Pontiac or south to Toledo."

"Maybe we should go to another country," Sara offered.

Denise smiled. "Sounds great, but I doubt Genar would spring for that kind of protection. He wasn't even real happy about agreeing to have the department pay for a roach motel, should the need arise."

"I own a beach house in the Bahamas. All we have to pay for is airfare and food."

"Are you serious?" Denise asked in astonishment. "You actually own a house in the Bahamas?"

"Yes. It was my parents' home. It was bequeathed to me, much to my older brother's disappointment. The Florida estate, ski lodge in Denver, and townhouse in New York weren't enough for him, I guess. But that's neither here nor there," she smiled coyly. "So, what do you say?"

"I don't know," Denise said, leery of the idea.

"I can pay for our tickets, and it will be less expensive in the long run. We can stay at my beach house a thousand miles away, or we can spend as much money, if not more on hotels in another city only hundreds of miles away."

"I still don't know," Denise said, shaking her head.

"Look at it this way: Toledo and Pontiac are both within driving distance. It will be easy for someone to follow us. But if they tail us to City Airport or Metro, they would have to search thousands of destinations."

Denise paused. Sara had a valid point, an excellent point. But being trapped in Paradise with this captivating woman could be too much temptation to withstand.

"I don't want you to have to spend your own money, Sara.

That's not right," Denise said, proposing one final argument. "And I can't afford a trip at the moment."

"I'll consider it a vacation, so you can rest at ease," Sara chuckled. "Besides, I think it's safer for us this way."

"Safer for us?"

"Yeah, your life is in danger here, too, Lieutenant," Sara teased. " I don't think you've really stopped to consider that."

"I have, but to you...I just haven't shown it."

"Why is that?"

"It's my job."

"But it's your life, too. And I happen to care a great deal about you, in case you haven't noticed."

Denise smiled. "I have noticed." She considered all the options and reached her decision. "All right," Denise began, "we'll go to your beach house."

Sara grinned wildly at the news.

"However," Denise continued authoritatively, "I call the shots. You have to promise to do everything I say, when I say. Understand?"

"Whatever you desire, Lieutenant," Sara cooed, leaning closer to Denise.

"I'm not kidding," Denise replied, trying to ignore Sara's seductive tone.

"Neither am I," Sara whispered up to Denise's ear.

The elevator doors opened to an apparently empty hallway. Sara swept her palms to the hallway, indicating Denise should exit first. Denise crept out with Sara tucked right behind her. As Denise unlocked the door she asked, "What's in the black bag?"

"Survival gear," Sara responded with a smile as she walked into the room. "One more of my many quirks. Don't worry."

Denise watched her walk back to the bedroom. She listened as dresser drawers opened and closed. Within minutes, Sara emerged. "All set?" Denise asked.

"Yes, I should have everything. Wait, my passport."

Sara opened her purse and thumbed through until she found it.

"I don't have a passport," Denise said, concerned.

"Do you have a birth certificate at home?"

"Yeah, someplace."

"That's all you'll need. I keep this passport because I travel often, but your birth certificate will be sufficient."

"Well, tonight I'll start to make arrangements within the department to get Customs clearance. It shouldn't be a problem. Now let's get going before more folks decided to pay you an unscheduled visit."

"Thank you," Sara said, stopping in front of Denise. "I really mean that. You saved my life, again."

Even as she did it, Denise knew it meant trouble, but she slipped an arm around Sara's waist as she studied Sara's eyes. Sara's gentle request earlier in the evening came back to her. Denise pulled Sara to her and gently took possession of Sara's lips, feeling the softness against her own.

Sara sighed in Denise's embrace. She couldn't tell who was more captivated as Denise's teeth tugged on her bottom lip.

As they broke apart, Denise pulled back slowly, fastening her eyes on Sara's lovely face. "You're welcome. And please don't ask for a repeat performance of this kiss. I think we needed to get that out of our system. The attraction needs to end here. I just wanted to...I don't know..." Denise paused, and Sara could tell by her scrunched eyebrows she was trying to find the right words to say. "This attraction is not just on your part, Sara, but we can't explore it. You're my witness. Agreed?"

Sara's mind was still dazed from the kiss, but she mustered a nod. "I'll do my best."

"Good. Now, let's get back to business and go get my things." Denise led Sara out by the hand. Speechless in her wonder at what had finally transpired, she followed.

Just as silently, DeVittem watched the news report that flashed onto the TV screen in the rec room at the jail. Reports were sketchy, the newswoman announced...an unknown assailant...a witness in protective custody.

Yadayadayada. Looks like round two went to the good lieutenant...again, he mused silently. He let out a long sigh and rubbed his temples. *Fucking bitch.*

He looked up to pay careful attention to Sergeant Michaels of the Detroit Police Department answering some reporters' questions as evasively as possible. *Ah, the third thorn in my ass. Wonder how long it will take for her to pay me a visit.* He chuckled. Suddenly the television went off, and he turned menacingly toward a guard behind him.

"Something you find funny, DeVittem?" he asked.

"No, sir," he replied in a patronizing tone. "Nothing at all."

"It's lights out. Back to your cell." The guard pointed with his nightstick.

DeVittem looked up at the blackened TV screen and blew a kiss. "Sweet dreams, ladies." *I've got options...lots of options.*

Chapter
6

September 28

The only aircraft to the Bahamas that had any seating available for the next day was an evening flight, but that actually worked out quite well for them. After going to Denise's place to pick up necessities, the two headed south, spending the night in Toledo. While Sara slept fitfully, Denise spent most of her time on the phone with a succession of people in what seemed like every department the police had. Unable to reach anyone with the authority to make a decision, her tongue tired and her mind overloaded with information, Denise finally fell into bed around 5 a.m., only to have to get up at 7 a.m. to make the additional calls to the numbers she was given by the people she *had* been able to reach. Picking up the phone receiver again, she sighed. She had so many damn numbers it seemed like one big circle that lead her back to the same place—one huge bureaucratic mess.

The more people for whom she filled out forms that Angie faxed to their hotel, the more she considered just saying she was going on vacation so she could avoid dealing with any of it. There was no rule that said she couldn't take a witness with her. No *written* rule, but DeVittem's attorney would have a grand old time in court with that bit of information.

After the run around she had gotten from the department, Denise expected Customs to feel like a lobotomy by the time they were finished, but the Bahamian inspectors didn't take as long as either of them had anticipated. Since Denise was "packing heat" as Sara teasingly put it, the officer was sure it would be another day of phone call after phone call. But after a series of pointed questions and a small stack of paperwork, they were on their way. They rented a car and drove toward Sara's house. It was still quite warm for September, and the fact that the car had no air conditioning made it much worse. That, plus the recent rainstorm, made for one humid night as they drove through the darkness.

"Although you really can't see it, it's very beautiful here," Sara said as she drove the small compact down the mostly empty highway. The greenery looked tropical and moist, with the headlights providing the only means of seeing the lush nature around them.

Denise smiled. "I'll take your word for it."

They drove a while longer in silence, the flapping windshield wipers providing the only sound. Though conversation had been a cornerstone of their relationship so far, a lack of sleep, a three-hour plane trip, and the possibility of murderers in pursuit left little room for lighthearted conversation. Sara tried not to read too much into the silence. She knew that Denise wanted to maintain the distance that she had spoken of in Detroit. *Surely she didn't mean* this *distant, did she?* Sara considered. *Nah,* she decided. *You're just being paranoid, Langforth.*

"There's a bed and breakfast up ahead that is owned by a family friend. I thought we could stay there for the night while I get the house opened up; I'm sure there are nasty critters living in my parents' place."

No, Sara reminded herself, your *place.* She still hadn't gotten used to it being her place. She rarely came to the beach house. It was just another reminder of the life she had left behind years before. Or more to the point, the life that she was cast from, due to her "evil" ways. She was surprised when her parents left her the beach house and a trust fund, but as soon as the shock wore off she saw the gesture for what it actually was. It wasn't about love or compassion; it wasn't about a final acceptance. If her parents had cut her out of the will, that would have verified that the family had skeletons in the closet, and—oh my—her parents wouldn't have tolerated being remembered that way. It sickened Sara, but she figured if she never had their respect, the least she could do was take the money. She had scruples, but she wasn't stupid.

"Won't the B & B be filled with vacationers?" Denise asked, drawing Sara back from her thoughts.

"Perhaps. But if so, I'm sure Nancy will let us stay in the den for the night," Sara replied.

They drove up the circular driveway towards a big structure that seemed to get larger and larger. It looked like a large southern plantation house: white with black shutters, and a white picket fence lining the huge property.

Denise looked around at the immensity of it with a sense of awe as she and Sara made their way to the porch. Sara stepped inside the front door and a bell jingled, noting their arrival. An old woman moved toward them from the shadows. Sara smiled as she moved forward to greet her friend.

"Little Sara Langforth!" the woman exclaimed, keeping her voice muted, so as not to wake the vacationers.

"Hi, Nancy."

"Oh, darlin', it's been ages since I've seen you. How have you been?"

"Good," Sara said with a nod. "And you?"

"Can't complain too much," Nancy replied as they hugged.

"How's Chester doing?"

"He passed away about a year ago, honey," Nancy said with a forced grin, trying not to make Sara uncomfortable with the bad news.

"I'm so sorry," Sara said, reaching out to the woman, stroking her arm in sympathy. "I had no idea."

"I'm okay. Sometimes it gets lonely in this big old house without him, but the vacationers keep me company. I've also got a staff that helps me out. They've been a Godsend at times."

"Well, I'm glad you're doing all right," Sara said.

They exchanged smiles for a few seconds until Nancy spoke. "What brings you here in the middle of the night, honey?" Nancy made sure to include Denise in her look, as well.

"Oh!" Sara exclaimed, realizing she'd forgotten proper introductions. "Pardon my manners. This is Denise VanCook. She's a police officer who's looking after me." Nancy and Denise exchanged pleasantries and a handshake, although it was evident that Nancy was bothered by the fact Sara required police protection. "I happened to be in the wrong place at the wrong time," Sara explained. "I became a witness for the prosecution, and it's safer for me here than in the city."

"Are you okay?" Nancy asked quickly, her concern apparent in her voice.

"Fine. However, we do need a place to stay until I can get my house cleaned up."

"My rooms are all filled, dear, but you're more than welcome to the study."

"That would be great," Sara said with an appreciative smile.

"No trouble at all. I'll be back with some blankets and pillows. You gals just help yourselves."

As Nancy left, Sara and Denise headed to the den. "She seems like a good person," Denise said as they walked along.

"Nancy's the best. I've known her for as long as I can remember. When I came out, my parents were a bit upset, to say the least. Okay, they were downright pissed, and they disowned me."

Denise couldn't help but smile at the theatrics that Sara displayed as she made the admission.

"Once my parents realized it wasn't just a phase, I know they talked to Nancy about it and things got better. They never liked me again, but we did remain civil with one another. Nancy's a good friend; she was never one to judge," Sara added with a far off look, obviously remembering the past.

Denise didn't have a chance to comment on Sara's story. Nancy reentered the room, weighed down with linens that the ladies promptly took from her.

"I'm going to bed, but don't take off anywhere tomorrow until you've had breakfast. Promise?"

"We promise."

"Good," Nancy said, turning to leave. Slowly the older woman began to walk away.

"Hey, Nancy," Sara called out, making her stop. "Thanks a lot...for everything."

"No problem, mon," Nancy said, mimicking an expression that ran rampant on the Bahamian island. "It's good to see you again. Sleep tight. We'll talk in the morning."

Denise and Sara watched her leave, then climbed under the sheet of the makeshift bed on the floor. Sara thought she would get a protest as she snuggled into Denise's shoulder. She was relieved to feel Denise stay loose and relaxed, going so far as to get comfortable herself by wrapping her arm around Sara. A few moments later Denise was out, a light snore floating through the room. Sara had to smile as she lay there wrapped in the warmth of the officer. *She's protecting me*, Sara thought wistfully. *That's all...nothing more.*

It was hot. It was humid. It was the Bahamas. They had been there three days at Nancy's insistence, since they had no utilities at Sara's place yet; and Denise was adjusting well to the Bahamian lifestyle.

She stood barefoot on the back deck looking at the water. The sun was just beginning to rise, and she could tell it would be another scorcher of a day if the rain clouds that passed through on and off during the early morning hours stayed away. Yellow and orange already filled the horizon over the blue of the ocean and white sand of the beach. Denise stood silently taking it all in.

"Ever been to Paradise before?"

Denise turned around to see Nancy smiling at her, bringing her a glass of iced tea.

"Can't say I have," Denise replied.

"I've lived here most of my adult life. My husband and I left our home in the Keys and moved down here to start the inn. It was rough at first, but we managed. When you start new ventures, the beginning can always be difficult to a certain extent, wouldn't you agree?" The woman had a mischievous gleam in her eye as she glanced back inside the house to where Sara was seated at the table, making a list of some sort.

"Yes, it can be rough," Denise answered with a smile of her own. "Not knowing what might lie ahead—it's not easy."

"No, it's not; but the rewards..." Nancy sighed. "Sometimes the rewards make it all worthwhile."

Denise had liked the woman the first night. She had to admit she was growing quite fond of her. Sara had described her perfectly. Yet another thing that Denise was smitten about: Sara's ability to capture the essence of someone. *Perhaps even capture someone totally—mind and spirit.*

Nancy cleared her throat. "You know, Sara thinks a great deal of you. I can tell by the way she looks at you when you're not watching."

"When she thinks I'm not watching," Denise corrected.

"So you've noticed?"

"I'm a cop. I notice things."

"Are you sure that it's all about being a cop, my dear Lieutenant?" Nancy teased, giving Denise a slight nudge with her elbow. "I've caught you looking, too, you know."

"Perhaps I'm not the only one with observational skills around here."

"You don't have to be observant to see the obvious, Lieutenant VanCook. Why don't you let down that guard of yours?"

"I need it. Sara is my witness," Denise said firmly.

"Is it really about her witness status?"

"What do you mean?"

"Could it be that your reluctance is based on something far deeper than protocol? Something you can't quite acknowledge?"

"Are you a shrink?" Denise laughed.

Nancy chuckled and gave Denise a friendly pat on the back. "Believe it or not, once upon a time, I was."

"Well, just don't start asking me questions about my relationship with my mother," Denise answered in deadpan before giving a small grin "Trust me, Nancy. I think Sara has one of the sweetest temperaments in the world, but she's not a pushover. She'll stand her ground when need be, and she looks at life each moment as it comes. Most folks say they can roll with the punches, but few actually do. Sara is one of those exceptions. And I think she's a very rare find."

"Just remember, precious gems are the ones most likely to be stolen. But then again, you're a cop; you already know that, I'm sure?"

Nancy didn't wait for a response. Denise knew she didn't expect one. She watched the old woman walk back into the house before turning her eyes out to the ocean again. *Yes, she is a precious gem, Nancy. She's smart enough to create a diversion to get away from a hit man. Other people might have totally freaked, but she held it together long enough to make him think she was in the shower. That 60 seconds might very well have been what saved her life. Plus, she's funny—makes me laugh when I least expect it, even if she is beating the tar out of me at a card game. And beautiful... Yeah, she's a looker, all right. Go ahead; call me shallow. So, where does that leave you, Denise?*

The officer continued to admire the ocean before her, contemplating her conversation with Nancy. For her part, Sara was inside doing some admiring of her own—namely, the woman on the deck.

"She's a sight to see, that's for sure," Nancy said softly. Sara just grinned. "And I can see you've got it bad, dear."

Sara chuckled. "Is it THAT obvious?"

"Oh yes," Nancy said blithely. "It's not one-sided, either."

Sara turned to face Nancy, suddenly much more interested in the casual conversation. "What exactly do you mean?"

"She and I spoke."

"And?" Sara prodded, when Nancy didn't immediately continue.

"Like I said," Nancy grinned widely, "she's got it bad, too."

Sara sighed in frustration. She knew Nancy well. The old woman wasn't about to divulge any secrets or conversations she'd had with others. Gossip was never one of the things Nancy engaged in. It was one of her best qualities...and, right now...one of her worst.

Nancy could only chuckle at Sara's reaction before turning more serious. "Hey, I hear we've got some rough weather coming in. You sure you gals don't wanna stay here for the time being?"

"How rough?" Sara asked.

"It's not a hurricane, but it might be pretty stormy this week."

Sara thought for a moment. "That's okay. We should be all right." They had set off a few fumigation bombs the day before and let the place air out. "Will you be okay here?" Sara asked.

"Sure. I've got lots of help here right now." She smiled to reassure Sara that she was just fine on her own. Sara nodded her agreement just before Nancy nudged the blonde. "Better go enjoy Paradise with her while you can."

Sara gave Nancy's arm a pat and took the older woman up on the suggestion.

Quietly, Sara crept up behind the lieutenant. "Beautiful, isn't it?"

The soft voice floated to Denise's ears, and she felt a small hand run down her back. "Yes it is. I don't think I've ever seen water that is actually blue," Denise said in amazement. She heard the tone in her own voice and she suddenly blushed, feeling like a child full of wonder. Sara cocked her head in question but didn't say anything. "I feel like such a tourist." Denise laughed out loud. "I have to keep telling myself I'm working here. It's not play time."

"All work and no play makes Jill a dull girl, you know? Besides, you do go on vacation now and then, don't you?"

"No, not really. I mean, not like this," Denise said, spreading her arms to encompass the view. "I'm a cop. I don't often get the time off of work, and when I do, I don't make enough to see places like this."

"Well, I make it a rule to visit a new place every year."

"Is that so?" Denise said, watching Sara strutting in front of her.

"Absolutely," Sara said with a firm nod of her head. "The world is a big place, life is short, and I plan to see as much of it as I can before I die...with your help now, that is. You gotta keep me alive, Denise. I've got an African safari planned for next year," the blonde teased.

Denise took a sip of her ice tea and raised her glass. "I'm working on it."

"Here's to you succeeding," Sara toasted, clinking their glasses together. "Perhaps I'll take you on the Kenya tour with me as a way of saying thank you." Denise's mood shifted from carefree to rigid in an instant, but Sara quickly covered for her unintentional insult. "I mean, I might need protection from those wild animals and it would be strictly as friends. Scout's honor." Sara batted her eyelashes playfully in apology for the off the cuff comment.

Slowly Denise began to smile. "I'll think about it," she mused. "But I'll only come if I can take my gun." She smiled mischievously.

"It's a deal," Sara said, shaking Denise's hand and then tugging it to draw Denise along as she walked. "Let's get breakfast and head to the store for some groceries." Denise didn't seem to mind the handlock, so Sara just enjoyed it while she could.

They ate breakfast then said goodbye to Nancy, with a promise they would return for dinner sometime before heading back to the States. The sky began to turn dark as they made their way to the grocery store for supplies. It was time to begin the big cleaning.

Sara didn't have a rambling estate like Nancy's, but it was larger than most of the dwellings Denise and Angie had been called to during their patrolling days in Detroit. It had a large porch that ran along the front of the three-bedroom home. The living room and dining room opened into each other, with a small kitchen off to the left. On the right, sat three bedrooms in a row. The master bedroom, of course, had a wonderful view of the ocean, even if it was a bit distant from the house. The living room contained a beautiful bay window next to the front door. As for the dining area, it had a large patio door that gave access to the beach and tropical vegetation outside.

Denise set the bags on the dining room table, releasing a sigh as she looked to the water and shrubbery outside. "It's only noon," she said, rubbing her eyes and yawning. "Why on earth am I so tired?"

"Maybe it's the fact your nerves have been on edge ever since Detroit?" Sara teased. "Granted, you've lowered your guard from time to time, but for the most part you've been very watchful."

"Maybe," Denise said, walking out to the living room to the phone.

Sara took one of the bags with her and began stocking the fridge. When she heard Denise yell, she dropped a head of lettuce and ran to the living room. "What is it?"

"We've got a dial tone," Denise said, showing the receiver off like some kind of prize.

"Oh, God! Don't do that again. I thought something was wrong."

"I guess my nerves aren't the only ones on edge," Denise teased.

Sara simply shook her head and went back into the kitchen. Denise dialed and waited, listening to the ringing tone and the rain outside the window. She hoped she would catch Angie in the office since she hadn't had the opportunity to check in with her partner since departing Detroit. She was relieved when she heard Angie's voice on the other end.

"Sergeant Michaels, Fourteenth."

"Hi, Sergeant Michaels."

Angie could hear the grin through the phone, but that didn't matter. She had issues. "Where in the hell are you!" Angie exclaimed. "Do you realize I've been worried sick about you? I thought DeVittem's goons got to you. You'd better have a damn good explanation!"

"Love you, too, Angie," Denise chuckled.

"All right, I guess I deserved that," Angie said, calming down. "I'm glad you're okay. Now, where are you?"

"The Bahamas. Freeport, actually."

"Freeport, Bahamas? Are you telling me that I gave up *my* Aspen trip so *you* could go to the Bahamas? Tell me I didn't hear that correctly."

Denise paused a moment, unsure of how to answer but certain of the reaction she would get. She licked her lips as she contemplated. "No, you heard correctly."

Sara couldn't hear the specifics of the conversation from across the room, but she could hear Angie's voice booming on the other end. She watched as Denise held the phone from her ear with a cringing look on her face.

"Sounds like you're in trouble," Sara teased as Denise tried repeatedly to move the phone back to her ear again, only to move it away as Angie continued to rant.

"Hold on a sec," Angie said, breaking off her tirade. Denise brought the phone to her ear again and tried to listen in on what was going on in her office back home. After a few moments, Angie returned her attention to Denise. "Okay, where was I? Oh yes, point three of rant—"

"Is everything okay in there?" Denise asked before she could continue.

"Yeah. Brenner and Wagner just walked in. Brenner got a suspect in the carjacking case."

"That's great!" Denise commended.

"Denise said that's great," Angie yelled to the others as they began to leave the office. "Anyway, how did you end up in the Bahamas?" Angie asked, steering the conversation back to Denise. She wasn't letting her off the hook that easily.

"Sara has a beach house here."

"Oh, really. Why the hell couldn't I be blessed and be the one who's bi? I could be the one getting the tan right now," Angie teased. "Seriously, though, it does sound safer than in the city. But then again, being together and stranded in Paradise sounds like it could be verrrry dangerous," Angie added with a laugh.

"Very funny," Denise replied. "How'd it go with Genar?"

"He wants to know where you are."

"Don't tell him. Don't tell anyone. If he asks, just say I'm working on getting the paperwork in line for the department. Besides, it will take him at least three weeks to get through all the damn forms I had to sign." Angie chuckled on the other end. "And of course, you could just flat out lie to him and say you haven't heard from me."

"Can I reach you?" Angie asked. "Do you have a number?"

"Yeah, it's 555-8796, but I don't have the area code."

"I'll find it," her partner replied.

"I'll call later this week for an update. You could try the cell phone, but we've got clouds all over the place so it's hit or miss. Anyway, hopefully the courts will push this one through." Denise could hear the sigh on the other end. "Yes, I know you're frustrated, but right now it's for the best. Maybe you could get a cell phone, and I could call you back on it."

"Nuh uh. You'll probably drag me out of bed at 3 a.m. on some wild goose chase stakeout, and knowing my luck, it will be the one night that I manage to land a real date."

"Hey, I only did that once," Denise argued. "If he couldn't understand that duty called, he wasn't the guy for you."

"Yeah, you keep telling me that, but I have to admit that I kinda saw his point, too. Coincidentally, that was actually the last time I saw *him,* too. Go figure, huh?" Angie prodded.

Denise sighed. "How many times am I gonna have to say I'm sorry for that?"

"Until the guilt trip no longer works or next year, whichever comes first," Angie replied.

Denise could hear Angie's grin through the phone and had to smile herself. "I wish you were here, Ang," Denise said sincerely.

"Hell, you and me both," Angie chuckled. "I could use a few weeks in the Caribbean. Look, Denise, I want you to take care of that witness *and* yourself, okay?"

"I will," Denise said firmly.

"I love you," Angie said after a brief pause. "When you hadn't called, I really did worry."

Denise smiled. "I'm sorry I didn't call sooner. We've been staying with a friend of hers, and I didn't want to call from there. And crappy phone connections didn't help. I promise I'll stay in contact from now on. And yes, I will take care. Everything will be all right. You'll see."

"Okay... I'll talk to you on Wednesday?"

"Wednesday sounds good. Bye, Angie."

"Goodbye, Denise."

Hearing Denise hang up the phone, Sara peered out of the kitchen. She watched Denise stroking the top of the receiver after she hung up. Her shoulders were slumped and she had a long look on her face. Sara could tell Denise didn't like working without Angie.

Denise mulled over how good it made her feel just to talk things over with Angie for a few minutes. When they had first met, they weren't instant friends. Only a handful of women had been on the force at the time, and most couldn't take the pressure—not just the pressure of walking the beat but the heat from their fellow officers. In fact, Denise had wondered if Angie had what it took to make it as a cop. As time went on though Denise respected Angie—even admired her on many levels. Angie was great at reading a situation and was seldom wrong. They could interview someone, and within minutes Angie had them figured out, knew what made them tick. She could console them or put them off balance, depending on the nature of the interview.

For Denise, it felt like she was missing an appendage when they weren't together. Angie was the yin to her yang. Without the other, there was a loss of balance. She never would have guessed that Angie would become such a pivotal part of her life. Denise knew, if it was not for Angie, she wouldn't be where she was. They had made great strides in the last ten years. Denise also knew that they could go higher, if everything on the DeVittem case worked out. Denise knew she had to stay focused. Sara's approach pulled her from her thoughts.

"How's Angie doing?" Sara asked gingerly, sensing Denise's melancholy mood.

"She's okay. She's a tad miffed," the detective chuckled, "but she's okay."

"You really love her, don't you?" Sara said sincerely, wondering if there was a deeper aspect to Denise and Angie's working relationship.

"Yeah, I do."

Sara studied Denise a bit longer. "Am I causing problems for you two?"

"What do you mean?" Denise asked, unsure of the intent of Sara's question.

"I can't help but notice how close the two of you are. Does the fact that we're together make her jealous? Does she see me as a threat?"

Denise was confused and it showed. As Sara waited for an answer, the light bulb clicked on. "Do you think Angie and I are lovers?" Denise asked with a grin.

"I've had my suspicions," Sara replied. *Suspicions*, Sara berated herself, *Now you sound like the jealous wife. Just shut up, Langforth, before you choke on your foot any more.*

Denise laughed and shook her head. "No, Angie and I are not lovers. Never have been. Never will be."

"Good." Sara nodded and started back to the kitchen.

Denise gave herself a shake and followed after Sara, wondering what in the world that conversation had been about. "Why the curiosity?" Denise asked, making Sara stop and turn around.

Sara considered just why she had asked. "I've never been a woman who enjoys coming between people," Sara explained vaguely. Denise wanted distance, and Sara was trying her damnedest to keep that distance; yet she wanted to get some answers in the process. "Be it friends or lovers; and sometimes I just feel like I'm a sore spot for her."

"Not to worry. Angie and I are the best of friends. I love her deeply, but it's totally platonic. It would be detrimental to our partnership if we were anything more than friends."

"I guess it goes back to the pesky thing about maintaining a certain distance?" Sara added.

"Exactly. Plus, she's as straight as they come. She's not homophobic, she's just undoubtedly hetero," Denise explained with a smile.

"What if Angie changed her mind?"

"About what?"

"About your relationship?" Sara grinned, prodding Denise for more information. "Say she decided she wanted more than a friendship with you. Would you take her up on the offer?"

Denise smiled again. "Two years ago, she broke up with a guy she'd been dating for about three years. She was drunk and said some things that could have melted a stone, but I turned her down. She fell asleep on my couch." Denise grinned as she remembered that night. "The next morning, she could only remember bits and pieces of the evening, but she did remember some of the things she'd said and she thanked me profusely for not taking her up on any of them. People can say lots of things about me: I'm stubborn, I'm hot tempered at times, I can hold a grudge with the best of them... But it must also be said that I have tremendous self-control."

"Well..." Sara began, "in the time we've known each other I'd have to say that's all true, especially the self-control element. You've displayed that all too well," Sara grinned. "For the most part," she threw in as a slight tease.

She was relieved when Denise didn't take offense and smiled

as well.

"Come to the kitchen," Sara said with a wave of her hand. "Lunch is almost ready." Lightning and thunder struck at the same instant, shaking the floor and rattling the windows. "Whoa!" Sara chuckled. "That baby was close." Her grin vanished when she saw Denise's face was full of fear. "You okay?" Sara asked the detective.

Denise paused a moment and looked out at the storm through the large bay window. "Yeah," Denise said, trying to shrug off her reaction. "Just caught me off guard, is all. Seems like the storms are getting worse, huh?"

Sara noted the concern in Denise voice, but dismissed it. "It's just a little water and wind; we'll be okay. Now, how about that food?" she asked, re-entering the kitchen.

Denise let out a deep sigh, then followed. "Yeah, I'm sure the bad weather will pass," she told Sara. On the inside, however, Denise was doing her best to steady her breathing as she prayed that it wouldn't last much longer.

October 6

The rain never lifted. A week had passed since she and Denise had moved into her beach house, and the storms were still sweeping across the island. Some were short and some lasted all night, but one fact remained the same—each one was more powerful than the previous. They'd lost their power twice since arriving, and Sara was reading by candlelight for the second evening in a row when the phone rang.

Denise looked over at Sara, concerned. No one had their number, so why was the phone ringing. "Maybe it's a wrong number," Sara said, noting Denise's wariness.

The officer waited until the third ring and snatched the receiver up. "Hello?"

"Hello. Sara?" a woman asked.

"Who is this?"

"Sorry. It's Nancy. Is Sara there, please?"

"Hold on," Denise said, placing her hand over the mouthpiece and looking at Sara. "Why in the hell is Nancy calling us? You gave her the new number, didn't you?"

"She isn't public enemy number one," Sara said, rising and crossing to the phone.

"Didn't I tell you NOT to give this number out...to anyone!"

"Let's fight later, after I'm off the phone," Sara said, snatching the receiver away from Denise. "Hi, Nancy. What's going on?"

Denise darted to the kitchen, shaking her head. *What am I gonna do with her? She promised she would listen, and she didn't. I swear, one way or the other this woman is gonna send me to the nuthouse.* Denise was convinced that Sara's fierce independence would be their undoing. The officer could feel her irritability growing. However, anger began to take a back seat to curiosity when she heard the concern in Sara's voice as she talked with Nancy. She went back into the living room and waited for Sara to finish.

"What's wrong?" Denise asked, even before Sara could hang up.

"We have a major storm coming," Sara whispered as she placed the receiver down.

"There's a news flash. We've had storms for the past week. Stuck in Paradise, and I can't even get a tan."

"No, Denise," Sara answered, starting to look around the living room. "We have a deadly storm coming. Nancy said there are weather conditions that started in the Atlantic this week, and they're heading this way...fast."

"A hurricane?" Denise asked, rising and starting to pace. "Or storm conditions?"

"Right now, they're just conditions. It hasn't reached hurricane proportions, but..."

"But what!"

"Late summer, early fall, is hurricane season."

"What do you mean? You knew there was a hurricane coming and you brought us here anyway?" Denise accused, growing angry again.

"Early autumn is hurricane season, Denise, but it's been years since the Bahamas has seen one. I didn't think it would be a concern."

"Well, it is now!" Denise yelled. "What are we supposed to do?"

Even as they spoke, the wind was picking up. They watched the palm trees outside beginning to bend to one side. "We'll cover the windows with the sheets that were on the furniture," Sara said, running to the bedroom.

Denise stood by, watching Sara throw the sheets out into the living room.

"Go out to the shed and get some hammers and nails," Sara ordered. It was an odd experience for Denise to be the one taking orders, and she stood unmoving, watching Sara continue to search for more sheets. "Go now, before it gets worse outside!" Sara yelled.

Denise went to the kitchen and got the key to the shed, then ran back through the living room. With a deep sigh, she opened the front door. It slammed against the house, tearing at its hinges. She tried to close it behind her, but the wind was too strong for her. Finally Denise put her shoulder behind it to slam it shut. Her feet slipped on the wet grass as she raced to the shed. The force of the wind blew her long, dark hair into her face, making it difficult to see to unlock the door.

She finally got the lock free and stepped inside. Another gust whipped through, taking the shed door along with it, but Denise didn't notice. She was too busy trying to remember to breathe. Once she had the requested supplies in hand, she turned to close the shed, only to find the door missing. She watched as it tumbled across the lawn.

Suddenly something hard hit her from behind, nearly knocking the wind out of her. She turned around to face the house. When she did, she saw that the shingles—that had kept the weather out—had become dangerous projectiles. To her left, she saw the electric and phone lines snap and begin to dance wildly in the gale. Denise lost her concentration. She felt paralyzed, dizzy. After a few mesmerizing seconds of watching, she closed her eyes to muster what was left of her self-control.

With her fear in check she began to run back to the house. Or at least, she tried. It had been easy getting to the shed, the wind had been at her back. Now she had to walk into it. The heavy rain that had just begun didn't help, either. She was almost around the corner and hanging on to the end of the house, when Sara came out. She grabbed Denise by the hand and helped pull her to the porch. Her strength startled Denise as Sara gripped her tightly and tugged her inside. They stood at the doorway and together managed to pull the door shut. Safely inside, they could still hear ripping and cracking sounds around them. They looked outside to see that the palm trees that earlier were only bent, had now completely snapped.

Sara was pretty impressed—Mother Nature was certainly on a rampage. It was dangerous, no doubt; but Sara felt a sense of awe as well. She turned to make a smart aleck comment about the weather to Denise, but she stopped before she uttered a sound. Sara was a bit worried, but her companion looked downright petrified. Here was a woman who had stood her ground against a gunman outside an apartment without fear. Yet this same woman was now physically shaking because of some strong wind and rain.

"Are you okay?" Conjecturing that maybe she'd been hurt

outside and hadn't realized it at first, Sara quickly inspected Denise's body. Denise was drenched by the rain and looked like a dripping Popsicle, but more delicious. She would have dwelled on that image a bit longer if Denise hadn't been so emotionally on edge. She lightly pushed Denise's wet hair from her face, causing her to jump.

"I don't like storms," Denise confessed as Sara continued to stroke her hair. "Not at all." Denise couldn't meet Sara's gaze. Her eyes kept shifting around the room. She only looked at the blonde when Sara cupped her chin so they could look eye to eye.

Sara wanted Denise to concentrate on her and not on what was going on around them. Something had really spooked the officer, and Sara felt an overwhelming urge to protect her. *Not unlike what she's done for you, huh, Sara?* "I don't like them, either," Sara confessed aloud, "but it will pass. Just remember how you stood up to those bounty hunters at my apartment and at the office. You're very brave, Denise. You're the bravest person I've ever met."

"It's not the same. People are much more predictable than Mother Nature," Denise said as she listened to the wind moan and the rain pound. Her eyes kept shifting around the room and outside to the windows, practically ignoring Sara.

Sara realized that the more time Denise had to think about the storm, the worse she would feel. Denise was someone comfortable with control. The weather was not currently giving her that option of controlling her own destiny; and that loss of control was making her a wreck. Sitting and waiting would only make things worse so Sara knew what she had to do. *I'll make you feel better, Denise. I promise.*

As lightheartedly as she could muster, Sara announced, "Let's get to work. We have lots to do before the real storm comes." Just as soon as she'd said it, she regretted the wording.

"What do you mean the 'real' storm?" Denise asked, looking urgently to Sara for an answer.

"I won't lie to you. It's going to get worse before it gets better, Denise," Sara confessed. "If it is a hurricane, at some point it will grow calm as the eye passes over and then—"

"It will get worse again," Denise finished. "I understand. I just thought that this was the worst, is all."

"It may just be a tropical storm," Sara said. She walked to the kitchen and turned on the battery-powered radio. "There. We'll listen for updates. Is that okay, or will it make you more uncomfortable?" Sara asked, genuinely desiring an answer.

"No, that's good." Denise nodded. "We'll know what we're

up against."

"Okay then," Sara said, rubbing her palms together. "We've got matters to attend to. We'll start by cracking the windows in here to relieve the pressure. Then we're going to nail up the sheets for protection in case the windows break. I don't want to spend the afternoon dodging glass, do you?" Sara teased. She prayed Denise wouldn't take offense, and she was relieved when the officer's lips curled ever-so-slightly into a grin.

"No, I agree. Where should I start?"

"Jane go north," Sara pointed, acting like Tarzan in hopes of lightening things up. "Me go south."

Denise tried to join in, asking, "Can you do the yell, too?"

"Yep," Sara answered confidently. "But not damn near as good as Carol Burnett," she smiled.

The rest of the evening proceeded in a similar way—Sara gave the orders, trying to evoke humor as Denise did the tasks. By the end of the evening, they had formed a mock bunker using the sofa and the kitchen table. Sara had stuck to her plan of keeping Denise calm by keeping her busy, but the time had come when there was nothing more they could do, and Denise began to grow tense again.

Sara climbed under the table and motioned for Denise to follow her. "C'mere," Sara said, pulling Denise close and wrapping an afghan around them. "Wanna tell me why you're so spooked by storms?" Sara said casually. "If not, that's okay."

Denise took a deep breath, then exhaled it in a sigh. "I'd really rather not think about that now."

"That's okay, that's okay," Sara quickly reassured her. She began a gentle rocking motion as she held Denise close to her, stroking her hair, playing with the ends now and then. After a period of silence, Sara cleared her throat.

"When I was five, I got stuck on a Ferris wheel with my brother. The very top car, too—just my luck," Sara laughed with a hint of melancholy. "They tried several times to get it moving, and it ended up catching fire. People were running and screaming... They called in a cherry picker to get everyone out, and managed to empty the cars closest to the fire while they were getting it under control. Since we were the highest, we were the last to leave. My brother jumped into the picker with no problem, but when I jumped...I didn't make it inside. I caught the edge. The fire was out at that point, and instead of taking the chance of pulling me inside they just lowered the basket until we were both on the ground. Ever since then I haven't been any higher than six feet off the ground. Hotels? Office buildings? No problem. But outdoors?

Well, I'm scared to death, as you already know." Sara grinned as Denise looked up at her.

"Getting down that fire escape had to be pretty damn scary for you."

Sara frowned as she considered it. "Yeah, it was. And I know if it hadn't been for you that night at my apartment, I don't think I could have made it—not just because of the gunman, but because of that damn fire escape," Sara said, starting to chuckle then turning serious. "We all have fears, Denise, things that go bump in the night. You helped me with mine; I pray that I can help you with yours now."

Denise was touched by Sara's obvious sincerity. She was quietly considering her response when an inquisitive look washed over her face. She moved from Sara's embrace, and soon the two of them were standing in the living room.

"You hear that?" Denise asked with a grin.

Sara paused a moment to listen, then it struck her. "I hear...nothing," she smiled.

"Exactly!" Denise ran to the door with Sara right behind her. She opened it and found a light breeze and the sound of water dripping off the house. It was full dark, and the sounds of the insects had returned as well.

"Let me turn up the radio," Sara said, stroking Denise's arm then rushing back inside. Denise stayed a moment longer to take things in before joining Sara.

"The storm that struck the Bahamas has cleared the islands and is weakening. News is coming up next in—"

Denise and Sara didn't hear the rest. They were too wrapped up in their whoops and hollers. When they settled down, Sara found herself engulfed by Denise's arms. It was a warm, wonderful feeling to be jubilant in Denise's embrace, and she realized that the longer she stayed there the more reluctant she would be to leave. So Sara pulled back and took Denise by the upper arms, getting a firm yet friendly grasp on them.

"Told you we'd be all right," she said, smiling at the officer.

Denise reached up and stroked Sara's hair, for the moment ignoring the little voice in the back of her mind, the voice that was telling her that her behavior was totally inappropriate. Her gut reaction contradicted her conscience. *But it is appropriate. She kept you safe—not from the storm, but from your ghosts.* "Thank you," she whispered quietly.

"For what?" Sara asked, trying to downplay the effect the gratitude had on her.

"For sharing your story, for keeping me busy...for keeping me sane." As Denise moved closer, Sara was certain that Denise was going to kiss her. At the last second however, Denise changed her destination and planted a grateful kiss on Sara's forehead. "Thank you."

Sara knew the kiss was a simple thank-you, but something else burned hotter and brighter behind it. Sara's impulse to push the limits of "distance" brought goose bumps to the surface of her skin that she was sure Denise could feel. The most frustrating part, however, was that she could tell Denise felt the same desire. Her touch, her kiss, they were light, but they contained the depths of Denise's heart. Of that Sara was sure. But just as with times past, no sooner did she feel Denise come closer, than she felt the officer retreat within herself. Helplessly, she watched as Denise released her and began to set the furniture upright.

If Sara had had any doubts before, she now knew with undeniable certainty—Denise wanted her, too. *It may not be tonight or even tomorrow, but eventually it* will *happen.* The infamous self-control of Denise VanCook would be relinquished to Sara Langforth when the lieutenant was ready. By the heat in her eyes, the feel of it in her fingertips, Sara knew the duty-bound officer would be worth the wait.

October 9

The storm three days before hadn't done as much damage as its sound and fury would have had them believe. Except for the trees, the shed door, and a few shingles, everything looked the same. The phone and utilities were operating again, although it had taken the entire three days to restore service. Even the cell phone now managed to pick up a decent signal so Denise had been lucky enough to check in with her partner. Everything was peaceful back home, which was also a blessing.

Sara was making dinner when Denise sidled up behind her, their bodies nearly touching. "Where did you learn to cook?" Denise asked as she sampled the Parmesan sauce.

Sara watched as Denise dipped her finger in the white gravy then sucked it dry. She masked her arousal with a playful smack, intended to condemn Denise's lack of manners. "Why do you insist on teasing me?" Sara asked in frustration. She knew Denise was fully aware of her excited state. *No sense in trying to hide it,* Sara figured. "Just remember that turn-about is fair play," she threatened, waving a wooden spoon.

"I'm sorry," Denise said, picking up the salad bowl. "I'll keep my lips to myself."

"Are you kidding?" Sara mumbled to herself. "That's exactly the problem."

"What's that?" Denise asked from the dining area.

"Nothing," Sara replied in a strained voice. "Could you please get the wine out?"

"Sure," Denise replied. She went to the refrigerator and extracted the bottle with smooth grace before strutting back to the dining table with it. For her part, Sara stood in the kitchen dishing the meal onto plates.

Denise set the bottle on the table and turned back to help Sara with the dinner just as the bottle exploded all over the table. "What the hell?"

Sara looked over her shoulder to see shattered glass covering the linen cloth.

Denise's eyes, however, instinctively looked to the patio door behind the table...and the pea-sized hole in the screen that had not been there moments before. "Get down!" Denise screamed as she took her own advice and hit the floor.

Chapter
7

Sara followed Denise's lead and hugged the tile of the kitchen. Denise went into a roll to avoid another round aimed in her direction. She instinctively reached to the left side of her body for her gun, but came up empty. She silently cursed as she realized that she had gotten far too comfortable over the last week: her holster was hanging on her dresser, not her shoulder where it belonged.

She darted to the bedroom at breakneck speed, and with a quick swing of her arms the holster was in place. Hearing another shot, she dashed back to the living room and picked up the phone. It was dead.

Very slick. You've cut the phone line, Denise thought as she moved into a defensive position by the patio door. She ripped down the drapes to give herself a wider field of vision. That's when she saw someone scurry through the shrubbery.

The small breakfast nook that separated the dining room from the kitchen was also serving to protect Sara. She crept along on her stomach, watching Denise pick up a dining room chair and hurl it through the screen.

"What are you doing!"

"I told you to get down," Denise snapped. Quickly she fired two rounds into the bushes. "C'mere!" Denise ordered.

Sara ran over to Denise and got behind her, awaiting the next order. Denise pushed the button on the cell phone. Frustrated, she slammed the lid closed against her thigh.

"Fuck! Low battery—that figures." Denise turned to Sara. "Stay low. Go into the bedrooms. Pack our clothes and make sure to grab my folder first," Denise instructed, being quick and precise.

"Where are we going?"

"Any place but here," Denise barked before firing two more

shots. "Now go!"

Sara dashed to one bedroom and then the other. In each room, she haphazardly piled their clothes into a carry-on bag. As her hands worked as quickly as possible, she heard more shots exchanged, both inside and out. *Please keep her safe. Please keep her safe,* her mind chanted as she thought about Denise in the living room.

Denise was holding her own in the firepower melee, and she uttered a small thanks that this person had gone with a rifle for sharpshooting and not an automatic weapon. A barrage of bullets would have certainly done them in. But as it stood, trading shot for shot, Denise knew they had a very good chance.

She was reloading her weapon as Sara returned with the flight bag in hand. Denise spoke to Sara without looking up, as she loaded more rounds into the chamber. "Got everything? The folder, too?" She had to have their Customs paperwork, or they wouldn't get very far.

"Yes... No, wait. My satchel," Sara said, running back to her bedroom. Moments later, she appeared next to Denise again.

"*Now* have you got everything?" Denise asked sarcastically, rolling her eyes. "What the hell is in that bag, anyway?"

Sara didn't have time to answer. The assassin was moving closer as round after round hit the house.

"Go open the front door, but use the wall as cover. Someone might be out there," Denise instructed. She fired another round as Sara darted over to the front door. "Ready?" Denise asked when she saw Sara's hand on the knob.

"Ready," Sara replied, swallowing hard. Her mouth had become arid and the adrenaline rush sang through her body.

Denise moved to the other side, pointing her gun outside. "Now!" she said sharply.

Sara flung the door open as Denise crept up to the frame, ready for anything. She scanned all directions, seeing no one. "Now's our chance—go!"

Denise started out first, running in a zigzag pattern that Sara mimicked. If anyone was out there, Denise wasn't going to give them a clear shot. Once they were at the car, Denise tossed Sara the keys and said. "You drive. Head for the airport."

Sara threw the car into reverse and floored it. Once they were on the pavement, she slammed on the brakes and shifted into drive. It was then that Denise saw the gunwoman beginning to give chase on foot, hoping for a lucky shot.

"Gooooooo!" Denise yelled. Sara tromped on the accelerator, leaving the attacker in a cloud of gray smoke as the tires found traction. They both sighed in relief when they turned the sharp corner, escaping any shots from behind them.

"Floor it and keep it floored," Denise ordered. "We need as much of a lead as possible." She reloaded her gun as Sara raced along the bare stretch of road. "I wonder how they found us?" Denise muttered, her heart pounding in her chest. "Are you sure this house isn't in your name?"

"Positive," Sara answered. "Like I told you back in Detroit, it's still in the trust account. I don't know how they got to us here," she panted, just as hard as Denise.

"Be honest," Denise began. "Did you tell anyone at home where you were? Did you call anyone in the States?"

"No."

"No one?" Denise pressed.

"No. Not a single person. The only one who knows we're here is Nancy," Sara answered. Soon she realized that statement wasn't entirely true. The realization made her a bit nervous. "And Angie," she added quietly, not daring to look at Denise's reaction. When Denise didn't say anything, curiosity got the better of her and Sara had to glance over.

"Well, it's not Angie," Denise said confidently, yet fidgeting in her seat.

"Okay. Then who else knows we're here?"

Denise didn't answer. It was obvious she was lost in thought. "Maybe someone found out about the trust and decided to look here, since you're not in the city anymore."

"Perhaps," Sara answered. The fact that Denise's partner was the only person to know still loomed in the air, although neither woman focused on it for the time being. For five minutes, not a word passed between them.

"I know it's not Angie," Denise said firmly, breaking the silence, trying to convince Sara, and maybe even herself. "I know it's not her."

Sara simply nodded in agreement. They made it to the car rental station and quickly dropped off the keys at the front desk, cutting ahead of everyone in the line. People grumbled in protest, but Denise's stature and steely gaze shut them up almost as quickly as their gripes began. Moments later, they were dashing inside the airport to the nearest ticket counter. This time Denise flashed her badge to the waiting queue and took a spot in front of everyone.

"When's the next available flight out of here?" Denise asked the ticket clerk, showing her brass to the clerk as well.

The agent punched something into the computer before turning back to Denise. "In a half an hour," she replied. "Boarding has begun."

"Okay," Denise said, tossing her credit card on the counter. "Give me two tickets and tell them to hold the flight. I'm an officer with the Detroit Police Department and I have to get through Customs."

"Yes, ma'am," the clerk said as she punched in the information.

Denise's fingers nervously tapped the counter as they waited for their tickets.

"What's the destination for the flight we've purchased?" Sara asked the clerk politely.

"Montreal, Quebec."

Denise and Sara looked at each other. "Canada?" they said in harmony.

"We're going to Canada?" Sara asked Denise.

Denise turned to the clerk. "Don't you have a flight going to the U.S.?"

"There's a flight going to JFK in New York. But that doesn't leave for another two hours."

"Looks like we're going to Canada," Denise informed Sara nonchalantly. Denise's impatience grew as the clerk walked away and began talking to a co-worker. The fact that she started giggling as she talked only made Denise's temperament worse. "Can we get our tickets *before* the plane leaves the ground?" Denise hollered across the counter.

"I'm waiting for the boarding passes to be printed," the clerk snapped, obviously unhappy with Denise for interrupting her conversation.

Denise paced in frustration as the clerk took longer than necessary to get her signature for the purchase. A few moments later, the clerk handed them their tickets and pointed out directions. Sara opened her ticket and examined it carefully.

"What? No first class?" Sara teased.

Denise rolled her eyes and she pulled Sara by the arm. "Will you come on?" Denise ordered, dragging the blonde away.

They ran frantically, dodging around slower human traffic. When they saw the metal detectors, Denise slowed down and got her paperwork in order. She waited impatiently, tapping her foot again until they gave her clearance to go to the Customs office. After a series of questions and numerous sets of eyes examining her paperwork, Denise had Sara by the hand and the pair took off running again. When they turned the corner to their terminal, they saw the attendant shutting the door to the gangway.

"Hold on!" Denise yelled. The young man turned, then began to open it again. Denise came to a quick stop, quicker than Sara, who bumped into her as the attendant took the boarding passes. They jogged down to the plane, both panting as the flight attendant pointed them towards their seats.

"I want the widow seat this time," Sara called out in a ragged breath.

"Fine. Hey, wait! You have acrophobia?"

"Yes, I do," Sara said.

"Then why—"

"Because I told you," Sara began, "being indoors is different. I'm not out in the open. Besides that, the chances of us falling are astronomical."

"I wouldn't say that," Denise argued. "With our luck, I'd be surprised if this sucker didn't fall out of the sky over Boston."

"Well, thank you very much, Ms. Optimism," Sara replied. "I know our luck hasn't been all that great, but we are doing okay. We're not dead yet, are we?"

"I notice that you used the word 'yet,'" Denise rebutted, unable to hide her chuckle.

"Very funny," Sara retorted. "I think things will be okay, now. If you're right about Angie, no one is going to find us."

"Perhaps," Denise agreed. "But let's not get too comfortable again, okay?"

"Fine. I'm going to take a nap now so I won't get comfortable later." Sara grinned, snuggling into Denise's shoulder. "It might not be a bad idea for you to get some rest as well," Sara said before closing her eyes.

Denise quietly studied Sara's beautiful face. Instead of exhibiting signs of panic, which most people would be experiencing, her face shone with hopefulness. It was refreshing, to say the least. Denise had spent so many years as a cop listening to people that had given up...given up on the system, given up on each other, and given up on themselves. To be around someone with so much optimism and spirit was delightful. By being around Sara, Denise realized that she, too, had begun to give up.

Denise had rooted herself in the theory that she would never find anyone who would want her as much as she wanted them. Denise had given up on love...at least until Sara Langforth had stumbled shoeless into her life. That fact made Denise realize that this "love" could be nothing more than infatuation—a hormonal rush brought on by extreme circumstances and a pretty face. *Great. My life is becoming a bad B, sex scandal movie*, Denise considered with a quiet chuckle to herself. *Of course, I'd be the*

Michael Douglas/Bruce Willis character, and Sara would be the pretty young rising star of the day that's half the age of either man. Hypocrisy. Gotta love it. But she realized that aside from raging hormones and the impending case, maybe there was another element that should serve as a warning signal. Maybe her reluctance came from the fact that she did truly love Sara, maybe too much. Perhaps she cared so deeply that she could never put Sara through the wringer of having a relationship with a cop—the late nights, the close calls, all of it. But then again, maybe she was just going crazy. *Worry about the case for now, Denise, not the girl.*

Denise tried to sleep, but her mind was too busy compiling a list—call Nancy to close up Sara's home, check with the authorities in the Bahamas to see if they could track down anyone at the house, and of course, call Detroit with the latest developments. Denise looked over at Sara again, finding her curled up. Quickly her sense of duty slipped away. She sighed in a light whisper, "Sara Langforth, whatever am I going to do about you?" The soft-spoken question was open to many interpretations, but the case was the last thing on Denise's mind as she, too, closed her eyes to get some rest.

Hours later, Sara sat in bewilderment as Denise spoke to the taxi driver who was racing them through the streets of Montreal. "I didn't know you spoke French!" Sara exclaimed.

"Yeah. I'm bisexual and bilingual. There's a lot of duality in my life."

"Je parle Francais, aussi," Sara said.

Denise's eyes got wide. "Vous parlons Francais, aussi?"

"Oui," Sara nodded. "But I'm not bisexual or bilingual. I also speak a little Spanish and German. And I'll never really like men."

"Okay, first off, how is it you speak three languages?"

"Four," Sara corrected. "Let's not forget English," she teased.

Denise chuckled. "Okay, four."

Sara soaked up Denise's smile for a moment before answering. "My family traveled a lot in Europe—that's where I picked up my French and German. My Spanish came from our housekeeper, Maria. When I was old enough, she taught me swear words, too, after extracting a promise that I'd never use them," Sara chuckled.

Denise nodded. "Okay. As for men, you don't like them? At all?"

"Well, I like men. I have a fair number of male friends; but

I'll never be sexually attracted to them. Never have and never will."

"You've never had a boyfriend? Ever?" Denise asked in disbelief.

"When I was a teenager, I dated a couple of guys; but it never felt right. You know...no electricity or fireworks."

"Maybe it was just the guys you were seeing?"

"Are you campaigning to make me straight?" Sara teased.

Okay—that was funny. Denise started to laugh and shook her head. "No, I'm not; but I like to at least experience something before I formulate an opinion about it."

"Well, I've had experience, and it just didn't do much for me. Besides, I remember how all my friends would gossip about all the cute guys. I never felt an attraction to any of them. But Mary Tompson...now, she was perfection in my eyes, but I didn't dare mention it," Sara said with a smile.

"How many boyfriends did you have?" Denise prodded. "If you don't mind my asking," she added, realizing that the conversation was getting a tad more detailed than she'd expected.

"Let's see," Sara said, looking up and thinking as she chewed on her lip. "There were Tom, Dave, and John. Tom was the first guy I dated and kissed. It was okay, but nothing like when I kissed Jennifer at summer camp. She wanted to practice kissing so she'd be ready for the real thing. We practiced a lot that summer," Sara chuckled. "I realized at 14 I was different... Or should I say, happily unique."

"What happened with the other two guys?" Denise asked.

"Well, Dave, I dated him in high school, but he was more interested in my anatomy than me. And John, I loved John dearly. He became my first lover, and my fiancé, actually."

"You were engaged?"

"Yep," Sara replied. "Hard to believe, huh?" she laughed.

"What happened?" Denise asked, shifting in her seat to face Sara. This was getting good.

"Rachel happened." Sara grinned devilishly. "John went to the University of Michigan, while I went away to school back east."

"Where?"

"Yale," Sara replied. "My parents wanted me to be a lawyer, so I went to law school for them. That's when I was in my 'I've gotta make Mom and Dad proud' phase."

"Wait a second," Denise said, holding up her hands. "You have a law degree from Yale, but you sell real estate?"

Sara chuckled. "I said I *went* to Yale. I didn't say I *gradu-*

ated," she answered. "Now let me finish, so it will all make sense."

"Sorry," Denise said sheepishly. "Please continue."

"Okay," Sara sighed. "Now where was I? Oh yes, John. Anyway, while I was at Yale, I met my roommate's friend, Rachel, and instantly felt all those sparks I'd heard people talking about. One night while we were together studying for a test, I could feel her eyes all over me. I asked her what she was thinking, and she said she was wondering what it would be like to make love to me. Just hearing her utter those words turned me on more than any sexual experience in my life. And my entire life changed that night.

"At Christmas break, I went home and told John I loved him but I couldn't marry him. He thought it was his fault...that he had somehow driven me to a woman. But I explained that he had fallen in love with a woman who realized she was really a lesbian trying her best to be straight. He was a good man, and he deserved to find the kind of love he needed. And with the engagement off, I knew I had to tell my folks the truth...so I did."

"They didn't take it well, I assume?" Denise asked, already anticipating the answer.

Sara sighed long and deep. "My parents were *old-fashioned.* They couldn't see how their daughter could leave a wonderful man for a perverse lifestyle. They pulled my college funding. Hence, my relationship with Rachel fizzled out. Seems that since I wasn't going to an Ivy League school, I wasn't worthy anymore."

"That's terrible. She just dumped you after you came out for her."

"I came out for me, regardless of her," Sara corrected. "And yeah, it did hurt; but like most things, I got over it. I got upset, I cried, I moved on. After that, I spent a few months wandering until I decided real estate looked like a good option. I took the classes, passed the exam, and found a broker to work for. After a few years, I was able to take the broker exam and become my own boss; and there you have it."

"I'm sorry it didn't turn out better with your folks. Did you ever make up?"

"In their minds," Sara began, "they did. They kept me in the will to a certain extent. It would have looked far too scandalous to the country club set if they'd learned I'd been disinherited—might mean we weren't the picture perfect family," Sara chuckled. "So I'm sure that's why I got a slice, while my brother was given the rest of the pie. You know, I've seen more and more people come out—celebrities and such—and things are getting better. Don't get me wrong. We've got a long way to go, but I think education is the key to a better life for everyone. Ignorance is the basis of all social problems in the world, whether it's about race, religion, or sexuality."

Denise smiled, but she couldn't meet Sara's eyes. "I know you're going to be offended," Denise warned as she played with her fingernails, "but I have to say you sound a bit hypocritical."

"You think I'm a hypocrite," Sara queried in astonishment.

"Well, maybe 'hypocrite' is a bit harsh," Denise conceded. "Perhaps just a little stereotypical in your views."

"Oh, really?" Sara responded, obviously offended. "What makes you say that?"

Denise paused to choose the right words. "When we met, you asked what it was like to sit on the sexual fence, as if I couldn't make up my mind to be gay or straight. Maybe you've been fed by the stereotypes of your gay and straight friends?"

Sara smiled. Denise had her. Sara couldn't understand bisexuality, so she had made assumptions about Denise.

"You're absolutely right," Sara willingly admitted. "And I apologize."

Denise nodded. "Apology accepted."

"But then again, perhaps you're not entirely correct about my stereotypical behavior," Sara added.

"How's that?"

"Maybe I wanted you to be a lesbian because I knew how I felt the moment I saw you," Sara cooed.

Denise smiled nervously. She was knocked slightly off balance by the sexy confession, as well as the possibility of an impending argument.

"But why wasn't my bisexuality enough?" Denise offered. "I think you must have a lot of friends who also think that bi's can't make up their minds. Be honest, Sara. If we got involved romantically, would you feel comfortable with your friends knowing that I like men, too?"

"Got me again," Sara agreed. "Guess I am a bigot, huh?"

"No," Denise countered. "You're not a bigot. You're just misinformed. Let me spell it out for you: I'm looking for the right person, not the right gender. In actuality, my life is much easier because I'm not surrounded by a box. My dating options are wide open," she chuckled.

Sara chuckled too. "That's one way to look at it." The cab grew quiet for a moment until Sara asked, "So, do you think you'll ever find the right person?"

Yeah. I might be lookin' at her right now. "Someday," Denise answered aloud with a fair amount of careful neutrality.

The taxi came to a stop in front of the hotel, and Denise paid the driver. They walked into a lobby that was tastefully decorated with antiques with an 1800's feel—warm and rustic. At the registration desk, they were greeted by a woman.

"Do you have a double room?" Denise asked.

"No, I'm sorry. All that is available this week is two suites," the woman said in a heavy French accent.

"How much is the suite?" Denise asked, fearing the answer.

"Five hundred and ninety dollars a night."

Denise turned to Sara wide-eyed, "She actually said that figure with a straight face."

Sara grinned. "Let's not get into another 'straight' discussion, dear," Sara teased, patting Denise's arm before turning to the attendant. "Do you have a weekly rate?" she asked the clerk in French.

"Oui," the clerk said as she looked through a ledger on the counter. "3,500 dollars American for the week, and it is available."

"We'll take that," Sara said handing over four one thousand dollar bills.

"Jesus," Denise whispered. "You carry that kind of cash on you?"

Sara just grinned. "Why not? I have an armed guard on duty. Besides, I told you I was loaded," she teased.

"No kidding. But still, are you sure you want to stay here?" Denise asked in a whisper. "It's more than a bit expensive, don't you think?"

"Not really. Any place we visit here is going to cost us just as much, if not more. This way we know we have a room for the week. We can do searching and pricing later. It might not be a bad idea to hop from place to place, even head toward Ontario. We'll put the room in your name...Jane Smith," Sara winked.

"I always wanted to check into a hotel using an alias. It makes me seem...naughty," Denise chuckled.

"I've got lots of ways to make you feel naughty," Sara cooed, pulling Denise down so she could whisper in her ear. "All you have to do is ask."

The tiny hairs on Denise's neck stood on end at the ardent words and the feel of Sara's breath in her ear. The lieutenant couldn't have moved if their lives had depended on it. At that moment, the clerk came into view again to interrupt them. *Thank God,* Denise thought in a silent prayer.

Denise handed the registration form to the clerk as she gave Sara a receipt. The bellhop grabbed the key and their bags. Arriving at the room and getting settled, Sara tipped the man $100 and asked that he bring up some more bath towels and pillows. He was more than happy to oblige.

Finally, Denise and Sara were alone again. Sara announced that she'd take their bags to the bedroom while Denise checked out the lay of the land.

Denise started on the left end of the suite, going into the bathroom. "Huge" failed to adequately describe its size. It had a Jacuzzi surrounded by mirrors in the far right corner and, directly across from that, a stand up shower that looked big enough to accommodate the Detroit Lion's entire offensive line. She smiled as she imagined Sara's body covered in bubbles.

Sara caught Denise's grin in the mirrors' reflection as she walked up behind her. "Looks like fun," Sara said with a mischievous grin. She began to play with the ends of Denise's chestnut-colored hair. Sara giggled at the officer's attempt to lose her smile. "Relax, Denise," the blonde soothed. She gently gripped Denise's arms as she stood behind her. "I won't bite. Not unless you ask me."

Denise smiled again. Sara released her hold and began to run her hands up and down the well-defined forearms instead. As Sara continued to caress her skin in silence, goosebumps appeared on Denise's flesh.

"Cold?" Sara asked, shattering the quiet, filling the large room with a small echo. "Should I turn up the heat?"

Denise couldn't respond verbally, but her body was telling Sara everything the blonde wanted to hear. Denise closed her eyes. She knew Sara could still see her facial expression in the mirror, and she didn't want Sara to see her eyes. They would say far too much. Suddenly Denise felt her hair being pushed to one side in delicate strokes. She didn't resist.

Sara wondered if Denise would flee, like she had in times past, but for now she remained stationary, so Sara pushed on. Standing on tiptoe, Sara began to plant light kisses on Denise's exposed neck and upper back. Denise's eyes remained closed, even as her breathing grew more and more rapid and uneven. Sara watched as Denise tilted her head invitingly and licked her lips softly, as if preparing to be kissed.

"Sara," Denise struggled, trying to get her name out to break the spell she was falling under.

Sara ignored the attempt. "So I lied," Sara whispered. "I do bite."

Sara pinched Denise's flesh harder between her teeth, letting her tongue dance around the captured skin. The moan that escaped Denise's open mouth urged Sara to go further. Her hands eased down and around Denise's hips, pulling the officer against her body.

Denise could feel the twin points of Sara's arousal through the thin material of their blouses, and she sighed again. "We have to stop."

The protest was weak, and Sara saw through it. "Can't stop," she whispered, tickling Denise's ears with the words, her desire making her short of breath and unable to form a full articulate sentence. "Want you too much."

Sara's hands slunk up the front of Denise's body, stopping at her breasts. Sara squeezed the globes softly, feeling their breadth and firmness. She continued to slide her lips over Denise's neck while teasing the hardening nipples with steady fingertips.

Denise didn't flee. She didn't argue. She simply placed her hands over Sara's. Their fingers intertwined and continued caressing Denise's body.

Watching Denise aid and instruct her on how she liked to be touched aroused Sara even more, and she could feel the wetness between her thighs. They both groaned as Denise threw her head back, resting it against Sara's.

Sara took the cue and began to slowly unbutton Denise's shirt, from top to bottom. Once again, to Sara's delight, Denise was more than willing. "I need you," Sara sighed hungrily. She continued to nip at Denise's earlobe, feeling Denise letting go with each button that came loose; and her spirit soared.

Denise could feel Sara's wet lips and hot breath against her ear. She couldn't even consider refusing Sara. Denise knew she was moving further and further away from control with each tender touch Sara delivered to her body, which grew slick with perspiration. Sara had Denise free of her shirt, and they could finally feel the contact of skin on skin. Denise began the journey at arousal then traveled to enjoyment. The next stop was Utopia.

"Am I making you wet?" Sara asked with seductive confidence, running her hands up Denise's sides.

"Very," Denise confessed in a whisper.

Sara moaned and gathered some of Denise's long hair in her fist. She turned Denise's head toward her and kissed her savagely.

Denise didn't fight. Far from it. She joined Sara in her feverish need. Sara was the quintessential seductress, and Denise belonged to her now. That voice, those fingers, and those lips took hold of Denise's senses. In the truest sense of the word, Denise was captured. She was being consumed by her desire for Sara, feeling her want multiplying over and over within herself. She ached to scorch Sara with her lips, to share all the passion she'd felt since the first night they had met.

As their tongues began to dance, Denise turned the rest of her body to face Sara. They were only inches away from the long countertop beside the sink. Quickly, and without breaking the kiss, Denise took hold of Sara's backside and lifted her up. She deposited her in a seated position on the counter. Denise shot down to Sara's breast, nibbling and biting Sara through her blouse, trying to taste her salty skin through the material. In seconds, Denise's saliva made the garment feel non-existent, as if Denise's lips were fastened directly to Sara's flesh.

Sara ran her fingers through Denise's long, silky locks, pulling her closer, arching her back to meet Denise's hungry mouth. Sara had her eyes closed as her head rested against the mirror. It felt exquisite, but soon it wasn't enough. Sara wanted to feel those long locks against her upper thighs as Denise drank in her sweetness.

"Let's go to the bedroom," Sara whispered. "Let's make love, Denise."

Chapter
8

"Housekeeping."

A loud pounding on the door followed the announcement, making both women jump.

Damn it. Sara cursed silently in her mind as Denise retrieved her shirt and quickly pulled it into place. Sara realized that if she had just taken Denise by the hand to the bedroom, they would be making love right now. Instead, her butt was starting to grow cold on the bathroom counter.

Denise excused herself to answer the door. When she returned to the bathroom, she had an awkward smile and a handful of towels.

"I'm sorry," Sara finally whispered running her fingers through her blonde hair in frustration. "I just want you so much."

"If you haven't noticed yet, the feeling is mutual," Denise said, trying to grin. "But that doesn't excuse what I just did here."

"You're blaming yourself for this?" Sara answered. "For your information, I, and I alone made the moves here."

"Oh really," Denise smiled. "I don't remember you being the one to put yourself on that sink," she argued, pointing to Sara as she sat with her legs still spread, encircling the space that Denise's body had so recently occupied. Self-consciously she closed her legs and hopped from the counter, readjusting her garments.

"Look," Denise began as she stepped closer. "You might think you've done...this," Denise said, waving her hands between them. She would have continued, but Sara cut her short.

"This," Sara said, mimicking Denise's gesture, "this is my fault. You asked for distance. You asked me to follow the rules, and I couldn't do that. You've been nothing but gallant. Loads of chivalry." Sara chuckled sadly. "While I, on the other hand, have been nothing more than a tease."

Denise watched Sara's grin fall as the woman tried to walk away.

"Sara," Denise said, grasping her by the upper arms, "I don't think you're a tease. I do, however, wonder if what's going on between us is real. Desperate situations can lead to feelings that might seem genuine but, in truth, are just an adrenaline rush. Plus, it's not ethical. You are my witness; I am your protector. If anything more were to happen, DeVittem's lawyers would have a field day and he might walk. And by the way, let's throw in that pesky problem about focus somewhere in there, too," Denise added with a grin, trying to lighten things up. "Point is, I should have stopped sooner; and I'm sorry if you're mad at me. I would understand if you were."

"I'm not mad," Sara whispered, still looking despondent. "I'm just frustrated—frustrated with the case, frustrated with traveling, and frustrated with life. But you, I'm not frustrated with you at this point."

Denise pulled back and studied Sara's face. She knew Sara wouldn't be smiling anytime soon, so she made a suggestion. "Why don't we get ourselves together and go out to get some food? All we had for dinner was a bag of airline peanuts and a stale ham sandwich. What do you say?"

"I already know what I want for dinner," Sara said suggestively and without forethought. Immediately, she slapped her forehead. "Okay, forget I said that," she apologized. "It just slips out naturally when I'm with you."

Denise chuckled. "As I said, the feeling is mutual; but let's stick to pasta or poultry. It's safer at this point."

Sara nodded. "Agreed."

Denise gently stopped Sara as she started to move again. "Are we...okay?" Denise asked, pointing back and forth between them.

Sara mustered a smile for the officer. "Yes, Lieutenant Van-Cook," Sara replied, the good-natured teasing tone back in her voice. "We're okay. Now let's go eat."

Denise started to follow, then stopped. "The cell phone. We need to charge it up." Denise realized at that point that the charger was probably still sitting in the Bahamas. "You didn't by chance remember to bring—"

"Yes, I packed the charger. See? I'm good for something," Sara smiled.

"I'm lucky to have a subject who thinks as quickly as you, so don't think you're not an asset."

"Well, the phone should be ready by the time we get back. If you want, I'll set it up."

Denise gave a nod and walked out to the door. "Let's stop by the boutique downstairs first. We need some clothes that are a tad warmer, I think."

"No arguments here," Sara called from the bedroom. A few minutes later, she reemerged. "All set?"

"All set."

"Let's roll, Lieutenant."

"Hey, I'm the cop—that's my line."

"A thousand apologies," Sara said, opening the door for Denise.

The open-air café was busy. Sara and Denise both agreed the duck in wine sauce was superb. The waitress had just brought their dessert order of chocolate mousse along with café au lait, when Sara turned to Denise.

"So, tell me your story."

"What do you want to know?" Denise asked, licking some mousse from her spoon.

"When did you realize you were bisexual?"

"Probably the same time as you. Perhaps a little sooner."

"I guess I was a late bloomer, then," Sara chuckled. " Does anyone in your family know?" she added, growing serious again.

"No. They've met a few women I was really good friends with, but they never knew our true relationship. I always felt it wasn't really any of their business."

"Are you scared to tell them?"

Denise paused. "I don't think it's fear. It just never came up. I never had a burning desire to walk into my parents' house and say, 'Guess what, I'm bisexual.' I've never had a serious enough relationship with a woman where I felt the need to do that. But I think my mother has her suspicions."

"Why?" Sara asked, puzzled.

"You mean besides the fact that I'm 36 years old and have never married?"

Sara smiled. "I guess I could see that. Though maybe you just never met the right person. You mentioned your mother, but not your father."

"My father's dead," Denise said flatly.

"I'm sorry."

"I'm not."

Sara took a nervous drink from her water glass, unsure of what she should say in response to Denise's answer.

"I'm sorry," Denise began, realizing she had made Sara uncomfortable. "That response kinda put you on the spot."

"It just caught me off guard is all," Sara said, returning to her drink.

"My father and I never really had a close relationship. He was a good man...when he was sober. Unfortunately, that was rare. He liked to drink. Then he liked to fight. And when I got old enough to fight back, things got a little bit better because Mom and I weren't his targets anymore. He knew I'd kick his ass."

Sara let out a chuckle, but quickly apologized for the reaction.

"That's okay," Denise reassured her. "It was pretty damn funny, actually. Especially the first time I went up against him. He looked like a deer caught in headlights. He never saw it coming. I threw him head first into an end table.

"By the time I got the badge, he'd quit the hard drinking under doctor's orders, so at least I never had to arrest him. But his quitting came too late. The bastard basically pickled his liver."

"Don't take offense, but I'm still sorry," Sara commented.

Denise took a sip of her coffee before answering. "Why's that?"

"Because I think our parents play a much bigger role in who we are than we care to admit."

Denise pondered her statement for a moment. "I think what you do with how you've been raised plays the larger role."

"How do you mean?" Sara asked, going back to her mousse.

"My dad was a drunk. I don't drink at all. My father was abusive, and I try to stop abusers. It's not so much where we're from as where we're going that matters," Denise answered.

Sara smiled. "And where are you going, Lieutenant Van-Cook?"

"All the way to the top," she grinned. "Chief of Detectives. Perhaps Commissioner. Maybe even Mayor someday. Well, perhaps not Mayor. I like to think I'm too honest to play political games," she grinned.

"Well, then," Sara said, raising her glass, "here's to Commissioner VanCook."

"I'll drink to that." Denise said, raising her glass and finishing the last of her ice water.

The waiter brought the check and Denise reached for it. Sara was quicker, however, and snatched it away.

"Hand it over," Denise ordered playfully.

"Nope," Sara said, putting the money on the table and securing it with her glass. "My treat. Now let's go."

"I thought I was the one who gave the orders around here," Denise teased as she rose.

"Not when it comes to food," Sara teased. "Isn't that what

Angie says?" she asked.

"Oh boy." Denise smiled. "Looks like I've got another feisty woman in my life when it comes to eating."

They walked down the street back to the hotel in quiet companionship until Denise spoke. "Okay, I told you most of my story tonight. So, what happened with your last relationship?"

"Andrea? The one I caught with someone else?"

"Yeah. How long were you together?"

"Five years. We were introduced by a mutual friend. It was a blind date, and we met in one of the local gay bars. When she walked in, I prayed she was the one. Imitation Barbie dolls annoy me, but I like women who have feminine features with stature. Not just height, but a sense of presence. You know, the kind that control a room as soon as they walk in.

"Her red hair was short, and she had this sexy, confident walk. As soon as we spoke, it was instantly intense. Six months later, we moved in together. I thought I'd spend the rest of my life with her, but my long hours began to take their toll.

"I realized what was happening to our relationship, so I decided to turn over a new leaf and surprise her by coming home early one Friday night. I stopped at the florist for her favorite flowers, and our favorite restaurant for a bottle of the wine she always loved... She was surprised all right. So was I. So was the woman in our bed. I remember dropping the wine and the flowers on the floor. I walked out and didn't look back."

"Did you ever try to get back together?" Denise asked in a gentle voice.

"She wanted to, but I couldn't. I couldn't trust her. How can you love someone you don't trust?"

"I don't think you can."

Sara sighed and looked up at the full moon above them. "She hurt me badly, but that was a while ago. I've gotten past it."

"Sounds like you're still in pain."

"Well, there's always going to be a scar. I guess I should say that I've gotten over it the best I can. At least I've begun to think that I can find someone out there who'll be faithful to me. Time does heal all wounds, despite how clichéd that sounds," Sara chuckled.

They arrived at their suite and Denise went in first and turned on the lights, inspected everything, and gave the all clear.

"Do you mind if I spend a few moments alone?" Denise asked.

"No, of course not. Are you okay?" Sara asked with concern.

"I'm fine," Denise grinned, flattered by Sara's apprehension.

"I just have to call Angie."

"Which phone did you want to use?"

"I'll go in the bedroom," Denise said as she locked the front door. "I'll be done in a few minutes."

As the officer made her way to the bedroom, Sara walked over and turned on the radio, giving Denise more privacy.

Denise's heart was in her throat as she picked up the phone. It would probably be the most difficult conversation in their partnership. She had to ask Angie if she any idea how she and Sara had been found. Part of Denise hoped that Angie would still be at the office; the other part wished she could just postpone things for one more day. She swallowed hard when she heard Angie's voice.

"Hi. It's Denise," she began, hoping Angie would start the conversation. As always, Angie was dependable.

"Hey! You're lucky you caught me. I was just finishing up our backlog of paperwork. Do you realize how many trees I've put to death today?" Angie said happily. Her voice quickly changed to one of concern. "You were going to call tomorrow. Did something happen?"

"You could say that," Denise answered.

"Are you okay? How's Sara?"

"We're both okay," Denise answered. "We left the Bahamas."

Angie could tell by Denise's sober tone that something was wrong. "Why? What happened?" she asked.

"They found us again," Denise replied.

Angie could hear the distance in Denise's voice by the curtness of her words. "How?"

"That's what I needed to ask you." Denise did her best to hide her suspicion. "Did you tell anyone where we were?"

"No!" Angie replied, offended. "You said not to say anything to anyone, so I haven't."

"Well, Sara says she didn't tell anyone."

"Do you believe her?" Angie asked with a hint of anger.

"Yes." Denise didn't add more. She couldn't. She was too frightened by what she might say. The silent tension was maddening.

"So you think I said something," Angie said, her voice rising with her distress.

"All I know is that Sara didn't tell anyone, and you're the only one who knew where we were."

"I don't like what you're implying," Angie stammered, growing more upset.

"I'm not implying anything," Denise answered.

"The hell you're not!" Angie countered quickly. "After all

these years together, you're going to take the word of a woman you've known for about a month!"

"Look!" Denise yelled into the phone. "I'm hundreds of miles from home with no way to find out who the leak is. So far, the only lead I have is you, and—"

"Me!" Angie shouted.

"Goddamn it, Angie, let me finish!" Denise took a deep breath, calming herself down so she could continue. When Angie didn't say anything more, Denise repeated, "The only lead I have is you, and I know it's not you, so I need your help."

Angie could tell Denise was trying to defuse the conversation, but Angie wasn't ready for that quite yet. "Are you sure she didn't call anyone?" Angie asked, the irritation still heavy in her voice.

"I'm positive. I've been with her 24 hours a day. You have to help me," Denise pleaded in a soft tone.

Angie remained silent on the phone. Maybe it wasn't a suspicious tone she'd heard from Denise. Slowly she was beginning to feel reassured that Denise was deeming her innocent. "What do you need me to do?"

"See the judge," Denise instructed her. "Tell him what's going on out here, and see if he'll move the trial up. I think someone may have tapped the line. Bring someone in, independently of the department, to check it out."

"All right. As for the judge, I'm not sure when I'll be able to get an appointment with him," Angie replied.

"I'll call around 5 p.m. tomorrow, so stay at the stationhouse until at least 6, just in case. Let me know when you can see him, okay?"

Angie didn't say anything. She was still hurt by Denise's accusing tone.

And Denise knew exactly what the frosty silence meant. "I know it's not you," Denise began, "but I don't know who it could be. I'm really frustrated here. Hell, I can't even tell you where *here* is," Denise added in frustration.

"I understand," Angie finally muttered. "If I was the one out there, I wouldn't see the situation any differently. I'll wait for your call tomorrow."

"Good," Denise replied. "Now tell me how things are going back home."

"Oh, fine," Angie began. "Genar is in my face every day wanting to know where you are. Everybody else thinks you've been locked up in a loony bin, and Wagner is wandering around like a moron."

"So not too much has changed, then," Denise chuckled.

Angie let out a small chuckle, too. Denise knew an unspoken truce was taking shape. "No, not really," Angie agreed.

"Well, just keep your eyes open and watch your back, okay?" Denise said with deep concern.

"You, too, Denise."

The pair said their goodbyes, and Denise walked towards the living room.

Sara looked up from her magazine when she saw Denise in the bedroom doorway. "I couldn't help but overhear some of the conversation," Sara confessed.

"I hate it when Angie and I fight; but I think she understands that I wasn't accusing her. I just have to get home to figure out who's tipping off DeVittem's thugs."

"If Angie is innocent like you say, I'm sure she'll figure it out."

"I know she's innocent," Denise said firmly, taking a spot on the sofa next to Sara.

"I believe you," Sara replied. "And I know how much you mean to her. She'll catch whoever it is. If not for the sake of this case, then definitely for your well-being. I don't think I've ever seen two women who love as deeply as you two do who aren't either related or sleeping together."

Sara stroked Denise's hair in sympathy, not seduction as she had hours earlier. "I can tell you're tired and frustrated. Why don't you try to get some sleep? Go to bed early. We'll share the bed, and I promise I'll keep my hands to myself," Sara grinned.

Denise smiled and hoisted herself off the sofa. "Are you coming?" she asked.

"No. I won't be held responsible for my actions if I see you undress. Like you said, it's safer at this point; so I'll stay on the couch for now." Sara winked. "Seriously, get some rest, Denise. I'll be okay."

Denise nodded and offered a goodnight as she slipped into the bedroom. Sara reciprocated as she watched Denise move confidently and gracefully, even in her tired state.

Stature, Sara thought as she went back to her magazine, giving it a slight ruffle to focus her attention. *Another gal with stature.*

October 10

It was 7:00 a.m. sharp when Angie showed up at the Wayne County jail and was shown to an interrogation room. It was of modest size, with one barred window to the outside, one table, and three chairs. The walls were made of cinder block, and the entrance was a metal door with a frosted glass window.

Angie heard one of the guards outside the door announce, "There's a detective here to see you, DeVittem."

DeVittem walked in, adjusting his blue jail clothing as if he was royalty—a Latin lover, the three top buttons undone on his shirt to show off his curly chest hair. He seemed to tower over the guard. Not the least bit intimidated by his size, Angie casually waved him to a chair across from her. The guard was going to stay, but Angie asked if he could wait outside, and the officer obligingly took up a post outside the closed door.

"I'm surprised you could fit through that narrow door with that chip on your shoulder, DeVittem," Angie began as he took a seat. "Actually, I'm surprised to see you here at all. I'm sure your fancy suited sharks could have found a way around that bail problem."

"You'll have to check the record better. Folks on welfare don't have money just lying around. It's hard for an honest man to find work these days, or a good attorney."

DeVittem had spent years manipulating the welfare system so that he never had to formally declare what he did for a living to the IRS. As he proceeded to lean back on two legs of the chair, Angie was tempted to knock the cocky grin off his face. Instead she retorted, "When I find an honest man, I'll ask him if that's true."

DeVittem gave the sergeant a grin that brought bile to her throat. His cavalier attitude was making her sick.

When she didn't add more, DeVittem spoke. "So, what brings you here today, Sergeant Michaels?"

It was Angie's turn to grin. "I don't recall telling you my name," she commented, hoping to snare him into saying something incriminating. "Care to tell me how you know it?"

"Your reputation precedes ya, dear Sergeant. That, and the fact I saw ya on TV the other night," he said with a wink.

"Oh, really," Angie replied, keeping her cool. She was sure that DeVittem had known her name long before her recent television appearance. He probably knew everything about her—from her shoe size all the way to her favorite color, blue.

"Yeah," DeVittem said as he folded strong arms across his large, tan chest. "Seems a couple of windows got busted out in the 'burbs. That's what ya said on the news broadcast wasn't it, Sergeant Michaels? Some folks just have no respect for other people's property, huh?"

He was a piece of work, all right. Angie maintained her grin and rose, walking around the table to stand by DeVittem. She leaned down, getting close to his ear. "Between you and me, Carlos, off the record," she said softly, "who was it?"

"I have no idea what you're talking about, Sergeant," he grinned. "But I will say this, since ya seem to have a problem of some kind," he said vaguely. "In my experience, it is prudent to keep your friends close, but keep your enemies closer."

Angie hadn't come for cryptic messages. "Call it off. You're not gonna get to this witness," she warned him in a menacing tone. "You're not gonna win this time. If you help me out now, you might get a more favorable sentence recommendation for being a 'decent' man."

DeVittem continued to rock on his chair with his grin firmly in place. "What's that saying? Oh, yes... 'Accidents happen.'"

Angie lost her reserve at that point, and with a firm kick the teetering thug landed flat on his back—chair and all. The guard burst into the room to find out what had caused the commotion.

"It's okay. Mr. DeVittem went just a little too far," she informed the guard, pointing to the chair. The irony of the statement wasn't lost on DeVittem. "Accidents happen, right, pal?" she asked DeVittem as she offered her hand to help him up.

He batted it away and rose by himself as she made her way to the door. "Take him back to his nice comfy cell," she directed the guard. "The one he's using now, before we ship him out to the state prison in Jackson," she added with a final jab at DeVittem.

As Angie exited, she could have sworn she heard the word "Bitch" uttered, but she knew that couldn't have come from DeVittem. After all, he was an honest, decent man. The interrogation wasn't as fruitful as she had hoped, but knocking DeVittem on his ass was cathartic: it made her grin—a grin that stayed with her all the way to her car.

October 13

Sara and Denise decided to do some window-shopping along St. Catherine and Sherbrook Streets. Denise's eyes never stilled for a second. She inspected every passerby, every parked car. After a while, she relaxed enough to enjoy the city scenery—architecture of centuries past combining with the latest designs of the past few decades.

Boutiques and cosmetics stores lined the avenue. They were filled with all the latest fashions, in bold colors at outrageous prices. Sara stopped in front of one of the windows as Denise kept walking.

"Did you find something?" Denise asked as she rejoined her charge.

"Not for me," Sara said, taking Denise's hand and tugging at it. "For you. Come on."

Sara led a reluctant Denise into the store. They were met by a woman whom Denise felt had a snobbish air, although she didn't have the chance to mention it to Sara.

"Do you require help?" the woman asked in a thick French accent.

"Yes. Do you have that green dress..." Sara looked Denise over, assessing her, "...in a size 8?"

"Yes, Madame," the clerk replied, walking over to a rack.

Denise leaned down and whispered to Sara, "What are you doing?"

"I want you to try this on," Sara whispered back, before abruptly making her escape to speak to the clerk. Shaking her head, Denise followed.

"Here, Madame," the clerk said, handing the dress to Sara.

"Here, Madame," Sara echoed, handing it off to Denise. Denise rolled her eyes in response, not immediately accepting it. "Please," Sara pleaded. "Try it on for me."

Denise sighed but took the outfit from Sara just the same, and proceeded to the changing room. After a few moments, Denise emerged wearing the garment. The deep forest green ensemble was designed with short sleeves and a short skirt. The color brought out a hint of jade in Denise's blue eyes, and the style showed off her gorgeous figure. Sara felt her jaw drop, but she regained herself quickly and turned to the clerk.

"Do you have accessories that would complement this outfit?"

"Of course, Madame," the clerk said, leaving again.

Denise turned to look at herself in the mirror as Sara walked up behind her. "Do you like it?" Sara asked.

"I don't know. What do you think?" Denise asked with a smile.

Sara studied Denise's reflection in the mirror to see the front of the outfit while using her direct view to see the back. "You want the truth?" she asked.

Denise nodded as she continued to examine her new look in the mirror.

Sara studied Denise a moment longer. *Oh, what the hell...* "Damn, you look hot!" Sara exclaimed in a heated whisper.

The admission made Denise giggle bashfully, but she quickly quashed it as the clerk returned. Sara took the necklace the woman had brought and slowly clasped it around Denise's neck. She gently gathered up Denise's hair, pulling it up so the jewelry sat in its proper place. Next, Sara handed over the matching earrings, and watched as Denise tilted her head to one side and then the other as she clipped them in place.

"Shoes," Sara considered out loud. "Do you have shoes?" she asked the clerk.

"Yes, Madame," the clerk answered before turning to Denise. "What size do you wear?"

"9 1/2," Denise answered.

"Pumps or flats?" the clerk asked.

"Pumps," Sara replied before Denise could. She examined the tall woman's legs as she spoke. "Definitely pumps."

"I will return shortly," the clerk announced in choppy English before scurrying to the back of the store.

Two more customers entered the store, but Sara was too wrapped up in Denise to notice them. Denise, however, kept an eye on them until she decided they were nothing more than fellow shoppers. Returning her attention to the task at hand, Denise noticed the price tag for the first time. "Oh, God!" Denise exclaimed loudly.

"What?" Sara asked nervously, looking around the store.

"This is $450," she whispered to Sara.

"So what?" Sara replied in a disinterested tone.

"So what?" Denise hissed. "That's a month's car payment. I'm not spending $450 on a dress, let alone adding accessories and shoes."

"Who said *you're* buying it?" Sara said with a smile.

"Well, I'm not gonna let you buy it," Denise argued.

"You can't stop me," Sara countered. "It's my money. If I buy an outfit that just happens to fit you and looks fabulous on you, that's my prerogative."

"Sara," Denise sighed, "please don't buy this. It's too expensive."

Sara placed her hands on her hips in defiance. "Do you think you're going to *owe* me something if I buy it?"

"No," Denise answered quickly. "You're not that kind of person."

"Well then, I'm going to buy it. You look too damn sexy in it to pass it up." Denise was about to argue again, but Sara placed a finger across her lips. "End of discussion," she said, cutting the lieutenant short.

The clerk returned and Denise slipped on the shoes.

"How do they feel?" Sara asked.

"Perfect," Denise grumbled, throwing her hands in the air, giving up. "Just like the rest of it."

"Great!" Sara replied, not letting Denise's negativity affect her in the least. Sara handed her credit card to the clerk, who took it to the register. "Let's get the tags off," Sara added as she began to remove them.

The clerk beckoned to Sara, so the blonde walked to the counter, continuing to glance at Denise as she signed for the merchandise. Sara quietly admired the officer as she adjusted the skirt and blouse, totally enchanted by the tall beauty. It was more than just Denise's outward appearance. The outfit seemed made for the brunette—showing off Denise's broad shoulders and curvy waistline, almost as if it was a testament to both Denise's strong demeanor and her more feminine features.

After the transaction was finished, Denise's street clothes were placed in a shopping bag, and Sara turned to the clerk. "Thank you for all your help."

"No, thank you," the clerk replied graciously.

"Shall we?" Sara asked Denise, with a grand sweeping gesture of her hand toward the front door.

"I don't know what to say," Denise told Sara, gazing into her eyes. "'Thank you' doesn't seem to suffice...but, thank you."

"You're welcome, and don't forget it. You're worth every penny and then some." Sara smiled, and Denise's cheeks got red as she smiled back at Sara. "Let's go to the café in Place Ville Marie for lunch. What do you say?" Sara suggested.

"Sounds great!" Denise replied enthusiastically, grateful that Sara was changing the subject. She didn't want her red cheeks to be the next topic of conversation.

Sara and Denise left the store, passing two young men outside the entrance. They noticed the young men turning to watch them.

"Told ya you look hot," Sara teased playfully, intertwining her arm through Denise's.

"I think they were looking at you," Denise replied conspiratorially.

Sara glanced back to find the young men still watching them. She stopped, turned Denise around to face her, and placed a slow, burning kiss on Denise's lips. When she broke away, she gave a slight wave to their admirers. Denise and Sara chuckled as the men grew wide-eyed and slack jawed, then made their way down the street, again arm in arm.

"I love to do that," Sara laughed, as she jerked a thumb

toward the guys behind them.

"You're wicked," Denise chuckled.

"Serves them right for being so rude," Sara said. "Plus, it lets them know they don't have a single hope in hell of picking either of us up."

"But does it always work?" Denise asked. "Many men have the 'lesbian fantasy.'"

"I've learned that straight men are much more intimidated by a woman's sexuality when they are in the company of other men. I'm not sure why that is, but remember this for future reference: if a man is admiring you and your female lover when he's alone, he'll move heaven and earth to try to engineer a threesome." Denise began to chuckle at Sara's theory. "It's true," Sara insisted, joining in Denise's delight.

"Well, I think men have a hard time taking no for an answer under any circumstances," Denise replied.

"Is that a quality you like about them?"

After a short period of thought, Denise replied, "Yeah, I like perseverance. Men can be very persistent."

"But so can women," Sara countered with a devilish grin.

"Believe me, I know," Denise acknowledged, looking at Sara accusingly.

"Oh, I've been very good on this trip," Sara replied. "I won't be canonized any time soon," she admitted, "but on the whole I've been very good."

"If you've been good, I'm not sure I could handle bad," Denise confessed.

"What's the tired cliché? 'When I'm good, I'm very, very good, but when I'm bad, I'm even better'," Sara chanted with a sly smile, playfully bumping into Denise as they walked.

"Is that true?" Denise asked invitingly, getting caught up in the game again.

"I'd love to show you," was the silky response.

Denise stopped walking for a moment, admiring Sara's smile. A light breeze was pushing Sara's short blond locks into her face. Denise gently brushed them away, caressing the skin as she did so, then started to shake her head in disbelief. Sara didn't give up. And although Denise's official party line was that she wanted to avoid any entanglement with her witness, her body cried out for contact. She loved the sexual fire that scorched through her veins when they were together like this.

"You know how I feel," Denise answered. "And you know what's at stake."

Sara nodded silently. *I'll be good, but I won't be an angel.*

"You really do look beautiful in that outfit," she added with a becoming grin.

Denise shook her head at the response. *What have you gotten yourself into this time, Denise?* the cop wondered to herself for a moment. "You're impossible," she told Sara.

"And you love it," Sara countered, wrinkling her nose, daring Denise to say otherwise.

Denise knew she couldn't. In spite of what she told Sara, she did love it. "Come on." Denise smiled as she lightly pulled Sara along. "Let's go get that food before we get ourselves into trouble again."

Denise felt Sara's eyes raking over her all day. Although Sara said she'd bought the new dress for Denise, it was obvious that she had purchased it for herself, as well. Denise could see the pleasure Sara got from admiring her in it. After an entire day of shopping and talking, they were finally back at the suite, and still Denise could see Sara looking at her in the mirror of the living room as she took off the accessories—the necklace first, and then the earrings. She took her time removing them. It was slow, seductive. Denise's movements enthralled Sara, yet Denise was the one who was reveling in her role. Denise continued to watch Sara in the looking glass. She saw a sudden change wash over Sara that reflected sorrow in the blonde's eyes.

"What's wrong?" Denise asked, turning around to face her.

Sara grinned for show and shook off the lapse. She was being silly, pining for something she couldn't have—a stunningly beautiful and brave woman who was too damned noble for both of their goods. "I'm okay," she replied, hoping that would be enough to dissuade Denise's curious nature.

"No you're not," Denise said sympathetically. "What's the matter? Homesick?"

Sara smiled gently. "No, the best part about home is here with me now, taking out her earrings," Sara complimented Denise with a warm grin. "I'm not lonely with you around."

"What is it, then?" Denise persisted as she leaned against the small accent table under the mirror.

Sara paused. Denise could see that she was troubled. And the blonde knew Denise wouldn't let it go until she had the truth. She admired Denise for a moment longer, unsure if she should give voice to what she'd been feeling. *Be brave,* Sara decided. "I'm falling in love with you."

Chapter
9

Denise was questioning what her ears had heard, and she found herself tensing from her relaxed stance against the table.

"Did you just say—"

"I'm in love with you," Sara repeated in the same quiet tone.

Dead silence ensued. No sound came from either woman—not even a breath or a sigh. Sara knew she'd caught Denise totally off guard with her declaration. She didn't want to make any sudden movements that might frighten the noticeably shaken brunette, so she gingerly moved closer with tiny steps.

Denise didn't know what to say. *Stop!* That was in the forefront of her mind, but deep inside, she wanted Sara to come closer. She wanted the small blonde to take a stand, initiate an advance, and tear down the protective walls she'd built around herself. Her stomach quivered with each step that Sara took toward her—a feeling of dreadful nausea mixed with hopeful anticipation.

"That scares you, doesn't it?" Sara asked as she walked over to the officer.

Denise didn't reply. She didn't move.

"Yes, I can see it does" Sara continued. "But believe me when I tell you: I've wanted you from the first moment I saw you, and every moment since." Sara ran her small fingers through Denise's thick, dark curls, never breaking the gaze she held fixed on the tall woman.

Denise tried to look away—she had to. The churning inside her, the conflict, was far too powerful.

But Sara placed gentle fingertips under the dark woman's chin and turned Denise to face her. "Please, don't be scared. Please look deeper, because I think you feel the same."

"Sara, please don't," Denise begged. She didn't need this—not now. Even if it was what she wanted.

"Don't what?" Sara whispered around the nervous lump in her throat that felt like a boulder. "Don't tell you how much I want you, or how beautiful you look in this dress..."

It was far too intense; she had to break the connection. Denise moved away before Sara could continue. She was almost to the sofa when she heard Sara slam her hands down on the table, rattling the small vase of orchids that rested there.

Maybe it was just the stress of the trip, the situation in general, or Sara's certainty about how Denise truly felt and the frustration it caused. In any case, the blonde felt something inside snap. She'd taken all she could in the cat and mouse game they had been playing since they'd met. Enough was finally enough for Sara, and she couldn't be the "duck" any longer when it came to Denise. "That's it!" she shouted in disgust. "Run away again, Denise!"

"I'm sorry!" Denise yelled, just as loudly. *I have to run away. Because if I don't, I might just implode.* "Look, I told you I couldn't get involved because I have to keep my distance and—"

"Come on!" Sara retaliated, closing the space between them with forceful strides. "You got involved the minute you kissed me in Detroit. And the all-fired important distance you keep preaching about is getting narrower each day we're together."

"I told you—"

"Yeah." Sara cut her off to save her the time. "Here comes the speech about how you have to keep your distance to keep your mind focused, right?" Denise didn't argue. She just turned away. That was, until Sara forced her to meet her eyes again with the rising volume of her voice. "That's bullshit, Denise. You're already involved. The evidence is irrefutable!"

"That is not true!" Denise raged, going toe to toe with Sara.

"The hell it's not," Sara countered, not backing down an inch. "I see the way you look at me, and I ache. Not so much for me, but for you. I see the want in your eyes, Denise. I hear it in your voice. And the worst part is, I would gladly give myself to you, but you can't accept that! You want me and you need me, but you won't take me!"

Denise felt shell-shocked by the impact of Sara's words. The room got quiet except for the heavy breathing evoked by their anger. When Denise didn't immediately answer, tensions began to ebb.

"I can't Sara," the officer whispered, running her fingers through her dark, disheveled hair, trying to think logically. "What you're feeling...what I'm feeling...it might not be real."

"Why isn't it real, Denise?" Sara asked, frustration thick in her voice.

"Because adrenaline is a powerful drug. It makes you see things and feel things that aren't really there. We might think that it's love, but in truth it's just a physiological experience," Denise explained. "I don't want to hurt you by having you think it's 'true love' if it isn't. I can't take the chance of getting involved with you any more deeply than I have."

"Yes, you can, Denise," the blonde countered. "And as for the 'real' element, you couldn't be more wrong. Maybe you don't love me," Sara added, swallowing down a sob with that realization. "I can accept that. But don't you dare stand there and tell me that what I feel is hormonal when I know it's genuine."

Denise released a heavy sigh of frustration and whispered, "I'm sorry."

"I don't want your pity." Sara groaned in misery at the situation, because she felt Denise was still missing the point. "I just...I want you. All of you. But I'm fooling myself if I think you'd ever open up to me more than you have."

"Jesus, Sara." Denise threw her hands in the air, getting angry again. "I told you my father was an alcoholic. That's not revealing enough for you?"

Sara considered for a moment. "No, because you've told me lots of facts about your life, but you haven't shared your feelings. What's it like to grow up in a household like that? What do you prize most in your life? Why *are* you so damn scared of storms? And why don't you trust me enough to open up?" Sara paused a moment to regain her equilibrium so she didn't end up in a shouting match again. That would get her nowhere. The more she thought about it, the more she realized that's where this relationship was heading...nowhere. She would be Denise's witness, and Denise would be her protector. *End of story... yet again.*

Sara sighed. "Forget I said anything tonight, okay? It seems pretty pointless."

The defeat was heavy in Sara's voice, and Denise could feel her own heart break as she watched the blonde walk into the darkened bedroom. After the bedroom door closed, Denise collapsed on the sofa with Sara's words still ringing in her ears. She gazed at the door to the bedroom. *Don't do it. Don't go in there. Sleep out here tonight.* That's what her mind kept repeating, but she continued to watch the door. She struggled, as if in some macabre tug-of-war between her conscience and her desire.

And it was not so much the physical desire she'd had weeks earlier when she'd met Sara, but something more, something deeper. Denise realized that maybe, just maybe, she was in love with Sara, too. The way she smiled when she was teasing, the sound of her laughter as they joked, even the way Sara continued to play with her fingernails when she was nervous or upset: it was all so perfect.

Too perfect, Denise told herself as she stood up and started to pace. *She's too perfect, which means that something must be wrong. Right? Right. Jesus, Den, you're not even convincing yourself anymore, and your arguments sound more like bullshit to your own ears.* Denise grabbed a pop from the mini-fridge and opened it. She took three long drinks and set it down. *It's not about the case—it's about her. Maybe Nancy was right—maybe it does go deeper. She doesn't need a fucked up cop with a string of bad relationship as a suitor. But she doesn't need to go on believing she's unloved, either. She's not unloved. In fact...I do love her. Problem is, I love her more than I should. I love her exactly the way she wants—but I can't.*

Denise felt tears well up, and she wiped them away quickly. *Goddamn, DeVittem, I hope you rot in prison for the hell you're putting me through. It's your fault—the reason I met her, the reason I can't have her—it's all your fault, you bastard. But you're not gonna win. I won't let that happen. She needs me close, and I'll give her what I can. I have to—for her and for me.* Without conscious thought, Denise suddenly found her feet standing at the bedroom doorway with the doorknob turning in her hand.

Sara was lying on the bed curled up in a ball. She'd opened her heart; and instead of feeling the embrace she'd hoped would come, she felt like she'd been sucker punched in the gut. She physically hurt from the emotional jolt; and the more she thought about it, the more the pain intensified. *Boy, you really struck out, Langforth. When two people love each other, it shouldn't be this complicated. But maybe what I said was right, maybe she doesn't love me. Maybe it's just lust. Maybe she'll never care.* Sara could feel her lip starting to quiver at the possibility, and she closed her eyes against continuing that train of thought. *Maybe you should just go to sleep and forget it happened—just like you suggested to her. It's obvious she—*

"Are you asleep?"

Sara was so wrapped up in her thoughts, she hadn't heard Denise enter. She was uncertain of how to respond—should she turn and face Denise, or just lie there silently? *Will she retreat again? Only one way to find out, I guess.*

"No," Sara answered, slowly moving to a sitting position. When Denise didn't automatically move forward, Sara tendered an invitation by patting the foot of the bed and sitting cross-legged so Denise would have a space.

Denise walked over to Sara's side of the bed and gingerly took a seat. They sat in silence for a long time, neither uttering a sound.

Sara silently watched the officer try repeatedly to say something, but each time Denise stopped before any words emerged. She didn't push. Denise had come to her; she would let Denise do the talking this time.

"Fear...uncertainty...in some warped way—feeling responsible for my father's drinking...that's what growing up was like for me. I felt embarrassed to bring friends to my house, because I didn't know what to expect from one day to the next. When my father died, I felt cheated that I never had the chance to have a 'real' father, and that made me feel selfish in a way because I did know my father, whereas some folks never even see their dad."

"Denise," Sara whispered, "you don't have to do this. Look, forget what I said. I'm not gonna bully you into this; it's not right. If you don't want to talk about it, I'm not going to hold it against you."

Denise smiled and rubbed her thumbs over each other repeatedly as she spoke. "I'm not being bullied, as you call it." Denise had to admit she was scared, but she would continue. She'd continue for Sara. "Few people in this world can make me do things I don't want to do. I want to share these things with you, but you have to understand that I've never really...opened up. So it's not something I'm gonna be real good at," Denise added, throwing in a nervous chuckle to try and lighten the mood.

"I'm sorry for interrupting," Sara replied softly. "Go on, if you want."

Denise took a moment and rolled her head, shoulder to shoulder, to release the tension before she began again. "Anyway, it wasn't a picnic living with my father. My mother did the best she could with the situation. Maybe that's why I've been so focused on my work. My mom had no outlet, no means of supporting herself. She depended solely on my father for pretty much everything. I didn't want to feel helpless like that. I never wanted to be at someone's mercy.

"As for what I prize most: Angie—because she helps keep me grounded, centered. I egg her on, and she holds me back." Denise chuckled with fondness. "But between the two of us, we get results. A yin to a yang, almost." Denise smiled. "I feel a great sense of pride about what I do. It makes me feel good to know I'm trying my best to do good. I'm not sure if you understand that— there aren't many people who do. Being a cop isn't something that

I do for a living, it's something that I *am*—something that keeps me alive. Angie understands that because she feels the same way."

Sara allowed herself to grin as Denise spoke of Angie, but she remained quiet.

"As for my fear of storms..." Denise paused a moment and took a deep breath. "When I was 12, I spent the summer with my aunt and uncle in Indiana—my mother's sister. One night, a bad storm hit and we were all running outside to the shelter. My uncle was getting my aunt and my cousins inside, when this board came out of nowhere and...I watched my Uncle Danny get staked by a piece of picket fence during a tornado. That image still haunts me whenever the weather gets bad, and I feel like that kid who ran for her life that night."

Sara's lip trembled as she watched Denise's shaking hands. She climbed out from under the covers and scooted closer to Denise, taking a spot beside her. Sara reached out and covered Denise's trembling hands in a show of support.

Finally Denise had the courage to continue. "Ever since then I've been scared to death of storms. I just freeze up and feel like I have no control over my life or those around me. And I don't like that feeling." Denise freed one of her hands and wiped her eyes with her fingertips. Slowly a grin came to her face.

"What is it?" Sara asked, unsure of what the small smile meant in light of such a tragic tale.

"You know, I've never told anyone that story before. Even Angie doesn't know why storms bother me so much. Guess you can't say I won't open up to you," Denise teased, lightly bumping Sara with her shoulder. "You gotta way of bringin' it out of me."

"I'm glad you shared with me," Sara answered. "Are you?" she asked tentatively.

Denise considered the question. "Yeah, I think so." She grinned. "Thank you, Sara."

Sara smiled and worked her way back to the head of the bed. "I'd like to take credit, Denise, but you have to realize something. You did that opening up all by yourself. You didn't have to do it, you know, but you did anyway. And I'm grateful...even if you don't love me," Sara said, unable to disguise her melancholy at the last statement.

"Sara, let me be totally honest," Denise began. She paused briefly and waited until Sara nodded for her to continue. "You are absolutely gorgeous, and the spirit that's inside that beautiful package is one I've looked for years to find. If the circumstances of our meeting had been different—if I had met you at a store or a bar or a baseball game, whatever—I would have jumped at any chance you might have given me for a love affair. But things being what they are, us practically running for our lives, I'm not sure—"

"Is it Joseph? Do you see the possibility of me being another Joseph?"

"How the hell—" Denise muttered.

"Angie told me."

Denise shook her head. "Remind me to kill Angie when we get home," she sighed. "And for the record, no. It's a similar situation, yes, but I don't think it's the same thing at all. My reluctance here with you is that maybe we're just sexually attracted, with little else in common."

"I understand," Sara offered. "You're not sure if it's real. As I said, that's fine. I'm not gonna push. Can't promise I won't still flirt with you outrageously. I won't let DeVittem or his attorneys, who might use our relationship to their advantage, spoil *all* my fun," Sara grinned. "But I see where things stand right now, and that's fine. I'm willing to wait," she grinned coyly.

Denise chuckled softly and rose from the bed. "It could take years, waiting around for me, you know?" Denise teased.

"Yes, I know."

The honesty of Sara's words threw Denise off kilter. Sara was dead serious. By the tone, Denise realized for the first time that the words the blonde had spoken earlier were true: Sara *was* very certain about her feelings. Denise was on the verge of saying "to hell with the world" and just climbing into bed with the beautiful woman, but her sense of duty got the better of her, and she walked around and picked up her pillow.

"Where are you going?" Sara asked as she watched Denise.

"To sleep on the sofa," Denise answered. "It's late."

"Denise, please stay here," Sara replied. "I promise to be nothing more than a good friend. After everything you said tonight, I think you need to be close to someone. Let me hold you...nothing more. You have my word," Sara said fervently.

Denise considered for a moment and decided that the invitation was far too inviting to pass up. "Promise?" she asked, just to be sure of Sara's intentions. She knew that she herself was on the verge of losing her self-control. If Sara had seduction in mind, it wouldn't take very much to push the officer over the edge at this point.

"I promise," Sara said, crossing her heart with her pinky before patting the other side of the bed. "Now get over here before I drag you in. But take off the dress." Denise's eyebrows shot up into her bangs. "You'll wrinkle it, silly," Sara pointed out.

Denise did as Sara had asked, and joined her in bed attired in her camisole and panties. She snuggled against Sara's soft shoulder while Sara gently stroked her arm. It was only after Denise was breathing deeply and steadily that Sara found she could rest, too. When sleep finally claimed her, Sara had her fingers tangled in the officer's hair as the smell of Obsession perfume and light perspiration filled her nose. Denise could say whatever she wanted, but Sara knew the truth as she drifted off. It was love.

October 14

"We checked it all out. Everything looks fine. No loose wires or extensions running off. Seems like the phone is in perfect working order," the technician said as he handed Angie the work order to sign. They stood in the middle of the precinct where Angie was conferring with Detective Estephan on a case they were moving up to the Vice Squad. Angie handed the order back to the tech; he gave her a copy, thanked her, and made his departure.

"Lemme guess," Detective Estephan joked. "You women talk so much, ya need two phones now, eh?" he teased in his thick Cuban accent.

"Careful, Estephan, or I'll have your tan ass deported," she chuckled.

"Ouch," he said, clutching his stomach in mock pain. "Guess I deserved that one," he answered not offended by her words. In fact, it had become quite the game between the two. In each other's eyes, Angie was the all-American, white bread eating WASP, and Estephan was the Communist, Latino, wanna-be lover.

"That one and many more I'm sure," she countered, playfully slapping him with the rolled up work order in her hand.

"Say whatcha will, Sergeant, my Sergeant, but I know the truth. It's luuuuvvvv," he cooed before laughing.

Angie smiled and made her way back to her office. "Estephan, not if you were the last man on earth," she chuckled as she closed her door.

Estephan turned to his partner, Edwards, who was sitting on the edge of his desk. "Oh yeah, she wants me," he said confidently.

Angie picked up her phone and heard the dial tone. *Sounds functional to me*, she considered. She promptly called the judge's office, hoping to get a meeting that week. The best she could do was the 28th. As she hung up, the picture of her and Denise that sat on the edge of the desk caught her attention. It was a photo of them at one of the departmental softball games. They both had their caps and their precinct T-shirts on, and their arms were draped around each other's shoulders in camaraderie. Smiles graced their faces over a job well done that day.

The departmental league... The department has records of the phone calls coming in and out. ... Maybe someone here... Nah, how could that be possible? Who would have ties to DeVittem?

Acting on that thought, Angie rose from the desk and left the office. She went over to the desk sergeant, who was working on some paperwork. "Hey, Wagner, I gotta question. All the calls that come in get logged, right?"

"Yeah, what about it?"

"Who has access to that information?"

"What do you mean?"

"Does anyone have to sign them out to see them?"

"No, it's practically a matter of public record. Why?"

Angie shook her head. *Well, that was fruitless.* "No reason, just playing a hunch that looks like a dead end. Thanks."

He gave a nod and she walked back into the office, picking up the picture to study again. Suddenly, something profound occurred to her. She had never taken the time to notice, but she realized that there weren't any other pictures around—no family members, no prized pets, nothing—just her and Denise. How many hours had she spent in that office before realizing that?

That recognition evoked a deep sadness that Angie hadn't realized she was feeling until that moment. Yes, she missed Denise; but she realized as she sat in the quiet of the office, away from the stationhouse chatter, she longed for her, too. Not in the way a lover longs for their mate, but with the need to be close to something in order to feel complete, whole.

During their last conversation, Denise had said she felt helpless to control what was happening; and Angie realized she felt the very same way. A nutcase with enough money to buy and sell anyone was sending people after her partner; and so far, she'd been unable to help keep her safe. Angie knew that if anything were to happen to Denise, DeVittem would never walk out of jail. Sure, he might make parole someday, but she'd break his legs to see that he didn't walk out. She would hound the man for the rest of his life and go as far as to give him an indecent exposure ticket if even his shoelace was untied. He might earn his freedom someday, but he'd never find peace...never.

Angie shook her head. *Focus*, she told herself. *Stay focused... Soon it will all be over.*

October 15

Denise was lying in bed on her stomach in a drowsing state when she heard the front door open. She quickly sat up and looked over for Sara. She wasn't there.

Denise darted to the dresser and grabbed her gun, taking a position behind the bedroom door as she heard approaching footsteps. Still half-naked, she stood waiting for the door to open. The doorknob began to creak as it turned slowly. Denise waited, taking a step back as the door opened.

"Denise?"

The officer recognized Sara's voice. "I'm back here."

"What are you doing?" Sara asked, peering behind the door.

"I was about to ask you the same question."

The sight of Denise in her cami, with her breathing labored, distracted Sara for a moment. She would have dwelled on it, but Denise didn't look too pleased.

"Oh...I went out and got you some breakfast. I thought you might be hungry."

Denise shook her head. Perhaps she wasn't fully awake and had heard the woman incorrectly. *She what?* "You went out? Without me?"

"I just went down to the bakery on the corner. I passed on the doughnuts because they seemed too cliché for you, so I got other goodies instead," she teased, as she took a seat on the bed, digging into the bag.

"Have you forgotten that people are trying to kill you?" Denise asked, her annoyance and temper starting to rise.

"Come on, Denise. I don't want to fight. I just—"

"No!" Denise snapped, cutting off the blonde. "Don't 'Oh, Denise' me here. I don't want you leaving without me. Do you understand?"

Sara dropped the bagel she had begun to retrieve back into the bag. It rattled around the paper as she spoke. "I'm sorry," Sara said, unable to hide her hurt. "I just wanted to do something nice to surprise you. That's all."

"You're far too important to be walking around alone," Denise explained, belaboring the issue to get her point across. "I don't want to lose you," she added firmly.

Sara had said she'd give Denise the distance she wanted, but suddenly it was just too much to ask. She knew Denise cared for her as a person; she just wouldn't take her as a lover. And that fact had started to weigh on Sara tremendously, seeping into harmless conversations like this one. Even at this moment she wanted much more than the officer would give, and she lashed out in frustration.

"Yes, I know," Sara replied sarcastically, now trading hurt for anger. "I'm too important to the goddamned case. You can't lose the star witness. I get it already, so let's drop it." The blonde wondered silently how they were ever going to survive this trip. She tried to rise to avoid another senseless argument, but Denise kept her in place by putting her hands on her shoulders.

"Do you really think all I care about is the case?" Denise asked in astonishment.

"I'm not sure what to think anymore."

"Oh, Sara," Denise chided, gently taking Sara by the upper arms. "I wasn't talking about the case, sweetheart."

The endearment naturally fell from Denise's lips, and Sara tried her damnedest not to smile. Inside she felt like she was doing cartwheels, like a giddy schoolgirl on the playground who had just gotten her first kiss. Soon, however, she was struck by the realization that she had let Denise down, and she began to hang her head, feeling even worse than before with this new declaration of how much Denise did care.

Denise left the endearment unchecked and decided to comment on Sara's growing depression instead. "Look," the officer began. "I appreciate the gesture, honestly, I do," she said, releasing her grip and pointing at the bags on the bed. "It's been a long time since I had someone bring me breakfast in bed." The officer paused a moment in thought and gave a quiet chuckle. "Come to think of it, I've never had anyone bring me breakfast in bed. I should take advantage of this, huh?" she grinned.

Feeling Denise's mood lighten helped Sara considerably, and soon she too smiled. "Shouldn't you be *in* bed to receive breakfast in bed," Sara said, pitching a thumb toward the mattress behind her.

"Good point," Denise said, darting back to the sheets. "Should I act like I'm still asleep, or will just being under the covers suffice?"

Sara grinned and took a spot on the bed. "That's your call. You're the boss."

Denise snatched the bag away and peeked inside. "What do we have here?"

"Crepes, croissants, and bagels," Sara said, peeking inside, too, their heads touching, bangs to bangs. "I put some coffee on before I left, so let me see if it's done," she said, rising and going out to the kitchen area.

Moments later, Sara returned with two mugs in hand. She

caught Denise stuffing her face with one of the croissants and handed her a cup. "Here," she grinned. "You'll need this to wash it down with."

Denise could only nod as she chewed.

"Hungry?" Sara asked, as Denise tried her best to consume her food quicker to resume the conversation.

"Yes," Denise answered when it was safe to reply. She took a drink of her coffee and emitted a sigh. "This is really good. We'll have to go back again tomorrow."

"Together," Sara added with a smile, to let Denise know she understood the lieutenant's lecture moments before; and the officer gave a warm grin. A small silence ensued until Sara spoke. "Look, I know you've got your rules about us you feel you have to follow," Sara began, "but I'm really frustrated here. Like you said, if we'd met under different circumstances, things between us would be different. And I do understand your reasoning, but reason has become a big pain in the ass," Sara chuckled as she finished.

Denise had to grin. She could certainly say she felt the same. "I understand. And if it makes you feel any better, I give you permission to flirt as wildly as you want."

"Do you honestly think you can handle that?"

"Well," Denise sighed, "I don't have a choice at this point."

Sara cocked her head. "What do you mean?"

Denise took a moment to compose her thoughts. "I think the trip will go much more smoothly for both of us if we can act as naturally as possible. And let's face it, Sara, you need to flirt like you need to breathe."

That drew a laugh out of the blonde. "Boy, have you got me pegged."

Denise smiled. "Well, I am a detective, I'm supposed to have a keen eye for detail. But in all honesty, a blind man could see what makes you tick."

"Am I that telling of a person?" Denise simply nodded. "I should learn to hide my emotions more," Sara said ruefully.

The officer shook her head. "Don't you dare change one bit. It's rather endearing, actually. After meeting so many people who spend most of their time trying to lie to me, it's wonderful, actually."

"So I can flirt, then?" Sara asked, with her eyebrows shooting into her bangs. Her expression was hopeful, and Denise smiled in response.

"Yes, you can flirt. Why make this trip harder on you than it has to be?"

"But what about you? Can you handle it?"

Denise smiled. "I think I can take whatever you can dish out." Another silence grew between them, and Denise looked at the two of them—first herself, then Sara, and then herself again.

"What's wrong?" Sara asked.

"I feel underdressed," Denise teased.

"Well, then," Sara said, rising and pulling her dress from her shoulders and pushing it slowly down past her hips. Denise held a croissant at her mouth, unable to complete the task of eating it. "Better?" she asked coyly. With that, she leaned over in her lace bra and panties, and nibbled on the opposite end of the French pastry. Denise could feel it start shaking in her hand as she watched the blonde. "Ummm," Sara hummed as she chewed. "Delicious."

"You're telling me," Denise sighed, not realizing she had spoken the words out loud. Sara's chuckle brought Denise from her dazed state. "You do realize that when I said I felt underdressed, I was going to put on a robe?" Denise asked, although it sounded more like a statement.

"Perhaps," Sara nodded. "But you gotta admit this is much more fun...and I have been given express permission to flirt outrageously, Lieutenant VanCook."

Denise couldn't argue with that. She just shrugged her shoulders and tried to go back to her croissant. Between chews, she tsked the blonde with her finger and told her, "You're bad. I might have to sleep with you just to prove it's nothing but sexual chemistry," Denise teased.

"That's not a bad idea," Sara countered. "Sounds like it could be a wonderful learning experience. And speaking of flirting outrageously," Sara continued, "I thought we could have a picnic today. The weather is supposed to be beautiful. There's that park by the St. Lawrence River where I could feed you grapes and you could feed me strawberries; and as for the rest of the time, we can continue to work on that 'just being friends' thing," Sara teased. Denise almost spat the large swallow of coffee she had just taken, but managed to gulp it down. "So, what do you say, Lieutenant? Are you up for it?"

Perhaps a roll in the hay was just what they needed. It would help decrease any pent up longings and prove once and for all that it was just hormones and nothing more. She'd show Sara she could give as good as she could get in this little game. "Oh, I'm up for it and then some," Denise countered.

Upping the ante, are we, Lieutenant? "Good," Sara answered. She rose from the bed and stripped off the remainder of her clothes. Denise took a sudden interest in examining her croissant with intense scrutiny, at least until her pulse slowed and she could keep her wits about her. "I'm going to shower. Wanna join me? It will conserve water, you know."

Tongue-tied and totally flabbergasted by the naked display before her, all Denise could do was nod yes while her voice gave out a meek, "No."

Sara chuckled before picking up a little piece of croissant to nibble. "You can't blame a gal for trying to help the environment." She winked.

Denise's eyes were fixed on Sara. Her heart had been pounding since she'd woken up to find Sara gone, and it seemed that that fact hadn't changed since Sara's return. In actuality, the drumbeat had intensified to the point that Denise found herself shedding her clothing.

If she wants to play, then I'll play, Denise considered deviously. *Thinks she can parade around in that gorgeous birthday suit... I'll show her.*

After making her way to the front door to check that it was secure, she proceeded to the bathroom and the sound of the running water. Denise could envision an angel on one shoulder and a devil on the other—each giving their suggestions on what she should do, running down the list of pros and cons. This morning the devil was making a lot more sense. She'd teach Sara once and for all that she could be a seductress, yet keep her desire in check. She could take the game all the way to the edge, too, but she wouldn't tumble over it.

Sara stood under the water, head tilted back wetting her hair. She heard the shower door open and immediately opened her eyes. She didn't expect to see Denise standing there, and totally naked at that. It caught her so off guard that she didn't have a witty reply or retort she could sling at the officer. All she could do was silently admire Denise's well-proportioned form.

"May I come in?" Denise asked, confident of how Sara would answer.

Sara blinked to make sure the image and the question were real and not just a figment of her lust-filled imagination. When she opened her eyes and Denise was still standing before her, she knew it was real. "By all means," she said, offering the cascading water to the brunette.

Casually Denise stepped inside and proceeded to let the water sluice down her body from head to toe. When she opened her eyes, she found Sara admiring her and licking her lips. Denise couldn't help herself; she chuckled in spite of her attempts at a serious seduction. Denise found that throwing the blonde such a curve when Sara had initiated this whole game, was downright comical.

"I'm just doing my best for the ecology," Denise teased. When Sara continued to stay rooted, Denise took the soap in her hands and began to work up a lather. She'd arrived in the bathroom with the idea of teaching Sara a lesson, but the longer the soap slipped across her fingers, the more her desire blazed into an inferno.

Even within her passion, she started to second-guess herself. Perhaps she was the overconfident bug who flew a little too close to the web. The longer she stood there, the more she realized she had trapped herself. There would be no turning back today: she wanted Sara; Sara wanted her. Case closed, and to hell with the rest of their mixed up, crazy lives. Either one of them could be dead tomorrow or the next day. Ignoring her passion for this lovely woman was no longer an option. She'd revel in it, with no regrets.

"Would you like me to wash your back?" Denise offered, scooting over to give Sara access to the water again.

"Certainly," Sara replied, recovering her bearings a little. The water cascaded down her front as she felt Denise's strong hands begin making circular patterns on her back. It felt like a bizarre water torture of sorts, nearly maddening. Sara couldn't contain her moan when Denise's hands slipped further south than she'd expected and cupped her buttocks.

That moan floated into Denise's ears and imbedded itself in her well of desire. She leaned in, pressing her high, firm breasts against Sara's soapy back. Her slippery hands snaked down Sara's curvy hips and then around to her stomach. Her head tilted down to Sara's ear, her moist lips resting against Sara's earlobe.

"I can't promise forever, or even tomorrow, for that matter. All I have to give you is the here and now. Anything can change in an instant," Denise whispered heatedly as the vibrations rattled against Sara's flesh.

Sara closed her eyes, soaking up the feeling of the water and the bombardment of Denise's sensory attack. "Then give me right now," Sara replied softly; and using all of her strength, turned around to face Denise.

The officer looked like a goddess towering over her, dripping wet, her raven hair slicked back from her beautiful face. Sara thought for a moment that she noted Denise's eyes grow darker with her desire. If one day was all she could have with this woman, she would take it. And take it she did.

Sara tugged Denise to her lips forcefully, by the back of the head. After a mélange of light kisses, they began to deepen the buccal caress as their tongues searched for each other. When Denise began to suck on Sara's tongue, the blonde felt her knees go weak.

Denise felt it, too, and scooped Sara close to her body. The innocent gesture to steady the woman soon turned into a passionate grinding motion as they pressed their thighs together. Denise could feel the wetness of the water as well as the wetness that had welled between Sara's legs. When tongues were no longer enough, Denise felt Sara's lips abandon hers and make themselves at home on her taut nipples. Responding to the onslaught, her head fell back against the shower stall. Soon their hands began to roam slippery flesh, joining in a primal rhythm.

"Oh God, Sara," Denise sighed, feeling the tiny waves beginning to take hold of her as they continued to stroke each other, touching any area of flesh they could reach. After minute upon minute of tantalizing each other's flesh, the water was beginning to run cooler, but still, for Denise, it was far too soon to experience ecstasy. "We have to slow down, sweetheart," Denise begged.

Sara's voice was firm. "No." She plunged harder and deeper and faster against Denise's flesh. "We've got all day," Sara replied, locking eyes with Denise's.

The officer felt hypnotized; she'd do her bidding.

"Come for me, Denise. Please, give it to me."

Any reserve that Denise was holding broke free in that instant. The waves came hard and fast, rippling through her body.

Sara paused in her movements and simply watched as the quakes rumbled through her lover. "Oh God, Denise," Sara sighed as she watched her lover. "You're so sexy, so beautiful," she whispered as she rested her head against Denise's chest.

After a few moments of just holding Sara, feeling her pulse pounding, Denise turned off the water. She stepped out of the stall without a word and offered her hand to Sara.

The blonde took it without comment and stepped out to join her lover. Sara was unsure if Denise's silence was a good thing, but soon the officer was all smiles. Next, Sara felt her feet go out from under her.

Denise wasted no time in lifting Sara up into her arms, which brought a giggle from the shorter woman. Without taking the time to dry off, Denise began kissing Sara as she carried her toward the bed. "Don't think you're getting away that easily," Denise said between kisses.

"I'm all wet," Sara objected, her hair dripping along as they moved.

"I'm sure you are," Denise retorted lecherously. Any reply Sara might have offered was muted by the smoldering kiss Denise planted on her lips.

The pastry remnants in the bags from earlier that morning were pushed to the floor to make space. Denise licked and kissed the water from Sara's shoulder, nibbling her way down both breasts and across her stomach. Sara's legs reflexively spread wider the further south that Denise proceeded. Soon Sara's ankles were wrapped around Denise's back, stroking her, titillating her, encouraging her to continue her journey.

The scent of Sara's arousal tickled Denise's nose, and the officer's desire ratcheted higher than it already was. Just the smell of Sara wanting her created a new fire within Denise, and she couldn't hold back the whimper. Her whole body hummed at the prospect of tasting the delicate woman that had stumbled into her life and wangled her way into her heart. Yet even in the throes of her desire, Denise felt a moment of insecurity. She knew, at the moment she couldn't offer Sara everything, maybe she never could.

Sara felt the sudden tension and refused to let Denise's doubts get the better of them. "Please," Sara whispered as she buried her fingers into the back of Denise's hair. Sara's back arched as she pleaded with her body, straining to connect with Denise, needing to feel her hands.

Denise's palms worked a slow path down Sara's body, and the blonde quaked with every touch. Seeing Sara's desire displayed before her was enough to make her put those little negative voices away and to prompt Denise into action. She plunged her head between Sara's legs, but took her time in delighting her palate with the blonde's exquisite taste.

It might have seemed like a slow torture or a tease, but Sara understood what Denise was doing—she was savoring her. The more Sara thought about it, the wetter she got; and the wetter she got, the more there was for Denise to savor. It got to be too much for the little blonde, and she found her hand cupping Denise's head and guiding her to her engorged clit. Her body bucked against Denise's mouth and the officer felt a new throb between her own legs at the thought of Sara's mouth against her in a similar fashion.

When Denise began to make hungry noises, that was enough to put Sara over the edge. Her legs wrapped tightly around Denise as her body shook, and a light dew of perspiration covered her skin. Her breathing labored, Sara's head fell back against the bed with a final thud.

The long deep sigh of satisfaction she emitted brought a smile to Denise's face as she worked her way back up to lay beside Sara, where Sara curled up in her arms. Both women lay unmoving and unspeaking. Denise opened her eyes and stared at the ceiling. She still felt unsure of where things were going—perhaps even more now than before. But in spite of her misgivings, she also felt a comfort in being this close to the woman in her arms.

"Are you okay?"

"Yes," Denise answered, trying to put reassurance in her voice. "Are you?"

Sara pulled the sheet over both of them and snuggled in closer. "Very much so," she mumbled in a sleepy voice.

Another silence passed between them, and Denise grinned when she heard a light snore come from Sara. *Oh yeah, Denise, you really taught her a lesson, didn't you?* Denise had to smile for a moment. She'd been caught, trapped, but she quickly pushed those emotions aside. *You're not trapped, really— you could get up and walk away from here if you wanted. But for some reason, I don't want to, do you? Hell, no! This feels right. It's warm, it's loving, it's...it's what you've been waiting for, isn't it? So what if it's not in the ideal situation you'd prefer. Joseph was the right situation, and in the end it fell apart anyway. You'll keep her safe. You won't let any harm come to her—no matter what.*

Denise closed her eyes and listened to the woman's breathing, matching the rhythm. When Denise finally opened her eyes again, she looked over at the clock to see that an hour had passed. Their hair was still damp but beginning to dry. "Sweetheart?" Denise asked, giving a light shake to Sara to rouse her.

"Hmm," Sara hummed as she opened her eyes and looked at her surroundings. She made note of the fact that she and Denise were still lying together. "Tell me I'm not dreaming," she replied as she looked between the two of them curled in each other's arms.

"No," Denise answered, giving Sara a reassuring kiss on the forehead. "You're not dreaming. We should get up, though. You had a picnic planned, if I remember."

"Does this mean you'll let me feed you grapes?" Sara asked coyly.

Denise chuckled. "You can feed me anything you like," Denise said, raising Sara's chin and placing a light kiss on her lips. "Come on, sleepyhead. Let's get moving."

With that, the pair got ready to face the day. It was a bit chilly down at the river during their picnic lunch in the park, but neither seemed to notice. They managed to find a secluded spot where they could flirt and tease each other without the disturbance of portable radios or barking dogs.

After a wonderful day of play, Denise knew she had to get back to work; and she called Angie. After exchanging update information, Denise gave Angie the phone number and told her to call after the appointment with the judge on the 28th to report whether she was successful in getting the trial date moved up. After the call, Denise and Sara ordered room service, and sat back to watch *African Queen*. When the movie faded to black, the television was all but forgotten as Denise and Sara spent the night making love—on the sofa, the kitchen table, and finally, when they made it to the bedroom, in the bed.

For the first time in weeks, life seemed normal, despite the new turn in their relationship. Denise's life, for the first time in years, felt totally transcendent. *Perhaps those hormones could be a good thing*, Denise considered with a wily grin before she drifted off to sleep.

The next morning the sunlight shone through the vertical blinds, kissing Denise's bare back as she slept. She rolled over to pull Sara close to her, but her arm came up empty. She opened her eyes to find Sara gone. Denise smiled as she reflected on the night before, and she rubbed her hands across her face trying to wake up.

"Sara?" she called out to the living room. There was no response. She slipped on her white hotel robe and walked to the bathroom. "Sara?" she called again. Again there was no answering hail.

Denise peered inside the bathroom, but she wasn't there, either. Concern flooded Denise. Sara had promised she wouldn't sneak out again, but she wasn't anywhere to be found.

Denise went to the living room to look. No Sara there, either. Denise was standing in the middle of the room with her hands on her hips, growing angry, assuming that Sara was rebelling against her again. Suddenly the phone rang, startling the officer. "Sara?" Denise answered.

"Denise."

"Sara!" she exclaimed, recognizing the voice. "Where the hell are you?"

"She's with me," a gravelly voice said on the other end.

"Who are you?" Denise asked, trying to keep her cool.

"Someone looking to make a deal. Your dyke here says she's got a hundred grand tucked away in a satchel in your room. Give it to me, and I'll forget I ever saw her."

"Where are you?"

"Where I am isn't important. Where I'm going *is*. Meet us at Mount Royal by the Stark Cross at 8 a.m. You've got two hours; and make sure you bring your girlfriend's little black bag."

"Let me talk to her," Denise ordered.

"No can do."

"If you want your goddamned money, you'll put her back on the fuckin' phone!" Denise shouted. It worked, because the next voice she heard was Sara's.

"Denise?"

"Are you okay, sweetheart?"

"Yes," Sara answered, trying to put up a positive front.

"Where's your satchel?"

"It's under our bed. There's $100,000 inside. I brought it for emergency money, but I never thought I'd be trading my life for it. DeVittem offered him $50,000."

"How did he get you?"

"He got a key from the maid cart. He was in the living room when I woke up, and he said he'd kill you if I didn't go with him, so—"

"Enough already," the man's voice broke in. "Mount Royal at 8 a.m. by the Stark Cross. If you're not there alone, she's dead." The next sound Denise heard was the thundering of her heartbeat over the buzzing of a dial tone.

Chapter
10

October 16

Denise ripped the phone cord from the wall and threw the entire unit across the living room. Her pulse was pounding, making her whole body shiver. She wasn't sure which was stronger, her rage or her fear. She took one shaking breath, and then another and another. Finally she was able to breathe in and blow out to slow her heart rate. She had to calm down if she was going to think clearly and pull off Sara's recovery.

"Okay, jerk-off, you wanna play?" Denise said, going to the bedroom to retrieve the satchel. "I'll play. I'll bring the money...along with a few close friends." With that, Denise checked her revolver and tossed it on the bed along with the case.

As Denise hastily threw on a sweatshirt and a pair of jeans, something the caller said to her echoed in her mind. *"Your dyke." How could he possible know about Sara and me? Unless... Oh, Jesus! He must have walked right into the bedroom. He saw the two of us sleeping, and I didn't hear a single thing.* The more Denise thought, the more she pieced together the most likely scenario.

He didn't want to kill her here, and he didn't want a double homicide on his hands for killing the both of us. That would be too noisy and messy. And he knew if he missed me, I'd surely kill him instead. So he waited until one of us woke up and came out, and that's when he made his move. Goddamn it! Well, you certainly fucked up this time, Denise. Fall for the girl and get her killed as a result. Well, no more. That's it. It's over. If I get Sara back alive, I'll have to make her understand that we can't go on like this.

She looked at her watch. She had just over an hour to put her plan in motion. With all the confidence she could muster, she picked up the bedroom phone. She had a few calls to make before she trudged up the hill for the confrontation.

The wind blew Denise's long ponytail around as she made her way towards the two figures beneath the supports of the huge steel cross at the top of the hill. Every minute felt like an hour as she watched the man who stood carefully tucked behind Sara. Because he was too well shielded by Sara's body, Denise had to abandon her plan to take him out with a single shot without getting too close. Her eyes never met Sara's, never left the captor's.

When she was about 10 feet away, the man spoke. "Let me see the money," he ordered.

Denise opened the satchel, took out a wad of bills, and tossed it back in.

"Throw me the bag," he sneered.

"How do I know you won't kill us both once you've got the money?" Denise asked casually, keeping her cool.

"You don't."

Denise stared him down. His cocky attitude was just one more thing to fuel her growing temper. She wanted to provide some reassurance to Sara, but didn't dare look at her. Denise knew that if she did, she would lose the control she had fought all morning to wrestle into place. Of all the situations they had been in, here it was crucial to maintain the distance Denise had repeatedly spoken of.

"Send her over here," Denise barked.

"Give me the bag first."

Denise smiled and shook her head. "Fuck you," she said, as she started to walk away.

Sara couldn't believe her eyes. Denise was leaving her there! Leaving her to die. She was on the verge of crying out, but the man beat her to it.

"Give me the money, bitch!"

"Give me the girl!" Denise yelled as she spun back around, closing the distance between them.

The man got frustrated and pushed Sara toward Denise. When Denise saw Sara heading in her direction, she pulled the gun that had been hidden in the back waistband of her jeans.

He saw the gun come out, and he pointed his weapon but didn't fire. "Now give me the money," he yelled nervously.

Not so arrogant anymore, are you, asshole? Denise didn't raise her weapon. She didn't want to make the man more edgy than he already was, because that could have disastrous consequences. Besides, she didn't have to raise her gun. She was one of the best hip shooters in the precinct. Now that he was in the open, she could pick him off from any angle, if need be. Her anger urged her to shoot, but her logic won out. She wasn't going to put Sara in the middle of a fire fight.

Instead, Denise instructed Sara to get behind her, and with a mighty heave she tossed the satchel down the hill. Denise kept her attention focused on the bounty hunter, who was in turn watching the airborne black bag instead of her. He watched with a look of disbelief and more than a bit of disgust as it traveled through the air. The satchel landed about 20 yards away from him.

"Go get your money," Denise taunted, waving her gun toward it. "Go on," she repeated when the man remained stationary.

"I should shoot you right now for doing that, you fuckin' queer."

Denise watched him twitch nervously as he pointed his weapon at them. "Look," she said in a more gentle tone, "I got what I came here for; you got what you came here for. Let's call it a day."

The man stood shuffling from one foot to the other, trying to decide what to do.

Denise put it all together. If he were the type of man that pursued a target for the kill of it, then Sara would have already been dead; but his greed was much stronger than his drive to use force. Denise knew she could use that against him.

"I'm a woman of my word, and I swear I will not harm you as long as you don't harm us. I can't promise I won't do my damnedest to track you down after you leave, though," she added with a wicked grin. "None of us here thinks that money is worth dying for. Do the wise thing, take the money. It's what you really want anyway. Deal?"

That seemed to calm the man a bit, and he began to gingerly walk backwards down the hill. His eyes didn't leave Denise for a single moment. The only time he looked away was to glance at the satchel to pick it up. When Denise didn't make a move on him, he realized she was going to let him go...for now. Still, he wasn't going to take any chances, and once the bag was firmly in hand, he sprinted down the hill.

Only after he had climbed into his car at the bottom of the hill did Denise pull Sara into a strong embrace. "Are you okay?" she asked the blonde, making a quick inspection of her body. "He didn't hurt you in any way, did he?"

"No, I'm okay. I'm doing much better now," Sara said with a relieved grin. "It would be nice if I still had my money, but it seemed like a fair trade."

"Oh, I don't think your money is going very far. Watch," Denise said, pointing down the hill.

The man hadn't even managed to put the car into drive before uniformed officers swarmed around the vehicle. A small group of mounted police from the park patrol burst over the hill on horseback. One rider stayed behind to speak to Denise as the others proceeded at a more leisurely pace towards the car below.

"Gee, when you send in the cavalry, Lieutenant, you really send in the cavalry, don't you?" Sara teased, watching the arrest below her.

"Good work, Lieutenant VanCook," the man said as he dismounted.

"Thank you." Denise smiled at the Mountie. "Will you be needing us any longer? Given the situation, we'd like to leave the area as soon as possible."

"By all means." He grinned warmly. "One of our officers will drive you wherever you like, ma'am. If we need your testimony, we'll contact you in Detroit. It's been a pleasure to help you," he said, gently shaking her hand in a gentlemanly fashion.

Denise watched as he left to oversee his men and sighed. "I've always been a sucker for a man in uniform."

"Yeah, right. You and me both," Sara chuckled.

Denise smiled, enjoying having Sara near her again...until the thought of the talk they needed to have came to the forefront of her mind. There was no reason she couldn't be professional and friendly, too, she told herself. "Come on," Denise urged. "We've got a train to catch."

"Aren't we forgetting something?" Sara asked. When Denise gave her a puzzled look, she offered, "My bag?"

"Oh, shoot!" Denise said, slapping her forehead. "Come on."

The duo proceeded to walk down the hill, watching the Mounties handcuff the kidnapper. "So tell me," Denise said casually, "how did you manage to have a hundred grand just lying around your office? Hell, I'm lucky if I have a thousand dollars in my savings account at one time," she chuckled.

"Like I said," Sara answered with a bashful grin, "I'm loaded. And I've always kept money stashed in different places. Never put all your eggs in one basket."

"Yes, and a stitch in time saves nine," Denise bantered. "I'm great at passé clichés, so you'll never win."

"A bird in the hand is worth two in the bush," Sara volleyed.

"Don't bite the hand that feeds you."

"Never look a gift horse in the mouth."

"And...and...argghh! I ran out of clichés," Denise chuckled.

"I thought you were going to win, Lieutenant? Guess this is a case of 'Don't count your chickens before they hatch'?" Sara jabbed, with a playful chuck to Denise's arm.

"Well, it takes one to know one."

"Sorry, you already lost—a day late and a dollar short," Sara said triumphantly, picking up her pace to walk ahead of Denise. All the officer could do was shake her head and smile.

Collecting Sara's bag and filling out all the required releases, they walked to the car the RCMP had loaned to Denise for the operation. A driver opened the door for them and they both climbed into the back seat, where Denise soon found Sara's fingers intertwining with hers. A gnawing feeling grabbed hold of Denise's gut. *You've gotta say something. You've gotta tell her you've gotten far too close.* But instead of speaking her mind, Denise transferred her focus to the case, like she often did in her life. Work was much easier to deal with than love.

"Train station please," she told the driver.

He nodded and checked his mirrors for traffic before pulling out onto the road.

"Tell me what happened," Denise asked as they drove along.

"Well, you were still asleep and I was going to call room service to bring us some breakfast. I would have gone to the pastry shop, but last time I got into trouble for that," Sara teased with a playful grin, able to relax now that things had drawn to a successful conclusion. "Anyway, I went into the living room, and he was just sitting there on the sofa. He whispered for me to be quiet and he wouldn't hurt you. Then he told me to get dressed, and he stood in the bedroom doorway and watched me to make sure I didn't say anything."

"He watched you dress? You mean he saw you—"

"Naked," Sara finished. "Yes. In truth, I was so scared that it didn't really register with me. I just wanted to get my clothes on and get out of there before he hurt you. Anyway, he kept his word. After we left the suite, I just kept talking to him—rambling, trying to keep him off-balance. At first he said nothing, but I kept pushing. He didn't say much, but what he did say was interesting."

"Like what?"

"He got in with a room key from the maid cart. I'm not sure how he knew where to find us; but he mentioned that he had been in town for the past few days, so chances are that he cased us the last day or so."

Denise released a sigh. *So much for thinking you were focused again*, the officer berated herself. "What else did he say?"

"Let's see... At one point, when I was getting frustrated with him, I asked why he didn't just kill me there, get it over with. But he said his deal was to bring me back alive. He said something else about you."

"What?"

"That you'd be dead, Denise, if it wasn't for the deal."

"The deal?"

Sara chuckled slightly. "Yeah, that's what I wondered, too—what deal? So I asked."

Denise chuckled at that point. "So you just chatted him up, did you?"

Sara shrugged. "What did I have to lose?"

She's got a point. "Well, what did he say?"

"He said there's a condition on the hit—his words not mine. You weren't to be harmed. And the reason I was being taken back to Detroit alive was so his boss could have the pleasure of seeing the job finished. Of course he never named DeVittem as his boss, but I figured that's just a given."

Denise couldn't believe it. Despite all the trouble, the heartache, and the sheer terror at times, Sara could still smile and joke. Denise felt a lump form in her throat when she realized that she had to maintain a strictly professional relationship with this woman who brought such light into her life, otherwise she would be endangering Sara.

Putting her roiling emotions on hold, Denise considered the strange terms of the contract. "Conditions?" she repeated out loud, working out just why DeVittem would be hesitant to have her killed. *Perhaps it's a stipulation his source in the department put on providing our location. Maybe I know the informant; maybe it's someone I thought I knew better than anyone. But why would Angie sell me out after all these years? It just doesn't make sense.*

"Anyway," Sara sighed, in the face of Denise's silence, "we got to talking about just how much my head was worth. I told him I could beat DeVittem's offer, and we ended up haggling." Sara chuckled. "Don't get me wrong, I was scared shitless at the time; but to hear it now, it sounds quite humorous. He wanted to know how much I'd give him, but I wasn't about to go that route! I wanted to know what amount DeVittem had fixed. Finally he gave in and told me it was $50,000. I told him I'd double it if he'd let me go, but we had to call you to get the bag. And that's when he made the call."

Silence filled the car. Sara could see Denise's mind whirling with thoughts, computing everything.

"So he...saw us? I mean, together?" Denise asked.

"Yeah," Sara answered. "But that doesn't mean anything."

"Oh, boy."

"What's the matter?" Sara asked.

"If he saw us, then that means DeVittem will probably hear about it. And if DeVittem's lawyer questions you on the stand about our relationship—"

"Then I'll tell the truth," Sara replied. "It's none of their damn business."

Denise smiled and shook her head. "It's not that simple," she began. "What I did with you..." She shook her head in disgust. "I disregarded so many of the rules governing the officer-witness relationship; and DeVittem's suits are sure to run with it. They'll discredit you as a witness and me as an officer, and he might walk."

"I won't let that happen," Sara answered. "I don't care what DeVittem's lawyers try to do. All I care about is the two of us getting through this safe and sound. That's all that matters, Denise."

Tell her now. If she really means that, then she'll understand. Now's the perfect time to tell her.

"I love you, Denise."

Oh, she had to say it, didn't she? Denise closed her eyes but, despite her misgivings, couldn't help the tiny smile that appeared. "I love you, too, Sara," the officer whispered sincerely. *You've still got lots of time before you get back to Detroit. Work up your nerve, Denise, and tell her later.* When she opened her eyes, Sara was eyeing her curiously.

"Where are we off to now? The Klondike seems like a safe bet."

"We're going to take in a doubleheader with the Blue Jays," Denise answered softly.

Sara considered the reply for a moment. "Ahhhh," she said out loud. *We're going to Toronto,* Sara thought. However, she said, "So, we're going to Baltimore, huh?"

Denise gave Sara a look of disbelief.

"I'm teasing. I'm teasing," Sara said, holding up her hands as she chuckled. "I'm vaguely familiar with our nation's pastime."

The rest of the morning went quietly and smoothly. They made idle conversation until they arrived at the train station, where they thanked the Mountie for playing chauffeur. Gallantly, the officer insisted on carrying their bags into the train station, then wished them a good journey and took his leave.

Once seated snugly in their spots on the train headed west, both women released a deep sigh. Sara rested her head on Denise's shoulder, and Denise's hand reflexively found its way to Sara's knee. It was just so easy to be relaxed and affectionate with this woman—more so than with anyone she'd ever met.

This was a close one. I almost lost her, Denise thought as she kissed Sara's forehead. *I love her. I know that now, but I have to let her go. It's the only way to keep her safe. She's going to hate it. She might even hate me; but I hope that some day she understands: I have to do it...for her.*

Chapter
11

Even though the sun was beginning to set, the reflections from the glass-windowed skyscrapers were blinding as the duo stepped out of Union Station and onto the Toronto sidewalk. An information kiosk was situated to the right, and Denise picked up a list of hotels. Making a few calls, she found a vacancy at the Royal York. It was a wonderful location—only steps from the train station, and a rental car facility was nearby if they needed to leave town fast. Of course in the traffic that surrounded them, perhaps "fast" wasn't quite the word; but they did have a ready means of escape.

They were escorted to their room, and Sara tipped the bellhop for helping with what little luggage they had. After he left, Denise looked out the window while Sara sprawled out on the bed. The officer turned to see Sara displaying a seductive smile.

"Wanna try it out?" Sara asked, doing a little bounce on the bed.

Denise tried her damnedest to smile back, but couldn't. After a few moments of silent regard, she gave a reluctant sigh. *Get it over with, VanCook,* she told herself. "We have to talk."

"Uh oh. It's never a good sign when people say, 'We have to talk,'" Sara replied, assuming a sitting position on the edge of the bed.

"And this time won't be any different," Denise answered truthfully. The officer knelt between Sara's legs and took the woman's hands in hers before she spoke. "I thought if I acknowledged my desire, it would make me more observant. I thought I could stay focused."

"Denise," Sara said, trying to stop her. "You've done all that anyone could do."

Denise let the comment pass without remark. She had to explain, had to express her thoughts and concerns. "That man got into our room, crept to our bedroom, and I didn't sense a thing. If I had been awake instead of sleeping in your bed, that never would have happened. For the rest of the trip, things have to be different. I can't be your protector and your lover. And protecting you has to come first."

"So that's it, huh? A one night stand is all there is for us?" Sara lashed out, immediately regretting it. "I'm sorry," she muttered, looking at Denise's fingers locked tightly around hers. "You told me it could all change in an instant. I accepted that. I just...I hoped it would work out."

Denise took a deep breath. "I want you. Lord knows I want you. But with things the way they are—with us being lovers—I can't guarantee your safe return. I almost lost it at Mt. Royal. I let my love and my anger start to get the better of me. And control is something I have to have, now more than ever. Besides, I've violated about 20 ethics codes by not ignoring my attraction to you. Add to that the fact that being involved with a cop is a stressful way to live even on a normal basis... Anyway, please tell me you understand."

Sara looked at Denise, trying to read something in her eyes— anything—that would give her some kind of hope for their future. She came up empty. Denise showed nothing. She was all business again.

"I understand perfectly," Sara gritted out. "You're saying goodbye, and you're not even gone yet."

Denise felt Sara's pain, but she couldn't let herself show any reaction to it. It was a new game now, with new rules. It had to be—for both of their sakes. *This is hard enough as it is.* "This isn't how I wanted it to be," Denise offered in a whisper.

"Whatever you think is best, Lieutenant VanCook. You're the boss," Sara answered as she darted up off of the bed. She couldn't stay. She knew she'd turn into a puddle at any moment, so she dashed to the bathroom.

"Sara, wait..." Denise sighed. When Sara didn't hesitate, Denise just let her go. She didn't have the strength to follow; and if she did, what could she offer—empty promises? *No. Sara deserves better than that,* Denise considered. *She needs someone to love her without reservation, and that can't be me—not now, maybe not ever.*

Sara locked the door behind her and looked at herself in the mirror. *I told you not to get involved with her,* she said to her reflection. *Don't you dare start to cry over a part-time dyke that can't make up her mind. She's not worth it.* Sara tried to convince herself; but the more she tried, the more pain she felt.

She did feel something real for me, something genuine. And yes, she is special. But you won't have her again. You can't have her again, no matter how much you want her. You'll never have her in your life the way you want—she won't let you inside. She's afraid she'll hurt you. She's afraid she'll hurt herself. And there's not a damn thing you can do about that. Despite the stern warning she had issued herself when she'd first looked in the mirror, Sara disregarded her own admonition...she did cry.

For her part, Denise finally rose to her feet. *You had to do it,* she told herself. *For everyone's sake. It's better she knows now; you'd only hurt her worse in the end. She's your witness; and even after all this is over, you know it's hell being a cop's wife. Do you really want to put her through that? Do you want to risk another Joseph?* Denise sighed and ran her fingers through her hair. *Focus, Denise.* Soon she did focus—eyeing the phone intently. *Get back to work, VanCook,* she told herself. With that, she picked up the phone and dialed a familiar number.

"I'm not in Montreal anymore," were the first words from Denise's mouth. No hi. No hello. No how's it going. She couldn't hide the suspicion that consumed her.

"What!" Angie exclaimed. "You were going to stay there for the week."

"Does our change of location throw off your plans?"

"Denise, what are you talking about?"

"You know exactly what I'm talking about," Denise snarled. "No one—do you understand—*no one* but you knew of our location. And still we were fingered. Tell me what the hell is going on! Did he get to you? Did he offer you the world and then some? Or was it just a lousy couple grand to make up for the lost skiing trip?"

"Did you ever consider that you were followed?" Angie shouted.

"Oh, come on, partner o' mine," Denise argued. "From the Bahamas to Canada! Get real!"

"It is *not* me!" the sergeant shouted. Her voice had such intensity that she could be heard outside of her glass-enclosed office.

"Oh yeah?" Denise hollered back. "Then prove it!"

Sara heard Denise shouting and came out to inspect. She stood in the doorway of the bathroom, but Denise didn't even notice Sara's presence.

"I shouldn't have to prove it, Denise. I'm your partner."

Denise paused. Yes, Angie was her partner. They'd spent many years together—caring for each other, protecting each other. A small flicker of hope rose in Denise's heart that perhaps, just perhaps, Angie was telling the truth. "Then find out who it is and how they know where we are. I'll call after you meet the judge, but I won't tell you where I am."

A long silence passed over the phone. "You really think it's me?" Angie asked, both offended and angry. Most of all, she was hurt. This was a woman she was willing to lay her life down for, accusing her of endangering it instead.

"I'm not sure what to think," Denise choked out, her pain sizzling through the phone line, threatening to become sobs. "All I know is that I can't tell you where I am until we find the leak."

"I can't believe after everything...all these years...you think I've been setting you up."

"Then tell me what to believe!" Denise shouted. She couldn't hold it back any longer; she began to cry.

Sara had watched Denise tear up. She had heard her sob. But never once had she seen Denise actually cry. She could only see her protector's back, but she could tell Denise was wiping away tears as she gripped the phone. "Well, do what you like," Sara heard Denise say before she slammed the phone down. Not even a goodbye was uttered.

Sara knew that Denise loved Angie. Of that, there was no doubt. She believed in her, counted on her, and found a confidante in her. Being a woman who had given up on believing in so many things, the loss of her best friend—the one thing she still had faith in—was monumentally heart wrenching for Denise.

Sara paused as she considered approaching Denise. She was still feeling a fair amount of hurt at Denise's calling things off, but she recognized that Denise was doing what she thought was best. She also realized that Denise hadn't lied to her or betrayed her. She'd said up front that everything might change in an instant; and it had. There was no sense in making their trip any more difficult than it already was. The problems she had with Denise began to pale in comparison with what had just transpired with Angie. She could still be a friend to Denise. With that thought, Sara made her way over to the officer.

Denise felt Sara's hand start at her shoulder and run the length of her arm as she began to regain her composure.

"Shh," Sara soothed. "It's okay."

"I don't want her to be the leak," Denise said with a heavy sob.

"Maybe she isn't," Sara replied optimistically. "Maybe there's some other explanation that neither one of you have had time to consider."

"Well," Denise began, finally turning toward Sara, "if it's her, I just lost my best friend. And if it's not her...I still just lost my best friend."

Denise put her face in her hands, slumped down at the edge of the bed, and cried. All Sara could do was hold her.

"I'm going out, Wagner!" Angie yelled, dashing through the stationhouse.

"Where you going, in case Genar asks?" he said, following behind her.

"Judge Harris' office," she replied, dodging around her fellow detectives.

"I thought your appointment was next week," he replied, getting tangled in the human traffic.

"It is," Angie said, stopping at the door and turning to face Wagner. "But he's gonna see me now."

Angie arrived at the judge's office in record time. She stormed through the first set of glass doors, then the second. An elegantly decorated hallway led to a reception area where a secretary was seated, but Angie wasn't paying any attention to the décor. She was on a mission.

"Is Judge Harris still here?" she queried. Her tone indicated that her unspoken request wasn't open to debate.

"Yes, he is, but—"

The receptionist didn't get any further before Angie was crashing through the chamber doors. The judge—an older gentleman with graying hair around his temples—sat behind a large bureau. A set of chopsticks was perched at his mouth when Angie burst inside.

"Can I help you?" he asked, setting the utensils down in his take-out box.

"Yes, I'm Sergeant Angela Michaels."

The secretary, who had entered on Angie's heels, spoke. "I tried to stop her, your Honor," she explained, "but she barged her way in."

"It's okay, Bridget," the judge answered. "Give us a few minutes. It's all right."

"Yes, your Honor," she nodded obediently. She made sure to direct a disapproving glare at Angie before leaving.

"Your name sounds familiar," the judge began.

"I have an 8 a.m. meeting with you on October 28th, but I

can't wait. I apologize for bursting in this way, but I am just about out of options at this point, sir."

"Well, I don't like having my dinner interrupted, but you look pretty upset," he noted. "What's the problem, Sergeant?"

"I have to have a court date moved up to as soon as possible." Angie was still feeling angry from her conversation with Denise, but she didn't want to transfer that anger to the judge so she steadied herself for his reply.

"I don't like to rearrange the court schedule," the judge said sternly.

"I understand, your Honor, but the lives of two people are on the line here. You see, about a month ago my partner, Lieutenant Denise VanCook, removed a witness, Sara Langforth, from this jurisdiction in order to protect her. Since that time, several attempts have been made on their lives. Sara is the only witness in the Carlos DeVittem murder case; and he's doing everything possible to see that she doesn't testify. DeVittem doesn't play by the same rules we have to, your Honor. I'm hoping you will do everything within your power to see that DeVittem is brought to trial."

"That's where I heard your name," the judge said, snapping his fingers and pointing at Angie. "The buzz in the D.A.'s office is saying you and VanCook did a wonderful job on that case."

"Thank you," Angie responded, "but all the work will be for naught if we can't keep the witness alive, your Honor. There's a leak somewhere, and the lieutenant and Ms. Langforth keep being found. They've been followed from Detroit to the Bahamas to Montreal, Quebec. We need your help, Judge. If there is anything you can do to push things along, I hope you'll consider it."

"How soon do you want to go to court with this?" he asked.

"As soon as possible. The D.A. already has all the information. It's a matter of scheduling."

Judge Harris leaned back in his leather chair and examined Angie for a moment. Finally he nodded, making the sergeant beam.

"How does two weeks sound?" he asked with a smile of his own. "I was supposed to go on vacation, but this might be worth delaying that for."

"Thank you very much, sir," Angie said, taking his hand and pumping it vigorously. "If it's any consolation, I had to cancel my vacation plans too because of DeVittem," she grinned.

"An autumn trip to New England. And you?"

"Skiing in Colorado," Angie grinned.

"Well, I'd love to see DeVittem off the streets. The guy is a serious dirtbag. Being a judge, I realize it's important to stay unbiased, so for the record, you never heard that."

"Heard what?"

"Exactly," he answered with a smile. "I'll help you out," he added. Just then the phone rang. He glanced down at the Caller ID box, then turned back to Angie. "Don't leave yet," he instructed before picking up the phone. "Hiya, Eddie. How's life treating you?" the judge said into the receiver.

Angie waited until the short conversation ended and the judge turned his full attention to her again.

"You know, ten years ago I broke down and bought a CD player. I never regretted it. I can hear Nat King Cole just as clearly as the day he recorded 'Unforgettable.'"

"Great song," Angie commented. "Actually, his daughter Natalie recorded a duet with him on that very song."

"He's dead," the judge answered. "How'd they do that?"

"They engineered it in a sound studio, with her voice and his mixed together. It's pretty good."

"Well, I'll be," he grinned, pausing for a moment. "Anyway, as I was saying, I bought my CD player, and I thought it was the best device ever...until I got this baby," he said, pointing to the telltale box. "If someone calls that I don't want to speak to, I can just let it ring," he chuckled.

"I know what you mean," Angie replied. "My partner and I..." Angie stopped mid-sentence.

"Are you okay?" the judge asked, concerned. The officer in front of him had just turned a ghostly white.

"I'm fine," Angie said, shaking her head to move past her shock. "Have you ever received an international call on your ID?"

"Let me think," the judge replied, scratching his temple but coming up empty. "Why do you ask?"

"I couldn't figure out how my partner's location was being uncovered, but we have one of those in our office at the station."

The judge looked speculatively at the telephone device. "I don't know. If an area is heavily populated, like Paris or London...or Toronto, I assume they have Caller ID available. In fact, I know Canada has it, because I've seen the ads for it on the Windsor, Ontario television station."

Angie sat silently, her mind racing, taking a few seconds here and there to kick herself. She hadn't once considered that damn little box. When the repairman had performed his inspection, he had just checked to make sure the phone functioned properly without any offshoots to other lines—nothing more. *Oh Christ,* Angie thought silently. *I can't believe it's that simple.* "Did you need anything else from me?" she asked the judge, getting a bit antsy.

"No," he replied. "I just wanted to tell you to call Bridget tomorrow about the court schedule. Late afternoon would be best. We'll know more by then. Also, go to the D.A. and prepare them for a possible date change, if you would."

"That's not a problem, your Honor." Angie rose and shook his hand. "Again, thank you very much."

"You're welcome," he said warmly.

Angie left just as quickly as she had come. She had to get back to the squad. She had to remove that last phone number from her ID box. But more importantly, she had to call it and warn her partner.

After Denise's exchange with Angie on the phone, she and Sara spent most of the time in silence. Sara wanted to hold Denise tight and love away her problems, if only for a short time, but she knew that was out of the question. She understood the new ground rules, and she would abide by them.

As a 1950's sci-fi thriller came on the television, they settled back and made jokes about the "oh so scary" monsters while they ate junk food. They both were tentatively feeling their way in handling the friendship route their relationship was taking.

Denise had just gotten another soda and was just about to settle back on the bed, when the phone rang. She looked to Sara with uncertainty.

"Maybe maid service wants to turn down the sheets?" Sara offered in a tone that indicated she was also leery.

Without comment, the officer walked over to the phone. "Hello?" she asked, unsure of what to expect.

"You are staying at the Royal York Hotel in downtown Toronto."

"Angie?"

"Yes, ma'am."

"How in the hell—"

"The goddamned Caller ID is how. I got your number off the box. If I hadn't found you at the number that showed up here, I was going to call—room by room—until I got you. But lucky for me the first one worked, so my damn finger won't fall off."

Denise was in total shock, without a clue as to what to say. "I don't believe it," she muttered.

"Well, believe it."

"Why didn't I think of that?" Denise berated herself.

'Is it Angie?' Sara mouthed silently. Denise nodded.

"Because you were in another country to begin with," Angie replied. "I didn't think of it, either. I thought maybe someone got the phone log; but since anyone can see that without notice, following up on that possibility felt like trying to find a needle in a haystack. Even so, I had the line checked; and when the service folks didn't find a tap, I pushed the idea of our leak coming via the phone out of my mind. We've never made use of the damn ID since they put it in. I feel terrible, because it's sitting right here by the desk and I never considered it. But here comes the worst part..."

"It has to be someone in the squad," Denise said, finishing Angie's sentence.

"Yes, but it's not that easy," Angie continued. "Your location in the Bahamas was never logged. It says "Caller unknown." The phone records just list it as an international call. Montreal logged in, but the Bahamas *did not*. And despite our earlier conversation, I can assure you that it is *not* me."

Denise searched her memory for a moment. "That's not true!" she answered finally.

"Oh no, we aren't going to get into this debate again, are we?"

"No, no," Denise answered quickly. "I'm not pointing the finger at you. I'm saying you're not the only one who knew Sara and I decided to hide out in the Bahamas."

"What do you mean? Because I didn't tell anyone."

"I distinctly remember you talking to Wagner and Brenner at some point in our first conversation from the Bahamas. Brenner had caught that carjacker, remember?"

"Oh, God, you're right! Do you really think it could be one of them?"

"Who else?" Denise answered knowingly.

"Well, if it's Wagner, I'm sure he knows you're in Toronto because I told him I was leaving the office as I was heading out, so he knew he would have the opportunity to check the ID. You might soon get another unannounced visitor."

"How long were you gone?"

"About an hour. By the way, I got the court date moved up. That's where I was—in Judge Harris' chambers."

"How did you manage that?" Denise inquired with pride in her voice.

"A lot of pushing and a little persuading," Angie chuckled. "He's a Nat King Cole fan, by the way. When this is over, we should buy him an album."

"Hell, if I make it out of this and get DeVittem behind bars,

I'll get Natalie to personally deliver copies of all her dad's CD's," Denise chuckled.

"Actually, that's how the idea of the ID came up. He was talking about CD's and his caller ID, when it clicked that we had one in our office."

"Do you think Sara and I should leave now?"

"No," Angie answered. "You need to get some rest. It's taken him at least 24 hours to put someone in place each time. But you might want to ask for a room change. Advise the staff of the situation so they keep your current room vacant tonight. That way, any hit man he sends will have to check all the rooms, like I would have," Angie jabbed in fun. "I'd just stay put for right now."

"Okay. I'll stay awake just in case. We're about five hours from home now, and I'd rather be on my guard tonight. Sara can sleep, and then I'll rest tomorrow while she drives. Should we come straight home?"

"Definitely," Angie answered. However, as a plan started to form in her mind, she backtracked. "On second thought, let's see if we can find out who the leak is."

"How are we going to do that?"

Angie considered the possibilities before she spoke. She had a "super spy" beau she was dating in an on again/off again fashion. He did work in home surveillance and things of that nature—new video cameras that were the size of an ink pen and such. She was sure that he could come in and set something up for her, even though they were off-again. "I think Steve might help."

"The peeping Tom?" Denise asked, trying not to laugh. It always seemed to get Angie's goat when Denise referred to his job in that manner.

"He is *not* a peeping Tom," Angie chuckled.

"I know, I know," Denise conceded. "So, what's the plan?"

"I'll have Steve rig up a camera in the office and close off one of the interrogation rooms so I can watch from there. I'll tell Wagner in front of Brenner, that you'll be calling me with your new location, and that I want your call and only yours. After you call, I'll wait and see who goes to check the phone ID."

"Please be careful."

Angie could hear the emphasis Denise put on the words. "I will," Angie replied. "I'll go by the book. You'll have to call me from a populated area, though, so I know the identification will be transmitted."

"Is there a populated area between here and Windsor?" Denise asked her partner.

Angie searched a mental map. "Niagara Falls," she finally

answered.

"You want us to go to Niagara Falls?"

"Yeah. It's only an hour south at the most. Leave Toronto tomorrow morning and go to Niagara. Make a pit stop and call me. Take in a few sights, if you like," Angie teased. "Then drive straight through and come back here to the station. I'll wait here until you get in."

"And what if the leak doesn't fall for it?"

Angie paused a beat. "Then we're screwed."

Denise had to laugh. "Beautiful," she replied sarcastically. "Wonderful plan."

Angie joined in chuckling. "You have to admit, it's one of our better ones."

"That's a pretty sad commentary on our careers, you know that?"

Angie continued to chuckle. Once their laughter died down a bit, she said, "I'm glad to hear you happy again."

Denise didn't say anything immediately. "Look, about earlier—"

"You're tired, you're strung out from the road, and if I know you, you haven't actually eaten anything of real nutritional value. I'd bet that right now you've got a bag of potato chips in your hand," she chuckled.

"Pretzels." Denise grinned. "You were close."

"Ah ha. I thought so. Just forget about earlier. I have. I know you're frustrated, paranoid, and about ten other adjectives. And in light of the way the situation has presented itself, I'm surprised you didn't suspect me sooner. So don't worry; all is forgiven, partner."

Denise felt herself tear up a bit. Angie really did understand—like always. "You know what?" Denise said, choking back a cry of relief.

"What's that?"

"You're the best."

Angie smiled at the compliment and cast a glance at the picture of the two of them on her desk. "You're not so bad yourself, Lieutenant VanCook," she replied. For a moment, neither woman made a comment. Angie cleared her throat, turning the conversation back to business. "Anyway, I have to see the D.A. I called and he's staying late to see me tonight, so I'm going to let you go. Just think, by this time tomorrow, you'll be home again. I'm looking forward to seeing you."

"Me too, you," Denise replied sincerely. "It feels like forever sometimes."

"Take care, and have a safe trip home."

"You take care, too. No playing the hero, okay?" Denise said firmly.

Angie knew what she meant. Denise didn't want her to become a target if she did discover the leak. Angie assured her otherwise with, "By the book, I promise."

"Okay, then," Denise answered. "I'll see you tomorrow."

"Goodbye."

"Bye, Ang."

Sara only heard one side of the conversation, but for the most part was able to put together the gist of what was happening. They were going home tomorrow—back to the real world. Despite the trauma of everything they had been through, Sara felt a bit saddened to see their time together coming to an end. She could feel that things would change once they got back to the city, and not for the better. Chances were Denise would become more detached and more businesslike in their dealings.

After the movie ended and they had eaten their room service dinner, Denise called the front desk and they were escorted to a new room.

"Why don't you get ready for bed?" Denise advised. "I'm gonna stay up tonight. Make sure everything's okay."

"Do you plan on sleeping at all, Lieutenant VanCook? Or are you going to keep playing Wonder Woman?"

Denise gave a soft grin at the thinly veiled concern. "Tomorrow you drive, and I'll rest. We're not that far from home, and Angie can take over from there for a few hours."

Sara gave a slight nod before rising and retrieving her pajamas from her flight bag. Returning from the bathroom dressed for bed, Sara began to turn the lights out in the room. The city lights from the window illuminated the room to provide some much needed lighting for Denise if someone should enter, but it wasn't enough that it would prevent her from sleeping. Denise took a spot in the recliner, looking out at the skyline as Sara crawled under the sheets.

Denise didn't know what to say to Sara. She was sorry that they'd gotten involved? Truth was, she wasn't sorry. For the first time in ages, Denise was happy. Perhaps she should tell her witness that her hands were tied? That was pointless, though. Sara already knew that. Denise decided the best course of action was to let things ride—no action, no words.

Sara watched Denise, who was studying the city from their window. They were going back to being individuals again; and Sara's heart felt a sudden aching. She silently told herself she was strong. She'd already proven it time and time again on this journey. She'd survived a fire fight on her apartment landing, a shootout at her office, and a bounty hunter's gun pressed against her. And she had managed to get through each event without shedding a single tear. But this time, watching Denise look upon the city with a frustrated, perhaps even, despondent look was too much to bear. Not wanting the officer to see her tear-filled eyes that threatened to spill over at any moment, Sara rolled away so her back was to Denise.

Denise heard her shift in position and looked over. She felt a sharp pain under her ribcage as she stared at Sara's turned back. *What a telling statement that is,* Denise thought silently. But she didn't blame Sara. She knew if the roles were reversed and Sara pushed her away, even if it was unwillingly, she would have a difficult time being cordial.

It wasn't until Denise felt a drop of water on her forearm that she realized she had began to cry silently as she watched Sara. She wiped her cheeks with her fingertips and took a deep breath. She didn't need Sara seeing her like this. She had to pull it together. She was a professional. She had a duty to perform. The longer she watched Sara, the less her duty was playing a role. She wanted to return to her. Tell her she was sorry. Tell her they could start over again. Denise even rose to her feet, but the image of the bounty hunter came back to her. And she knew the reason Sara had been put in that position in the first place was because of her own lack of professionalism. Yes, she loved Sara; but she wasn't about to take the chance that the woman would be killed over that love.

So, instead of joining Sara in bed as she had considered doing, Denise turned and looked out over the city again, her forehead rested against the cold, slick glass of the window. She was frustrated. She was tired. She was trapped. But most of all, she was sad. She could never be what Sara needed. Tomorrow they would get their long awaited wish: they would finally be home. But neither woman could say they were happy about it.

Chapter
12

October 17

"Sergeant Wagner?" Angie called out across the stationhouse. Wagner stood next to Brenner's desk, and Angie silently patted herself on the back for perfect timing. She felt confident as she walked up to them. "VanCook will be calling to give me her new location today, so hold any other calls I get. I don't want to speak to anyone else until I've spoken to her. Got it?"

"Yes, ma'am," he agreed with a nod.

"If it's important, take a message. Otherwise, tell them to try again tomorrow. Oh, and whatever you do, don't tell Genar. He'll pester me for her location, and I'm under strict orders from her not to tell anyone. The less Genar knows at this point, the better. Understood?"

"Crystal clear," he grinned.

"Good man," she replied. As Wagner started back to his desk she turned to Brenner. "What's the status on that carjacker?"

"Judge set the prelim for the 29th."

"Ahhh, looks like we have another good man," she complimented, giving him a chuck on the shoulder. "If you need me, you know where to find me," she added as she walked away.

DeVittem's words came back to her: *Keep your friends close, but your enemies closer.* Now they made sense. One of the men she had just praised was her enemy. *I'll do just that,* she thought. Everything was in place. As always, waiting was the hardest part.

Denise managed to doze off and on during the night, yet she'd gotten no solid sleep. Sara slept in. Denise considered waking her up so they could get moving, but like Angie had said, it would take a while before a hitman would make a move. Besides, Sara needed her rest.

Angie also had to put things together at her end, and Denise wanted to give her ample time. From the map in the phone book, it looked like Niagara Falls was an hour's drive, tops. She didn't want to arrive too early. Denise still found it inconceivable that either Wagner or Brenner would betray her. She respected both men and enjoyed working with them. *How on earth could either one of them do this? What would drive someone to harm a fellow officer? Good God! The things they faced from the outside world were bad enough. You had to believe in the people that watched your back.* Denise was certain, however, that it had to be one of them; because if it wasn't, then the only suspect left was Angie. And she'd already traveled that path. She was certain that Angie wasn't to blame.

Denise looked away from the window to see Sara stirring. Slowly the blonde opened her eyes and yawned.

"Good morning," Denise called softly.

"Good morning," Sara replied, looking around. "What time is it?"

Denise looked at her watch. "9:30."

"Why didn't you wake me up?" Sara asked, leaning her weight on her forearms.

"We're in no rush," Denise said. "I want to make sure Angie has things set up. We'll hang out here a while, grab a bite to eat, perhaps. If we get into Niagara around 1 p.m., that should be in plenty of time."

Sara nodded, wiping some sleep from her eyes. "Do you want to get a shower first?" she asked.

"No. You can go ahead. I'll go in after you."

Sara was on the verge of making another conserving water argument, but fought against it. *New rules, Sara*, she reminded herself. *New rules.* Instead she rose, not quite fully alert, and headed to the bathroom.

When the water started, Denise's mind took her back to the shower in Montreal: the way Sara looked, the way she smelled, the way she tasted. Denise closed her eyes against the memory. *You know it was stupid to begin with. You know the two of you would never make it. Sexual attraction. That's all. Nothing else. Get it out of your mind, VanCook.* Maybe if she said it enough, she'd believe it. With a deep sigh, Denise found a vacation brochure to occupy her thoughts.

When they were both ready, they packed their belongings and headed downstairs for some breakfast at the hotel restaurant. It was a quiet affair consisting of some scrambled eggs and fruit. Neither woman was quite sure of what to say to the other, how to begin a conversation, so the weather was the key topic of the day.

Soon after, they were at the car rental station and on their way. Denise didn't get much sleep on the drive to Niagara, but she did manage to rest her eyes a bit as she had done the previous night. Her energy level was too high and her nerves were on edge at the thought of the upcoming conversation with Angie. She wasn't sure if all of the elements necessary to set the plan in motion would be in place, but she knew Angie would do everything in her power to make it happen.

Sara pulled into Niagara around 12:30, and they found a hotel. Denise explained the situation to the check-in clerk, and she was gracious enough to let them use the hotel phone to make the call to Detroit.

Angie heard the phone ring in her office and started a little at the sound. Denise's nerves weren't the only ones wired that afternoon. She stood up to make sure everyone in their area knew that she was on the phone. "Hello?" Angie said nervously, hoping it was her partner.

"Hello, my darlin', hello my honey, hello my ragtime gaaaaal," Denise sang into the receiver before starting to laugh.

"You seem awfully happy," Angie chuckled.

"Is there a reason I shouldn't be?"

Angie understood the question and all the implications of it. "No. Everything is in place and on schedule. They both know you're going to call...and...right now Brenner is looking at me. Keep talking until Wagner comes in, okay?"

"Sure," Denise replied. "What would you like to talk about?"

"How's the weather?"

"The weather? It's clear and a sunny 62 degrees with a 10% chance of showers later in the day," Denise answered, imitating a weatherman. "Humidity is relatively low at 20%," she added.

"Very funny," Angie grinned. "Did you have any problems last night?"

"You mean except for listening to Sara snore all night? No, " she answered as she winked at the blonde and the disparaging comment earned her an elbow in the ribs.

"That's good," Angie replied. She looked up to see Wagner walking through the squad room.

"Do you have any idea of who it is yet?" Denise asked.

"No," Angie answered, "but Wagner now seems to be taking an interest in watching me. I don't want to be wrong about this. I'm not making any assumptions until I see one of them standing in my office."

"You mean my office?" Denise teased.

"I'm sorry. I meant *our* office."

"It's *my* office," Denise insisted.

"Is not."

"Is too."

"Is not."

"Is too!"

"If it's your office," Angie taunted, "then why am I standing in it, huh?"

"Ooh, touché."

Angie chuckled. *Figured she'd give up after that one.* "I'm glad you're coming back today. I've missed you." The smile was evident in her voice.

"I've missed you too, sweetcheeks," Denise rejoined playfully. Then her demeanor changed as she suddenly remembered what lay ahead. "Please be on your guard today, okay? Anything could happen, so just be ready."

"I will," Angie promised. "I'll see you in a couple of hours."

"Take care," Denise cautioned.

"Yeah, you too," Angie replied sincerely.

A silence hung over the phone for a moment until Denise spoke, "I know I don't say it much but...I love ya, Ang. Be careful."

Angie felt herself choke up at the declaration and swallowed down her emotions. "Love you too, Denise. See ya soon."

With that, both women hung up, and Sara had to admit she was a bit baffled by the closing sentiment. She knew that Denise and Angie were just partners, the best of friends. But something else lay behind that. Perhaps this plan was much more dangerous than she'd assumed. She didn't want to question Denise about it. *At least, not now.* So instead of grilling the officer, she made a suggestion. "Why don't we get some lunch before we head back?" she offered.

Denise grinned. "Told you that you should have had more than that bagel and cantaloupe."

"I told you, I don't eat a lot in the morning, Miss 'My Cholesterol Is So High I'm Working On A Massive Heart Attack,'" Sara prodded.

"I like to eat real food in the morning," Denise retorted. "And as you can see, my stomach isn't the one growling right now."

"Don't make me give you my pathetic puppy dog eyes," Sara warned.

Denise chuckled. "Oh, please, don't let it come to that! Come on. I'm sure they'll have some restaurants or something on the strip out there."

As they walked down the street to Clifton Hill, they took in the sights before finding a hotdog vendor. With their franks and drinks in hand, Sara nodded toward the bottom of the street. "Come on," Sara waved, careful not to spill her soda. "Let's go see the Falls."

Denise looked around, but she didn't pick up on anything that seemed out of place. *Oh, what the hell*, she figured. *It's only 15 or 20 minutes out of my life.* "Have you been here before?" she asked.

"Nope. Never. And you?"

"Really?"

"No. Why? How many times have you been here?"

"This would make my...hmmmm...let's see...first time," Denise grinned.

"You've never been here, either? You made me feel like I'm the only one alive who hadn't been here," Sara chuckled.

"I figured that with all your money, at some point your folks came here," Denise answered. "My folks could never afford it. Well, maybe they could have if Dad hadn't spent all that money at the bar." Denise grinned ruefully. "And I never had a reason to come here—no honeymoons to speak of," she teased. "Why haven't you been?"

"Niagara Falls was far too touristy for my parents. It was always trips to the Australian Outback, or Venice, or some little island out in the Pacific that no one who speaks English can pronounce," Sara replied. "I missed out on fun stuff that kids usually do."

Denise smiled. "Maybe after lunch I'll take you to the wax museum."

"Oh, really, Mom! Could we, could we?"

"Not if you don't calm down, young lady," Denise answered, joining in on the pretense.

Although the Falls were nowhere in sight, they could hear the rush of water and feel a cold breeze from the east. They followed the sound, and soon they could see a deep ravine. A few feet further and they could see the giant cascades across the river.

"Come on," Sara said, holding her aluminum-wrapped dog and soda in one hand and using the other to take Denise by the elbow. She picked up speed, pulling Denise along with her.

Denise loved the way Sara could see the world through a child's eyes. The officer found herself paying more attention to Sara's excited reaction than to the scenery surrounding them. But then Denise looked up the river.

A sense of awe came over her—something that she hadn't felt

in years—perhaps since the time she was a child. She couldn't believe her eyes. She had gone on hiking trips and seen a few waterfalls in her time, but nothing compared to this. Even the pictures Denise had seen of Horseshoe Falls paled in comparison to actually standing here.

"Isn't that beautiful?" Sara said, squeezing Denise's hand. "Let's go get a closer look."

They walked toward the huge water mass, nibbling on their lunch. With every step they took, the thundering noise got louder. Denise was surprised. The railing that guarded the river wasn't very high. People peered over the edge, but no one dared to lean too far over. As Sara and Denise finished their lunch, they continued to walk through the maelstrom of different nationalities—Asians, Indians, and Europeans. The air was humming with many different languages—French to her left, Hebrew to her right. Families, lovers, and lone individuals all flocked to the water's edge.

The river ran right next to the edge of the embankment, and Sara and Denise finally made it to the edge of the Falls. From there it would be nothing to splash right in and go head first over the Falls. In fact, Denise was surprised to see that people weren't lined up with barrels hoping for a shot at fame. It seemed most folks, however, were smarter than Denise had given them credit for, and everyone was spectating from behind the railing. Mist sprayed up, getting them a little wet, so they opted to visit the large gift shop behind them. At least that's what they had planned to do, before Denise felt something poking her back.

"Don't move," a gruff voice said. "Don't even breathe."

Denise glanced over at Sara, who was looking behind them.

"He's got a gun in his pocket," Sara said in a hushed tone.

"That's right, and if you don't do as I say, I'm gonna splatter her heart across all that pretty water. Do you understand?"

Both women nodded silently. The burly man then proceeded to search Denise, finding the gun in her shoulder holster. He took it discreetly and stuffed it into his waistband, covering it with his sweatshirt. With the natural wonder around them, no one even noticed the action. "Let's walk," he ordered.

They began to turn around in compliance with the command, but then Denise jumped, grabbing at the arm that held the weapon on them. She pulled his hand from his jacket pocket, exposing the weapon, then cracked his hand over her knee to relieve him of the gun. He retaliated by punching her in the face with his free hand. His gun fell to the ground, but so did Denise.

Tourists around them noticed the commotion and began to scream and run in the opposite direction to avoid the confrontation. The attacker reached for his gun, but Denise kicked it over the edge of the walkway and into the water. She got a boot to the stomach for her trouble, and curled up on the cement as the pain exploded in her belly.

Sara saw the attacker reach to pull Denise's gun from his waistband. She didn't give her action a second thought: she saw Denise was in trouble, and she reacted. Before he could get a shot off, Sara jumped on his back and delivered two solid blows to his face.

He flipped Sara over with ease and the blonde landed squarely on her back, knocking the wind out of her. He cocked the gun and pointed it at Sara, momentarily leaving his own torso fully exposed.

Denise saw the opening. The assailant was poised with his arm outstretched, ready to fire at Sara, and the lieutenant charged. She tackled him and the two of them tumbled to the ground, the weapon falling from his hand in the process. Denise landed on top, but the gunman managed to backhand her so hard she fell off. Blood dripped from Denise's nose and eyebrow as she lay on the ground next to him. "Run!" she yelled to Sara, who was upright and trying to catch her breath.

Sara knew the best course of action was to get help and explain which of the combatants was on the side of the angels, so she forced herself to her feet and began stumbling towards the gift shop.

In the brief moment that Denise's attention was on Sara, the attacker managed to retrieve the gun. Intending to prevent any outside interference, he raised the weapon and took aim at the fleeing woman.

Denise turned back to resume the fight just in time to see the danger. Heedless of the scraping of the concrete, she swiveled her body around to kick the man's legs out from under him. As he tried to catch himself, the weapon flew from his hands, sending it flying out of arm's reach.

They both saw it; and they both glanced at each other before focusing on the weapon again. Both officer and attacker knew it— it was all over for whoever failed to regain possession of the gun.

Nah-ah, bastard, Denise thought. Both breathing hard, they struggled to their feet, trying to scrabble forward at the same time. Neither of them could get traction on the wet cement, and it appeared as if they were crawling. The attacker gained his balance first and kicked Denise's head into the ground, but she succeeded in grabbing his leg and pulling him back down. She climbed his body to inch closer to the weapon. He emitted a howl of pain as her foot found purchase on his hand and she got enough traction to stand up.

He tried to pull her down, but Denise hurdled his out-stretched hand. Unfortunately, in doing so, she slipped on the damp surface and fell. Only inches away from the gun, she stretched with all her length, but came up just short. *Jesus Christ, let something go right*, she pleaded silently, trying to wriggle her way toward it. As the gunman dove over her, she executed another roundhouse kick, swiveling her body and legs to thrust the gun away. This time, however, it sailed toward the gift shop where Sara was returning from calling for help. Denise gave the erstwhile attacker a wicked grin as they both scrambled to their feet.

Sara picked up the gun, made sure it was uncocked, and tossed it to Denise in one easy heave. The assailant tried to inter-cept it, but came up empty as Denise caught it with one hand and took aim. Seeing the situation spiraling out of his control, the man desperately rushed her before she could get a shot off.

Denise fought to maintain her balance as the attacker pro-pelled her backward. She could hear his scream of frustration and the sounds of sirens getting closer, but the sound that was thun-dering above them all was the rushing water behind her as she stumbled toward the guardrail.

Denise's back slammed against the stone embankment. The thug sent an uppercut to Denise's chin, then followed with a left hook. Denise tried to point the weapon and shield herself from another blow at the same time. She didn't dare fire blindly with the scattering of bystanders so near. Sara regrouped and raced over to the attacker. Before she could get a good hold on him, he elbowed her in the face, sending her back to the ground. Suddenly, instead of another punch, Denise felt herself being lifted, and she shook her head to clear the blood that had dripped into her eyes.

"Oh, God!" Denise heard one spectator yell. "He's gonna throw her over!"

Denise grasped the man's jacket as tightly as she could. "If I'm going, you're going!'" she yelled.

"Like hell," he shouted back, as he tossed her over the edge.

Denise lost her hold on the man's coat, and the gun as well, but she managed to hook her arm over one of the iron railings. She fell hard against the cement barrier and heard a loud splash. She felt her running shoes being sucked from her feet as they dangled in the water. Her armlock was slipping fast, and if any more of her body went in, she didn't think she could maintain her grip against the current. She looked up to find a way to crawl back to safety, but all she found was the assailant pointing her gun at her.

"Let go," he ordered.

"Let me think about this a minute," Denise answered, behaving as if she had the upper hand.

"Now!" he yelled.

Denise closed her eyes and quickly ran through her options. If he fired at her, she would be dead. If she didn't die from the gunshot, she wouldn't be able to hold on, and she would be dead. If she did as he asked, she would go over the falls and chances were...she would be dead. Her heart threatened to pound out of her chest as she concluded that she really had no options. But she wouldn't leave Sara as long as she was alive; and so her choice was made. She held on, heard him cock the gun, waited for the inevitable.

"Freeze!" a voice ordered. "Police! Drop the weapon and turn around."

The man stared down at Denise. "I think I'd do what they say," Denise said, struggling with her words and her grip. *The current is getting stronger or I'm getting weaker*, Denise considered. She desperately tried to tighten her hold as she watched the thug drop the gun and slowly put his hands in the air.

Denise could only see feet rushing toward them. The gunman was cuffed and led off to the side, as people crowded around the guardrail to get a better look at Denise.

"Can you reach my hand?" a police officer asked Denise as he stretched over the side.

"I can't let go," she managed to reply. "Current's too strong."

"Okay," he said. "Just stay calm. We're coming to get you."

The officer stepped back as some park rangers showed up with an odd-looking contraption. One was suited up in what looked like mountain climbing gear. He exchanged a few words with Sara, then climbed over the edge to Denise while three men held his line.

"Denise," he said calmly "we're gonna get you outta here, but we need your help. Can you lift your foot?"

"I think so," Denise sputtered. "But there's no support to set it on." She nodded toward the other side of them.

"Get a man over here!" the rescuer yelled. Within seconds, another man was over the railing to Denise's right.

"Okay," the ranger instructed, "use Tony's leg for support once you get your foot up." With that, the officer let go of his grasp on his line and fell back to try to get as far behind Denise as possible, while his team members on shore held his line taut.

Denise tried to raise her leg as Sara looked on in speechless terror. "You're too close!" Denise yelled.

Tony moved down as the first rescuer reached under Denise's arms. "You're going to be okay. Try again," he coaxed.

Denise took another shot at the cement and finally got her foot on Tony's knee.

"That's it," the first rescuer encouraged. "I've got you. Push on up. Push on up."

Tony didn't move, staying as still as he could so Denise wouldn't slip. Three workers came over and grabbed at Denise's arms.

"On three," the rescuer told the group. "One...two...three!" With that, they all heaved Denise up with their combined strength.

"Arghhhh," Denise howled in painful determination. The rescuers leaned over the rail and grabbed the rest of her body as soon as they could. The police officer caught her as she fell to the sidewalk...on the safe side of the railing.

Denise barely heard the cheering crowd. The pain in her arm and shoulder was too great. She figured one or the other must have been dislocated or sprained during the fall or the rescue. But she immediately pushed the pain aside to attend to a more pressing issue. "Where's Sara?" she demanded.

"Who?" the cop asked, hearing the fear in Denise's voice.

"The blonde I was with." Denise tried to see past the emergency medics who were now examining her. "Sara!" she yelled out.

"I'm here," Sara shouted, pushing through the crowd around Denise and dropping to her knees beside her. "I'm right here," she said, giving Denise a tender kiss on the forehead.

"Are you okay?"

"Am I okay?" Sara echoed, starting to cry. *You're nearly tossed to your death, yet you ask if* I'm *okay?* "I am now that you're safe."

"Shh," Denise soothed, seeing the tears come to Sara's eyes. "I'm all right. My arm hurts like hell, but I'll be fine."

Sara nodded silently. She wanted to stay strong for Denise, but as her adrenaline began to wear off, she felt her emotions brewing and her nerves physically twitching her right eye and her limbs. "I'm so sorry," Sara told her.

"Well, what did I expect? All these little outings you take me on always go awry," Denise teased before mimicking her. "Let's go to my office. Let's go to the Bahamas. They'll never find us in Montreal..." Sara started to sob again, which was the last thing Denise wanted. "Calm down," Denise whispered. "I was only kidding."

"But it's all my fault. This whole trip has been my fault."

"Has the whole trip been that bad?" Denise asked sincerely.

Finally a smile crept to Sara's face. *No, it wasn't all bad.*

Denise gave Sara a grin before the EMTs began putting a neck brace on her.

"What in the world do you think you're doing?" Denise asked, clearly annoyed.

"We don't want to take any chances," the medic replied. "Can you lay down on this board?"

"No, I cannot. I have to be in Detroit in a few hours."

"If you're lucky, you'll get to leave the hospital in a few hours," he told her.

"I'm not going to the hospital," Denise said, starting to sit up. She put her weight on her bad arm and felt a shooting pain that made her cringe.

"What hurts?"

"Nothing," Denise answered. "Get out of my way."

Sara put a gentle arm on Denise's shoulder, making sure not to hurt her but wanting to get her full attention.

"Please let them look at you," she asked softly. "Tell them what hurts."

Denise sighed and relented. "My arm and shoulder. I got pulled up a little too hard; but other than that, I'm fine."

"Take a deep breath," the medic told her. Denise gave a little wheeze in the process of complying. "No arguments. You need to go to the hospital."

"Fine. But she's going with me," Denise said, pointing to Sara. "She's not leaving my sight."

"That's fine. She can ride in the ambulance, if you like. However, Detective—"

"I'm a lieutenant, thank you very much," Denise corrected with uncharacteristic pique.

"I'm sorry, *Lieutenant*," the medic said. "In any event, you're going to the hospital, so lay on the board."

Denise did as instructed, but not without a roll of her eyes. When they got to the hospital, her cooperation didn't improve. When they tried to get some x-rays, Denise refused to have Sara leave the room. "Put a lead apron on her if you have to, but she's not leaving my side." They soon realized it was easier to let the officer have her way.

After two hours in the emergency room, during which time the police took their statements and returned Denise's gun, the doctor finally arrived. She was an older woman, perhaps in her early fifties.

"How ya feeling, eh?" she asked conversationally.

"My arm hurts. I'm tired. And I want to go home."

"Sounds like someone's a little grumpy. Maybe you got up on the wrong side of the bed this morning," the doctor countered with a friendly smile.

The bedside humor wasn't flying with Denise. "See? That's where you're wrong. I didn't get up on the wrong side of the bed, because I haven't been to bed in about 36 hours."

"Come on. It didn't take me THAT long to get here," the doctor joked.

Sara could see Denise beginning to boil over. The doctor's chipper attitude wasn't helping the situation any. Sara knew her growing smile would only fuel Denise's irritability, so she turned away and took a special interest in the cloth divider that enclosed the gurney.

"Look, lady," Denise said, gently grabbing the physician's smock, "I'm only gonna say this once, so listen carefully. I am an investigative detective with the Detroit Police Department. I am the ranking lieutenant in the Homicide Division. This woman standing to my right is a key witness in a murder trial. Since all this began approximately a month ago, I've been in two different countries, and I've run from one side of this continent to the other. I've been awake the last 36 hours straight protecting her, not to mention that I nearly took a header over Niagara Falls today. So believe me when I say: cut out the optimistic attitude and tell me the results of all those little tests you ran to scam my insurance company." Denise released her and smoothed out her smock where her grip had wrinkled it.

"Well," the doctor said nervously, "on the whole, you're fine."

"I knew that!" Denise said, shaking her head in disgust.

"However," the doctor added, "you've got a separated rib. It's pressing on your lung, which is why you can't take a deep breath. It's not life threatening, but it can be extremely painful."

"Like she had to explain the pain aspect," Denise said to Sara. "Just fix me up so I can go," she told the doctor.

"Gladly. We have a chiropractor who's coming in to straighten you out."

"Someone to make me straight," Denise grinned. "And just when I thought my day couldn't get any worse."

Sara had to chuckle at that remark, which went right over the doctor's head.

"He'll be here in about an hour," the physician replied.

"An hour? I've already been here for two," Denise complained.

"Look, lady," the doctor mimicked Denise, "I'm only gonna say *this* once. I could keep you here overnight because of the head trauma you sustained in that brawl, but I've decided to release you after the chiropractor is finished. Now if you have a problem with that, let me know; and I'll have the nurses get a room ready for you."

Denise didn't reply. She watched the doctor slam the medical chart down on the end of the bed and head for the door, fuming.

"He'll be here in an hour," she repeated as she slammed the door shut on her way out.

After the doctor was gone, Sara turned to see Denise's reaction. She just laid back on the bed, tapping her foot against the mattress in impatience.

"You have to admit," Sara began with a small grin, "she's kinda sexy, especially when she let you have it." Denise stared at Sara with a serious frown and bloodshot eyes. "I'm kidding," Sara added. "She's a Barbie doll type. It wouldn't surprise me if she drove a pink Corvette."

Denise tried to stay angry, but ended up cracking a grin.

"Don't smile too much. You might strain that rib," Sara prodded with a wink.

Denise gave a soft chuckle, but it didn't last long. She clutched at her side almost immediately. "Please don't make me laugh. It hurts when I laugh. I just want to be home. We're already four hours late as it is. And that's *if* the other doctor gets here on time."

Sara took a spot next to Denise on the bed. "I feel so guilty, Denise," she whispered.

"Why?" Denise asked, raising the automatic bed up a bit.

"If we hadn't gone to the Falls, none of this would have happened. You said it yourself today."

"I was teasing," Denise replied in a soothing voice. "Besides, if we hadn't gone to the Falls, it could have been much worse," Denise countered.

"How?" Sara asked in disbelief. "You almost went over the Falls without the barrel."

"Since that thug was undoubtedly following us from Toronto, he may have tried to run us off the highway later on. We wouldn't have had any back-up or any cover. You have to stop blaming yourself for all this," Denise said, reaching out for Sara's hand. Without hesitation, Sara took it. "Believe me, it turned out for the better."

"I just wish there was something more I could do," Sara

sighed.

"You did pretty good out there today," Denise grinned. "It took a lot of guts to try to take on a guy that big."

Sara grinned. "Well, as you can tell, I'm not the greatest fighter of all time, but I can do some pretty mean eye scratching."

Denise started to chuckle but stopped abruptly, holding her side again. "Look, Sara," Denise began sincerely. "Your time to shine will come. You will walk into that courtroom in Detroit. You will tell the truth, the whole truth, and nothing but the truth. And you will put that murderer behind bars."

Sara smiled again and Denise joined in her enthusiasm, but not for long. The smile slipped from her face.

"What's wrong?" Sara asked, sensing the change.

Denise looked at Sara for a moment. "I wonder what Angie is doing right now."

The night before, Angie had ordered Interrogation Room Two closed until further notice. She explained that she and Denise had a hot lead on one of their cases and wanted to make sure it was available, as they were closing in on the perpetrator. Everyone believed her, but they didn't especially like the idea of Sergeant Michael's pulling rank and having a reserved room.

The truth was, Steve had come in the night before during the midnight shift, and installed a tiny camera in her office and a monitor inside the closed room. The squad wasn't shut down during the late shift, but rarely was anyone around, so the timing was right. Angie sat watching the monitor. She waited, and waited, and then waited some more.

At 3 p.m., she told the squad she was going out and if she wasn't back by 4 p.m., she was officially gone for the day. Of course, she never left; she just went around the back and crept up the stairs without being observed. Angie yawned and looked at her watch—4:06 now, and not a single incriminating movement had been made. She knew Denise would be arriving soon, and she still had no idea who was leaking information to DeVittem. The longer she looked at the small screen, the more tedious the stakeout became.

She had just finished rubbing her eyes for perhaps the ninth time that hour, when she saw someone standing behind her desk. She leaned closer for a better look, watching as the man nervously looked around. He pulled out a pen and paper and began writing down the information from the Caller ID.

"I'll be damned," Angie whispered to herself as she watched

him. Suddenly the door burst open, and Angie thought she was going to go into cardiac arrest. She turned to see Captain Genar.

"What in blazes is going on here?" he asked.

"Shh," she said, running to the door and pulling him inside before closing it.

"Look," she said, pointing to the monitor. "He's been tracking Denise and our witness using our Caller ID, then he's been leaking the info to DeVittem."

"Him? Are you sure?"

"Unfortunately, yes, sir," Angie answered firmly.

"You're sure he's a leak?" he asked again in disbelief.

"Yes," Angie answered, just as convinced as the first time.

"Wait a second," Genar recalled. "You told me you didn't know Lieutenant VanCook's location."

Angie nodded. "I lied," she replied frankly. His arched eyebrow was all Angie needed to see to realize she had some explaining to do. "We couldn't be sure who to trust. So, what should we do now, sir?" she asked her commander before turning back to the monitor and studying the black and white screen.

"Oh, Jesus," he said, shaking his head, watching the monitor. "Are you absolutely sure? We can't just come out and make unfounded accusations."

"Everything you just saw has been recorded and will support any charges that the department brings. Denise and I set this up. She was to call during a quick stop in Niagara Falls, then leave immediately to come back here. Only two people knew that she was going to be calling, and therefore would know to check the Caller ID for her location: Wagner and Brenner. Lieutenant Van-Cook should be arriving any moment, so I'm wondering if we should wait for her."

"No," Genar decided. "Let's take him down now. But get him outside first. Who knows what might happen if we confront him here in the squad room. Tell him you've got car trouble out back or something. Let him go ahead of you, then cover him from the rear. I'll wait outside to move in on him from the front. Agreed?"

"Yes, sir."

"Okay. Give me five minutes, then slip downstairs and meet with him."

Captain Genar left to take up his position, and Angie waited impatiently. Finally, she proceeded downstairs. She had to keep her emotions in check, not giving any cause for suspicion. She looked into the squad room and saw the informant standing near his desk. She could feel herself begin to perspire, and took a deep, calming breath.

"I'm having a lousy day," she began as she walked up to him. "Not only did I lose my perp, but my car is making a funny noise. I didn't wanna chance going home, so I thought I would stop here. You're pretty handy. Could you come out back and give me your opinion?"

"Sure," he answered. "Lead the way."

Angie led the way, and he calmly followed behind her. Once outside, Angie stepped aside to let him move past her. That's when he saw Captain Genar near the bottom of the steps. Angie backed up a bit, blocking the door so he couldn't reenter the building.

"We need to ask you a few questions," Genar said.

Angie's colleague turned around and read the suspicion in her eyes. He knew he was busted. He dove down the steps and onto Captain Genar, trying to flee.

"Don't run!" Angie yelled. "It will only make it worse." Angie watched him stop and pull his weapon as he turned to face them. She didn't want to die, but she didn't want to kill him, either. She decided talking to him, trying to get him calmed down would be the best solution. As a gesture of good faith, she left her gun in her holster. "Let's talk about this," she said in a conciliatory tone, taking a step towards him.

"Don't move!" he said sharply, looking around for any other officers that might be lurking there to detain him. A uniformed team that was standing by their cruiser saw the commotion and rushed over.

Genar yelled over to them, "Hold your ground!" Obediently they stopped immediately.

"See? No one's gonna move," Angie reassured. "No one's gonna hurt you. Just put the gun down so we can talk about this. I'm sure you've got your reasons for what you've been doing."

"What the hell would you know?" he began. "You and Van-Cook—you always get the right cases. You always get the honors and decorations. I get nothing, year after year. Except for this time—this time I got three years' salary for three phone numbers."

Angie was boiling mad, but she didn't want to show it. He'd sold them out. And over something as inconsequential as money. Sure, the department didn't pay well; but that was part of the job. That was something you accepted, because you knew the real value was the good you could do for the people you were there to protect. For some reason, that realization had been lost to her associate. She knew this situation could blow up at any moment, and somehow she had to bring it to a close soon. She could see his trigger finger actually shaking. "Relax, okay? So maybe you didn't get all the glory, but you're a wonderful officer."

"Wonderful? You think I'm wonderful! I'll show you wonderful, you arrogant bitch!" he yelled scornfully.

A single shot rang out. Angie didn't have even a second to react. Detroit lost one of its finest; and though she didn't know it yet, Lieutenant Denise VanCook, had lost a dear friend.

Chapter
13

Sara drove up to a line for the customs booth as Denise woke up.

"Where are we?" Denise asked, trying to open her eyes.

"We just left Windsor," Sara replied. "Another 15 minutes, and we'll be at the station house."

"Are we at the bridge or the tunnel?" Denise asked, rubbing her eyes and looking around.

"I took the bridge," Sara answered.

"Switch places," Denise instructed as they came to a stop. Sara put the car in park and got out to take the passenger seat.

"What time is it?" Denise asked as both women re-buckled their belts.

"8:30 p.m. We made good time."

"Should I issue you a speeding citation, Ms. Langforth?" Denise teased.

"You're out of your jurisdiction, Lieutenant VanCook," Sara countered playfully.

"Point taken."

As they pulled up to the window, Denise flashed her badge and asked to go to the customs station. After getting processed there, they headed to her precinct. Denise was certain that Angie would still be there waiting. When Denise drove past the front of the stationhouse, Sara asked where they were heading.

"I'm going to park around back," Denise explained. "There will be a lot less traffic this time of night."

At least that's what she'd thought. When she reached the lot where the officers typically parked their personal cars, she saw that police from other precincts and news film crews were swarming all over the place; and Denise knew that whatever had happened wasn't good.

"What's going on?"

"I don't know," Denise answered. She could sense Sara's nervousness, and she reached out to touch Sara's arm. "Just stay close to me, okay?" she added.

Sara gave a nod, and they exited the car. She took Denise's hand as they walked up to the stationhouse where they saw uniformed officers trying to control the newshounds. Police tape was clearly cordoning off a crime scene. Denise led Sara through the tide of humanity, pausing only to clip her badge to her waistband. As they approached the steps, she saw the chalk outline. Denise looked at Sara with dread in her eyes.

"Angie!" Denise yelled as she ran up the steps, pulling Sara along with her. She moved at breakneck speed, dodging people in her intent search. "Angie!" she yelled again, it coming out more like a cry than a call for attention.

Denise grabbed a nearby uniformed officer. "Have you seen Sergeant Michaels?" she asked as her eyes scanned the area.

"Who?"

"Sergeant Michaels!"

"I just arrived from the 22nd," he answered. Denise didn't give a damn where the man was from. She wanted to know where her partner was. Knowing he would be of no use to her, she pushed him aside and resumed her search. Denise tried to find a familiar face to discover what had happened, but she didn't recognize anyone from the day shift.

"Do you see her?" Denise asked Sara.

Sara swiveled her head all around. "No...but I'm sure she's okay."

"Angie!" Denise yelled again as she stood still in the center of the room. She couldn't shake the sinking feeling that was overwhelming her. Then she felt a hand on her shoulder. She looked back. "Oh, God!" Denise wept. "What happened?"

"It was Brenner," Angie sighed. Denise could feel the anguish in her partner. "When I confronted him, he ate his gun in the parking lot."

"Brenner?" Denise said. "I saw the outline, and I thought it was you. Thank God you're all right!"

Denise and Angie shared a tight embrace. Never in their partnership had Denise had the feeling of Angie being ripped from her life. She felt herself begin to shake as her nerves began to relax all at once. With the adrenaline fading, she also began to feel the pain of the sore muscles and bruised bones that had taken a beating earlier that day, and she pulled away.

"Let's get outta this commotion," Angie said, tugging Denise along. They all proceeded to an examination room on the second level. Once away from the uproar, Angie told Denise about having planted the camera and Captain Genar discovering her monitoring the office. Then the conversation inevitably turned to Brenner.

"I can't believe it was him," Denise began. "I've known him for years. I can't see how he could do it."

"Yeah, I know," Angie agreed. "You two went through the Academy together. But it looks like he had a price...and he was bought."

"I always thought of him as a friend," Denise said, rubbing her eyes.

"We all did. Everyone here is in shock right now. There's going to be an investigation by Internal Affairs. In fact, they already came in to talk to me and Genar."

"Genar? What did he have to say about all this?"

"He backed me up, Denise." Angie grinned. "He saw everything that happened, and he says I'll be cleared of any wrongdoing."

"How can they hold you responsible for suicide?" Sara asked.

"They could say that she pushed him into the act," Denise explained. "If that were the case, they could bring her up on charges of willful neglect of duty, or some kind of crap like that."

"Right," Angie agreed. "But Genar saw how I tried coaxing him to calm down. And in his statement to the investigators, the captain even said that my behavior was above and beyond what could have been expected. I never even drew my gun on Brenner, Denise." The room grew quiet until Angie spoke again. "So, tell me your story. Why are you four hours late? More trouble?"

"You could say that."

"She almost got pitched over Niagara Falls," Sara explained. "And I don't see how she can be so casual about it," she added, adopting a disapproving look.

"All in a day's work," Denise said. "Sometimes you eat doughnuts while you type reports. Sometimes you get thrown into the Niagara River. It happens."

Angie sat slack-jawed. "You mean you were tracked again? Looks like Brenner got to make one last phone call. Probably while I was seeing the judge, I'd guess."

"That's what I assumed, too," Denise replied. "But hopefully things will be quiet now."

"Are you tired?"

"Yes," Denise admitted wearily. "Are you finished here?"

"Yeah, there's nothing more I can do here tonight."

"Then let's go to my place. We'll sleep in shifts. And since I just woke up, you can sleep first," Denise told Angie.

"Wait a second," Sara interrupted. "I've slept more than both of you. I'll stay awake, and if anything happens I can wake you."

Denise and Angie looked at each other. "Okay," they agreed in concert before cracking small grins.

They all rose from the table to make their way to Denise's apartment, but Angie stopped Denise, pulling her into another hug. "I'm thankful you're home," she said as they embraced.

Denise swallowed down her tears. "I'm thankful you're safe."

October 29

"Okay," said the young district attorney. "Let's go over it one more time."

Sara and Denise groaned. "If we keep this up, her testimony is going to sound so rehearsed tomorrow no one will believe it," Denise protested.

"I just don't want any surprises on the stand," the prosecutor said. "Now, tell me what happened on September 16th of this year."

The three of them sat in a small office as Sara recounted, one more time, all the incidents that had taken place since the murder, leaving out only that she and Denise had become lovers. That would undoubtedly be extremely detrimental to their trying for a conviction.

After Sara finished her account for the third time, the prosecutor smiled confidently. "You've gotta wonderful witness," he complimented Denise. "But I do see one thing."

"What?"

"Make sure you refer to Denise as Lieutenant VanCook or the lieutenant. I know you two must be close after everything you've been through. I don't want the defense to use it against us to sway the jury. Okay?"

"Strictly business, then?" Sara suggested.

"Exactly," he replied. "The facts in this case are irrefutable, and I want to keep your testimony succinct, and as impersonal as possible. When you call the lieutenant by her first name, it just seems too personal. Do you think you could handle that?" he asked Sara.

"Yes," Sara replied.

"Same applies to you, too, Lieutenant VanCook. It's Miss Langforth, not Sara."

Denise nodded in agreement.

"Now," the prosecutor smiled. "Let's go over it one more

time." Denise and Sara looked at him as if he had lost his mind. "Just kidding," he teased. "Go home and relax, and I'll see you both bright and early in the courtroom tomorrow."

"Thank God," Denise sighed in relief.

"Thank you, Lieutenant. It's cases like this that make my life a little easier. You've done a wonderful job."

"I only hope I can say the same thing about you after tomorrow. DeVittem is a slick one," she cautioned.

"Your case is safe in my capable hands," he said, shaking Denise's hand. "And you, Miss Langforth," he continued, taking Sara's hand, "just relax tomorrow and tell your story. Okay?"

"Yes, sir," she answered respectfully.

The attorney and Denise thanked each other once more, and she and Sara left. The air was cold for October, and they hurried to the car. When they were driving through the neighborhood where the shooting had taken place, Denise sensed Sara's discomfort. "Are you okay?" she asked with a sidelong glance.

"Yeah. Just remembering," Sara replied.

"Don't worry. You're going to be just fine on the stand, and then this will all be behind you."

Denise and Sara shared a smile, which faded quickly as the car was jarred from behind.

"What the hell?" Denise said, looking in the rearview mirror. The car behind them sped up, smashing into their bumper again. Denise tried to control the car, but she was beginning to veer wildly to one side. The attacking vehicle struck again, sending the police unit crashing against a vacant building.

Sara watched helplessly as Denise's head slammed into the side window. "Denise!" Sara screamed as the car skidded to a full stop. But Denise lay limp at the wheel. "Denise! Please wake up!" Sara exclaimed, distraught. She didn't want to move or shake her, being wary of making her injury worse. She did the only thing she could: she screamed again. "Denise!"

Sara looked out her side window to see a man there raising a gun toward her. With as much speed as she could muster, she yanked the door handle and kicked the door open with all her might. The surge of force toppled him to the ground.

She knew she couldn't fight the man. He had the advantage of size and weight and strength. Her only option was to run and pray that the man ran after her, leaving Denise unharmed. She heard the man still groaning in pain as her feet carried her away from the car.

Mere seconds later, she felt the man closing in on her. She felt herself jerked to an abrupt halt, felt the weight of the man upon her. She rolled away, only to be stopped by a wall behind her. The man stood up to tower over Sara.

"You don't really want to do this."

"Yes, I do," he sneered as he aimed his gun.

Sara took one last look back at the car and closed her eyes. She silently prayed for Denise's life. *Please, Lord, keep her safe.* She heard the hammer of the gun set, and waited for the impact of the bullet. But the impact didn't come. Instead, she heard a loud thud that forced her eyes open.

"Son of a—" the attacker howled as he spun around.

Sara leaned to the side to see what had startled the gunman. It was Rick, the homeless man, holding a crowbar.

"No one's gonna hurt my angel," he said defiantly.

Sara scrambled to her feet and knocked the assailant's arm up as he tried to take a shot at Rick. For his part, Rick took another swing with the metal bar, knocking the gun from the outstretched hand. Rage didn't begin to describe the look on the thug's face. That look, however, turned to one of fear as a car entered the other end of the alley and screeched to a stop near the frozen trio. The rear doors of the vehicle opened, and a man stepped out from each side. Within seconds, two shots were fired, and the would-be assailant fell to the ground. Sara and Rick both jumped back, unsure if they were next on the hit list. But just as quickly as the car had arrived, its passengers got back in and the vehicle disappeared.

Sara and Rick looked at each other, puzzled as to what had just happened, but Sara didn't dwell on it too long. The immediate danger to her had passed. She needed help for Denise, and she needed it fast. She ran for the radio in Denise's squad car as Rick, crowbar in hand, followed protectively behind her, scanning the area warily. "Is anyone there?" Sara called into the microphone. There was no response. "Is anyone there?" she repeated more frantically.

"Who is this?" a voice asked from the speaker.

"My name is Sara Langforth," she replied. Forestalling the inevitable questions, she quickly explained the situation and gave their location. Denise was still unconscious when the emergency teams showed up three minutes later.

As they loaded Denise into the ambulance, Sara turned to Rick. No one deserved to lead the duck-and-cover life she'd been forced into—least of all this homeless man who had only been coming to her aid. "We didn't see who was in that car, did we, Rick? We didn't see who shot this man, right? We can't even remember the color of the car, correct?" Sara coached.

"Whatever you think is best," he told her.

"Trust me. The less you saw, the better," she said, putting her hand on his shoulder. "Thank you for being there," she added.

He blushed and grinned. "My pleasure, angel."

"I'd stay, Rick, but..."

"I know," he said, pointing to the ambulance. "Go with her."

Sara smiled and gave him a nod of thanks as she climbed into the back of the emergency transport. "Can you call Sergeant Michaels at the 14th? Have her meet us at the hospital?" Sara asked the driver.

"She's on her way now, ma'am," he answered.

Sara gave an approving smile, and in a few moments they were pulling up to the emergency room entrance. Sara walked alongside Denise's gurney, waiting for some sign that she would be okay. Angie was in the waiting area when she saw them come in, and she rushed over.

"Are you okay?" Angie asked Sara as she watched them wheel her partner away.

"I'm okay," Sara said.

"How's Denise doing?"

"I'm not sure. She hasn't woken up, but she's breathing fine."

"Well, let's go and sit," Angie said, heading back to the waiting room. "You can fill me in."

Sara recounted the details of that afternoon's events, then she and Angie sat nervously in the empty waiting room.

The sergeant had noted Sara's intense concern over Denise's condition, and had been trying to delay commenting on it until they had some word from the doctors. Now that it looked like it would be a while before that would be forthcoming, she felt she had to ask.

"You're very upset about Denise, aren't you?"

Sara studied Angie's expression. The sergeant was fishing for information.

Angie, for her part, could tell Sara was considering her answer. "It's okay," Angie said comfortingly. "You can tell me. You love her, don't you?"

Sara didn't break her eye contact. "Denise and I have been through a lot together."

"You didn't answer my question," Angie chided gently. "Do you love her?"

Sara was unsure how much of her soul she should bare. Could she trust Angie to remain quiet and keep her comments in confidence? She stuttered at first, trying to figure out what to say without pouring her heart out. But in the process of trying to hide her emotions, they were completely exposed. Confession seemed the best solution. Sara had witnessed Denise and Angie's first reactions upon seeing each other the night of the suicide. She knew any initial anger Angie might feel as a result of her love affair with Denise would pass.

"Yes, I do," Sara admitted. "Very much."

Although Angie didn't need confirmation, she asked the question anyway. "Are you lovers?"

Sara looked offended. "That's a bit personal, don't you think?"

Angie's silent pursuit of the truth showed in her eyes without her saying a single word. The sergeant's stare was relentless.

"Yes," Sara finally answered before standing up and walking to the observation window near the ER.

Angie shook her head back and forth in disapproval. "I knew it."

Sara turned around swiftly, making Angie look directly at the blonde across the small room. "Denise didn't want to tell you! Besides, it's over. On the way back, she told me she didn't see a relationship in our future. Some garbage about dangerous situations and hormones. Point is, she doesn't think I truly love her...and she's truly wrong. But then again, maybe she's the one who's not in love. Maybe it's her way of letting me down easy."

Angie watched Sara look out the window again, toward the area where Denise was being worked on. The woman was obviously in pain, although she appeared angry; and Angie's heart went out to her. She rose and stood behind Sara. "I don't know about that," Angie commented. "I've never seen Denise as happy as when you're around. I saw it the first afternoon we spent together...and I still see it today."

"Then what's the problem?" Sara asked, dragging out each word, aching for an answer. "And don't give me any crap about ethics and cop oaths and so on. I've heard too much of that already."

She's certainly a spitfire, Angie thought with a grin. *A perfect match for Denise, if I do say so myself.*

"I can't read her thoughts," Angie answered. "I only see her emotions."

Sara sniffed and wiped back some tears before they spilled. She felt Angie put an arm around her, giving her a gentle hug.

"She's been searching for the right person for years," Angie explained. "Perhaps she's frightened by the fact that she's finally found her."

"But why would that scare her?" Sara asked. "She should be

happy. Hell, I know I am. At least, I was," Sara corrected herself.

"Well," Angie began, "in the ten years I've known Denise, I've watched her drift in and out of relationships. With each one that came along, I hoped she'd find the happiness everyone longs for. But she never did, and she never discussed why. She'd simply say it was over, and it didn't matter why. And she's said that many times. Maybe too many times. Maybe she can't handle another person she loves walking out of her life. Maybe she wants to be the one to walk away, before she gets hurt.

"I know that fiasco with Joseph left her shattered for quite some time. He'd gotten threats, but never said anything to Denise. When they finally got to him, Denise was devastated. Her love for someone had caused them to be hurt. Joseph survived. The man was arrested again. But Denise never forgot. They called it quits, and she shut down after that; she gave up."

"How is that her fault? He should have said something to her."

"What? And have his male ego bruised by running off and telling his girlfriend someone was hassling him? Yeah, he should have done that. And you're right—it's not her fault at all. But if you know Denise...and I think you do...you can see how she would take the fall for it. In her mind, it was her responsibility to keep him safe...and she failed."

Sara considered Angie's words in silence for a moment. "Please don't tell her I told you," Sara begged.

"I won't say anything," Angie agreed with a faint smile.

Sara nodded her thanks as a nurse came in. "Denise Van-Cook?" she called out. Sara and Angie both moved to her quickly through the vacant waiting room.

"She's fine," the nurse began. Angie and Sara both sighed in relief and smiled at each other. "She's got a big knot on the head and a light concussion, but she's conscious now."

"Can we see her?" Angie asked.

"Yes," the nurse replied. "But keep it brief, please. We gave her a sedative for the pain, so she's a bit groggy."

"That's understandable," Sara said. Of course it wasn't just the drugs that had Denise tired, she was sure. The last few weeks had been more than anyone could take—both physically and mentally.

The nurse took them to the area where Denise was resting, and motioned them around a linen divider. "Please don't stay too long," she whispered in reminder.

Angie and Sara crept to Denise's bedside. Denise's eyes were half closed but she smiled when she saw them.

"How ya feelin?" Angie asked.

"Like someone drove me into the side of a building," Denise joked, cracking a grin. "What happened?"

"Well," Sara began, "one of DeVittem's thugs ran us off the road in a last ditch effort to knock off your witness, namely me. When I ran to draw him away from you, a homeless man came to my aid. It's good to have friends in low places."

"Is he all right, your friend?"

"Yeah, he's okay," Sara answered. She looked to Angie. She wasn't sure if she should fill in the blanks for Denise. Angie gave her a nod indicating she should continue.

"Then what happened?" Denise asked.

"Well, it seems I must have a guardian angel someplace, because a car came out of nowhere and its occupants killed DeVittem's man."

"What did it look like? The car I mean," Denise asked, willing her eyes to open wider to better focus on the story.

"I don't remember."

Denise looked at Sara and frowned. "You don't remember? You? Miss Keen Observer of Detail?"

"It was sleek, sporty...silver I think. Maybe light copper in color. One of those expensive type cars, but I'm not sure what kind."

"This from the gal that drives a BMW," Denise said to Angie before turning back to Sara. "Why are you lying?" she asked the blonde. As she began to piece together what had transpired, Denise felt a rage growing inside her—not so much with Sara, but with the situation. Sara looked down guiltily, unable to meet Denise's scrutinizing eyes. Sensing how uncomfortable she was making Sara, Denise relented. "You're okay, right? Your friend's okay? That's all that matters, I guess."

Sara looked up at Denise. "Yes, I'm okay. And you're gonna be okay, too," Sara said, beginning to whimper. She felt like Denise had lost respect for her because she didn't want to give her all the information. But she couldn't. She just couldn't go through it all again.

Denise sensed the emotional overload the woman was suffering under, and she wanted to calm her. "Sara, look at me," Denise said. Hesitantly, Sara raised her eyes. "C'mere," she motioned with her head. Sara worked her way to the head of the bed. Denise reached out and stroked Sara's cheek. "Thank you," she said sincerely. "You've done all the right things today. I'm alive because you made all the right moves. So don't worry about anything else, all right?"

That did it. Sara had used up her reserves and began to cry openly.

Denise wiped her tears away gently. "Promise me you won't beat yourself up over what happened today, okay?" Denise added a grin, hoping Sara would return the expression. Denise was grateful when she saw a small smile pull at the corners of Sara's mouth. "Good girl," she added. Denise cleared her throat and raised her bed with the remote control.

"You're supposed to be resting," Angie chastised. "That nurse is gonna have our butts tossed outta here if she sees you sitting up."

"She's little," Denise teased. "I could take her." She grinned, then chuckled. Denise turned to Sara, "Do you mind if I have a word with Sergeant Michaels in private, Sara? Just a few minutes."

"Sure, no problem."

"Be back in exactly two minutes," Denise said, looking at her watch. "If you're not back, I'm getting out of this bed to find you. Got it?"

Sara knew that although there was merriment in her voice, Denise was also dead serious. "Yes, Lieutenant," she promised with a grin as she walked out.

Once Sara was out of earshot, Denise turned to Angie. "So the bad guys managed to do something I couldn't—keep Sara safe, huh?"

Angie shook her head fiercely. "Don't even go there, Denise. I didn't see any of them getting pitched off the Falls for Sara. Don't you dare lie there and start to belittle all the work you've done protecting her. I won't hear it. We both know that's not true."

"A silver or copper, sporty, expensive car... It was Sarchco's men. They protected Sara because she'll put DeVittem away and pave the way for them to take over his rackets. With DeVittem out of the picture, guess who moves up to the top spot?" Denise began to chuckle at the sad irony of it all. "What do I do now? Go after the men that saved Sara?"

"Yes," Angie answered. "As hypocritical as that sounds, yes, that's exactly what *we* do. Because they break the laws that govern this society. That's what we do—we uphold the law."

Denise didn't answer. Her head just fell back onto the pillow. "Well, at least I know Sara will never have to worry again about DeVittem after the trial. I think she'll have a guardian angel for some time, thanks to Sarchco."

Two minutes had passed, and Angie watched Sara reentering.

"Should I make myself scarce again?" she asked as she slowly stole in.

"No," Denise called out. She couldn't see Sara, but she could hear her approach. "Watch your ass," Denise warned Angie. "They may still be crazy enough to make another attempt before tomorrow."

"We will," Angie replied. "And make sure you follow nurse's orders. We need you at the trial tomorrow, so do everything they tell you."

Denise nodded silently.

"I mean it, Denise," Angie said, taking a commanding mother tone with her partner. "I know how you get."

Denise chuckled. "I need a new partner," she quipped. "You know me too damn well; I can't get away with anything anymore."

Angie chuckled. "Sorry, babe, but you're stuck with me. Took me over ten years to train you, and I sure as hell ain't gonna start all over again at my age." She winked. "Get some rest," she said sincerely. "I'll be outside, Sara," she added to the blonde.

Sara and Denise watched Angie leave before they looked at each other.

"It's almost over," Denise said softly. The duality of her words almost made Sara weep, but she wanted to stay strong in front of Denise. After all the risks Denise had taken, it was the least she could do.

"Yes, it is," Sara agreed in the husky voice that Denise had grown to love. It was just one of the things that had Denise smitten with the blonde. Soon they would all be out of her reach. "Like Angie said, get some rest," Sara added before patting Denise's hand and walking out to Angie. "Tomorrow will be a busy day."

Chapter
14

October 30

Opening statements had been made, and Angie was called to the witness stand to open the prosecution's case. The D.A. had hoped to put Denise on the stand before anyone else, but she hadn't been released from the hospital by the time court was called to order.

Angie breezed through the prosecutor's questions and the defense's cross-examination with ease. The next witness for the county was Sara. She walked to the stand confidently, not backing down from DeVittem's glare.

The intense stare the defendant gave her showed more of his fear than his anger. He knew this woman would be the death knell to his freedom. He had counted on his contacts to handle her—to make sure she never testified in court. What he hadn't counted on was the determination and strength of Denise VanCook, or the will and spirit of his target, Sara Langforth.

Angie smiled as she listened to Sara's testimony. She was good on the stand. Damn good. Denise would have been proud. The defense was unable to pose a single objection. She remained neutral, factual. She used the term "defendant" when she referred to DeVittem while answering the district attorney's skillful questions. But the sharp edge her tongue put on the word "defendant" cut through the courtroom, stabbing all who were listening—especially DeVittem. All DeVittem and his attorney could do was sit and wait for their cross-examination. The D.A. finished and DeVittem's lawyer finally had his turn.

"You say this man is the one you saw in the dimly lit alley on the night of September 16th of this year, correct?" he asked, trying to shake her recollection.

"Yes," Sara answered, making sure to add, "but it wasn't dimly lit. Evening was just beginning to fall, but there was still plenty of light."

The attorney ignored the additional comment Sara had added for the jury's benefit.

"You told the detectives that night was beginning to fall, so how could you have had plenty of light?"

"As I said, it was evening—not night," Sara countered.

"Now at the station house, you identified the alleged perpetrator from an eight year old picture. How can you be so certain that the man you saw in that dark alley was my client?"

"As I explained to the detectives when I was looking at the picture, I mentioned the man I saw looked about ten years older...but that's already been established in Sergeant Michael's testimony." Sara was quick, confident, and articulate. Strike one on the defense.

"But how can you be sure?" the attorney asked with a cocky grin. "Ten years is a long time. It's a known fact that the human face can change every six months."

"Children's faces change every six months until age twelve, not adult's. I took human phys in college, too, Mr. Connely."

Angie stifled a chuckle. *Goddamn, she's good.*

"Objection," Mr. Connely told the judge. "Ms. Langforth is not testifying as a medical expert. Her testimony is without foundation."

Before the judge spoke, Sara chimed in. She couldn't help it. If the attorney wanted to go a few rounds, she was game. Hell, she'd been through much worse. "Then your question should be disallowed for lack of foundation, too," she told him.

The D.A., who had begun to rise, sat back down. Sara was even handling his objections for him. He had to snicker when Sara's retort to the defense counselor elicited the same noises from the jury box.

Mr. Connely did his best to mask his surprise at Sara's statement, turning to the judge. "Permission to treat Ms. Langforth as a hostile witness, your Honor."

The judge smiled. "Are you sure you want to go there, Mr. Connely?"

"I can give as good as I get," he answered firmly.

"So can I," Sara muttered.

The judge knew he had to rein things in, but he also had to admit he was enjoying this. Usually things weren't so lively in his court. "Ms. Langforth," the judge cautioned, "I'll ask that you keep your answers strictly to the questions that are asked of you, or I'll be forced to hold you in contempt. Consider this your first warning."

Sara had the overwhelming urge to lean over and smack the

arrogant smile off of Connely's face. Instead she answered quietly with a "Yes, your Honor."

Connely cleared his throat and began to stroll the length of the jury bench, moving across the room. "Now, as I said, how is it possible to identify a man from a ten year old picture?"

Sara grinned. She debated about mentioning something she had told Denise. They had entered the mug shot as evidence, as well as the two reports—one submitted by Angie and one by Denise. *Oh, what the hell*, she figured. *Go with it.*

"Ask Mr. DeVittem to unbutton his shirt," Sara requested. "The man who killed Jimmy Bakker had a cross tattoo, or a design similar to it." Sara turned to the judge. "Do you have a piece of paper, your Honor, so I could draw a picture for the court?"

The judge looked to both attorneys for approval. The district attorney was leery, but nodded his acquiescence. Connely was a different story.

"This isn't an art class, Ms. Langforth," Connely replied condescendingly.

"Yes, I understand that. But you asked how I could be sure of your client's identity. With the judge's permission, I'd like to answer your question. It requires a picture—which I'll be happy to explain to you and the court."

"Objection, your Honor. The perpetrator having a tattoo that the witness remembered is not mentioned anywhere in Sergeant Michael's report," he told the judge.

"Because it wasn't in Sergeant Michael's initial report. She didn't know." Sara added.

"Well if it's not in the report—"

"It's in Lieutenant VanCook's notes, which were added before trial."

"What?" Connely asked. "I object, your Honor. We were given no prior notice of this evidence."

"Yes, you were," Sara blurted. Quickly she apologized to the judge. "I'm sorry, your Honor. No disrespect was meant. I'll be quiet now."

"May I see the report?" the judge requested. The bailiff handed it over and he looked through it. As testified, the information was there. "Objection overruled. You posed the question, the witness will be allowed to answer it."

"Then I withdraw the question," Connely replied.

"Permission denied." With that, the judge handed Sara a sheet of paper and a pen.

Connely closed his eyes and shook his head. The glare DeVittem gave him was icy, and it turned the attorney's blood cold when he opened his eyes and saw it.

The prosecutor wiped damp hands on his trouser leg. His witness could be destroying his case. It was a chance, a big chance. But this whole case had been filled with big chances. If DeVittem didn't have such a marking, that would cast doubt on Sara's identification, and that made the D.A. exceedingly nervous. At least he felt that way until he looked over and saw DeVittem's reaction.

As Sara drew the top half of the cross, DeVittem undid his collar and pulled down his shirt to expose what looked like a Celtic cross on his right breast. Sara finished her picture and looked to the jury, holding up the sketch. "May I step toward the jury," she asked the judge, who gave his approval. She continued to hold up the picture for them as she walked over.

"This line here," she pointed to her picture, "was his shirt line, and this design above is what I saw." The jury ooohed and ahhhed at how close Sara's picture came to the tattoo on DeVittem's chest who, under bailiff's orders, was now facing them.

His attorney looked worried, but soon dredged up an explanation. "You could have seen that on the mug shot," he challenged Sara.

"Yes, I could have." Sara nodded before casting a glance toward Angie. "But this tattoo is recent...well, perhaps not recent. Let's just say that he didn't have it the last time he was arrested, because his arrest record lists a skull on his arm and a dagger on his ankle, but it says nothing about the cross on his chest. You can refer to Exhibit... I'm sorry," Sara said, facing the D.A. "I don't remember what exhibit number the mug shot book was given."

"Exhibit F," he answered.

F for fuck you, Sara thought as she smiled at DeVittem.

At that, Angie nodded at the D.A. Sure enough, Sara was on the money and the district attorney stood up. "Your Honor," he began, "in addition to Miss Langforth's testimony, I'd like to introduce her sketch into evidence along with Exhibit F."

"Objection," the defense attorney cried out. "Your Honor, we've been given no prior notice that this...chicken scratch...was to be formally submitted, and I ask that it not be allowed into evidence."

The judge paused a moment, reviewing the legal precedents. "Overruled," he answered. "You wanted to know why the witness was so certain of her identification, and she provided you with the answer. This arrest record isn't anything that isn't available to be seen by any member of the public. The picture is only a physical representation of what Ms. Langforth has described. I'm overruling your motion. Bailiff, please take the book and show the jury the page which points out that DeVittem didn't have a cross tattooed on his chest at that time."

Strike two on the defense.

"Mr. Connely," the judge told DeVittem's lawyer, "you may continue."

Mr. Connely now looked as nervous as his client did. He had to take desperate measures to discredit Sara as a witness in order to salvage the case. It was time to bring out the only ammunition he had.

"Ms. Langforth, are you and Lieutenant VanCook intimate?" the defense attorney inquired.

"Objection, your Honor," the prosecutor said, standing up. "This question is irrelevant to the case."

"Sustained. Please restructure the question, Mr. Connely."

The defense attorney paused a moment. It was imperative that the jury be given a reason to question Sara's testimony. He had to pursue his point. "What is the nature of your relationship with Lieutenant VanCook?"

"Same objection, your Honor! I cannot see the relevance of this line of questioning."

"Will both attorney's approach the bench," the judge ordered. The D.A. joined Connely in front of the judge. "I can't see the relevance to this, either," the judge agreed. "Mr. Connely, where are you going with this?"

"It goes to motivation, your Honor. They did spend over a month together. I'm trying to establish whether Miss Langforth's testimony is being affected by any emotional or physical attachment she has to Lieutenant VanCook," the attorney said, still looking at Sara.

"No," Sara replied. The D.A. tried to mask his wince at Sara's outburst as he returned to his seat. Having his main witness volunteer information was something he wanted to avoid.

Connely saw the reaction from Sara and pursued it. "Your last relationship lasted 5 years and was with a woman. You just spent nearly two months with Lieutenant VanCook, a very attractive woman," he persisted. "You were together day and night. Surely you couldn't help but form an emotional attachment, perhaps even an intimate relationship?"

Sara tried not to look surprised, but it was useless. *How the hell does he know that? What a muckraking bastard.*

"Regardless of how you may try to portray my life," Sara replied, keeping herself in check, "my 5 year relationship was not with Lieutenant VanCook."

Angie was literally on the edge of her seat when she felt a tap on her shoulder, and she gave a little jump.

"How's she doing?" Denise asked, taking a seat next to her partner, right behind the D.A.

"Beautifully, so far. But Connely is asking her how intimately you two got to know each other. And he's digging into her past relationships," Angie whispered.

Denise didn't reply. She just looked at Sara, who saw her and looked back.

"You didn't answer my question. Do you and Lieutenant Van-Cook—"

"Lieutenant VanCook and I spent over a month together, that's true," Sara interrupted. "We spoke intimately on many life issues. But if you think for one moment that she's coerced me into getting up here to tell falsehoods about that man over there, then you're crazier than your client."

The jury smiled and chuckled at Sara's response.

"Objection!" the defense attorney cried out.

The courtroom giggled, and the judge tried not to chuckle himself. "To what are you objecting?" he tried to ask in all sincerity.

"She can't talk to me like that. Who do you think you are?" the attorney asked Sara.

Sara looked past Mr. Connely and straight into DeVittem's eyes. "His worst nightmare." Casually she turned back to Connely again. "And you both know it."

DeVittem's attorney realized too late that he had kept Sara on the stand too long. Strike three on the defense. He was out. "No further questions, your Honor," he said to the judge, walking back to his seat next to DeVittem. He didn't even reserve the right to recall the witness, because he knew there was no way he was going to put her back on the stand.

When the prosecutor turned back to smile at Angie, he saw Denise. "Yes! You made it," he whispered to her.

"Your next witness, Mr. Prosecutor," Judge Harris ordered.

David Rose, the prosecutor, rose confidently to his feet. "The prosecution calls Lieutenant Denise VanCook to the stand, your Honor."

Sara and Denise passed each other with an acknowledging nod, as Denise took her place in front of the witness stand.

DeVittem sank lower into his seat with every step she took. As the officer gave her sworn oath, he felt his freedom slipping away. He did what he could to keep his anger at bay. He listened intently as Denise gave the breakdown of the events that had followed Sara's arrival at the precinct house, and their subsequent investigation. When the prosecutor announced that he had no further questions, DeVittem grabbed his attorney by the arm.

"You'd better fucking go for the throat," he warned his attorney. "No goddamned tap-dancing this time; 'cause if I'm going down, then the good lieutenant is going with me. Got it?"

Connely nodded his understanding. "Got it," he answered softly.

"You'd better pray you crack her on the stand," he threatened. "It's either her or you."

Connely took a deep breath, rose, and walked to the witness stand. "Lieutenant VanCook," he began, "is it true you've had sexual relations with Ms. Langforth?"

"Objection!" the prosecutor said, bolting up from his chair. "Didn't we go through all this a few minutes ago? The point is moot."

"I instruct the jury to disregard the question," the judge told them. "Mr. Connely, you had better have a very good reason for continuing this line of questioning."

"I'm trying to establish if Ms. VanCook—"

"That's lieutenant," Denise corrected with an acidic tone.

"Apologies. I'm trying to establish if Lieutenant VanCook has an intimate relationship with the witness. If so, her testimony, as well as Ms. Langforth's, could very well be collusion and not admissible in this case."

Sara, Denise, and DeVittem knew he couldn't come right out and say the two had been seen together. The only one to have seen them together was an assassin that DeVittem couldn't admit to having a connection with. Of course that didn't mean that the attorney wouldn't make the most of the knowledge in some way.

"Any *hypothetical* relationship I *might* have with Ms. Langforth is irrelevant to what she witnessed."

"I agree," the judge ruled. "Unethical perhaps, but it doesn't make the testimony of either witness inadmissible."

"Your Honor, according to an inside source, Lieutenant Van-Cook and Ms. Langforth engaged in a passionate love affair. At the very least, that supports professional misconduct on the lieutenant's part. I think that it is important to this case," Connely argued.

"That source wouldn't happen to be one of the many bounty hunters Mr. DeVittem contracted to kill Ms. Langforth, would it?" Denise interjected angrily.

"Just answer the question! Are you engaging in sexual relations with Ms. Langforth?"

Denise paused a moment and looked at Sara. She wasn't

going to let this shark get the better of her by making her lose her temper. She answered the question as it was posed. "No. I am not sleeping with Ms. Langforth."

"Have you ever had sexual relations with Ms. Langforth?"

Before Denise could answer, the judge intervened. "Okay, that's enough, counselor! You're one question away from contempt. Do you hear me? Now—do you have anything further to ask that is of real relevance to this case? If not, then I suggest you save the taxpayer's time and money, and have Lieutenant Van-Cook step down from the stand."

Connely considered his options. He knew the judge wasn't going to let the speculation go any further. He'd done all he could. "No further questions, your Honor."

"Bullshit!" DeVittem shouted, darting up from his seat. He was so angry that the jury could see his pulse beating in the standing veins on his neck. "I'm not going down thanks to two fucking dykes!"

"Yes, you are," Denise taunted from the stand. The words were out before she had a chance to bite them back, but she tried not to show her regret.

"Mr. DeVittem, please sit down," the judge ordered.

DeVittem didn't listen. He continued to rant. "Hear that? She *did* do that bitch, and now she's going to make me take the fall."

"Mr. DeVittem," the judge replied, getting angry, "you'll sit down this instant or you'll be removed from the courtroom. Justice will be served here."

"Justice? Where's the justice in that lesbo getting her girlfriend on the stand to testify?" Connely went over to calm his client down, and DeVittem turned his rage on him. "Don't even touch me, you sorry sack of shit suit," he warned.

"Should've spent more money on a better lawyer, rather than wasting it on unsuccessful bounty hunters, DeVittem," Denise prodded from the stand.

At this point the bailiff came over to restrain DeVittem, who was forcing his way towards Denise. The judge pounded his gavel repeatedly, yelling for order. Finally a hush fell over the room and everyone caught their breath.

"Now are we done with your witness Mr. Connely?" the judge asked.

"Your Honor," Connely began, "I move for a mistrial, based on the comment made by Lieutenant VanCook. Her personal relationship with the witness constitutes misconduct and collusion."

"Oh really?" Judge Harris queried in a stern tone. This trial was the biggest circus he had ever been a part of. He had to admit that at first it had been amusing. Now it had become downright annoying. "How do you figure?"

"Because of their relationship with each other, the key witness was coerced into perjured testimony by Lieutenant Van-Cook."

Sara bolted up from her seat behind the D.A. "I would have never met Lieutenant VanCook if I hadn't witnessed your client commit a murder!"

"That's enough! Everyone sit down, or you're all going to be held in contempt," the judge thundered.

Sara obediently took her seat as Connely tried to get DeVittem to do the same.

"In response to your motion for a mistrial, Mr. Connely," the judge began, "there is no evidence to suggest that Ms. Langforth's testimony was in any way coerced by Lieutenant VanCook." Connely looked like he was going to speak, but the judge held up a finger. "Furthermore, I suggest you get your client to relax, because he is not helping his case by his actions here."

Reluctantly, DeVittem finally resumed his seat. "You're not walking away unscathed," DeVittem muttered toward Denise, who was still on the stand.

"Mr. Connely," the judge asked, "do you have any further questions for Lieutenant VanCook?"

"No, your Honor."

"Mr. Prosecutor," the judge said, turning to the D.A., "do you have any further questions for any of your witnesses?"

"No, your Honor."

"Lieutenant VanCook, you may step down. We're going to take a fifteen minute recess, and when we resume, we will all have ourselves under proper control. Court is in recess," the judge said with a bang of his gavel.

As Denise left the stand, she flashed a small grin at DeVittem. He looked like he was going to charge her, but Connely grabbed his arm to prevent him from moving. Denise lost her grin however when she noticed Captain Genar's disapproving look as he rose in the back of the courtroom and filed out with some others who were leaving.

Oh shit, Denise sighed inwardly.

"I'm worried," the D.A. whispered to her as she took a seat behind him.

"You and me both," she answered.

"Madame Foreperson, has the jury reached a verdict?" Judge

Harris asked. Only an hour had passed since the jury had heard the closing arguments and been taken to the deliberation room.

"Yes, your Honor," she replied. "On the charge of murder in the first degree, we the jury, find the defendant, Carlos DeVittem, guilty."

Angie clapped her hands together once in victory before twining them together as if in prayer, giving thanks. The sound merged with all the other commotion in the courtroom that resulted from the announcement of the jury's decision.

Denise embraced Sara hard. "I told you you'd do it," Denise whispered her congratulations. Sara didn't have long to dwell on the praise. DeVittem tipped the defense table over, pushing Connely out of his way.

His eyes focused on Sara—nothing else—as he charged. The bailiff and two other guards were on their way as DeVittem reared back to take a swing at Sara. Before he could deliver the blow, Denise jabbed him squarely in the face, knocking him off balance and allowing the guards to restrain his arms. Kicking and screaming obscenities, DeVittem was led out of the courtroom.

In his twenty years on the bench, Judge Harris had never seen anything like the display before him. He didn't even call for order. He just watched his courtroom in disbelief as DeVittem was led away.

"Our thanks to the jury," the judge pronounced, once things had settled down. "You're all free to go." The judge opened his notebook and scribbled something. "Sentencing will be set for November 30th at 9 a.m. Court is dismissed." As Judge Harris banged the gavel, the D.A. turned around and thanked Denise and Angie.

"And you," he said, looking at Sara. "You were great. You had me a little worried now and then, but you were brilliant. I hope we never have to do this again," he teased.

Sara laughed. "You and me both."

"I have to go," the prosecutor said, rising and gathering his papers. "You ladies take care now."

They watched him walk out with everyone else. Moments later, they were the only three souls left in the vacated courtroom.

"I'm heading out, too," Angie announced. "But first I have to thank you," she directed to Sara, shaking her hand.

"It was my pleasure. I'm glad I could help."

"Shame you didn't get here sooner," Angie told Denise. "You should have seen her. She was phenomenal." Denise and Angie shared a brief smile. "Well, I'll see you outside," she added to her partner.

They watched Angie leave in silence before turning to face each other. It was as if they were memorizing each other, knowing they would probably never meet again and hoping to capture the moment forever.

"I guess that's it," Sara sighed as she stroked the top of one of the bench seats with her fingertips. "I've fulfilled my civic duty," she asserted with a small smile.

Denise continued to examine Sara—her light blonde bangs, her oval face, and slender lips. "We'll notify you of the sentence as soon as we find out," Denise told her. "And as for DeVittem's hired hands, don't worry. He's smart enough to know that harming you now would only cause him more trouble. He'd never get a shot at parole. Besides I think your guardian angels from the other day will be looking out for you for quite some time."

Sara nodded and began to make her way out. When she reached the double courtroom doors, she stopped. She turned slowly, taking a last look at Denise. She wanted Denise to follow, but the lieutenant didn't move. She remained where she was, etching every detail of Sara Langforth on her mind and in her heart. As Sara pushed through the doors and disappeared, Angie's voice echoed over and over in Denise's head: *She was phenomenal. She was phenomenal.* She was... But Denise let Sara walk away just the same. *It's better for Sara this way.*

February 20

Number in hand, Angie was standing at the deli counter when the blonde over in the far corner caught her attention. With a grin, she walked over to the table where the woman was sitting, staring off, deep in thought.

"Sara Langforth?"

Her concentration refocused as she looked up at the voice calling her name. "Hey, Angie. How you doing?"

"Pretty good. I just stopped in to get lunch for me and Denise."

"Where is she?" Sara asked, looking around.

"Oh, she's not here. She's at the station—as usual," Angie grinned. "So, how have you been? Still making a killing in the real estate business?"

"Actually, I left real estate, and I opened a soup kitchen down here. Eddie here," she said, motioning to the counter, "gives us leftovers for the folks who come into the shelter."

"Eddie's a good guy. I've been coming here for years."

A small silence fell between them until Sara spoke. "How's life going for you and the good lieutenant?"

"Not bad. And yourself?"

"Can't complain—no murder attempts, so that's always a good thing," Sara chuckled.

Angie gave a broad smile. "Well, that's good to hear. Things are going well for you?"

"Yeah. Things are okay."

Sara said the words, but they rang hollow in Angie's ears. "If you don't mind me saying, Sara, you look a bit tired for twelve o'clock in the afternoon."

Sara gave a sigh before mustering a grin. "I don't sleep much anymore. I..."

"What?"

Should I say it? Oh, go ahead. What difference will it make? Probably none, so just spit it out. "I miss Denise a lot. Is she doing okay?" Sara asked.

Angie could hear the concern in her voice. *Should I say it? Oh, go ahead. Just spit it out.* "No, I don't think she's doing okay. I think she misses you, too."

"Well, I haven't heard from her."

"She hasn't heard from you."

"Why should she?" Sara countered. "She called it off. I'm not going to go crawling back to her, begging her to give us a chance. It wouldn't be right."

Angie sighed and ran her fingers through her hair. "You know, Denise is still the most stubborn woman in the world, but you run a close second, Sara."

"What does that mean?"

"What that means is that you could both be happy if you *both* could put your pride on hold long enough to stop being pig-headed."

Sara considered the words. "Do you think she'd consider seeing me?"

Angie grinned. "With a little pushing and persuading—yes, I do."

"I don't want her strong-armed into contacting me," Sara grinned.

"Come on, you know, Denise. Spare the rod, spoil the lieutenant."

Eddie emerged from the back with a couple of gallon tubs of potato salad in his arms. "Sara, this is all I've got for you today. It's been busy. Maybe tomorrow we'll have more." He set it down on the table.

"Every little bit helps, Eddie. Thanks so much."

Eddie noticed who Sara was talking to. "Hey, Sergeant Michaels! How ya doin?"

"Can't complain."

He looked at the number in her hand and snatched it away. "Don't worry about that. Whatcha need?"

Angie smiled. "You know I don't want people thinking I'm on the take and getting preferred service."

"Nah, if you were on the take I wouldn't charge ya; but you'll get the bill, don't worry," he chuckled. "What did you need?"

"One ham on rye, one roast beef."

"You've got it, sweetie," he said, heading back behind the counter.

"So anyway," Angie said, returning her attention to Sara, "I can talk to her if you like."

"I'm not sure," Sara answered. "It's been quite a while."

"Think it over and let me know," Angie told her.

Sara picked up the containers. "I will. Look, I gotta get this food to the shelter and then head home to do some paperwork. Take care, Angie."

"You too, Sara."

Angie watched as Sara walked out of the deli, a sadness still visible on her formerly sunny features. A moment later Eddie returned with her sandwiches, wrapped and placed in a brown paper bag. She handed him a ten dollar bill and told him to keep the change.

"You know Sara?" he asked.

"Yeah, it's been a while since I've seen her, though."

"She's a sweet girl, but there's something about her."

"What do you mean?"

"It's like she's...sad. Really sad, like something is missing."

"Well, maybe she'll find that missing piece, Eddie," Angie offered. "Gotta hungry lieutenant to feed. Thanks. I'll catch ya later."

"Always welcome," he nodded, making his way back to work.

Angie zipped up her jacket, then picked up the bag from the table. *Missing something, huh? Well, that's up to her to fix.*

Denise heard a tap on the office door and looked up. It was Angie.

"Can we talk?" Angie said as she poked her head inside.

"Of course," Denise said, worried that something was bothering Angie. "What's wrong?"

"That's what I wanted to ask you," her partner replied.

"What do you mean?"

Angie took a deep breath. Knowing her pigheaded partner the way she did, she knew this wouldn't be easy. "Have you seen her at all?"

"Who?" Denise asked, avoiding Angie's gaze. She knew damn well who Angie was referring to.

"You know who," Angie began softly. "The one you've been pining over these last three months. The one who makes you stay here fifteen hours a day, sometimes all night."

"Still playing catch-up after my month's suspension for conduct unbecoming," she replied.

"Well, I'm worried about you."

"Well, I'm fine," Denise mimicked.

"You're not fine, Denise. I see it behind those depressed baby blues of yours. Why don't you go see her? You already paid for your so-called sin, and she's no longer your witness."

"Like you said, it's been over three months since I've seen her. Sara needs someone stable. You know this life is hard. The only thing harder is being a cop's wife. I don't want to put her through that."

"So, you love her, but you're making that choice for her? Shouldn't she be the one to decide if she can take it?"

"It doesn't matter. I'm sure she's moved on with her life by now."

"Why are you so sure about that? I know you haven't," Angie countered.

"Since when did you become Dr. Joyce Brothers?"

"Get as sarcastic as you like, but this needs to be said. I hate to see you lonely."

"I could never be lonely. I'll always have you to nag me."

Angie's first reaction was anger, then frustration, then sorrow. Sorrow for Denise. "She's not Joseph, if that's what you're thinking."

That name made Denise look away. "I know she's not Joseph."

"Do you?"

"Yes, I do."

"Good, then you can get over the thought that she might get hurt because you're on the job."

"She might get hurt," Denise argued. "It's happened once before, remember?"

"To Joseph, right?" When Denise didn't respond, Angie pressed her attack. "See, you are making comparisons?"

Denise gave a frustrated sigh. "Jesus, do you have a point?"

"Yeah, I do. I don't think Sara is the same type of person that Joseph was. I think if she ever found herself in a similar situation, she would come to you, just like she did with the DeVittem information. And if anything ever did happen to her as a result of your work, she wouldn't hold it against you. It wouldn't tear you apart; it would bring you closer together."

"What makes you so sure?"

"Like I said, it's been three months...and here you sit...miserable." Denise didn't reply, but she began to swivel side to side in her rolling chair, considering Angie's words. "Go to her," she begged softly.

"And say what? I have no reason to see her."

Angie looked around the office, casting about for a reason. That's when she saw it. "Her book!" Angie suggested. "Take her book back to her."

"Oh, God," Denise laughed. "That is so adolescent."

"What do you mean, it's adolescent?"

"I'd feel like a scared teenager conjuring up some stupid excuse to see her."

"You're not a scared teenager," Angie argued. "You're a scared adult... Besides, don't you think she'd like her book back? She told you it was one of her favorites."

Denise thought over the ridiculous plan, a plan that was getting less ridiculous the more she thought about it.

Angie could tell Denise was considering it. "Go ahead!" she urged.

Denise looked at the book as she mulled it over. "Maybe next week."

"No!" Angie said forcefully. "Not next week, tonight."

"Tonight?" Denise asked, pulling at her wrinkled clothes. "Look at me. I'm a mess."

"She's seen you in a lot worse condition, Denise."

Denise hated it when Angie was so goddamned logical; she knew for every con that she spewed, Angie would give a pro. She might as well quit now while she was behind. The thought made her chuckle.

"What's so funny?"

"You," Denise answered, shaking her head. *Might as well agree and get it over with, just to prove her wrong.* "Tonight, huh?"

"Yes, tonight."

Denise thought it over again. "Okay, but what happens if I get there and she's...not interested."

"Then you'll know. Because even if you tell yourself you've made the right choice by walking away, you're still wondering. This way, you'll know for sure. You can move on without wondering what could have been. You need some type of closure to all this, Den."

Before Denise could reconsider, Angie went over to the coat rack and grabbed Denise's coat. With a deep sigh Denise stood up, and let Angie help her with the sleeves and zipped her up.

Angie picked up the book, walked to the door, and waited for Denise.

Pausing to give another deep, deliberate sigh, Denise finally walked over and took the book. "I hate you."

"We'll see if you still hate me tomorrow."

Denise cracked a smile and left the office. When she was almost out of the squad room's double doors, Angie called to her. "Good luck!"

Soon Denise was standing in the hallway of Sara's new apartment. She'd been there once before to have Sara sign some paperwork regarding the case against their assailant in Canada. Denise raised her hand twice, but couldn't bring herself to knock either time. She took a deep breath, steeling herself to try again, and finally moved her hand forward. Before her knuckles could make contact, the door suddenly opened and Denise saw Sara hugging a tall brunette.

"Denise!" Sara exclaimed. "What are you doing here?"

Denise couldn't pinpoint what she felt. Anger. Hurt. Guilt. Embarrassment. Maybe all four. *Serves me right for listening to Angie,* she told herself. She eyed the embracing women a moment longer, then realized she had to say something. "Your book," she said, handing it to Sara. "I'm sorry for not returning it sooner. I didn't mean to interrupt," she added, as she turned to go.

"Do you have to leave?" Sara asked.

Denise stopped and faced Sara. "I'm sorry," Denise began. "I assumed you'd be alone. I should have called first."

"Well, she's about to be alone," the brunette said with a smile. "I'm going home, and Rick here is on his way to a meeting."

Denise looked beyond the two women into the apartment to see a man standing behind Sara. The dark-haired woman turned back to Sara. "Give me a call, and we'll have lunch next week." Then, giving Denise a wave, she departed.

"I'll let you know what the Red Cross says later today," Rick told Sara. He shot a glance at Denise as he left, then paused to take a closer look. "You're the cop!"

Denise smiled. She wasn't sure just exactly what the comment meant, but she accepted the handshake he offered.

"You look a lot better than the last time I saw you—slumped over a steering wheel," he grinned.

At first Denise didn't follow, but she soon realized this must be Rick, the homeless man that had come to Sara's aid. *Funny, he doesn't look homeless. He's dressed pretty damned well.*

"Nice to meet you," Denise answered, shaking his hand.

"Nice to meet you, too. I've heard a lot about you."

"Rick," Sara interrupted, "you don't wanna be late for that meeting. The shelter needs the support."

He accepted the cue to shut the hell up and move on with good grace. "Right," he told Sara. "Anyway, nice to see you, Denise. Sara, we'll talk later." Rick made his way down the hall with a silly grin on his face.

"Come on in," Sara said, opening the door wider in invitation.

As Denise walked in, she took a look around. Everything looked the same as it had before, everything except Sara. She was still just as beautiful, but her hair was much longer now and a darker shade of blonde, probably a result of the lack of sunlight during the winter months.

"How have you been?" Sara asked gently, drawing Denise's attention back from her observations.

"Good. Been busy," Denise answered. "Cop's work is never done, it seems. And you?"

"I've been working, too. I gave up real estate, though. I started a homeless shelter downtown. Rick works with me; he's doing a great job of getting us financial support. Can't say I'm making money, but I don't really have to worry about that, so it works out. Janet—she's the one who just left—helps me out, too. Old friend from my college days who used to be a social worker and now tries to make things better without having to cut through all the red tape," Sara smiled in her nervousness, feeling that she was rambling. "I'm sorry I didn't properly introduce the two of you, but I have to admit I was surprised to see you here."

"That's okay," Denise replied. "I'm a bit surprised to be here."

"Why? Didn't you want to come?"

Months earlier Sara would have put a teasing sexual spin on the expression, but now her words seemed detached, edgy, and Denise began to second-guess herself about being there. "Angie thought I should come."

"And you didn't?"

Denise considered how to answer the question. "I don't want to interfere in your life, but when I saw you with her it felt like that's exactly what I was doing."

"You mean Janet?"

Denise nodded.

"Like I said, she's an old friend. And you weren't interfering with anything. She's *my* Angie." Sara grinned. "As a matter of fact, there's no one your presence could interfere with. I haven't been seeing anyone. I haven't wanted to see anyone."

Maybe I still have a chance. Denise felt an overwhelming desire to pull Sara into her arms and thank God she hadn't moved on.

Sara was carefully watching for Denise's reaction and saw her eyes become suspiciously moist. "What is it?" Sara asked softly, hoping Denise would open up about what was in her heart.

"I lied," Denise said, starting to tear up but quickly regaining her composure.

"You lied? About what?" Sara asked, stroking the officer's arm.

"About things being good. That's a lie. I've been miserable. Genar questioned me about the two of us after the trial, and I told him the truth. I told him what had happened between us. He suspended me for improper conduct." She chuckled ruefully. "All that time I spent fighting my attraction, trying to maintain a professional distance, was for naught. As I drove here tonight, I realized that I should have followed my heart and let the consequences be damned. I told myself I would never fail to do that again. I'd do the right thing for me—not worry about what others might think."

Denise paused and took a deep breath. "I'm a decisive person, Sara. Every day I make choices that affect people's lives. But when it came to my own life, I was conflicted. I loved you. I wanted you. But I also knew I had a job to do. For someone who's so practical, my passion for you took me by surprise. So, like I said, it was a conflict. It confused me. It probably confused you. Plus, when I discovered that I truly loved you, it scared me."

"Because Joseph got hurt for loving you?"

"Yeah, well, I think that's part of it. It's hell being involved with a cop. It could be dangerous if you become a target. Plus there's lots of late nights, lots of worrying, and I didn't want to put you through that, so I decided to just move on. Go to work, do my job. But you know what? I love my job, but it doesn't make me happy anymore."

"Why not?"

"Since I've been back, I've spent hours at the office trying to

forget about you, thinking you had moved on. But I find myself
wondering where you are and what you're doing. I wonder who
you're with, and whether she could ever care for you as much as I
do. Everything reminds me of you; and I miss you so much I ache.
So, let me say, my indecisiveness is over. I've accepted what I feel.
And right now, I hope that you feel the same. Angie told me the
choice to stay or go should be yours. So, I'm giving you that
choice...if you want to take it, that is."

Sara was speechless. Never in their relationship had Denise
gotten so wordy, but after a three-month silence, it did seem fit-
ting. And it wasn't that she didn't believe what Denise had just
told her. She certainly could understand, because she felt the same
longing. Surprised as she was, she was having trouble finding the
words to say. Thinking of Denise's suspension and that she had
been the cause, Sara softly responded, "I'm sorry."

Denise gave a firm nod. "That's all I needed to hear. I had to
come here to make a clean slate of all of this. Thank you for being
honest," Denise said, starting toward the door.

At first Sara couldn't understand why Denise was leaving.
She wants me. She said so. So why on earth is she— Oh no! Sara
grabbed Denise by the sleeve of her leather jacket and turned her
around until they were face to face. "Don't you dare walk out of
my life again," Sara ordered. "I ache, too, Denise," she added in a
whisper. "Please don't get the wrong idea. I'm not sorry because
you came back, far from it. I'm sorry the department took your
badge."

Denise let out the deep breath she'd been holding since she'd
heard Sara's soft-spoken apology, afraid she might break the spell
if she even took a breath. A sense of relief flooded over her, and
she moved in closer until they were forehead to forehead. "Do you
still love me?" Denise asked after a few moments of just holding
Sara in her arms. "Does this feel right to you?"

Sara felt herself get choked up, too, and she cleared her
throat. "Yes. But you should know that I lied, too, when I said
there was no one I wanted to see...because I never stopped wanting you, and I know I never will. But I've got to know, I need to
actually hear you say it: am I the one you've been looking for?"
She smiled up at Denise.

Denise returned the smile and stroked Sara's cheek. "I've
found my Red Delicious," she answered playfully. "If you'll be
mine, I'll most certainly stop roaming the orchard."

"It's a big step for you. I just want you to be sure that—"

"Sara, I've never been more sure of anything. And I can handle anything that comes our way—be it your friends, who think

I'm doing nothing more than killing time as a part-time dyke or, God forbid, a pack of DeVittems chasing us across the world again. So, are you ready for the trouble I might bring?" Denise grinned.

Sara nodded and chuckled, but that soon turned into a hum of arousal as Denise claimed her lips with a tender kiss. As their passion rekindled, Sara gave a silent thanks to Angie for encouraging Denise's return. Sara knew that she would always love this woman who had risked her own life to keep her safe, providing protection not only for her body, but for her heart. She had finally found a place to call home, and it was in Denise's arms in moments like this.

Denise fell into the kiss with all her heart and soul. There were no conflicts, no pressure, and no urgency to do the right thing. This *was* the right thing—holding this woman, loving her. It hadn't just been the adrenaline high that had made her love this woman as much as she did; Sara was a part of her. Since their separation, she hadn't felt complete. And if she had her way, she would never let her go again—never.

"For the record," Sara said softly, "I think you're the strongest, most decisive woman I've ever met. And I understand completely about your sense of duty and sense of self. Honestly I do, Denise."

As Denise pulled back, she made a mental note to go back to the stationhouse to see Angie. The officer's fingertips lightly stroked the lips she had just been fortunate enough to kiss. Sara closed her eyes and gently captured them on one of their sweeps.

The desire to take Sara to bed after so many months was very strong, but Denise resisted. She'd resisted before, she could do it again. At least for the moment.

"Then, what do you say we do things properly this time around, hmm?" Denise said softly.

"What do you mean?"

"Let's do this the way normal people do."

"Well, what do *normal* people do, Denise?" she queried with a coy grin.

Denise smiled and gently relinquished her embrace, zipping up her coat. "Would you like to go out tomorrow night? Dinner and a movie perhaps?" Denise invited formally.

"Why, Lieutenant VanCook, I would be honored!" Sara grinned. "But I should warn you...I may not kiss on the first date."

"Shucks," Denise said, snapping her fingers.

"I might do more," Sara added with a wiggle of her eyebrows.

Denise chuckled and brushed Sara's chin with her fingertips before giving her a light kiss. "Until tomorrow, then?"

Sara gave a kiss of her own as she stroked Denise's face. "Tomorrow," she agreed.

Denise opened the door and Sara followed, leaning against the frame. "Where are you off to?" Sara asked.

"The precinct," Denise answered. "I think I owe Angie a big thanks."

"Make sure you give her mine as well."

"I most certainly will. Have a good night, Sara. I'll see you tomorrow."

Denise was halfway down the hall when Sara stopped her. "Hey! What are you doing this weekend?"

"I don't know, spending it with you perhaps?"

Sara smiled. "I was thinking... Maybe you could take a few vacation days. I happen to have a beach house in the Bahamas, you know."

"You don't say," Denise teased with mock surprise.

"Yes, I do. Weather looks clear down south. No storms coming. Think you might be interested?"

"Well, I'll have to think about it. A weekend getaway is a pretty big commitment, something you don't wanna rush into." Denise's face seemed to glow. "I'll let you know tomorrow."

Sara nodded with a growing smile. "You do that."

They stood a few more moments, admiring each other. Denise took two strides back towards Sara and grasped her waist to pull her closer. She locked her in a tender embrace, running her fingertips down Sara's cheek. "I love you, Sara Langforth," she whispered, as she placed a kiss on the top of the smaller woman's head.

"I love you, too, Denise."

With a contented sigh, Denise turned and paced down the hallway to the front door of the complex. She stopped and turned around to see Sara still watching her. She gave a small wave, then blew her a kiss. Denise opened the door and stepped outside. *Oh yes. I think a thanks is certainly in order for Angie.*

Sara closed the apartment door behind her, picked up the phone, and dialed, waiting impatiently until she heard the voice on the other end. "Hey, Denise was just here, and I wanted to thank you personally."

Angie smiled as she looked at the picture of herself and Denise on the desk. "You're very welcome. When you stopped being pig-headed and called, I was more than happy to help. She had looked too long to find the right one to let her slip away."

"Thank you, Angie, that means a lot to me," Sara answered.

"And the idea about the book—very clever."

Angie chuckled. "They pay me to be clever, you know."

Sara joined her merriment. "However, I wish you had told me about the suspension," Sara said seriously.

"I didn't want to bother you with that. Besides, you might have changed your mind—getting too wrapped up in guilt to do what you knew was right."

"In that case, thank you. And thanks to you, clever girl, I have a date tomorrow night. But you'll have to act surprised when she tells you. She's on her way there now."

"Oh, don't worry. I can pull it off. But you do realize that one day we'll have to tell her the truth."

"If she takes me up on my offer to go to the Bahamas this weekend, I'll tell her when she's out in the sun with a margarita. By then, she won't care."

Angie chuckled again and gave a sigh. "Whatever is she going to do with us?"

"Love us both. At least, I hope so."

"I'm sure she will, and I'm sure I'll see you again soon. I'd better look busy here for when she gets back."

"Take care, Angie. And thanks again."

"You're very welcome, Sara. Night."

"Night."

Sara hung up the phone, wondering for a brief moment, *Was it wrong to have gone into cahoots with Angie?* When she recalled that smile on Denise's face and how it had filled her heart with joy, she answered her own question. *Nahhhhh, not on our lives.*

Angie saw Denise enter the squad room, smiling. She quickly picked up a folder, stuffing her face inside, trying to get her own grin under control. As Denise entered the office, she put the file down and looked up at her partner.

"Well, you're smiling." Angie grinned herself. "Should I take it that things went well?"

Denise was on the verge of going into the story of what had transpired, when she stopped and cocked her head, examining her partner's smile. No, it wasn't a smile. It was a smirk. And not just any smirk; it was a knowing smirk.

"You knew." It wasn't a question. She took her coat off and hung it on the rack by the door.

"I don't know what you're talking about," Angie replied as she picked up the case folder again. This time she didn't have a chance to hide her grin.

Denise walked over and snatched the file away, tossing it on the desk. "You set me up."

Angie didn't say anything at first, and a silent, staring contest ensued. "I most certainly did not," she finally began. "I just gave you a push in the right direction, is all."

"Did Sara know?"

"If I told you yes, would you cancel your date this weekend?" Angie immediately placed her hand over her mouth in mock surprise for spilling the beans.

"She called you after I left?" Denise couldn't believe how sneaky and conniving her partner had been, or Sara for that matter.

"Oh, come on, Denise. She couldn't come back to you. You dumped her, remember? If anyone was gonna make a first move, it had to be you... Are you mad?"

"No," Denise answered honestly. "But I'm starting to wonder if you missed your calling in life."

"Oh really?"

"Yeah. I think you'd do much better working in Vice as a hooker or a drug buyer. You're quite the actress."

"Had you fooled, huh?"

"Yeah, you did," Denise chuckled.

"So when did you figure it out? On the way over?"

"Given my reputation as an outstanding detective I'd like to say yes. Truth is, it wasn't until I looked at you just now."

"Why? What did I do?"

"Oh, I don't know. The cat-that-ate-the-canary grin, for starters."

Angie laughed out loud. "You've got a little touch of 'permagrin' going on yourself there, partner."

"It shows, eh?"

"Yeah it shows. And it looks good on you."

Denise took a seat across from Angie on the other side of the desk. "She wants to take me back to the Bahamas."

Angie heard reluctance in Denise's voice she didn't like. "You are going, right?"

"I don't know," Denise shrugged. "There's a lot here I have to take care of, so it's not like I can just get away."

Angie stood and walked around the desk. She leaned down to Denise, taking her hands. "Listen to me carefully. This," she said looking around the office, "this is a job. It shouldn't be your life. And I know you've waited a long time for someone like Sara to come along. So take my advice, dear partner: put the job on hold and start living."

"I hear you, but—"

"No buts."

"What about this backlog of paperwork?"

"It will be here when you get back. Not all of it," Angie grinned. "I'll do what I can. The rest can keep until you get back."

"And the personnel reviews are coming up, too. I have—"

"Well over a month to get them done," Angie finished. "Are we going to play this game all night? Or are you going to realize I'm right, and give up now?"

Denise chuckled and squeezed Angie's hand before letting go and standing up. "No, I'll put in for my vacation time with Genar before I leave tonight."

"That a girl," Angie nodded in support. "Wanna grab some dinner?"

"Sure. You buying?"

Angie paused a moment. "Oh, what the hell. Since all I did was to hook you back up with Sara, the least I can do is buy you dinner, too," she teased.

"Fine. I get the hint. I'll buy."

"You're on," Angie said, going for her coat.

Denise didn't move. "Hold on a second. You're supposed to argue and insist you pay. That's how it works."

"Says who?"

"Says anyone. That's the rules."

"There are dining rules now?" Angie said, handing Denise her coat after she donned her own.

"Yes, there are rules of common and insincere courtesy."

Angie chuckled. "Is that so?"

"Absolutely."

"Well, since I'm just learning them, we'll go Dutch tonight. How's that?"

"Sounds good to me."

"Next time, you get the check," Angie added, quickly walking out of the office.

"Oka— Hey, wait a minute."

"Too late, you already agreed."

Denise just grinned and shook her head as she followed behind Angie.

Epilogue

Denise sat in the witness box, trading glances with Sara and Angie and watching DeVittem's outburst.

"Justice?" DeVittem shouted. "Where's the justice in that lesbo getting her girlfriend on the stand to testify?" Mr. Connely, his attorney, went over to calm his client, and DeVittem turned his rage on him. "Don't even touch me, you sorry sack of shit suit," he warned.

"Should've spent more money on a better lawyer, rather than wasting it on unsuccessful bounty hunters, DeVittem," Denise prodded from the stand.

At this point the bailiff came over to restrain DeVittem, who was forcing his way towards Denise. The judge pounded his gavel repeatedly, yelling for order. Denise saw DeVittem reaching into the bailiff's holster, his long fingers wrapping around the gun. She raced from the stand, her heart pounding. She almost made it to DeVittem before the gun cleared the holster. Almost.

She felt a painful fire spread through her chest before her mind registered the shot that rang out, the force of which pushed her back a few feet. Helplessly, she watched DeVittem turn the weapon towards Sara and fire again.

Unable to move, Denise saw Sara's head jerk back and blood begin to pour from her forehead. The expression on the blonde's face was blank—no light, no fire, completely devoid of life.

Denise screamed.

Suddenly, a light came on, and Denise found herself sitting upright in bed with Sara to her right. Her heart was pounding and she was having difficulty breathing. She felt a cool, coastal breeze coming through the window, which calmed her just a bit. She knew she wasn't in a courtroom. She was in Sara's beach house in the Bahamas, miles and months away from the trial.

Sara leaned on her elbows, watching Denise strain to get hold of her nerves. She continued to raise herself until they were sitting side by side. Denise still said nothing, and Sara began to run her hand up and down Denise's back reassuringly.

"Wanna tell me how I died this time?" Sara asked casually.

Denise gave Sara a disapproving look and ripped the covers back, darting out of bed. "How can you be so blasé about it?"

Sara sighed, "Because they're just dreams, Denise. That's all. We've been together for three months now. There's nothing wrong; we're both fine. You have to start to accept that."

"I'm trying." Denise ran her hands over her face.

Sara knew there was something more and decided it was time for them to face the issues, prompting, "But?"

Denise shook her head. "I'm just scared."

Sara was quiet for a moment. "So, tell me about this dream?"

Denise walked to the window, looking out at the beach. The sun was just beginning to rise, creating a mixture of orange and pink clouds on the horizon. It was beautiful. Life was beautiful; but for some reason...

"We were at the trial, and DeVittem got the bailiff's gun."

"And he shot me, right?"

"Both of us."

Sara didn't say anything. She rose from the bed and quietly made her way over to Denise, wrapping her arms around the slender waist and resting her head between Denise's shoulder blades.

"I'm right here. We're both okay."

Denise allowed her arms to cover Sara's. "I just don't want you hurt because of me."

"I'm already hurting, Denise."

That made Denise turn in the embrace so she could face Sara. Before she could speak, Sara silenced Denise with an index finger over her lips. "I'm hurting because I wonder if these dreams are something more, something deeper. Maybe you're not as worried about someone else hurting me as you are that you might somehow hurt me."

Denise shook her head. "No," she said firmly. "I don't think that's it."

"I do," Sara replied. "I think you love me. I take that back—I know you love me. But perhaps love isn't enough. Maybe you're not ready for a commitment, and the dreams you've been having are telling you that."

"What are you saying?"

Sara slipped from the embrace and went back to the bed. "I think maybe you're more scared by being in love than by watching me die."

"I'm not trying to push you away."

"I didn't say you were, but since you mentioned it...are you?"

Denise shook her head and quickly made her way back to the

bed, sitting in front of Sara.

"Listen to me, Sara. Please?" Receiving a nod, Denise continued. "I've never been more happy than I am right now. And I know everyone says that when they first get involved with someone new, but I really mean it this time."

"So you lied to all the others?" Sara teased.

"There haven't been that many others," Denise smiled. "And no, I didn't lie. I just didn't have a real basis for a comparison. Nothing has felt this good before. I mean...you fit me. You fit me more than anyone else I've ever met; and I don't see myself growing old with you. I—"

"Thanks," Sara said indignantly.

"Let me finish?" Denise asked. Sara gave a nod. "I can't imagine my life—the life I'm leading today—without you. I've led that other life. I know what it feels like; and after the trial when you left...I realized at that point what life would be like without you. And I was miserable. So I'm not looking at starry-eyed fantasies of gray hair and rocking chairs. The need I feel is here and now, and not somewhere down the road."

"If that's true, then how do you explain the dreams? You know I'll stand by you. But I love you enough to leave if it's too much for you to take. And I'll be honest, Denise, it's getting to the point where I wonder if my presence is more detrimental than supportive. Maybe if I left you'd be able to get a decent night's sleep."

Denise snorted. "I can't believe you're thinking of leaving me after what I just told you."

"I'm not thinking of leaving you. I said I wanted to stay. I want to help you work through it. I'm just concerned that I'm making things worse." Sara began to tear up. "My heart would break if I left, but I can't stay if I think I'm constantly hurting you. My well-being isn't a fair trade for your pain. So, if it was for the best...I would go."

Denise grinned and climbed across Sara to sit beside her. She pulled her into an embrace as they both reclined on the bed. "It wouldn't be best. I think you know that deep down."

"I just don't want to hurt you, Denise."

"I know the feeling," Denise answered as she began to run her fingers through Sara's hair.

"So, where does that leave us?" Sara asked.

Denise considered the question. "Think about what we've gone through together. We spent over a month running for our lives and nearly being killed. I don't think that goes away overnight just because DeVittem's in the state prison. Would you agree?"

"Most definitely."

"Then you see how it's a part of us, as individuals and as a couple. It's a history that we can't change. Please don't think that these dreams are about any reluctance at being with you. I honestly think it's just a way of coming to terms with all of it—the running, the hiding, the need for survival."

"Shell shock," Sara said softly.

"Hmm?"

"Shell shock," Sara said louder, rising slightly to face Denise. "Vets who've been in war go through it. When you spend a fair amount of time wondering if you're going to die, and you're repeatedly faced with deadly situations, it takes its toll on the psyche. It's called shell shock."

"Yeah? Well, I'm a cop who's had special training, and I can't handle it as well as you do. Care to explain that?"

"Yours is coming out in dreams. It's more noticeable when someone's screaming next to you in bed." Sara chuckled, trying for some levity. "With me, it's little things. I'll see something or I'll hear something, and it takes me back to incidents."

"Such as?"

Sara considered for a moment. "Yesterday when we were walking along the beach, I looked down and saw the water at my feet. Instantly, I flashed back to Niagara."

"You didn't say anything."

"No, I didn't. I just thought it was my way of dealing with it all and didn't need to drag you into it."

"But that's why I'm here; so you can drag me anytime you like," Denise grinned.

Sara chuckled and burrowed back into Denise's shoulder. "We're a fine pair, aren't we?"

"Like I said...we fit."

Sara was quiet for a moment, then cleared her throat. "Do you think it will go away?"

Denise thought about it. "It will get easier. I believe that. But I don't think it will ever go away completely. And as long as we have each other, that will help. So no more talk about leaving. Agreed?"

Sara kissed Denise's neck and tightened her arm around Denise. "You're the boss, Lieutenant VanCook."

"Not anymore," she chuckled. "I'm on vacation, remember?"

Sara rose and straddled Denise's hips. "In that case," she replied, hovering over Denise with a predatory look in her eyes that the officer had grown to love, "we should make the most of it."

"You know, I'm starting to think that these bad dreams have their advantages. They force me awake to find a beautiful woman leering at me."

"Accentuating the positive, are we?"

"Certainly. Gotta take the good with the bad."

Sara smiled down at Denise as her fingers played with the ends of her hair. A solemn look crossed her face that made Denise cock her head in wonder. "I've never loved anyone more. Do you know that?"

"Did you know the feeling is mutual?" Denise countered.

"I had a suspicion."

"Would you like some tangible proof?" the officer persisted, drawing one finger slowly along Sara's jawline, tracing the curve of her neck, and coming to rest on the upper slope of one firm breast.

Sara swallowed hard and settled back comfortably on the bed. "Present your evidence, Lieutenant," she said with a sexy smile.

Denise reached over and turned off the light, with the rest of the night...the rest of her vacation...the rest of their lives together to look forward to.

About the Author:

CN makes her home in Southeastern Michigan with her husband, daughter and a menagerie of pets. She began writing at age 10 after listening to stories her grandmother told about her journey to America. With an Associate degree in psychology and journalism she is now pursuing a full-time writing career in the areas of novels, short stories and screenplays. When not writing, she enjoys an array of music, movies and painting. Her Internet homepage can be found at http://www.wintersproductions.com.

Printed in the United States
17455LVS00003B/223-234